1968

This book may be kept

FOURTEEN DAYS

A fine will be charged for each day the book is kept overtime.

GAYLORD 142			PRINTED IN U.S.A.

Thunder on the Chesapeake

By David Divine

The King of Fassarai
Atom at Spithead
The Golden Fool
Boy on a Dolphin
Thunder on the Chesapeake

David Divine

Thunder on the Chesapeake

New York
The Macmillan Company
1961

Library of Congress catalog card number: 61–8108

To Harold Strong Latham
who in his garden first heard this story
and approved it.

Foreword

TODAY, a hundred years after the *Monitor* and the *Merrimac* fought out the tentative first battle of a new age of the sea in the shallow waters of Hampton Roads, the United States is the greatest naval power in the world.

That splendid eminence is built upon the achievements of Hampton Roads. I do not think that the people of America are properly aware of this. I do not believe that they have ever evaluated the influence of sea power in the War Between the States at its full worth. I do not believe that they know enough of the greatness of their naval tradition. These were some of the things that led me to attempt this book. The Battle of Hampton Roads was an opposition of differing elements of genius: the genius of the community of Portsmouth and Norfolk and the Elizabeth River that manifested itself in the *Merrimac,* the genius of John Ericsson and the beginnings of modern technology that manifested itself in the *Monitor.*

I have tried to see these things through the eyes of the people who brought them about, to see them as they were seen by the people of Portsmouth, by the lonely, angry brilliance of Ericsson. Because of this I have kept to the spelling of the name that was used for the *Merrimac.* Scholarship has decided that it was spelled with a final "k." John Porter, who raised her from a charred and sunken wreck, who conceived her metamorphosis, and who built her and sent her out to battle, wrote on his drawings "Merrimac." It is a softer, gentler spelling of the Indian original. I have kept it, as I have kept other contemporary spellings of ships' names, in defiance of the scholars.

1

The
Turbulent
Air

Chapter one

THE lookout lifted his head suddenly and searched the star-scattered darkness. The sound of wings was louder now, a strong beat, moving purposefully.

He said, "Canada geese, south boun'."

"Late in the season for geese," answered Stephen, "and they're not calling."

"No," the lookout agreed reluctantly, "they ain't callin'." He moved his head in an awkward sweep, as if trying to outline invisible shapes against the stars. After a little, he said, "Wouldn't be swans."

The wingbeat diminished, the sound merging in the ship noises—the rustle of water under the bow, the slow thud of the paddles, the occasional creak of blocks in the rigging.

Stephen said, "There's nothing to show she was ever there."

The lookout man lowered his head as if called sharply back to duty. "She was there," he protested, and after a pause added doubtfully, "sir. Last I saw of her she was end on, headin' straight up the channel. Rate she was goin' she'd be halfways to Charleston b'now." He strained at the darkness ahead of them.

There was a level in the sky where the stars faded and ceased. There was an area on the sea where the star paths began. Between them there was nothing—a vague, indeterminate darkness that was neither sea nor sky but that held, Stephen knew, the Carolina coast, and the entrance to Charleston Harbor, and the dark, low walls of Fort Moultrie.

The lookout asked, "D'you think they'll shoot, Lootenant?"

"No, I don't think they will." Stephen turned and began to walk back toward the pilothouse.

The ship was darkened. It gave her a secret look. The rigging of the

2

foremast moved very slowly against the stars as she rolled to the ground swell. The spars were dark against the sky. From her funnel he could see the black smoke moving lazily aft and a little to the starboard side. Under it the walking beams rose and fell with the awkward, angular gestures of a drunken man. Except for the soft ship noises there was silence. It was as if she moved by herself, controlling her own destiny. He walked as far as the windows of the pilothouse and stood there, waiting.

The captain's voice asked out of the interior darkness, "Nothing at all?"

"Nothing. She's anchored up under the guns of Fort Moultrie by now."

"What was she?" Stephen identified the voice as belonging to Woods, who commanded the troops on board.

He answered, "She was a guard ship—must have been."

"If she was a guard ship," asked Woods quietly, "why didn't she send up a rocket when she saw us, to warn them up at Moultrie?"

"Mebbe she didn't see us." Captain McGowan's tone was reasonable.

"She saw us," insisted the pilot, "else why did she turn and run? She knowed we was comin'!"

"How can you tell?" Woods asked.

"Hell! They've doused the coast lights, ain't they?"

There seemed to be no answer to that. Stephen peered at the pilot's face. It was lit very faintly in a green, pallid light from the compass. The light was too tenuous for him to see the man's expression, but the face looked haunted. He turned and went slowly back to his position in the bows of the ship.

This was the heart of the matter. The sea lights were out. Charleston beacon should have been clear on the southern spit of Morris Island, three miles or less from them. There was no light at Moultrieville— there was only the vague, uncertain blackness. As a seaman he felt there to be something wanton in this, an irresponsibility that was beyond politics and secession, beyond war even. This was something that was aimed at the fundamental understandings of the sea, something that was directed at all ships, at all safety, at all civilized usage. They should have sighted the buoy that marked the bar of the ship channel by now, but there was no buoy—he was sure of that. The buoy also had been destroyed. The guard ship was another matter; a guard ship was legitimate, proper perhaps: but to destroy the seamarks and the lights was the end of order.

The lookout asked, "What do they think back there, Lootenant?"

Stephen for a moment found it difficult to think of anything except the dousing of the lights. Finally he said, "They think that she was a guard ship, waiting for us."

"That means they're goin' to shoot."

The stars began to move from right to left: McGowan was swinging the ship. The *Star of the West* moved in a long, lazy circle. Toward the end of the circle Stephen heard the pilot call to the leadsman in the chains and heard the splash of the lead. He had lost all sense of time now—McGowan had silenced the ship's bell after midnight—and all sense of direction. Automatically he searched for the pointers of the polestar, fixed it, and fumbled for his watch. It was impossible to see the dial in the winter darkness.

The lookout muttered, "Stands to reason they'll shoot."

Stephen ignored him.

The ship was steady again, creeping slowly in. McGowan had not yet made up his mind.

Overhead they heard a voice high in the crosstrees shout, "Light!" and give a bearing.

Stephen saw it first—hardly more than a faint glow hanging halfway between the last of the stars and the first of the water.

The lookout said: "It's a shore light but it's behind something. Can't see the full of it at this level."

Stephen was aware that his heart had accelerated.

McGowan's voice called, "Mr. Knott, will you come aft, please!" and then repeated, as if for emphasis, "Mr. Knott!"

Stephen walked rapidly back to the pilothouse.

McGowan said: "It's a fixed light and it's high up. It's not on the water. Could be a light on Fort Sumter."

From the absolute darkness of the back of the pilothouse, Woods' voice said, "Anderson knows we're coming."

Brewer muttered harshly, "*They* know too."

McGowan seemed to have made up his mind. "I'll try in a bit, but we'll want light to go up the channel."

Though he could not see the captain, Stephen felt that McGowan's eyes were on him interrogatively. He thought for a second before he agreed: "Yes, you'll need light."

McGowan had apparently wanted the answer only in confirmation. He made no further reference to it, but said instead, "I guess they'll shoot."

"There's no telling." Woods' tone was doubtful.

Brewer cleared his throat. "They're South Ca'lina men! Anythin'," he added, "anythin'."

Stephen turned away from the pilothouse and walked aft. He fumbled for a door in the superstructure, listened for a minute to the gasp and withdrawal of the steam in the cylinders, and then, opening the door, went in. The air inside was hot and fetid—a scent of innumerable men, sweat, tobacco, urine. He closed the door behind him and saw through the darkness the gleam of the light on the deck below, and, groping, moved to the head of the companionway. There were bodies lying at the foot of it: men in every attitude of surrender, lying on their sides, on their backs, on their stomachs, asleep. The place was full of sound —mutterings, snores, harsh breathing—against the background of the engine noises. A haze obscured the dim oil lamps.

Ten Broeck, the Army surgeon, was sitting at a desk inside the door of his cabin. He nodded grimly at Stephen. "Recruits—they don't know enough not to sleep. If they were old hands . . ." He paused for an instant. "Give me recruits for the night before a battle!"

"There's not going to be a battle," said Stephen automatically.

Ten Broeck grunted. "How d'you know? Have you ever been in one?"

Stephen flushed slowly. "No," he admitted, as if it were something of which to be ashamed.

"I have. They'll fight."

"They won't fight! This is a merchant ship, a supply ship. They won't risk a war for a supply ship."

"South Ca'lina men?" Ten Broeck's tone was like an echo of the pilot's.

Stephen began to pick his way between the bodies on the deck. They were so close that it was difficult now and then not to touch a man. In the alleyway there were three men on their knees praying. Here and there a man sat up. Once, as he stepped over a body stretched out utterly flat, he saw eyes watching him, and a soft voice asked, "Will they shoot, Lootenant?" And he answered without pause for consideration, "No, they won't shoot."

They were young, most of them—artillerymen, drawn out of the depot at Governors Island. He wondered for an instant what he was doing among them, and then continued to pick his way, followed occasionally by faint questions.

When he came back to the foot of the companionway, Ten Broeck asked simply, "They'll do?"

Stephen nodded.

Ten Broeck held up a piece of paper. "My will. I write it every night before a battle. Six times now, most of them in Mexico. Tear it up the next night. One of these days I'm going to fall out of a buggy and break my neck. Nobody'll know what to do then."

Stephen went up to the deck, let himself out, and stood with his eyes smarting in the cold. They watered slightly, and he wiped them and, having wiped them, looked out toward the east and was astonished to find that the horizon was a hard bar of darkness against the pale suggestion of the dawn.

As he went past the pilothouse, McGowan called out, " 'Nother thirty minutes mebbe there'll be enough light!"

Stephen felt rather than saw that the *Star of the West* was slowed down again until she had barely steerageway. He went reluctantly back to the eyes of the ship.

The lookout said, "Mornin', Lootenant!" and Stephen realized by the changed voice that the watch had changed.

The blue light took them by surprise. Its sudden, urgent brilliance showed the upper works of a small ship, part in silhouette, part almost incandescent in its glare. As the lookouts from each post shouted, Stephen saw that the unknown ship was turning fast. The light blazed on, was obscured momentarily by a projection on the deck, and then grew brilliant again. It died at last, and he saw the swift parabola as the burning sheath of the flare fell toward the water. A red light began to burn in its place. The guard ship, then, had not gone as far up as Fort Moultrie. It had lain waiting for them inside the ship channel as they had waited outside for the dawn. It was heading up for Moultrie now.

The lookout next to him said, "She's goin' like a singed cat."

A second red light burned, then for good measure a rocket climbed. The lookout said, "Reg'lar Fourth a July!" Stephen grunted, and the lookout became suddenly garrulous. "If they didn't know we was comin' before, they know now. They goin' to shoot, mister?" He looked sideways at Stephen and corrected himself apologetically: "Lootenant?"

"No, they won't shoot. Nobody's going to risk a war over a single ship."

The lookout asked sardonically, "You ever been in Charleston?"

The *Star of the West* was moving well over half speed now. From the liveliness of the water and the feel of the ship Stephen knew they were crossing the bar. He turned and looked down the length of the ship. Its outlines were etched by the dawn. It was no longer secret. There was a noise about it: the wind in the rigging, the halyards slatting against the mast, the paddles that were urgent and angry. Smoke stretched far behind them, lowering down toward the water and very dark above the new silver of the morning.

The guard ship, none the less, was drawing away from them. She was small but she was fast. She was heading up for the entrance at flank speed, and he could see the broad spread of foam that lay in her wake. From her he turned to the lookout, who was tall, redheaded, lean.

The lookout said, "I didn't sign on for no fightin'."

"Maybe not," answered Stephen coldly, and turned to walk back once more to the pilothouse.

Though it was still dark in its shelter, it was possible to see the four men in it: McGowan, the pilot, Woods, and the man at the wheel.

McGowan's voice was almost satisfied. "She was the guard ship, all right. Must'a' been waitin' for us. They'll be awake on the beach. I'm goin' to keep over to the starboard side o' the channel far as I can. No sense askin' for trouble. There's deep water up to half a mile off the north end of Morris Island."

The lookout on the foremast called again.

McGowan said: "Light's on Fort Sumter all right. I didn't doubt it. Ain't no one else on this coast'd show a light. You goin' to have the troops up, Mr. Woods?"

"No, they'll stay below. They've got their ammunition. They can wait."

"And if Fort Moultrie fires on us?"

Woods answered carefully, as if he had rehearsed his opinion: "Major Anderson spiked the guns and wrecked the carriages before he abandoned Moultrie."

"Christmas, that was." Brewer's voice was gruff. "They've had two weeks to do somethin' about it."

"What does the Navy know?" asked McGowan obliquely.

Stephen nodded. "They told me at the Navy Department that the guns commanding Maffit's Channel were still in position."

"That must'a' been a week ago—full." The pilot's gruff voice had a hard note of common sense.

Woods considered it. "We have still the option of running ashore on Morris Island and taking the men in in the boats."

"Run my ship ashore!" exclaimed McGowan bitterly.

Not until the eastern horizon was alive with light was it possible to see the coast inshore of them, and then it was only a long, thin line of gray with a darker line above it. It had a remoteness, an inhospitable absence of anything human. It was a coast line, the boundary edge of a continent—nothing else.

It seemed to become clearer in abrupt stages. First it was a line of grayness, and then when Stephen looked again he could see white dunes and an overtopping of vague scrub, and the next time he looked there were house roofs, scattered and far apart. He was puzzled for a moment by the swiftness of the changes until he realized that between them he was concentrating on the almost invisible guard ship that was now between the headlands, still firing her silent rockets against the diminishing darkness of the west.

Quite suddenly he could see the northern coast—Sullivans Island and the cluster of the houses of Moultrieville. They shone brilliantly against the darkness over the mainland, and he looked behind him and saw that the east was very bright, almost gay in the moment before the sunrise.

Above them the lookout shouted a third time. Following the direction of his shout, Stephen saw a flag, and in that instant the sun rose. Through his telescope he saw that it was the red palmetto flag of South Carolina. It seemed to have no importance to him. Fort Moultrie was the point of danger. He switched back to Moultrieville, picking up the low black bulk of the fort. There was no flag there.

Behind him he heard footsteps, and after a brief silence Lonergan, the reporter who had sailed with them, asked, "D'you suppose those fellows have got a battery there?"

Stephen answered, not sensing the direction of the question, "That's Fort Moultrie."

"Uh-huh—on Morris Island, I mean."

"No, there's no battery on Morris Island—Navy Department would have told us." Stephen took his eye from the telescope and looked up at the forestay. It was glistening with spray and salt and the reflection of the low sun.

"How far are we out?"

"A mile and three-quarters," replied Stephen, adding quickly, as if it were enormously important, "There's no flag over Moultrie." Involuntarily he glanced back toward the flag on Morris Island. As his eyes reached the dunes, he saw a flash and a sudden puff of dark smoke that instantly became white and lovely in the sunlight.

Behind him he heard the reporter gasp, "Christ!"

There was a long pause. Then on the still blue surface of the sea spray leaped in a great luminous fountain. From the fountain they saw a ball move up in a long, slow, easy skipping movement, reach the top of its curve and fall slowly down toward the sea again.

"It wouldn't'a' hit," said the lookout. "It was fired ahead of us."

Stephen's mouth felt dry. All the tension of the morning was crystallized in this moment.

"It was a warning shot. The next one'll be aimed at us." The reporter's voice was full of surprise.

"There may not be a next one. They'd go as far as a warning shot. I doubt—" Stephen broke off.

He heard McGowan shout. The bos'n ran forward with the big garrison flag that they had found among the stores the previous day. With frantic urgency it was run up at the foremast, whipping out at once in a blaze of fresh blue and white and scarlet. Stephen looked aft to the old flag. It was drained of all color by this blazing freshness.

Lonergan, behind him, said, "They can't help knowing they're firing on the flag now!"

There was another puff of smoke ashore, a high plume, darker this time—a heavier gun. Again the spray sprang up between ship and shore. Again, as they watched, the ball lifted away from it—black, glistening, tiny; but this time it grew, and Stephen stopped breathing, almost consciously, as it lifted in a slow, inexorable curve toward the ship.

He felt Lonergan move and then stop as if he were trapped. The reporter cried, "My God, it's going to hit!"

Before he could finish the sentence the ball soared over the ship, and Stephen heard the whistle and rush of its passage. He stood quite still. The lookout had thrown himself to the deck. Lonergan had crouched down.

Stephen disregarded both of them. As if to himself he muttered, "They can't be such fools—they can't be!"

Lonergan straightened up. "They are."

Another gun fired. Stephen remembered now that he had heard the reports of the first two guns—faint, distant, hardly impinging on his consciousness. The wind was carrying the sound away. The small gun fired again. As Stephen ran back to the pilothouse, he was aware of a desperate longing to take refuge on the lee side of the midships housing. The new ball splashed into the sea short of them.

McGowan called out, "You must give us bigger guns than that, boys, or you can't hit us!"

Stephen realized that from the pilothouse McGowan could not have seen the second ball pass over the ship.

Woods came out of the pilothouse, as if he wished to avoid the suggestion of sheltering, and stood beside Stephen. Almost conversationally he said, "It's hard to believe."

As his voice ceased, a ball hit in the forechains. The leadsman leaning out, swinging his lead to make a cast, leaped for the deck, fell, and lay there, lifting his head from the planking, and waiting. The ship shuddered above the vibration of the engines.

McGowan bellowed: "Mr. Bragg, get below! See if she's making water—get the carpenter!" His eyes swiveled to the man on the deck. "Norden, get up! Get back where you were! They don't hit twice in the same place."

Over his shoulder Stephen heard Lonergan growl, "Begod, he thinks it's lightning!"

Another gun fired. Again they watched the swift succession of spray and ricochet. This time the ball floated between the funnel and the flail-like walking beams.

Woods said, "Another one like that . . ."

Again the ship shuddered. The hit was aft somewhere. Stephen remembered that there had been no splash. It was a direct hit: the gunners in the low sand dunes of Morris Island had got the range.

From the eyes of the ship the redheaded lookout shouted back, "There's a flag over Sumter!"

Woods directed his telescope toward the fort. He said abruptly: "Union flag—and they've got the casemate guns run out."

Stephen saw the fort distinctly for the first time. The sun was full on it. The brightness of the Union flag was very clear against the west. He thought that he could make out the spires of Charleston beyond.

He heard McGowan say: "Ain't no use runnin' her ashore on Morris Island now." There was a tone of relief in his voice.

Woods ignored him. To Stephen he said: "We'll be in range of Moultrie in five minutes' time. We'll get cross fire then. It will take us a long time to go through. What's the tide now?"

"First of the ebb," Stephen replied automatically. "It's running stronger every minute."

Lonergan, over their voices, demanded: "Why doesn't Sumter fire? Why doesn't Anderson help? If he covered us—"

"With what?" interrupted Woods roughly. "He's got sixty men and a brass band in a fort built for six hundred. What could he do?"

A ball whistled over the wheelhouse, and Stephen knew that he was afraid.

Lonergan was muttering, "If I was Anderson, I'd have been shooting by now."

The lookout shouted, "There's a cutter coming down in tow beyond Moultrie!"

The cutter must have been visible for some time. No one had noticed her. She was in tow of a tug.

Woods swore softly under his breath. Aloud he said: "That's it, then. We can't stand up to her too!" With a quick authority in his voice he called: "Take her out, Mr. McGowan—take her out!"

Stephen saw the bows of the *Star of the West* swing away from Moultrie, passing from left to right across the line of the houses of Moultrieville and the sand dunes beyond, and swing on past the line of the surf, past the shallows, past the entrance to Maffit's Channel—more and more swiftly, until at last they were headed down the ship channel toward the open sea again.

Another ball passed over them; the next missed on the starboard side; a third fell astern of them.

They were in the grip of the ebb tide now. The paddles had a swifter note, a harsher, more furious beat. Though the cutter was squaring away from Moultrie toward them, she was a long way astern. Stephen went wide of the pilothouse to watch her, and was aware that already Moultrie had diminished: the complex of its walls was less menacing; the houses, the land, the entrance itself had a decreasing significance.

A ball or two splashed astern of them as the battery in the sand-hills cleared its guns in a last futile firing. Then the morning was quiet again except for the noise of their passage.

Woods looked up at the bright flag that streamed overhead. Almost apologetically he said: "Wasn't anything else that we could do, the way I see it. We couldn't land on Morris Island—they were there already. We couldn't take on Moultrie and the cutter." There was a defensive edge to his voice. " 'Tisn't as if we had any guns. They ought to have sent a warship."

Lonergan mumbled hurriedly: "They fired on the flag. They couldn't not have seen it."

Stephen looked at him. "They saw it." His voice was bitter. "They wanted it that way. I don't understand it. I don't understand the way they think."

The pilot was leaning against the windows of the pilothousing. "They don't think. They just shoot. They knew they was goin' to shoot. Wasn't any thinkin' to be done."

"But"—Stephen's voice was baffled—"But it's an act of war! Whatever way you look at it, it's an act of war. It's rebellion!"

"Chasin' Anderson across into Sumter was rebellion," said the pilot sardonically.

"No, it wasn't the same thing. They've fired on the flag now—and that's war."

Lonergan, a little apart from them all, asked ironically, "With Old Buck Buchanan as President?"

"But he's got to do something about it. He can't just let it go," protested Stephen.

"Buck Buchanan and Toucey?"

"Navy ain't goin' to do nothin'." The pilot's rasping tone cut into the argument. "Not while Toucey's there they ain't."

"Nor while Buchanan's at the White House." Lonergan was contemptuous.

Stephen walked to the bulwarks and looked over the broad foam patch of their wake. The cutter was still coming steadily down the channel after them. "They're Americans, and they've fired on their flag," he persisted.

Lonergan, leaning against the pilothouse, said ribaldly, "You're a Southerner yourself."

"I'm a Virginian."

"They're South Ca'lina men."

"Virginia will stand by the Union." Stephen's voice was cold.

"Hell it will!" retorted Lonergan softly. "You won't make commodore."

Stephen stared at the newspaperman. "Why?" He wondered if Lonergan had seen his brief moment of fear, and a hot flush rose.

"You think too much."

Woods called out: "Webb, get your men up on deck! They might as well have a bit of sun."

Chapter two

THE girl eased herself forward and, parting the winter-withered grass stems, looked across the clearing. The boy, with a curious economy of gesture, moved one finger and indicated the farther end of it. Over against the dark, somber level of the swamp water Linden saw the doe take sudden shape. She was not sure what had betrayed it—perhaps the restless movement of an ear or a sudden flick of the tail. When she had looked before there had been nothing visible; now the doe was outlined in the cold silver light and, as she watched, it lifted its head and snuffed delicately with dark nostrils.

The boy whispered, hardly breathing, "Ol' buck's not here."

They lay silent, watching. The doe began to feed with an air of defiant security. Duck called to each other in the swamp, and a cardinal flashed across the glade, a warm scarlet in the gray coldness. A heron croaked a long way away, and the boy croaked instantly in return, in perfect imitation of the bird. The doe lifted her head, swiveled enormous ears, and settled once more to her feeding.

Linden laughed very softly. She inched forward again. With her short dark hair she looked like a boy herself. She wore an old coat, and ancient trousers two full sizes too big for her.

To their right something crashed in the undergrowth, a small noise—it could have been a squirrel or a chipmunk—but the boy said, his face lighting: "Ol' buck. Here he comes!"

There was a rustle and then silence. The doe watched, exquisitely wary, her head half raised, the eyes soft and wide. After the rustle there was absolute silence, yet when they saw him the buck was almost at the center of the glade. He was young; his coat was still unmarred by the winter, his antlers were broad and challenging. For a moment he stood outlined against the skeletal beauty of a swamp maple, then he moved proudly forward.

There was another rustle to the right. "Other ol' buck"—the boy's voice was rich with anticipation—"Other ol' buck comin'. I tol' you, Mis' Linden, I tol' you!"

The second buck was older by perhaps two full seasons. It moved easily and with a formal pride. The first turned and waited. The newcomer stopped five yards away. They began an intricate pattern of movement—backing, edging sideways, advancing and retiring. They made no acknowledgment of the presence of the doe.

Occasionally the older one snorted, a quick tearing noise in the winter stillness. There were little rustles in the undergrowth after each sound, as if the swamp edge were full of unseen watchers.

The older buck attacked first. The movement was so swift that Linden barely saw it before it was over. In the very middle of a slow sidewise passage, oddly like a chassé in the middle of a dance, it lunged forward, dropped its head, and brought the antlers up in a swift scything motion. The tip of the left antler grazed the belly and side of the younger deer, and it leaped sidewise in a convulsive evasion.

The evasion turned in a whiplash movement into an attack, and antlers clashed with a sharp sound like dead branches striking together.

The doe grazed with a careful indifference.

The younger buck gave ground first, and was pursued. The heads locked, freed themselves, and locked again. Linden looked obliquely at the boy. His eyes were glistening; his face was taut with expectation. His whole body was knit with excitement.

Once more the bucks clashed. This too was now resolved into a pattern. It was as formal as jousting, as improbable of danger as an exercise in the lists before the ladies of a court.

Then there was a sharp report like the crack of a branch breaking under snow, and Linden saw the older buck lift its head with a lopsided movement and stand bewildered. One antler was broken off short, close to the head. The buck made scarcely any effort to avoid the next lunge from its adversary, but accepted the blow, staggered a little, and then turned and plunged away.

The younger one stood immobile, watching the retreat. It made no attempt to follow. When the crash of the flight through the undergrowth was still, it lifted its head and snorted. The long rough noise held, it seemed to Linden, a derisive note.

The boy gasped, "Jesus!"

The doe moved. She stopped cropping at the winter grass, walked away from the swamp edge toward the center of the glade, and stood waiting.

Deliberately and with infinite care the young buck approached her. He sniffed the cold air close to her in a series of quick exploratory sounds. He walked past her, turned, sniffed again, and then snorted once more.

The doe waited, expectantly submissive.

The buck mounted her with a quick arrogant movement of extreme beauty. They coupled in an ecstatic rhythm, the buck's lithe body superimposed, the legs splayed, the triumphant antlers crowning the pyramid.

The boy turned, his face troubled. "Maybe we'd best be goin'."

Linden did not look at him. "Ss-sh!" she murmured. "Don't scare them!"

"They don't scare easy when—when they're—like that."

The girl made no reply. She watched, absorbed, feeling a hot flush at her neck and temples and a tingling in her breasts.

The boy said, as if compelled to defend himself, "It's nachrel." He turned away from the girl and watched the deer again. After a long silence he added, still under some obscure compulsion, "I seen that ol' bull of Mist' Choat's over to Deep Creek."

Fiercely the girl whispered, "Be quiet, Jeriel!"

He had the ordinary boy's resentment for a departure from custom: normally she called him "Jeri."

He grunted and lay silent, watching the antique, elemental power of the act. The girl was wholly caught now in the quickening, imperative rhythm. The climax was as sudden as the breaking of the antler had been. There was a moment when the buck was motionless, his head upstretched, his antlers thrown back, his nostrils wide. Then with a single convulsive move he freed himself and stood, his sides heaving in and out like overworked bellows, his head drooping slightly.

The doe stood beside him, flaccid, fulfilled. Again there was a moment of suspension, a moment out of time. Then suddenly she made a quick, absurd flirting movement, lifting her rump in a little idiotic gesture of pure happiness. Her tail flicked, and she began to lope slowly and gracefully out of the glade. The buck looked after her, apparently puzzled for a moment, then followed her. The cardinal flashed across the glade again like a scarlet punctuation mark.

"Finish," said Jeriel, getting to his knees. He stretched himself as if he were tired after long work, and jerked up onto his feet. The girl rolled over onto her back and lay there sucking a dry grass stem, quite unaware of him.

He walked slowly out to the middle of the glade and kicked at the broken antler. He looked smaller now that he was on his feet. He was thirteen, solidly built and strong. He stooped down and picked up the antler and examined the break, honoring it with a long low whistle. Over his shoulder he said, his voice uncertain: "Better be gettin' back. Your Aunt Deb . . ."

The girl picked at the grass stem. She was not thinking, she was feeling.

The boy muttered, "Clean break," and dropped the antler. He kicked it again, and it bounded away and lay still, presenting the whiteness of its broken end like a scar on the winter grass. "Your Aunt Deb—" he began.

Linden collected herself. "Go get the horses," she said dreamily.

He plodded away and she watched him go. When he was out of sight she got up and walked in turn over to the center of the glade. It was difficult to judge her age in the ill-fitting clothes; she might have been anything from fourteen upward. Actually she was almost seventeen. But though the clothes could disguise her age they could not hide the slender grace of her movement. Her body was precise and accurate in its muscular response. Her head was proud and she held it alert and instantly ready. She gave an impression of intense vitality.

The boy came back with the horses, their feet thudding dully through a damp stretch of grass. The heron flapped heavily over the trees thirty yards beyond them, and Jeriel watched its flight without expression, croaking malignantly as the bird reached the edge of the glade.

"That ol' bull of Mist' Choat's—" he began.

"Jeriel!"

They mounted in silence and began to pick their way back to the plank road. Halfway there Linden said distantly: "There's no need to be dirty-minded. It was beautiful—it's natural."

"Sure," he answered, as if the necessity to reach agreement was urgent. "Sure, ever'body does it."

They rode on in silence, skirting the edge of the plank road. A group of three carts came into sight around a bend, moving with the slow, unending plod of the ox.

The Negro who led the first team looked up as they approached. He took off his hat with a wide smile. "Mornin', Mis' Linden."

"Morning, Johnstone." Her father always called his Negroes by their surnames, maintaining that as freed men they were entitled to their dignity. The first two carts were her father's, the third belonged to Mr. Brayne: they were going to the swamp for shingles.

The ripple of greetings followed her down the road. Jeriel turned back to shout to the last Negro, and they rode on again in silence. Beyond the next bend Linden knew that they would see the outlying shacks of Gosport and, far beyond them, the masting shears and the roofs of the two great ship houses of the Navy Yard. She gave the roan mare that she was riding a little kick, as if the forward movement of her thought had communicated itself to her heels. The horse responded, and they rounded the corner rapidly. The flag at the Navy Yard was three-quarters of the way up the tall mast outside the headquarters building, creeping slowly upward. It was bright in the low sun.

She checked the horse at once and called over her shoulder, "Quiet, Jeri!"

Listening, they picked up, very soft and made sweet by the distance, the notes of the bugle.

Jeriel said: "You'll catch turkey. Your Aunt Deb, she'll be up. She'll take the stuffin' outta you."

"I can still go in the back window."

The boy nodded. The back window was an accepted part of their excursions, and so was the fact that Linden's Aunt Deborah never left her room before eight o'clock in the morning. If she saw Linden in trousers, there would be what Jeriel called "a screechin' match." The memory of the deer was eclipsed now by this other and more important interest. They cantered on, united in the necessity to defeat adults.

After reaching the spur that ran out from the railroad tracks, and skirting it until it stopped without apparent reason, they rode into an area of shacks belonging to freed Negros. The shacks appeared to be inhabited by children and hogs. The strong stench of the hog wallows flooded the morning air. There were chicken and dog smells, but their individuality was wholly subsidiary to the odor of hog. Slowly and by degrees the shacks improved until at length they came to a section of decayed houses and, after that, to the respectable houses of Portsmouth itself. There was little movement in the streets—a mule wagon and a cart or two, here and there a man on horseback, a few cold-pinched people on the sidewalks.

Behind them a mounted man came furiously out of a side turning and overtook them, going hard. He reined in as he drew level. "Linden," he shouted, "they've sunk the *Star of the West!*" He fumbled in a pocket and produced a paper, a telegraph form. Without actually looking at it, he read: "Coast batteries manned Citadel Cadets opened fire supply ship *Star of West*. Five hits."

Linden's face lit. "They've done it! Who sent that, Ulysses?"

"Mackenzie over at the telegraph. I've got to get to the paper. We'll be bringing out a special: '*Star of the West* Sunk!'"

"Are you sure she's sunk?"

Ulysses was already past her. He called back over his shoulder: "Must be—hit five times." Then, turning right round, he called back: "Your Aunt Deb, she'll be waiting for you. Better get those pants off!"

Linden laughed.

Jeriel asked, "You s'pose that's right—about the *Star of the West?*"

"Of course it's right! I knew she'd be fired on as soon as the news came from New York that she'd sailed." Again Linden's heels conveyed her excitement to the horse.

"That Ulysses's always shootin' his mouth off!"

They could hear him far down the road doing just that. By the time they had passed the next block, people were standing at their doors. Voices called out to them: "Linden, you heard? They've sunk the *Star of the West!*"

With her face alight she shouted back: "I heard. The North'll have to fight now."

Over and over again the exchange was repeated in different terms. The town was in the grip of a mounting excitement. It seemed to pass like a wave from either side of the street, washing into the cross streets and the back alleys. The town was awake, alive, almost roaring, by the time she reached the house. Excitement seemed to make the subterfuge of an entry by the back window unnecessary.

"Ain't you goin' round the back way?" asked Jeriel.

Joyously she said: "What's it matter, Jeri? What's it matter now? They've sunk the *Star of the West*. Take the horses round to Mullin—tell him I said for him to walk them!" She was off her mare and through the gate and across the narrow yard before she had finished speaking. She went in at the door shouting: "Father!" and then, more loudly, "Father, they've sunk the *Star of the West!*" The words were like a tocsin, full of omen, prophecy, and doom.

Her aunt came out onto the landing and stood with her hands clasped together and resting lightly on the rail of the balustrade. She was not tall, but by her taut uprightness she gave an impression of height. Her hair was parted precisely in the middle and swept in smooth, perfect swags over her ears to the pad at the back of the head that had been made popular by the young Victoria. Linden could not remember when Aunt Deborah's hair had ever been disarranged.

Linden stopped at the foot of the stairs, looking up. Only a very little subdued, she said, "Aunt Deborah, they've sunk the *Star of the West!*"

"Go to your room," ordered Aunt Deborah evenly, "and put on decent clothes!"

Linden's voice had something of a wail in it, a wail of incomprehension. "But Aunt Deborah, they've sunk—"

"We will discuss it presently when you are decent."

Rebelliously the girl demanded, "What's not decent about trousers?"

"It is indecent for a girl to wear man's clothing." Aunt Deborah's voice raised itself a fraction in pitch.

"It's a sight more indecent for a girl to sit in the bottom of a boat in skirts."

"Linden . . ." Aunt Deborah made a tactical error.

Before she could retrieve it, the girl said: "You've got to sit with your knees up. It shows everything."

Aunt Deborah plunged. "You are getting too old for the boat. You will be seventeen in a little. You've half lived in it since you were ten years old. It's time you grew out of it."

"Aunt Deborah, they've sunk the *Star of the West!* There's going to be a war. What does it matter what I wear?"

Aunt Deborah repeated implacably, "We will discuss it when you are decent."

"Aunt Deborah"—the despair that came into her voice whenever she found herself unable to communicate with an older generation overwhelmed her—"there's going to be a *war!*"

"Maybe"—Aunt Deborah shifted her ground with the skill of an old campaigner—"but you weren't out in the boat this morning."

"I was riding." The girl's voice was frankly rebellious. "I don't see that skirts are any more decent, riding."

"A lady would use a sidesaddle."

"I'd rather be safe than a lady," said Linden swiftly.

Unfairly Aunt Deborah took refuge in the rights of an adult. "Where were you riding?"

The girl abandoned discretion with an abrupt recklessness. "I have been watching white-tailed deer copulating," she said, her voice a cool, deliberate parody of her father's.

Her aunt disregarded the word; clearly its significance passed over her. "I see no reason why you should not have done it in a ladylike manner. I have told you not to wear those things. Go up to your room. And wash before you come to breakfast." She started down the stairs, ignoring the fury in the girl's eyes. At the foot she said distantly, "If you wish to be treated as a child, I shall continue to treat you as a child."

Linden began to speak, changed her mind and, bending forward, kissed her aunt on the cheek. Between her teeth she said, her voice mocking, "Dragon!" and went up the stairs two at a time.

Her father was standing at the upper landing. "One of these days," he murmured ironically, "your aunt will buy herself a dictionary."

"They've sunk the *Star of the West!*"

"Who says so?"

"Ulysses Hogan."

"An inaccurate young man."

"I saw the telegram—the Citadel Cadets, they hit her five times."

"And she sank?"

"It didn't exactly say she sank." Linden was constrained to a doubtful honesty.

"South Carolina men—" His face clouded. "Even if she's not sunk, they've fired on the flag."

"South Carolina men, North Carolina, Virginia—it's the South. It's a challenge!" The excitement made her eyes brilliant; her skin was flushed, and her eagerness was all but palpable.

He said slowly, "Lin, I'd better tell you before the whole town tells you—Stephen was with the *Star of the West*."

"Stephen!" She put the back of her hand to her mouth in an old childhood gesture. He saw the brightness drain out of her face. Her eyes became dulled, remote. She said again: "Stephen! But he went to New York."

"His orders were to join the *Star of the West* at New York. He helped to survey the Charleston entrance channel a year ago."

"He's a *Virginian!*"

"He's an officer in the Navy of the United States." Ash Cleave's answer was sad, as if in the grief of the moment he saw long perspectives of unhappiness.

"You should have told me." Her voice was diminished to a whisper.

"His orders were secret." Cleave watched her face. "I didn't know myself until Washington ordered the *Brooklyn* out to support the *Star of the West*." He paused for a moment with his forehead furrowed. "I don't think she could have reached her. Did Ulysses say anything about the *Brooklyn?*"

The girl shook her head as if the question were of no importance. "He shouldn't have gone."

"He was under orders," Cleave said with a patient reasonableness. "Lin, be sensible! You know what Stephen thinks about this."

"But he's a Virginian!"

"Virginia's a part of the Union."

"The Union's finished. The North's got to fight now." The words came with a rush. "Moment the North moves, Virginia will go with the South. She *is* the South!"

"I doubt it." His tone took on a gentle irony. "I don't think Virginia would split from the North because a lot of boys and a few grown fools fired on an unarmed merchantman. You know the *Star of the West*, Linden—she's been here a dozen times. Unless they armed her in New York, she's a plain, simple merchant ship. Looked at from any point of view, to fire on her was about level with murder."

"South Carolina," said Linden hotly, "has seceded from the Union. She has her rights. She's an independent nation."

Swiftly he answered, "No nation has the right to fire on another's ships without declaration of war."

"Oh!" The monosyllable was attenuated almost to a sigh.

"There's more to war than flags and trumpets, Linden." The words

held a deep compassion. "You'll have to think it out for yourself."
Cleave went slowly down the stairs. He had still to face his sister.

Aunt Deborah sat patient and—at a guess—resigned at the foot of
the table. The coffee and the hot cakes and the bacon were strategically
placed in front of her. She had an entrenched position.

As Cleave settled himself, she said: "Four—or three?" and without
waiting for an answer began to fill her brother's plate. "She is utterly
beyond my control!"

Cleave watched her tolerantly. "That's the seventh time you've said
it this year."

"She refuses to grow up."

"Sense, plain sense. If we'd known enough about it, we wouldn't
have grown up either."

"Please!" His sister regarded him frostily. "She will be seventeen in
a matter of months. She's—She's . . ."

"Marriage high?" asked Cleave speculatively.

"Old enough to behave like a woman—like a lady," snapped his
sister.

"I don't think she wants to be a lady," said Cleave gently. "I don't
think she even wants to be a woman. I think she's afraid." He looked
at his sister.

"Whether she's afraid or not," said Aunt Deborah with one of her
devastating flashes of frankness, "she has a woman's body."

Cleave nodded.

"She's getting too old to be runnin' round with men and boys. . . ."

"It could be better than sitting out with them behind the pot plants
at dances."

"Jeriel leads her into things."

"I doubt it," said Cleave. "I don't think he does more than suggest
possibilities."

"It's not right—not right for her to be going around with a young
boy. People talk."

"People in this town," Cleave answered tolerantly, "will talk through
the Day of Judgment. Would you rather she went around with Revell
Jordan?"

"Mercy!" Aunt Deborah put her fingers to her mouth in a gesture of
despair.

"Jeriel keeps her out of a deal of mischief that she could get into."

"He is beginning to grow up," returned Aunt Deborah, recovering
herself.

"He is the son of the best foreman I ever had. I owe it to his father to keep an eye on him. It's as good a way as the next."

"His father was a drunk and died in a drunken brawl."

For the first time Cleave fixed his eyes on his sister. "He died—that's enough. Be gentle with Linden today. The *Star of the West* . . ."

"Foolishness," said Aunt Deborah scornfully.

"Yes," he agreed heavily, "just foolishness. But she knows now that Steve Knott was with the *Star of the West*."

They ate in silence until Linden appeared. She moved uncertainly. In a loose brown dress her body seemed to have lost its vitality. Her eyes were puzzled.

She paused beside her aunt. "Aunt Deborah, I'm sorry," she said remotely and, without waiting for an answer, went to her seat.

The meal passed slowly. Cleave watched his daughter. It was clear that she was trying to think through her difficulties. There was nothing he could do to help.

Afterward she walked down the passage to the front door with him. As he took his beaver from the many-armed hatrack, she said, "They wouldn't be drowned in sight of the shore like that." And then: "He could swim miles."

"He was always a strong swimmer." Cleave was not sure whether he said it kindly.

The girl went out in front of him. Cleave heard a voice call, "Lindy!" and saw her start. Then she said, with a return almost to her normal voice, "Rev, what are you doing with that gun?"

"Didn't you hear?" The young man stood balancing with an eager, nervous energy on the balls of his feet. He was not more than twenty, six foot, strongly built. His face was carved in strong contours. A discerning eye would note that the flesh had not yet fined away from the contours at all points, but there was no question that he would make a handsome man. He was cultivating the beginnings of a military mustache.

"I heard," answered Linden, defiantly joyous again. "Ulysses told me—when the news came. Where are you going with that gun?"

"My guess is they'll call out the company by noon." The voice had an odd and unused authority. "Governor Letcher'll send an order through some time in the morning."

"He won't," said Cleave gruffly.

Revell jumped up the last two steps. "Sir, I didn't know you were there. Sir—why?"

"Because he's still got some sense." Cleave looked the young man up and down. "What are you going to do with Sam Jordan's squirrel gun, Revell?"

The young man flushed angrily.

Chapter three

CLEAVE turned away from the great mahogany sideboard and looked at Stephen with a faintly humorous eye. "Port, Madeira, brandy?"

"I should enjoy port, sir."

In the candlelight the room looked larger than it was. It had acquired a dignity. Even the wholly fictitious ancestor over the fireplace had assumed the character of a work of art. It was his sister Deborah's ancestor. To her occasional fury Cleave would admit no connection with it.

He lifted the decanter with an accustomed care and walked back to his place at the table. Stephen filled his glass and passed the decanter back. The wine had a bright beauty in the candlelight.

Cleave said: "Right. Now that the women have gone—what was it really like?"

"Madness," Stephen muttered hurriedly. "There was no sense to it. It was unreal."

Cleave looked at him curiously. "What did you think it was going to be like?"

"I don't know. I don't suppose any of us had thought it out properly. I never believed they would shoot."

Cleave nodded approvingly at the honesty of the direct statement. "It didn't make sense then; it doesn't now. Nothing in Washington makes sense either. They had me at the Navy Department for two days. They asked the same questions over and over again."

"Did you see the President?"

"No, sir. I don't think he wanted to see me."

"He wouldn't." Cleave's voice had a sour edge to it.

"I don't think"—the hurried tempo came back to Stephen's words—

"I don't think anybody wanted to see me. I don't think anybody wanted to know about it."

Cleave studied his wine with care, sipped a little. "If you were President, with only six weeks of your term to run, would you want to look too closely at a *casus belli?*"

"Sir," Stephen answered with a quaint formality, "I am only a Navy lieutenant of one year's standing. I don't know about these things. Has a State the right to fire on an unarmed ship belonging to the Federal Government?"

"Was it the State that fired or was it that old fool Stephens—namesake of yours?" He looked quizzically at the young man.

"A State has to take the responsibility for what its soldiers do." Stephen stared down at the white damask of the tablecloth as if searching for a nonexistent stain.

"South Carolina seceded formally from the Union."

"Under the Constitution she had the right to do so. At least, that's what they taught us at Annapolis." Stephen's voice was uncertain. "If she had the right, and she did it legally, that makes her a foreign power, but a foreign power hasn't the right to open fire on an unarmed ship without declaration of war."

"That's a way of looking at it—for myself I think it's the right way—but there's more to it than that. There's the rest of the South. I don't like Buchanan—never did, I think he's an old fool—but his hands are tied. He can't start a civil war six weeks before he leaves the White House. He doesn't want to, either."

"What's going to happen then?"

"I don't know"—Cleave shrugged, his hands turned palm upward on the table—"I don't know. I wish I did. I wonder if Abe Lincoln knows?"

Stephen looked down at the table again. "Civil war, the whole future of a country, sir—and it rests on the shoulders of a small-town lawyer from Illinois."

Cleave nodded. "That's how it looks from one angle. But it may also be that it rests on the shoulders of fools like Major Stephens. Did you see what the Charleston papers said?" He thought for a minute, and quoted: " '. . . who has thus had the honour, which he so much coveted, of opening the impending conflict.' "

Stephen drained his glass. He put it down without comment. The words seemed enough in themselves. Instead he asked, "What will Virginia do?"

"If you go round to Sam Wilson's place, you will get the general idea that the State of Virginia proposes to seize Washington next week."

"He's running for election to the State Convention?"

Again Cleave nodded.

"I've heard about that. I don't like Sam Wilson."

"He won't get in," said Cleave with finality, "nor Murdaugh either. Portsmouth's solid for the Union."

"I wonder." Stephen looked up at him with a doubtful eye. "I don't seem to believe in much these days," he offered apologetically.

Cleave pushed the decanter over. "What was it really like on the *Star of the West?*" he asked, going back full circle without explanation.

"The shells," answered Stephen slowly, "came up out of the spray. They were black and glistening, and they seemed to move slowly because they were coming straight at us."

"Were you scared?"

"No," answered Stephen automatically, and rejected the negative at once. "Yes, I was scared. I wanted to hide behind the deckhouse."

Cleave nodded. "But you didn't?"

"No," agreed Stephen very slowly, "but I didn't like myself much."

"Put it down to the shock of finding out that the world is full of fools," said Cleave. "That and the first battle, and having nothing to do yourself. It doesn't add up to much. Call it experience."

"That still doesn't make me like myself."

"Times are when I despise me," said Cleave sardonically. "I've looked at my face in the mirror every morning for twenty-eight years since I began to shave." He laughed. "That's off your chest anyway."

"Perhaps, but what do I do if Virginia doesn't stay in the Union?"

"She'll stay."

"But if she doesn't?" Stephen persisted.

"Then you'll have to decide which way your loyalty lies. Virginia or a Union which can't exist without Virginia—not as a Union, anyway."

"I've sworn . . ."

"You could always resign your commission." Cleave's voice was drained of expression.

Stephen jerked his head round and faced Cleave. "Would you advise that?"

"I advise nothing. You'll have to make up your own mind. You'll get a lot of advice thrown at you in the process. For what it's worth my own view is that Virginia won't go out. But secession's a disease—it's catching. A lot of the younger people have caught it already."

"Linden?"

Cleave nodded and pushed the decanter across again. When Stephen refused it, he said: "Right. Shall we follow the ladies?"

Aunt Deborah was seated at the pianoforte. She played with restraint, with a careful avoidance of feeling, and with some inaccuracy. It was a ladylike accomplishment. Linden made a pretense at embroidering. Stephen sat down next to her, and laughed. With long fingers he stretched out the linen. "One leaf and two petals since I went away. If I could hope that you'd remembered Penelope . . ."

"Fiddle! Steve, do the girls in New York spend all their time on embroidery?"

"I never met enough girls in New York to know. I was too busy."

Without coquetry the girl said, "You expect me to believe that!"

"I was. I had four hours in New York when I went up, and the rest of the time I was on Governors Island. I drove straight from the pier to the depot when I came back."

Linden looked full at him, abandoning small talk. "What are you going to do, Steve?"

"Do?" He flicked the embroidery away.

"When the South fights."

"The South's not going to fight," Stephen asserted. "Nobody'll be such a fool as to try to relieve Fort Sumter again. They'll talk and they'll go on talking. I've been in Washington." Bitterness crept into his voice with the last words.

"The South's going to fight," said the girl calmly. "Mississippi went out of the Union while they were firing at the *Star of the West*. Florida's gone. Alabama's gone."

"Deep South—they've talked about it for thirty years."

"Georgia's going out tomorrow."

"How do you know?" demanded Stephen quickly.

"Ulysses Hogan told me."

"Ulysses Hogan," returned Stephen flatly, "told you that we'd been sunk."

The girl's eyes flickered sideways to her father. "He's been telling you."

"All the town's been telling me," answered Stephen wearily. "Nothing will happen unless Virginia secedes. Virginia won't."

"Virginia will lead the South!" Linden lifted her head, her eyes sparkling. "You're a Virginian."

He sat silent, staring at the unfinished embroidery.

"Aren't you?"

"I'm a Virginian, yes. Born and bred in this town. But I'm an officer in the Navy of the United States. One of the things I'm supposed to do is help keep them united."

"Fiddle!" snapped the girl and, rising from the sofa, walked over to the piano, dropping the embroidery behind her.

Dutifully Stephen bent down and picked it up, then he too rose. The blue uniform showed off his strong body admirably, the bright gilt buttons shining in the candlelight. The gold bands on his sleeve were impressive.

Linden smiled charmingly at her aunt. "Aunt Deb, play this for me. I want to sing."

Aunt Deborah looked at her, surprised; then she looked at the music, resettled it on the rack, and began to play.

The girl's voice was true, delicate, but she sang with deliberate irony. Stephen listened to the words with their hammer-like cadence:

> *"Listen to the mocking-bird,*
> *Listen to the mocking-bird,*
> *The mocking-bird still singing o'er her grave . . ."*

Once he caught her eyes, and she looked at him defiantly.

Cleave, watching the two faces alternately, smiled to himself, but there was a sadness in it. When the song ended he said with a gentle malice: "That song was written for Harriet Lane. What's the talk of her in Washington now?"

"Pink tulle and apple blossoms," replied Stephen a thought too quickly, and Cleave saw Linden's eyes swerve instantly to Stephen's face.

"It's not true that she rules the United States," observed Cleave cynically. "She only rules the President."

Aunt Deborah began to talk families and gossip from New York and Washington. The evening became free of undertones, almost light-hearted.

But when Stephen rose to go, Linden said lightly, her voice as mocking as the song: "Georgia tomorrow and Virginia next. And you're a Southerner, Steve."

Cleave took him to the cloakroom.

Stephen, putting a scarf round his neck, murmured: "It's a disease. She's taken it."

"She's very young. She's"—Cleave used the word almost wryly—"reluctant to grow up." Both men were silent for a moment. Finally Cleave looked Stephen in the eyes. "The trouble is that she might grow up overnight sometime." Again there was a silence that was embarrassing before he ended, "It would be a pity if you weren't there in the morning."

He took Stephen to the front door and watched him go. Then he went back into the hall and stared at himself in the mirror. His wry, humorous face stared back at him, the eyes deepset, enmeshed in wrinkles. "You've gone as far as a father decently can in telling a man to seduce his daughter," he murmured. "Stephen's got scruples." Again he watched his face in the mirror, made a little grimace at it, and said, "Pander."

He walked slowly down the hall, putting out the lamps.

Chapter four

"DOC WHITE and Mr. Holladay," said Linden bitterly, breaking the silence, "I wouldn't have believed it—I couldn't have believed it! It doesn't make sense. Virginia's South."

"Nothing makes sense," said Revell Jordan, towering in the darkness beside her.

The street lamps that led away from the Court House were far apart and dim. Behind them the noises of the crowd, the cheering, the band, the drunks, mingled and crossed each other like orchestral variations on a single theme. The little group walked stolidly down Court Street.

A voice from the rear called, "We'd have done better without Jim Murdaugh."

"What d'you mean 'better'? That wouldn't have done us no good. Wasn't Jim Murdaugh that lost us the election."

A girl's voice said: "I gave out more favors; I kissed more men. . . ."

"Ah, what the hell!" growled the man's voice. "This town's Union."

Linden said, "Portsmouth will fight for the South when the time comes."

There was no response. One by one individuals drifted away, couples at times, turning up the side streets to their homes until at last Linden and Revell were left alone with Jeriel walking like a shadow three feet behind them.

Revell began to talk rapidly. "It doesn't matter what this town thinks.

There's the whole of Virginia. Doc White and Holladay, they're just two men. Two men won't make any difference. The Convention will vote out of the Union. You watch, Lindy! That Convention'll vote out, straight out—you watch! What can Doc White do at Richmond—or Jim Holladay? They're just two men, nothing special to them, just two men. You've got to reckon the men from Petersburg an' Danville an' Roanoke. The delegates from Richmond'll vote out."

Far down the road, in the momentary light of a street lamp, Linden saw a naval officer in uniform and knew that it was Stephen. They drew together slowly, almost, it seemed, reluctantly.

Stephen greeted them. " 'Lo, Lin! How's it, Revell? What happened? I've been down at the Yard."

"We lost," answered Linden. "Doc White and Mr. Holladay were voted."

Stephen said quietly: "That's sense. Doc White's a good man."

"He borned me," put in Jeriel, as if offering the fact in confirmation.

"He's a Union man," retorted Revell savagely.

"This is a Union town," said Stephen. "Haven't they proved that tonight?"

"Takes you to say that!" Revell grunted.

"It's a Southern town," said Linden.

"Look, we've been all over this, day in, day out for the last two weeks. You've got to take the result. It was a free election."

"Ah, hell!" exclaimed Revell scornfully. "Half of the folk were scared and the other half felt in their pockets."

Linden stood in the dim light of the lamp, looking with a puzzled anxiety from face to face. "We don't belong to the North. We've got a right . . ."

Stephen's voice cut across hers. Both men were ignoring her now. "Which am I? Scared or money-grabbing? If I'd had a vote, I'd have voted for Doc White."

"Then you'd have been a traitor to Virginia," Revell almost spat.

Stephen answered calmly, "Take that back."

"Damned if I will! You've been talking like a traitor ever since you came back from the *Star of the West,* and by damn', that's what you are!"

"Stop it! Stop it!" Linden was frightened.

The two men took no notice. They stared at each other uncertainly.

Stephen said slowly: "I can't thrash you here in the street in uniform, but there's an empty lot half a block back. Jeriel, come and hold our coats for us!"

"Stephen," Linden urged, "stop it! Stop it!"

Stephen turned, suddenly aware of her. "You run home, Lin. You oughtn't to be here."

"That's right," said Revell, as if surprised in his turn. "You run home, Lindy."

The two men wheeled together and strode down the street. They both knew the empty lot. Revell was breathing hard. Neither of them looked to see what the girl did. They turned off the road, crossed the sidewalk, and moved toward the center of the vacant ground in an intense, angry preoccupation. There was a clear space there, free of scrub, the grass dead with the winter. Stephen stripped off his uniform jacket and handed it to Jeriel. The boy took it eagerly. Revell did not speak except to say "Here!" as he handed over his jacket to the boy. He rolled up his sleeves, watching Stephen warily in the darkness. They stood silent, facing each other for a minute.

Stephen said: "You've wanted a thrashing for a long time. Come on!"

He lunged forward. Revell parried the blow awkwardly. The night was very dark, overcast. There were no stars. They could see each other only as darker shapes in the darkness. Revell hit back, and Stephen came in suddenly with a left hook that jolted him. They separated and came together again.

Jeriel heard the thud of the repeated blows, the groan as a heavy one landed. He crouched down so as to see them better against the faint glow that came from the last light in Court Street. They towered above him now, enormous, flailing, reeling backward and forward. At irregular intervals there was a gasp. He heard Revell clear his throat, break away and spit, and he guessed vaguely at a cut lip and blood, trying to piece together possibilities from his own experience of school fighting.

One of the shapes collapsed suddenly out of the faint glow of the light. It was impossible to be sure whether he had been struck down or whether he had stumbled. He was up again instantly. It was impossible even to be sure which of the two men it was. The pounding began again at once. They came closer, and Jeriel watched them, Homeric, above him—wheeling shapes, flailing savagely, grunting, thudding, stumbling. He could smell the sourness of sweat. He could hear every breath as it was drawn. He could hear his own heart pounding. Neither man spoke; there seemed no time for words, no purpose in them. The blows were continuous; there was no science in it, they were like blind men guided by the contact of the last blow.

When they separated, it was by no signal. It was as if they had reached an instant, imperative agreement. They stood facing each other, perhaps six feet apart, panting heavily. Stephen stood hunched forward a little, his arms drooping. Revell stood upright. Jeriel could just distinguish one from the other in the darkness.

It was Stephen who said at last, "Come on!" and went into the attack again.

He had given up trying to find the vulnerable points on Revell's head, and concentrated instead on his body. He fought coldly, as he had begun to fight, and brutally. The necessity to hurt Revell was very strong. He was in hard condition. The couple of inches in height that he gave away was made up by the length of his reach, by the weight of his hands. He struck out savagely, trying to land each blow with the full weight of his body behind it, using his feet as he had been trained to do. Once he missed altogether and shot forward with the weight of the blow, and Revell hit the side of his head as he passed. He recovered himself with his head ringing, and groped to make contact with his opponent again. Into his anger he crowded all his hates: the stupidity of the men of the battery on Morris Island, the failures at New York and at Washington, the interminable, infuriating debates in Portsmouth, in Norfolk, and in Gosport, the frustrations of Commodore McCauley and the Yard.

Revell changed his tactics suddenly. He came in through Stephen's guard and clasped him round the waist. They wrestled breathlessly. Stephen was shaken off balance, shaken out of the rhythm of his pounding. He went down almost on his back, found a purchase on the ground, and, twisting desperately, straightened himself, surged over on top of Revell and hit blindly, feeling his fist connect with Revell's cheek. He felt a knee under him and was thrust away. Revell came to his feet again, plunged in head down, and Stephen struck as he came, and missed. Revell butted him in the stomach, knocking his breath clear. He fell again. They tumbled about the closed space, slugging, missing, tearing their knuckles on the hard ground, one man having the vantage for the moment and losing it instantly to the other.

Jeriel, squatting on his heels, moved backward or forward as he sensed the changing vantage. They were breathing more harshly now, gasping at times for air. Revell got on top and closed his hands round Stephen's throat. Stephen struck up between the outstretched arms and connected with Revell's chin, jerking his head back with a snap that could be heard, and freed himself. As Revell came up on all fours, he swung and missed and fell. They writhed on the ground again. It was too dark to see where to grasp, too dark to judge positions, too dark almost to feel. Wearily they got to their feet, and by some telepathic sign drew apart and rested, heaving, hot, and spent.

The interval was longer this time, but once more it was Stephen who said, "Come on," and added, this time, "you bastard!" And he realized that he was no longer fighting for politics, no longer fighting for the Union, no longer critical of the South. He was fighting for Linden—and he knew this simple fact in a single, blinding flash.

This time Revell came in very low and took his legs from under him, and his head crashed against the ground. Revell felt a moment of triumph. For an instant Stephen's body was limp above him, and in the same instant, it seemed, there was a convulsive heave and Stephen swung over, and his body hit against Revell's head and both men lay still, breathing stertorously. After a long time they rose together and clinched, but there was no longer heart in it, no longer anger.

They fought on, exchanging blows in a purposeless, mechanical manner. They swung at each other, but there was no weight behind the blows. They clinched, but there was no strength in the clasp. They lurched groggily over the area, and Jeriel, crouched now on one foot, his other leg free to send him instantly out of the way, watched their strange gyrations against the almost invisible glow of the lamp.

Revell asked suddenly, "You had enough?" and was answered by a blow that took him in the stomach, and he doubled up.

Stephen was too weak to follow up the advantage. They separated again and stood crouched, infinitely weary, at the point of total exhaustion.

Stephen said thickly, "Come on!" But Revell made no move. They waited, growing slowly cooler. At last Stephen straightened painfully. "We don't seem to be getting any place."

Revell gave a croaking laugh and straightened himself in turn. He said: "We don't at that. Do we pack it up?"

"We pack it up."

Revell called: "Jeri!" and Jeriel darted forward with the coats.

Stephen muttered out of a swollen mouth, "Thanks, Jeriel."

Jeriel said: "Jeez, I wouldn't'a' missed it!" and watched the two men turn and walk away from him, striding through the undergrowth beyond the clearing toward Court Street. Aloud he said, "I guess that beats everything!" Without raising his voice, he added, "Mis' Linden, we better go home now."

Linden, between two small scrub trees, demanded, "How did you know I was here?"

"I heard you. You don't move that quiet. Heh, what a fight, what a fight! I couldn't see nothin', only hear it. Neither one of them's got a horn to break."

"Jeriel!"

"I don' mean nothin', but there wasn't anythin' to end it. They jes' stopped. Jeez, what a fight, what a fight!"

They reached the sidewalk. Far down Court Street the two men were walking together; a newcomer would have said that they walked in amity. The girl and the boy turned up to the Cleave house two blocks later.

A few yards before her gate, Linden said, "It's stupid to fight over politics."

"Sure—over politics."

Softly she said: "Good night, Jeri. See you tomorrow."

"Good night, Mis' Linden." Jeriel walked on, whistling to himself.

Linden went into the house, and her father called from the drawing room, "Doc White got in, did he?"

"Yes, and Mr. Holladay."

"My fellow townsmen," commented Cleave, "have shown a little common sense for once. Norfolk will do the same. General Blow will get the vote without any trouble." He looked at Linden with his head on one side. "You don't seem to be as upset as I thought you might be."

"Steve and Rev have been fighting over it," she offered incautiously.

Cleave looked at her, silent for a long minute, then grunted. Finally he observed softly: "My daughter, I love you very dearly, but you are still not too old to be put across my knee and beaten. I am not sure that it wouldn't be wise to do it now."

She looked at him, and smiled, and he felt his heart catch at the beauty in her face as she said, "I haven't done anything, Father."

"Go to bed or I'll get that hickory stick!"

Chapter five

STEPHEN knocked on the door, opened it and walked in, according to custom. Commodore McCauley was sitting at the desk, his head resting on his hands. He jerked up abruptly as he heard the sound of Stephen's entrance—too abruptly.

Stephen said: "Sir, I thought you'd be interested to see this." He held out the copy of *Harper's Weekly*. "The British have launched the *Warrior* ironclad. There is a fuller description than we have had. She carries four and a half inches of armor for more than two hundred feet of her length." He laid down the paper.

The old man looked at it, focusing his eyes with difficulty on the print. "I don't think . . ." he began. For a moment or two he read, then he seemed to lose concentration. He looked up at Stephen, and then away from him, out through the big windows that opened on the Yard.

Beyond the end of the first ship house, with its endless tiers of windows, the bows of the frigate *Merrimac* soared high out of the water. Her jib boom was unshipped, and only the stump of her bowsprit showed. A roof of light planking had been built over her to shelter the decks while her overhaul progressed. She looked ugly, ill proportioned, un-shiplike. Beyond her, well out in the Southern Branch, lay the *United States*. The old three-decker was heavy on the water, parish-rigged, unkempt, but she had an antique dignity.

McCauley said: "I've been fifty years in the Navy. Timber's good enough for me. God never meant iron to go to sea." He smacked the paper angrily so that it curled up on either side of the flat of his hand. "Eighteen inches of teak and four and a half inches of iron outside it—she'll never carry it, sir! She'll sink under it!" He became dramatically portentous. "Would you, sir, go to sea in a gale of wind in an iron ship?"

Stephen blinked. There seemed to be no answer that combined common sense and tact.

The commodore turned still farther round in his chair, the legs grating on the wooden floor. He looked right down the length of the ship house. "Time that they made up their minds to finish the *New York*," he observed crustily. "We get no orders." He wheeled back with a surprising agility and looked up at Stephen with his eyes narrowed, peering through the close lids under the wild growth of his eyebrows. "We get no orders from Washington—nothing that you can take hold of. This man Toucey—you ever met him?" The gruff abruptness of the voice dismissed Toucey. "Who's going to replace him? Does this man Lincoln know anything about the Navy? I heerd"—his voice took on a painful parody of a Midwestern accent—"I heerd he floated down the Mississippi on a flatboat. Who's he going to put at the head of the Navy Department, d'you know?"

Stephen shook his head slowly. The old man was having one of his bad mornings.

"Some grocer from New York!" McCauley sat silent, his jaws moving slightly as if he were chewing something delicate and soft. His lips were tightly closed. After a long interval in which there was neither sign of dismissal nor attempt to keep Stephen's attention, he said suddenly, "You're a Southerner."

"I'm a Virginian, sir," Stephen answered with careful dignity.

"What's this dam' Convention going to do?" McCauley did not wait for an answer. "Talk, talk, talk—all that conventions ever do is talk. Will White's a Union man, that's something. So is Blow. The West Virginians, they'll be Union men. Is Virginia going to stay in the Union, Lieutenant?"

"Sir, I don't know." Softly Stephen added, "I hope so."

"Half the Yard will go out if she doesn't." McCauley's voice changed. It was grim now, shrewd and to the point. "Half my officers—more—will go. What do I do about the Yard? I've had no orders from Washington. Even when they started that dam' nonsense with the *Star of the West* . . ." Suddenly he lowered his head again and narrowed his eyelids. "You were with the *Star of the West,* weren't you?" Disregarding Stephen's nod, he snorted: "God-dammed stupidity! Even after they ordered the *Brooklyn* to sea I had no orders, no instructions, no guidance. What do they want me to do?" He lifted the paper and held it between finger and thumb with an air of contempt. "Take this dam' thing away! Iron ships. Steam ships that can't keep the sea. Engines that break down three times in a watch. The *Merrimac* there!" He gestured through the open window. "Her engines broke down eighteen times in three months. Take it away, take it away! I don't care what the French have done—or the English."

*   *   *

The basement of the Vermillion House was given over to the company. Against the rear wall the badge of the Old Dominion Guard was painted in flaring colors. On the one side it was flanked by the flag of Virginia, on the other by the Stars and Stripes. Twice the Company had asked Vermillion to take down the Union flag. Twice he had answered: "Wait till we secede, boys! Plenty time for that." The Virginian flag hung down in rich folds. Somebody had draped the Stars and Stripes back on its staff—Vermillion had allowed that.

There were twenty-eight men of the Guard in the room; they sat on barrels, on the table, on the window ledges. From the seat next to Vermillion at the head of the table a gaunt, dark man harangued them.

He had the tight-drawn facial skin of a fanatic. "They'll rise any minute now. They got 280 men—definite! Most of them from Doc Beasley's crowd. Used t'meet over Beach's stables in the big hall there. You know it, Luther—where you got the sorrel. They're goin' to rush the White House first—Capitol next. Buchanan, he won't know what's happened to him. If the Vice Pres'dent don't open the c'tificates— ain't no President." His arms spread out dramatically, the fingers of his hands splayed back in tension.

"Don't believe it," Vermillion protested.

"Lootenant," said the gaunt man urgently, "I heerd them, I heerd them myself. All they got to do is burn the c'tificates and the thing's finished. Lincoln, he won't come to Washington—wouldn't dare. Washington's bin as full of plans as the bay's full of fish when the shad run. If *they* do it, *we* got to do somethin'!" The gaunt man was insistent. Voices from round the room supported him.

"Such as?" prompted Vermillion skeptically.

"If we wis to get together with the National Grays and the Rifle Company and Jim Choat's boys, and mebbe the Light 'Tillery, we could take the Navy Yard. Ain't more'n three hundred men there— Marines, seamen, they're a poor lot." He lifted one hand like a Baptist minister exhorting the brethren.

Revell, his face alight, shouted, "We could take the Yard in an hour!"

Behind him a man demanded, "And have the *Cumberland* and the *Pennsylvania* fire into Portsmouth?"

"We'll act legal," said Vermillion. "When Richmond tells us to do something, we'll do it."

The room dissolved in argument. It was almost impossible to distinguish individual words, to hear out single sentences. Men shouted, blared, hurled their words into the uproar.

In the middle of it a man came in and handed Vermillion a paper.

The lieutenant read: "Abraham Lincoln, of Illinois, having received a majority of the whole number of electoral votes, is elected President of the United States for four years, commencing the 4th of March, 1861."

The newcomer said: "There was no disturbance. The meeting was orderly."

*　　*　　*

Aunt Deborah sat upright, her hands resting neatly in her lap. Her body was exactly aligned; the feet close together, invisible under the wide-swept flounces of her dress; her back straight and centered, accepting no support from the arms or the back of the chair. Smoothly, blandly, she asked questions. She had an elaborate circle of acquaintance: Navy wives in Washington, Navy wives around the New York Navy Yard, Navy widows, Navy fiancées, Navy children.

Stephen liked her. In spite of her angularities, her occasional eccentricities, he could sense the real warmth in her. He could even—he found himself smiling very faintly at the thought of it—sympathize with her in her eternal conflict with Linden. She could not reach Linden's mind, she could not match its mercurial movement, she could not understand its evasions, its darts, its sudden twists. It was more than the ordinary division between the young and the elderly. Quite simply, she could not keep pace—she had admitted as much to him in a rare moment of weakness. In the six years since the death of Linden's mother during the yellow-fever epidemic, she had tried to keep pace. Most of the time, Stephen thought, she had been breathless.

She was breathless now. Suddenly she stopped the long catechism of birth and death and marriage and scandal. "I told her to be back at three o'clock!"

"She'll come," Stephen assured her tranquilly.

"She has no sense of obligation." Then, with a quick flash of perception, Aunt Deborah said, "The mind of a dragonfly."

"And the beauty," added Stephen softly.

Aunt Deborah thought for a moment, as if carefully weighing all the possible aspects of the question. "She has beauty of movement and light and color," she agreed surprisingly, "not a classic beauty. It's not" —she fixed her eyes on Stephen—"not restful."

Stephen laughed out loud. "Her father would agree with you. But it's exciting."

"I'm growing too old for excitement."

Again he laughed. "You have no need to fear growing old—not today nor for a long time to come."

Aunt Deborah allowed herself a grim chuckle. "You've been saying nice things to me since you were twelve years old. I like you, Stephen." Again there was a flash of perception. "Don't let that child hurt you!"

Stephen looked at her, startled. "What can I do?" He studied the elaborate convolutions of the carpet. "Anything can happen." He looked up at Aunt Deborah questioningly. "What's Lincoln going to do? Why doesn't he say something? Why doesn't he make his position clear? If the ultras at Montgomery get their way—" He paused lamely.

Aunt Deborah asked, without emphasis, "D'you think there's going to be a war, Stephen?"

"There could be—there could be easily. I don't think Abraham Lincoln's strong enough to stop it. I don't know enough about him—nobody knows enough about him."

"Men," observed Aunt Deborah, reverting to her chill normality, "are fools. Abe Lincoln included."

"Well," said Stephen wryly, "that's comprehensive."

They heard Linden's voice in the street outside, dismissing Jeriel. She sounded elated. There was a momentary change of light in the windows as she came up the stairs to the porch, and they heard the door slam.

Stephen watched Aunt Deborah, certain that she was framing rebuke, but Linden came in at the drawing-room door laughing and eager, and rebuke died. She stood framed against it, holding out a paper in her hand.

The paper was smudged with printer's ink, a newspaper galley proof. She read: "President Jefferson Davis, amidst the thunder of cannon and the tumultuous cheers of an inspired crowd, took the oath this morning as President of the Confederate States of America. Scenes of enthusiasm never before experienced in the city of Montgomery have today set the South on fire. The flames of patriotism, the glory of a new nationalism, the fervor and spirit . . ."

"Jefferson Davis is a fool," declared Aunt Deborah. "More'n that—he's a cold fool. Don't ever trust a cold fool!" She got up and swept out of the room. At the door she added, "I'm even sorry for that Varina Howell."

"Your aunt knows something of every naval wife in the Service." Stephen's voice was lazy. "Seems as if she knows something of politicians' wives as well."

"For a woman who sings as softly as she does in church Sundays—" Linden left the sentence in the air. Her expression changed; there was a quick anxiety. "Stephen"—she held out the blotched proof to him—"what are you going to do about this?"

He watched her face intently. There was an uncertainty in it that matched the new note in her voice. He had a sudden impression of fragility, a knowledge that she could be hurt. When he spoke at last his voice was gentle. "What *can* I do about it, Lin?"

"Ulysses told me Jefferson Davis is going to set up a Confederate Navy."

Stephen sat up abruptly, but he murmured, "That's just Ulysses—"

"No!" The eagerness was overrunning the anxiety now. "Captain Semmes' cousin Judith told him. She came down from Washington yesterday."

Stephen subsided again. "Cousin's talk!" He laughed briefly. "He'll try. Won't get him anywhere, though. You've got to have ships to have a navy."

She faced him like a fury. "He'll get ships. He'll get men. He'll get officers too. There's nothing the South can't do!"

He got to his feet, startled. "Lin, listen to me! I'm in the Union Navy. I'm an officer. What's Jefferson Davis's navy to me? 'Tisn't even as if Virginia was in the Confederacy. She isn't, she isn't going to be. You know how the Convention will vote."

"I'm sick of the Convention! I'm sick of everything. I'm sick of . . ." She stopped herself. Stephen was miserably certain that she had almost said, "you."

"Lin," he asked urgently, "why does it mean so much to you? Why's it so personal? Portsmouth has nothing to do with Charleston. It's not even as if slaves meant anything to you. Your father freed the last of his just after you were born. You've never had anything to do with them. What is it?"

"I don't know. I don't know. . . . We're not free. We're tied to the North. I hate Yankees. I hate . . . I hate . . ." She turned suddenly to the fireplace, rested her forearms on the high mantel, and pressed her face against them.

An enormous, flooding compassion took Stephen. He walked hesitantly across the room to her and put his hands round the cage of her ribs and felt, almost with the effect of a galvanic shock, the urgent life that they prisoned, the vibrant, beating energy inside them. Even as he felt and measured it he registered in incongruous parallel the fact that she was not wearing her stays, and that Aunt Deborah would explode if she knew.

For a long moment he held her, his hands giving to the quick pulse of her breathing. Then, with an inseparable mixture of passion and compassion, of pity and desire, he moved his hands up over the soft thin flesh of her ribs until they cupped the pointed breasts. In the brief permitted moment his mind recalled his desperate wish as a boy to stroke the breast of a bluejay, and the disillusion that had met experiment. Then the moment was gone.

As panicked, as angry as the bird, she snatched herself out of his hands, swept across the room, stood with her back against the wall and her hands splayed out for support on the wallpaper, and said in a voice that he had never heard before: "I won't be touched—I won't, I won't! Nobody must touch me. I belong to myself!"

*   *   *

Ulysses said hurriedly: "I'll find it—I'll find it! I cut it out. It'll be somewheres here." His hands raked uncertainly in an enormous confusion of papers. "Read the *Delta* whiles I look for it. It's good— b'God it's good!"

Linden looked down at the marked passage: " 'Mr. Lincoln's silly speeches, his ill-timed jocularity, his pusillanimous evasion of responsibility, and vulgar pettifoggery, have no parallel in history, save in the crazy capers of Caligula, or in the effeminate buffoonery of Henry of Valois. . . .' "

"Them's fightin' words." Ulysses offered up the old phrase vaguely, his hands continuing the search as if they were independent of his mind.

"What did Henry of Valois do?"

"Nothing for pure young representatives of Southern womanhood to talk about," replied Ulysses.

Linden allowed herself to be diverted; she was not altogether sure of her ground. She began to read another clipping: " 'People now marvel how it came to pass that Mr. Lincoln should have been selected as the representative man of any party. His weak, wish-washy, namby-pamby efforts, imbecile in matter, disgusting in manner, have made us the laughingstock of the whole world. The European powers will despise us because we have no better material out of which to make a President. . . .' "

"That was a Northern paper—Salem, no less—but when I write like that my respected editor, my sainted master, my immaculate boss says—"

" 'You're wastin' paper again, bo-o-y!' " Old Sam Davies, doubled over his composing stick, did not even bother to look up. "Not that you ever wrote like that. You ain't got the style—nor yet the learnin'." He hawked and spat with great accuracy at the copper spittoon. "Eff'n it's the *Noo York Times* you're lookin' for, it said, 'He wore a Scotch plaid cap and a very long military cloak, so that he was entirely unrecognizable.' That's exac'. I know—I set it 'bout an hour ago."

"A Scotch plaid cap!" The girl's eyes sparkled. "Honest Abe and a

Scotch plaid cap!" Her voice was bright with malice. "Has anybody ever made such a fool of himself?"

"Most of us," rejoined old Sam sourly.

"Most of us aren't President." Ulysses' voice was distant.

"Nor ever likely to be." The old compositor began to lead out a column. His fingers moved with the assurance and accuracy of fifty years of dedication. He slipped in the last of the thin brass strips and with the same precision lifted a folded paper from a shelf and handed it toward Linden. "He don't know the best of it," he said with a broad contempt. "He don't read the Kaintuck papers. He don't like Kaintucky."

She looked down at the sheet in her hands and read the name "*Louisville Courier.*"

Sam grunted. "Smart paper. You read the pome!"

She searched for a moment, unfamiliar with the layout of the paper, and then suddenly it leaped at her—a long poem, thirteen verses in the meter of "Yankee Doodle," thirteen acrid, blistering verses describing Lincoln's flight across Baltimore, the weeping of his friends, the scorn of his enemies, the idiocy of his advisers. She became utterly absorbed in it, avid, lost—and suddenly she threw the paper up and began to chant:

> "*Lanky Lincoln came to town,*
> *In night and wind and rain, sir,*
> *Wrapped in a military cloak*
> *Upon a special train, sir.*"

Ulysses stared at her open-mouthed. "Where did you get that?"

"Kaintuck paper that you wouldn' read," replied Sam acidly, "all about how Mr. Lincoln came to Washin'ton. Smart poet they keep on the *Courier,* I reckon."

Ulysses stretched out a hand demandingly. "Give! I'll take it in to the editor."

Sam's back began to shake with silent laughter.

"Have you shown it to him?" demanded Ulysses suspiciously.

"Set it up hour and a ha'f ago, sent him in a proof. He won't use it, though."

"Why? Why?" Ulysses threw up an impassioned face. "That's why this paper's going down the hill. Scared of its own shadow! No guts. No courage. No energy. Why? Why?"

"Reckon he's got more sense," observed Sam flatly.

Ulysses struck an attitude of despair. "Sense!" he exclaimed with dramatic overemphasis.

Linden stared over the fonts at the old man. "It's good or you wouldn't have set it up," she said accusingly. "Why shouldn't he use it? This is a Southern paper."

"Not that Southern, it isn't! Editor, he laughed. Twenty minutes' time he'll send out and tell me he wants a dozen proofs for the club. I've got 'em ready"—he slapped a neat pile of paper at his side— "but he won't print it. For why? Because he knows they got thugs in Baltimore. Hire a man to 'sassinate a President-elect for fifty bucks and a fifth o' rye."

"If he had a fifth of the stuff that makes a President in him, he'd defy a hired assassin." Linden's voice was scornful. "Marse Linkum!" She almost spat the Negro version of the name. "He's not President yet and he won't be in twelve months' time either! Not of the United States, he won't." Her voice took on an almost evangelical fervor. "There won't be any United States."

"I got a next-year's calendar to the house," said Sam calmly. "I'll mark that up. 'Mind you of it next April."

"Aa-ah!" Linden managed to roughen her voice almost into a snarl. "A President who sneaks into his capital like a thief in the night, with his tail between his legs."

"Mind your metaphors, Linden," said a deep voice behind her. "Sam! Run me off a dozen proofs of that Linkie Deedle."

"Got 'em here," answered Sam complacently. "I reckoned on twenty minutes. You goin' to eat early?"

"I'm going to drink," said the editor firmly. "Linden, you go home and don't keep my staff from idling more than his natural bent allows for. And don't take any more proofs home! I've had your Aunt Deborah complaining to me."

"That would be about the little girl who wrote to him about growing a set of whiskers."

" 'I'll put my trust in Providence, and let my whiskers grow,' " quoted the editor gravely. "She said it was blasphemous. I'm afraid of your Aunt Deborah. Remember that!"

*   *   *

The horse picked its way delicately between the piles of lumber. Steam from a leak in the pipe a yard from the big upright boiler hissed confidentially in the raw air. A flurry of rain swept over the Elizabeth River, pockmarking the silver surface of the water. Men were shouting down at a barge that was coming in with the tide toward the little wharf. The horse reached a long stretch of sawdust, and its hoofs ceased to make a sound. Cleave looked down at the angular head affectionately—he claimed that Beauty was the second ugliest horse in Portsmouth.

The four Negroes worked under the eye of Callaghan, the Irish foreman, close to the gate. They were working at a live-oak knee. The curved timber was raw from the adz.

Callaghan spoke as Cleave came parallel with him. "What's Abe Lincoln goin' to say this mornin'?" he demanded truculently.

Cleave looked down at him, frowning a little. "I don't know. Nobody knows."

"He'd better say somethin' definite."

Cleave rode out of the yard onto the unmade track that led up toward Crawford Street.

Almost at once a woman asked him, "What's Mist' Lincoln going to say this morning, Mist' Cleave?"

"I don't know—wish I did!"

At the corner of Crawford Street and the track a group of men called out: "Thought you'd be to Washington, Mr. Cleave. What's he going to say?"

He turned past them into Crawford Street and called over his shoulder, "I wish I knew."

Everybody, he felt, wished for knowledge—all the town, even the children. Nobody knew. For a moment he projected his mind through the town, thinking himself into houses and offices, saloons and clubs. Nobody knew: everybody was waiting. Beyond the town everybody was waiting. He thought suddenly of farms, and fishing boats in the Tidewater and ships beyond them, and other villages and towns and cities, endlessly spreading out through the mountains, down the valleys, along the shallows and creeks of the coast—seaports, farm towns, mining towns and cattle towns, spreading out and out down the long rivers to the Gulf, and beyond the Gulf to the new territories, and beyond the territories to the West. He had a vision of the whole country in the clarity and the brilliance of a medieval miniature, the vision of a nation waiting—waiting for war or perhaps for peace. Linden and Revell and young Vermillion and Jim Choat and some others were certain that it would be war. The mayor, Doc White still away at Richmond, General Blow, and some others believed that it would be peace. Between them was all the rest of the nation. Nobody knew.

He passed Atcheson, and Atcheson shouted: "I wish I'd gone up to Washington. This waiting's worse'n a battle."

Cleave nodded in abstracted agreement.

The name evoked a picture of the place. He thought of the dome of the Capitol as he had seen it last—unfinished, with the gantry rising in the middle of it and the scaffolding round about, and the timber and the iron and the stonework lying on the great lawn in front of the building. He thought—and smiled wryly at the thought—of the great bronze statue of Liberty, Liberty with a sword in one hand and a wreath of flowers in the other, that was to surmount the summit of the dome when it was built at last.

Another flurry of rain swept down the street, and he shivered, and knew that he was shivering not because of the rain but because of the communicable fear that held all the town in its grasp this cold March noon.

Neither the rain nor the wind nor the cold served to keep people off the streets. The sidewalks were crowded as he approached Main Street. Main Street itself was thronged with carriages, with men on horseback, with country carts. People leaned out of open windows. The place was noisy with talk. He himself was lost now in the crowd, as if his identity had lasted only as far as the end of Crawford Street. Main Street was the city itself, and the city was full of apprehension.

Just short of the telegraph office Stephen stepped off the sidewalk and greeted him. His face was set and anxious. Out of the saloon two doors down the street from the telegraph office came a roar of voices. Over it Stephen called, "Nothing's come through yet."

Automatically Cleave looked at his watch. "Not due to start till noon."

"Hitching post outside the telegraph office's jammed up with people. Better go round the corner and in the back way," advised Stephen practically. He took Beauty's bridle and led the ungainly beast between the carriages, mumbling a greeting as he passed each.

Mackenzie, the local manager of the telegraph company, was an old friend. He sat now at his desk, long ribbons of punched tape flooding out and trailing down onto the ground beneath it. He returned Cleave's greeting. "Nothing yet, Ashwell. Drizzling in Washington, same as here. Old Fuss-and-Feathers has taken"—he looked at a section

of the tape as if to refresh his memory—" 'all reasonable precautions.'
It'll be coming through any minute now."

Cleave looked round the packed room. Almost all of them were
Union men, and almost all of them looked doubtful now. He could
feel the communication of anxiety throughout the room. There was a
silence. In the silence they could hear the clicking of the instruments
in the operators' room behind them. The thin wooden partition cut
off sight but not sound.

Against that background Cleave tried to picture the scene at the
Capitol, superimposing it upon his earlier memory of the unfinished
building: a dais crowded with officers and politicians, with reporters
and friends and judges, and old Chief Justice Taney—shriveled, mum-
mified, desperately anxious—waiting to administer the oath. He tried
to brush in a picture of the new President: immensely tall, simian,
Lincoln the baboon, lanky Lincoln, Lincoln the rail-splitter, Lincoln
the mouthpiece of the cold, grasping, industrial North. The newspapers
offered no real guidance. The newspapers stormed or jeered or railed
or were querulous. What was this man like? Was there a man behind
the grotesque façade? Where was his humanity? What shape was it?

An anonymous hand thrust through the window with a length of
tape. Mackenzie studied it. "Procession's over. Reckon he's about
coming up on the platform."

"No trouble?" asked a voice.

"No trouble."

Outside in the street there was a brief roar. Something had excited
the crowd.

In the little inner room there was silence.

A fresh batch of paper came in. "Flub-dub," declared Mackenzie
scornfully. "Somebody's fell out of a tree."

They waited. Cleave watched Stephen, studying his face as if he
could find in it some solution to this problem. The younger man's eyes
were worried. For him there was no solution: he could not see a clear
way. Every possible course of action was overlaid with conditions
and exceptions.

Mackenzie pulled in another skein of tape and jerked himself upright in his chair. "Speaking! Taney's given him the oath. He's Pres'dent
now." His eye ran down the tape, stripping it from hand to hand with
a quick, practiced motion. The neat round holes seemed to leap together for him, to coagulate into words and phrases and sentences:
" 'Apprehension seems to exist among the people of the Southern

States,' " he read out, " 'that by the accession of a Republican Administration, their property, and their peace, and personal security, are to be endangered. There has never been any reasonable cause for such apprehension. . . .' "

"What's he mean by 'reasonable cause'?"

Mackenzie overrode the interruption: " 'I have no purpose, directly or indirectly, to interfere with the institution of slavery in the States where it exists. I believe I have no lawful right to do so, and I have no inclination to do so. . . .' "

Cleave felt as if pressure were lifting from his skin, as if under his coat he moved more freely, as if his body were lighter.

A sepulchral voice said, "If he sticks to that, what have we got to lose?"

Argument developed as to where the original statement about slavery had been made—friendly argument, overlaid with a particular approval. In the middle of it the machines began to click again.

Mackenzie waited until there was an accumulation of tape and straightened up to his desk to study it again. "Fugitive slaves—he's covering that one now—'shall be delivered up.' "

A man close to Cleave said, "Maybe he's not what the newspapers have called him."

"Is any man?" asked Cleave.

Mackenzie hammered his desk suddenly. " 'I hold,' " he read portentously, " 'that, in contemplation of universal law and of the Constitution, the Union of these States is perpetual . . .' "

"Jesus," exclaimed a voice, "that's speaking!"

" 'Can it, as a contract, be peaceably unmade by less than all the parties who made it?' "

"That's one for South Car'lina!" said the man close to Cleave.

And a new voice muttered, "That's one for Jeff Davis!"

Mackenzie read again: " 'The power confided to me will be used to hold, occupy and possess the property and places belonging to the Government, and to collect the duties and imposts; but beyond what may be necessary for these objects, there will be no invasion—no using of force against or among the people anywhere. . . .' " Mackenzie held up the skein of tape. "I read that means peace," he commented softly.

Cleave murmured, "Amen."

They waited, relaxed, almost cheerful, while Mackenzie scanned new lengths of tape.

Abruptly he said: "Listen! 'Physically speaking, we cannot separate. We cannot remove our respective sections from each other, nor build an impassable wall between them. . . .' " He ran a long length of tape between his fingers. " 'Suppose you go to war, you cannot fight always; and when, after much loss on both sides, and no gain on either, you cease fighting, the identical old questions as to terms of intercourse are again upon you.' "

Cleave said, "This is a man!"

The last skein of tape slipped by, and Mackenzie wiped his forehead. " 'In your hands, my dissatisfied fellow countrymen, and not in mine, is the momentous issue of civil war. . . .' " He was silent, his eyes flickering down the holes, the tape streaming through his fingers. The room was utterly silent with him; even the clicking of the machines beyond the partition was still. " 'We are not enemies, but friends.' " Mackenzie's voice was harsh now. " 'We must not be enemies. Though passion may have strained, it must not break our bonds of affection. The mystic cords of memory, stretching from every battlefield, and patriot grave, to every living heart and hearthstone, all over this broad land, will yet swell the chorus of the Union, when again touched, as surely they will be, by the better angels of our nature.' " Mackenzie flung up his head. "Message ends. That's a great man speaking."

Through the room there was something like a sigh, a deep breath of relief, a gust of escaping tension.

The deep sepulchral voice said, "Reckon that means peace."

Near the door a man growled, "I guess we can go now, Mac."

And Mackenzie said, "Yes, I think that's all."

The crowd in front of the telegraph office filled the street. No traffic moved. Here and there a man on horseback, penned in the crowd, towered above the sea of heads.

Cleave, coming out on the porch of the telegraph office, heard a stentorian voice shouting: " 'The Union of these States is perpetual . . .' What does that mean? 'Can a contract be peaceably unmade by less than all the parties?' What does that mean? 'The power will be used to hold, occupy and possess the places belonging to the Government . . .' What does that mean? 'I am not prepared to speak to those who want to destroy the Union . . .' What does that mean? It means war! It means that a damned Yankee lawyer is going to come round the back of things and force war. It means that he won't talk or discuss peace—he'll force war. It means that he'll relieve Fort Sumter and that'll mean war—and Fort Pickens, and *that*'ll mean war. It means that whatever we do or say . . ."

There was a flurry in the crowd, and a small group of men moved with a sudden purpose. The voice stopped. Cleave saw Revell shift from a position behind the speaker, and arms flailing. Then for no visible reason there was quiet. The crowd as a whole moved neither one way nor the other. There was no riot.

"Words," said Cleave softly, "mean different things to different people."

Chapter six

SHARP, lying back in the deep, uncomfortable chair, asked lazily, "What makes you think Virginia won't go South?"

"Everything that's happened at the Convention up to now," replied Stephen aggressively. "The vote to stay in the Union's been overwhelming."

"Wait till Honest Abe gets going!" Pegram, watching the younger man carefully, put enough cynicism in his voice to get a hot retort from Stephen.

"You've twisted the inaugural! That was a straight appeal for peace."

"I don't know whether it was or whether it wasn't." Pegram's voice was filled with a doubt that was wholly honest. "I suppose I've read it ten times now. It means something different to me every time. If you read the newspapers, it means something different to every editor and, if you talk to people, it means something different to every person."

Stephen said stubbornly, "It was clear enough to me!"

"Then why are we commissioning the *Pocahontas?*"

Sharp, from his position low down in the chair, offered a quotation: " 'The power confided to me will be used to hold, occupy and possess the property and places belonging to the Government . . .' "

"We don't know what service she's going on," said Stephen stubbornly.

"She might just be going out into the Atlantic for a nice quiet cruise" —Sharp's tone was acidulous—"but you know she's not and I know she's not. She's going to Pickens or she's going to Sumter; from the order for coal, I'd say Sumter. If Abe Lincoln tries that, there'll be war."

"You've no proof that the order has anything to do with the President. It's possible that it's simply a precautionary move on the part of Welles."

"Postmaster, editor, Secretary of State for the Navy"—Pegram's voice was full of scorn—"what does he know about it? What does he know about anything? Father Welles, Grandfather Welles—have you ever seen him, Stephen?" Stephen shook his head. "I saw him when he was Chief of the Bureau of Provisions and Clothing thirteen years ago—too far back for you, Stephen. He was an old woman then. He's older now."

"If you feel like that about him," said Stephen, watching Sharp's face while he spoke, "why don't you go down to Montgomery and offer yourself to Cat-o'-Nine-Tails Mallory?"

Sharp jerked angrily.

"All that was a long time ago," Pegram answered, his voice even. "Mallory did a lot of good for the Navy with the Retiring Board."

"Some of us," agreed Stephen softly—too softly, "wouldn't have got our promotion if it hadn't been for the deadheads he cleared out."

Pegram flushed angrily.

Sharp sat up, the lazy good nature gone from his voice. "The question is what you'll do if the Confederacy fights."

"The Confederacy won't fight." Stephen's voice was as hard as the other man's. "I'm damned certain it won't fight unless the Border States come in. Jeff Davis is not that much of a fool, and the Border States won't join."

"How do you know? How does anyone know?"

"The Convention knows," replied Stephen. "There'll be another vote two or three days from now, and you know what the voting's going to be. Everybody knows."

"And nobody knows," said Pegram, "what the Convention'll do if Abe Lincoln forces things."

"He won't," declared Stephen resolutely.

"Then what are we getting the *Pocahontas* ready for?" The argument had come back to its starting point in the normal Service circle.

Sharp cut across it again. "If Virginia goes with the Confederacy, what will you do?"

Stephen's face for the first time was troubled. "I don't know, because I don't know what the reasons would be that would make her go with the Confederacy."

"I'm a Virginian," said Pegram softly, with a vibrant warmth in his voice.

Stephen felt a quick irritation. "Hell, I'm a Virginian too, but I was born in the Union and bred in it and raised in it, and I elected to go into its Navy—and that goes for you and for Sharp too. What's all this about, anyway?"

"We want to know," Sharp replied, "what you will do if Virginia goes in with the South."

"I'll tell you when she goes," said Stephen curtly. "Ask me then."

"We're asking you now."

"Why?"

"The Navy Yard," said Pegram obliquely, "would be damned important in a war between the North and the South."

"Sure it would be damned important! D'you think Welles doesn't know that? D'you think Washington doesn't know it? You don't think they'll let Norfolk and Portsmouth go, do you?"

Sharp had slumped deep in his chair again. "Then why do they leave us with that eminent example of senility, Commodore McCauley, in command?"

"Because"—Stephen's voice had a trace of uncertainty in it—"because they're sure that Virginia won't go out. If they replace McCauley, I'd take it as a sign that they felt she might."

Pegram shrugged his shoulders and walked over toward the door. With his hand on the knob he turned. "I was over at Monroe yesterday morning. The talk there was that General Scott had decided to hold Fortress Monroe."

"Of course he's decided to hold Fortress Monroe!" Stephen snapped. "What else would he do?"

"He's decided that he has only troops enough to hold Fortress Monroe. He's got nothing to spare to garrison Portsmouth and the Navy Yard." Pegram went out and shut the door behind him.

"You going to think it over, Steve?" Sharp's voice was silken. "I hear Semmes has gone down to Montgomery and Catesby ap Roger Jones."

Stephen shrugged in turn. "Catesby Jones was one of the people Mallory's Retiring Board put out." A frown creased his forehead.

As he went to the door Sharp said behind him, "The early bird gets the promotion."

*   *   *

The boy on the stringpiece of the wharf caught the line expertly. Looking down at Linden, he called, "Convention is voted, Mis' Linden."

The girl jerked up her head. "How?"

"Stay in the Union, Mis' Linden. Reckon you'll be mad."

"I am mad," said Linden briefly. "Jeriel, throw the fish up! Don't stand there gawping."

The small boy whistled. "Shad! Whose nets you bin poachin'?"

"We don' poach," retorted Jeriel virtuously. "We bin helpin' Andy Macrae. Catch!" He threw up a basket and then commenced throwing fish in quick, silver arcs.

Linden busied herself making fast the mainsail. She moved angrily, jerking the knot on the lashing, dumping the rudder and the tiller with thuds on the bottom boards of the boat. Finally she went up the iron rungs of the ladder with a purposeful fury and stalked across between the piles of lumber toward the office of the wood yard.

Callaghan looked up from marking the end of a cedar log. "Aft'noon, Miss Linden. Your pa said for you to get dressed and come on back to the house."

"You've heard about the vote?" Linden asked.

"Sure I've heard about it! Somebody's got some common sense, anyways."

"Sense!" The girl almost snapped the word.

Callaghan grinned at her. "Jeff Davis, he'll have to think o' somethin' else now. Ain't goin' to be no war."

Linden turned on him. "Then what are they fitting out the *Pocahontas* for? What about the orders for the *Merrimac*? Came through yesterday morning. You've heard about them by now—everybody in the town's heard about them."

"I guess that's common sense too," answered Callaghan shrewdly, "jest common sense. If I was Abe Lincoln, I'd do the same. Ain't no use having ships if they ain't ready. *Merrimac,* she's been lying there too long anyways. Don't know what they bin thinkin' about."

Linden stalked on past him. As she entered the door of the ramshackle office she called back, "Yankees don't think."

Callaghan stood looking after her. "They think right smart sometimes," he said ruminatively, "right smart."

Jeriel came up with the small boy, carrying the basket of fish between them. "Two-three shad, Mist' Callaghan?" he offered.

"Sure. Put 'em in my hut. She's good and mad."

"B'n mad all day. Knew it was goin' to happen. We'd have got twice as many shad if she hadn't tangled with Andy Macrae."

"Her pa says for her to go to the house."

Jeriel considered this for a moment before he said with unexpected wisdom, "Reckon he don't want fer her to go stickin' her neck out an' get into more trouble." He sighed profoundly, while the small boy watched him with a measure of admiration. "She shore takes a lot o' steerin'!"

Callaghan got down on his knees again and resumed the cabalistic chalking of the end of the cedar log. After a moment he laughed. "Like that dam' little boat of hers. Well, it ain't my war!"

Linden stalked back to the house in South Street, Jeriel walking tolerantly half a pace to the rear. He was a connoisseur of Linden's moods. The small boy abandoned them.

Cleave looked up from the long horsehair sofa as she entered the drawing room. Revell, sitting in one of the fireplace chairs, got to his feet, hurried and awkward.

Distantly Linden greeted him. Even more distantly she greeted her father. "Callaghan gave me your message," she said in a thin voice.

Cleave looked at her with a gleam of humor in his eye. "I thought it would be safer."

"Safer!"

"It is quite possible," explained Cleave gently, "that there may be demonstrations in the town. This town likes demonstrations."

"A person has a right to say what he thinks."

"Something in that," admitted Cleave.

Revell's eyes moved from the girl to her father and back again. "That's democracy," said Linden, as one who drives an advantage home.

"It is"—Cleave's voice was almost humble—"but democracy also implies the rule of the majority, and there was a pretty big majority at Richmond—eighty-eight to forty-five to be exact"—he picked up a piece of paper with an almost illegible scrawl across it, as if to refresh his memory—"*against* a motion to introduce an Ordinance of Secession."

Revell sat upright. "It's not final!"

"Two to one"—Cleave's voice for the first time had a little edge to it —"if you will allow me the odd decimal points, seems pretty damn' final to me."

"It wasn't a vote against a Secession Ordinance!" protested Revell hotly. "It was only against a motion to bring one in."

"You can't vote against an ordinance if you don't bring it in"— Cleave's tone had a deceptive reasonableness—"but you can't vote *for* it, either. I'm strong on democratic principles myself. I have decided to accept the will of the majority"—Linden glared at him—"and that goes for my family too. I have decided that my family is not going to raise any more hell around this town."

Linden said, "Oh!" with a quick explosion of breath.

"I have already"—the sweet reasonableness in Cleave's tone continued—"expressed my views to your Aunt Deborah. She has given me her promise. I have, of course, no rights or, I suppose, even influence over Revell here, but as he informs me that he is about to secede personally to South Carolina—"

Linden broke in: "Are you going then? Why didn't you tell me? What are you going to do? When are you going? What's happened?" She turned from Revell and faced her father angrily.

Cleave held up a hand in mock defense. "Not my doing."

Revell muttered with clumsy apology: "I had another letter from my cousin 's mornin'. They want men for his company—want 'em bad. He says if I was to go down straightaway, there's a chance I'd make sergeant —third lieutenant, even."

"Third lieutenant of the Molasses Creek Fire-Eaters." Cleave's voice was utterly devoid of expression.

Revell flushed.

Linden turned on her father in fury. "How can you say such things? I—I think I hate you!" She turned on her heel and flung out of the room.

Cleave stared at Revell maliciously. "She's angry, really angry. If she wasn't, she'd have banged the door. There's a MacBayne and Reed boat leaving for Charleston Saturday morning's tide." His voice was politely informative. "If I can help in any way—matter of the fare, for example . . . ."

Revell rose, hot and red. "I think you've been cruel."

"She'll get over it," said Cleave grimly. "I don't think any good purpose will be served by discussing the matter. Your hat, I believe, is in the hall."

*   *   *

Stephen looked out across the Elizabeth River to the Norfolk shore. The City Hall dome, the spire of Christ Church, the Presbyterian Church cupola, all towered above the warehouses of the waterfront. He watched while a brig, moving easily under topsails alone, eclipsed building after building and released them again to the crisp sunlight of the morning. The harbor was full of ships and small craft. Sails moved everywhere. The water was alive and brilliant and full of movement. The day had a joyful air.

He could not feel joyful with it. He broke a long silence. "I still can't understand why Washington doesn't do something about McCauley. Seems as if they have forgotten us."

"Doesn't the vote tell you anything?"

"Should it?"

"It's plain enough," replied Cleave. "Lincoln's got to keep Virginia. He won't do a thing to spark tempers in Richmond. Suppose *you* try to balance a Navy Yard against a State."

"I hadn't thought of it that way."

"It's a gamble. Most things are a gamble at a time like this. Myself, I'd try for the State. If Lincoln keeps Virginia, he keeps the Navy Yard. If he loses Virginia, he'd have a hard time hanging onto the Elizabeth River. The British tried it in seventy-six. Best part of thirteen hundred houses got themselves burned over there." Cleave looked speculatively at the Norfolk skyline.

Stephen heard footsteps behind him, very soft on the compost of sawdust and bark that paved the wood yard.

Cleave, without turning, said, " 'Lo, Sam." The old compositor's morning visit to the yard was ritual. "We were remembering the Norfolk fire."

"Which one? Norfolk, she's always gettin' herself burned."

"The British," replied Cleave.

"Wasn't the British. It was the Minute Men burned her that time."

"Ah! But we blamed it on the British," said Cleave tolerantly. "That's war."

"Never could make up their minds which side they was on in Norfolk."

"We weren't too certain ourselves in Portsmouth." Cleave prodded the old man.

"Hell! We was certain enough, only some was certain one side and some was certain the other."

"Why?" asked Stephen.

"We're a long way from the rest of Virginia," replied Cleave cryptically, "the hell of a long way if you ask them in the Fall Line towns."

The brig was almost out of sight now, only her topsails showing over the houses and wharves of the Point.

Cleave said: "Partly it's being a seaport. You get different notions in a seaport. It's a long time since we felt tied up with the rest of Virginia except in political speeches."

"Lot of folk in this town still hankers after North Carolina," put in the old man. "You remember that meetin' Charlie Reid called. He was always big-mouthed. 'The Senate of Virginia have perpetrated an act of tyranny worthy of the Dark Ages of mail-clad despotism. . . .'" he quoted. "'Since we are to be taxed without participation, we ask that the ruling power of the land make us outcasts rather than slaves, by ceding us to North Carolina.' Hey-hey! He can call up powerful words, Charlie Reid."

"The meeting was enthusiastic," said Cleave slowly, staring out over the river. "Your father voted for the motion, Stephen." He waited for a moment. "So did I."

* * *

The stone curved up, described a neat, economic parabola, and disappeared through the six inches of open window. Jeriel marked its flight with satisfaction. There were times when he had a sinking fear that he might break a pane, but it was counterbalanced always by a feeling that it would be interesting to see what would develop if the worst happened. The disappearance of the stone was not followed by any reaction from within the room. Jeriel waited, studying the window in the light of past essays. Only after a considerable interval did he allow his eye to stray, conning the surface of the yard in search of another stone. His eye was still lowered when he heard the window open.

Linden thrust her head out. There was no association here with fairy tale, nothing of Rapunzel letting down her hair—Linden had no hair to let down; she was, moreover, blear-eyed and full of sleep. She asked almost wearily, "What's happened?"

"*Pocahontas,* she's sailin' 'bout ha'f-past seven."

"All right," said Linden remotely, "she's sailing."

"Lot of people goin' down to watch her go," offered Jeriel softly, muting his voice with the necessity of long experience.

"I'm not allowed to raise any more hell around this town." Linden's voice held a note of resignation.

Jeriel had a complete and perfect innocence. "Ain't nothin' said 'bout you watchin' other people raisin' hell," he suggested.

Linden considered the proposition for a moment. "What are you going to do?"

"Throw rocks and shout at 'em. Ain't nothin' else, I reckon."

"I'll come," she said abruptly. "Wait for me round in the street."

She straightened away from the window and considered the position.

The clock on the mantel said six minutes to seven. No point in trousers —she would never be home in time to change. Reluctantly she pulled a dress off the hooks in the wardrobe, slipped off her nightgown, and began to wash superficially and without enthusiasm. Almost consciously she waited until the shock of the cold water had finally awakened her before she began to think.

Revell said that the *Pocahontas* was ordered to Fort Sumter. Stephen said that there was no certainty as to her ultimate destination. The town was divided. For three days now the excitement had been working up. Twice her departure had been postponed. The town had had three nights to develop its theories or its anticipations, according to its allegiances. She had listened on the outskirts of crowds to Murdaugh and to Wilson, hovering clear of them, unembroiled, obeying at least the letter of her father's orders. She had heard Sam Wilson say: "If they was to hold the election again today, I'd get in." She was sure that that was true—she wanted it to be true.

That was as far as her thinking got, for the next moments were occupied in getting noiselessly down the stairs. She placed her feet with the certitude of long usage on the inside of each tread close against the wall, knowing that it creaked less at the point of junction. Even while she did it she knew that her father would be awake and would have heard her by now.

Jeriel was sitting on the front steps. Almost mutinously he said, "You bin a time!"

"I had to dress."

He headed down for Crawford Street.

"Where are you going?" Linden asked, again aware that she had lost leadership. She had been acutely conscious of that fact during the past days.

"Can't go to your pa's yard—that'd be as good a place as any. We'll try down by Mist' Allerton's."

Other people were moving down toward the river front, not only young people. She caught a contagion of excitement.

A man passed her whom she vaguely remembered seeing once before—she did not know his name. "Guess this is when the trouble starts, Miss Cleave," he remarked, and went past them, his head down, his shoulders forward, purposeful, important.

"It depends where the *Pocahontas* is going," Linden answered, and wondered at her moderation.

Jeriel had no moderation. "Fort Sumter—ever'body knows she's goin' to Fort Sumter! Reckon that'll start somepn."

Up in the Navy Yard a whistle blew shrilly, and Linden jumped. They could see smoke rising above the ridgeline of the Marine Barracks. More people were coming out of the houses. They were spread across the road now, a stream all heading in one direction, all heading for the riverside. There were boys in it, but mostly it was composed of adults, as purposeful, as full of importance as the man who had overtaken them earlier.

They passed a wall. Jeriel looked at it and looked at Linden with a faint disgust. "You can't go over that in those things."

Almost humbly she suggested, "We could try farther down by Mr. Catterick's boathouse."

"Have to." Jeriel's voice was caustic.

Two hundred other people had had the same idea. The waterfront next to Catterick's was crowded. Buildings, rooftops, sheds upstream and down were thronged. Across the river on the Berkley side the front was crowded. Far down across the mouth of the Eastern Branch, Linden could see that the waterfront of Norfolk in its turn was black with people.

The whistle sounded again in the Navy Yard. It was impossible from where they stood to see beyond the curve, but the smoke was blacker now, angry looking, lifting up in an ugly cloud above the intervening buildings. A tug went up the river, fussing and leaving behind her great swathes of broken water from her side wheels. A boat rowed across to the Berkley shore. A boat rowed from the Berkley shore across to them, moving sideways with the strength of the young ebb.

The *Pocahontas* came suddenly into view. One moment the smoke cloud was far back over the roofs of the buildings, the next moment her long bowsprit and the black forward curve of her bow were clear against a faint haze that hung over the water up the Southern Branch. Linden could hear shouting. It was impossible to discern its intention. The rest of her appeared: the three masts, the raked funnel, the gun ports along her deck, the Stars and Stripes, enormous and brilliant, whipping astern. She had a singular, hard beauty silhouetted in blackness against the morning light. As she came down the river, the shouting moved with her, a confusing medley—objurgations and cheers, taunts and good wishes.

The group in which she stood in Catterick's yard was, Linden thought, possibly representative. She could hear cursing, shouts, epithets, mostly from the younger men but with some of the women joining them—a third, perhaps, of the whole. The rest cheered, but the cheers, she thought, were uncertain. A fight broke out down near the boatshed. She could see Jeriel lobbing ineffective stones into the water, and she knew that he had promised his friends that he would throw stones and that he was fulfilling a promise. Twice he made them skip. All of them were a hundred and fifty yards short of the black hull that slipped past them, silent, aloof, and full of purpose.

The shouting passed them, and only the wrangle in the middle of the yard kept on. She heard it taken up in wave after wave down the river—shouts of warning, threats, cheers, encouragement. It reflected in an almost perfect exactitude the confusions and uncertainties of the town. The *Pocahontas* swept on, increasing speed steadily, leaving under her counter a froth of white water against the yellow-gray sullenness of the outgoing tide. Only the Stars and Stripes made brilliance in the gray light of the April morning.

*   *   *

Commodore McCauley looked doubtfully over the top of his glasses and said, "Be seated, gentlemen." He collapsed rather than sat down in his own capacious chair and fumbled at the long envelope, trying to insert a stubby forefinger into an inadequate ungummed space under the flap. Isherwood leaned forward and passed over a paper knife.

McCauley muttered, "Thank you, thank you," and then, with a touch of irritation, "I can manage." The paper ripped and he took out the folded orders that it contained and began to read.

Isherwood and Alden watched him, their eyes narrow.

He read carefully and methodically for a moment or two, then his eyes wavered back over a half-read page and began again, and he read aloud in a tone of expostulation: " 'Great vigilance should be exercised in guarding and protecting the public interest and property.' Who does this man Welles think that I am? I have exercised all the vigilance that any officer could have exercised. They give me no troops to protect the public interests—no troops." He was silent for a minute, and then repeated very softly and almost despairingly, "No troops."

He read on. After a long interval he spoke. "I must not give needless alarm—to me, a commodore in the United States Navy, he says that I must not give needless alarm, that I must exercise great vigilance! Does *anybody* know in Washington what is happening here? Does anybody care? Half my officers—more than half—are Southerners. Nothing happens in this office that is not known in Montgomery within a day. You cannot speak a word even in the open space of the Yard but it is telegraphed to Montgomery. How can I exercise great vigilance? How can I prevent needless alarm?" There was another brief pause, and again the soft repetition, "No troops."

He came at last to the end of the enclosures, and sat looking between the two men, looking so fixedly at the opposite wall that Isherwood had an almost irresistible desire to turn his own head. The engineer broke the silence at last. "Sir, I should like to begin an examination of the *Merrimac* as soon as possible with a view to ascertaining the ordering of the work."

"You are Engineer in Chief." For no reason at all McCauley made a courtly little bow to the surprisingly young man who was the senior engineer of the United States Navy. "Your orders are categorical. You must make your own decisions. Much work has already been done, much work." He paused for an instant, and then hedged. "I am not aware precisely of the degree of progress that has been achieved. My junior officers will inform you." He appeared to lose himself in contemplation.

Alden stirred uneasily in his chair, and the old man's head moved slowly in a half-circle until the eyes bored into the younger man. "Commander Alden, your orders also are categorical. I have now no responsibility for the *Merrimac*. They have chosen to take her out of my hands. It is irregular, it is most irregular." With energy he seized a small hand-bell and rang it.

The two men watched him in a blank surprise. It was as shocking as if a man in a coma had sprung from his bed.

McCauley was still ringing the bell when Stephen opened the door and entered. He stood at attention.

"You will take Engineer in Chief Isherwood and Commander Alden to the *Merrimac*. You will inform them of the progress of her repairs. You will give them every facility. I wish you to understand this clearly —they are to be given every facility." Once more he paused, and then allowed himself the echoing repetition, "Every facility."

"Yes, sir." Stephen relaxed enough to open the door.

The other two men said, "Thank you, Commodore," saluted, and passed into the wide passageway.

Stephen followed them, shutting the door behind him. As he closed it he saw McCauley slump forward over the desk, focusing his eyes on the papers from Washington.

Stephen said: "Straight down the stairs, gentlemen. I'll get my hat," slipped into his office, snatched his uniform cap, and joined them.

They went out of the headquarters building and into the open ground between it and the ship house. Through the litter of anchors, stacks of chain cable, old guns, and timber he indicated the way down to the *Merrimac*.

He was a little in front of them when he heard Isherwood's gruff voice. "Been drinking?"

"Me, sir?" Stephen's voice was startled.

"Not you. I know the story—can't afford to drink on a lootenant's pay."

Stephen realized that the gruff voice was, in fact, friendly, and he answered: "Not more than ordinary. I think he's worried himself into a state of nerves."

"I'll say!"

Alden disregarded the exchange disapprovingly. "Lieutenant, what's the state of the *Merrimac*?"

Stephen considered for a moment before he answered hesitantly: "Behind schedule, sir, a long way behind schedule."

"Why?"

Stiffly Stephen replied, "I haven't been working on her, sir."

"Ho!" exclaimed Isherwood brusquely. "And so you don't know the gossip and you haven't heard anybody say anything and you wouldn't know why birds fly! How long will it take to get her ready for sea?"

Stephen relaxed again. He liked this man. "I'm not enough of an engineer to be certain, sir, but I'd say you could do it, if you worked round the clock, in six days."

"Four," asserted Isherwood bluntly. "Do it in four."

Apparently at a tangent Stephen asked, "Was the *Pocahontas* ordered to Fort Sumter?"

Alden caught the intention quickly. "Meaning, if she was, there'll be trouble in the Yard?"

"There was trouble when she went out, sir."

"Shouting and a few stones." Alden's voice was acid.

Isherwood said, "You're a Southerner."

Very evenly and without emphasis Stephen answered, "I was born about five blocks from here, sir."

"And you're going South?"

"I was brought up in the Union and I accepted a Union commission. Virginia's still in the Union."

"But if she goes out?" Alden was very quick to search behind the overt meaning of words.

"I don't know," replied Stephen frankly. "I was born in the Union."
He repeated the words as if they had a talismanic meaning.

"She could have been ready by now."

"Yes, sir," he agreed without hesitation, "she could have been."

They had come to the seaward end of the great ship house. A gang
had just shipped the *Merrimac*'s jib boom; men were working about her
bowsprit, parceling the forestay.

Isherwood said: "Fine ship, fine ship—and the damnedest set of
engines that ever went to sea! Who's in charge?"

Stephen told him.

Isherwood sniffed; his nostrils spread wide and went white at the
edges with each sniff. "Knew him in Philadelphia," he said caustically.
"Are there enough men in the Yard to work nights?"

"I should think so, sir," replied Stephen slowly.

"Are there enough men in the base to man her?" Alden demanded.

"The *Pocahontas* just about swept the *Pennsylvania* clear, sir."

"I know, I know. They're recruiting a crew in New York, but I don't
think it will come through in time. They're trying something in Philadelphia."

They were almost at the foot of the gangway now. Stephen, looking
up, saw Pegram come across the deck and start down it. He said, "Commander Pegram."

Alden grunted. "My term."

"Southerner?" Isherwood cocked an eye up under his bushy eyebrows.

"Virginian," replied Alden tersely.

Isherwood asked, "How many of you Virginians are there in this
damned Navy?"

The words could have been offensive, but Stephen felt that there
was no more than an underlying humor behind them. Again he warmed
to the man.

Pegram reached the foot of the ladder, and stopped.

Alden said: " 'Lo, Bob. I didn't know you were here."

Isherwood looked at him testily. "I understand this ship's about
three weeks behind schedule."

Pegram looked at him with a thin smile. "I wouldn't say as much as
that," he murmured. "We've had certain problems."

Isherwood looked him up and down with a cold and studied malice.
"It will be necessary, then, to find certain solutions."

*   *   *

Jeriel heaved himself up onto the ridge with a grim and concentrated effort. The shortness of his legs put him at a disadvantage. He stood tiptoe on the ridge itself and, stretching upward, reached the sill. Then, feeling out to the left, he found a toehold on the collar of a downward rainwater pipe and levered himself to the sill. The top of the window was open. Sitting sideways and in a position that he knew with pride held an extreme danger, he began to edge the bottom of the window upward with the tips of his fingers.

It was halfway up when he heard Linden's voice—angry, urgent, secret. "Who's that?"

"Me. Couldn't wake you up nohow. Jeez, but you sleep heavy! What'd you have for supper?"

"Get down off that sill!" she ordered. "You'll break your neck."

"Ain't broke yet. She'll do. You get dressed."

"Why?"

"Rev Jordan's why. He says fer you to come—and jump to it."

Jeriel heard a scratch as she struck a match. It failed to ignite. She tried twice more and swore softly. Finally the match sputtered into flame and she lit the bedside candle.

"Get off the sill and get down below!"

"I'll wait."

"You will not. I've got to get dressed."

"Me, I'm not old enough to count."

"You get down on the ground!"

Jeriel leered at her, bending low down to look in through the open window, but the expression was lost in the dim light of the candle. Reluctantly he lowered himself to the ridge, found a foothold, eased himself away, and by gradations reached the ground again. He waited, whistling so softly that at times he lost the little unformed tunes himself. Presently he saw Linden move like a dark shadow over the window ledge and ease herself down in turn to the ridge. They walked silently away from the house.

Not until they were clear did Linden ask, "What does Rev want?"

"Up to the Navy Yard. He's got six or eight there. Wants you fer somethin'—I dunno what."

They went through the dark streets, moving fast and quietly. Even in her more outrageous excursions Linden had never been out so late as this. She admitted to herself that she was frightened, yet at the same time she was buoyed with excitement.

They were almost at the Crawford Street bridge when she suddenly remembered her father's order. She murmured doubtfully, "My father would call this hell raising."

Jeriel was silent.

Linden considered the point carefully. Something of the importance of the injunction seemed to have gone out of it since the departure of the *Pocahontas*. Cleave had made no comment on that episode.

She was about to phrase her doubt in another way when Jeriel said succinctly: "Hell's riz. We'll find Matty Walker far end o' the bridge. He'll know where Rev Jordan is." The slight tone of scorn that always came into his voice at the mention of Revell Jordan was obvious again.

At the far end of the bridge he stopped and whistled softly. A shape materialized out of the shadow—a boy perhaps a year older than himself.

Linden asked, "Where's Rev Jordan, Matty?"

The boy peered closely at her. "It's Mis' Linden? Said he'd be over to the far end o' the street, front o' the Craik house."

"I know," said Jeriel.

They turned and walked up the utterly empty road. The night was oddly silent. Ordinarily in the darkness there were incessant noises from the river—water noises, the splash of anchor cables, the creak of blocks, whistles, shouts. There were land noises too—noises from the railroad tracks, the bells of locomotives, the clatter and crash of shunted cars. But tonight there was only one area of sound, one focal point. Somewhere far in the depths of the Yard men were working. They heard the thud of metal on metal, muffled, mysterious.

"They're working in the Yard." Even Linden's whispered voice sounded loud against the background of the general silence.

Jeriel muttered, "Workin' on the *Merrimac,* nights!"

Out of a deeper patch of darkness Revell's voice said, "You've been the devil of a time."

Linden bristled.

Before she could say anything in her own defense Revell burst out: "Oh, my God, you've got those damned trousers on! I told Jeriel to tell you to dress."

Jeriel protested: "You didn' say what she was to dress in! You know she wears pants when she comes out like this."

"What is it? What d'you want?" asked Linden. "If you're bothering about Aunt Deborah . . ."

"Hell with Aunt Deborah!" interrupted Revell. "I had to have you because I wanted to have a woman who could walk past the main gate with me. I've got to see what they're doin' in there. They're so worked up tonight they'd arrest a man walkin' past by himself."

Linden said scornfully: "Is that all? I'll go. They won't arrest me."

"They've taken in two of my men already." Revell almost snarled, yet at the same time his voice managed a faint pomposity on the words "my men."

Linden felt a queer tenseness that extended down to her fingertips. "What's it all about? I haven't been told anything. What are you trying to do?"

"They've doubled the sentries round the Yard," whispered Revell, "and they're doing something at the main gate. There's a hell of a bunch of them there. We've got to know."

"Why?"

Revell was silent for a minute, but it was clear that his sense of importance was wrestling with discretion. "Jeriel, get along out to the small gate! Watch till the next change of sentries and then come back here." As the boy padded off into the darkness, Revell said, "Linden, I'll tell you, but you can't tell your father."

"Why?"

The repeated monosyllable seemed to infuriate Revell. "Goddam, don't keep saying why! I'm tellin' you—you're not to tell your father. You swear?"

"I swear," she replied automatically.

"Hell, it's no use askin' you to swear! You don't believe in anythin'. You can't tell your father because he's not with the South—and you know that. We're goin' to capture the Navy Yard." Again with the word "capture" the note of pomposity came back into his voice.

"Tonight?"

"No, not tonight, but we've got to know what they're doing."

"Who says?"

Reluctantly but with overwhelming importance Revell answered: "Ex-Governor Wise says. We got orders from him. The Richmond boys are goin' for Harpers Ferry. We're goin' to get the Navy Yard. Fortress Monroe after that, maybe, or maybe we join up with the others and go straight on to Washin'ton."

She looked at him suspiciously in the darkness; Revell's plans were always two sizes larger than life. Yet the very immensity of them this time seduced her imagination: Harpers Ferry and Fortress Monroe, and—and Washington. It was vital, it was gigantic, it was Southern. She could believe it of Wise. She remembered and rejected her father's criticism of him: "Bullfrog! Find a million like him in the swamp on a hot summer's night." The division between herself and her father widened.

"Get me a skirt, a dress—anything! It'd take too long to go home again."

Revell whistled. The whistle was formulated, clearly a signal. For a moment Linden felt disillusioned. There was an echo of boys' games in it: Indian fighting—pirates—slave hunting. For a fraction of a second she caught herself wondering if war were an Indian game.

A shadow drifted up out of the darkness. Revell's voice demanded: "You Grandy? You live hereabouts?"

"Down th' street."

"Can you get a skirt of your ma's, dress or something?"

"She'll whale me."

"Somethin' that'll fit Linden here."

The shadow stooped forward peering. "Evenin', Mis' Linden."

"We've got no time to talk." Revell's voice carried the authentic rasp of command.

The shadow drifted off.

They waited, standing there in the silent night. There were lights here and there in the Marine Barracks, a glow of light over the wall of the Yard, another glow deeper in, down near the waterfront. Again and again they could hear the soft dull thud of metal on metal.

Revell said angrily, and almost to himself: "They had no right to put double shifts on her. We've got to take the Yard before she's ready for sea. We need the *Merrimac*."

"How long will it be before she's ready?"

"I don't know—I don't know. Sharp, he was keeping the work slowed down. Now this new man's come from Washington. He's a driver. Listen!"

Again the thud of metal on metal came from the depths of the Yard, and the sound of men's voices with it, calling. It had a note of urgency.

"How soon can we attack?" she asked.

"How do I know?" For the first time there was candor in Revell's voice, candor and a sense of grievance.

They heard the sound of feet running, a soft hurrying noise, muffled and wary. Grandy came, breathing heavily. "My sister's"—he held out a shapeless bundle—"they'll fit her better. I gotta have 'em back before it's light. She'll beat th' hell out of me else." Linden shook out the bundle. Something fell to the ground. The boy stooped and picked it up. He said indignantly: "You shouldn' a done that. It's her meetin' hat."

"Won't hurt," said Revell gruffly. "Ground's dry."

Linden, feeling in the darkness, discovered that the bundle consisted of a short jacket and a skirt. "You used your head. They'll do. Turn your backs!"

"Hell!" Revell's voice reached a pitch of suppressed indignation. "It's dark as a cow's belly. You got pants on already."

"You turn your backs," said Linden firmly. She shed the heavy man's coat that she wore, and added, "Hold these!"

The skirt met reluctantly at the waist over the bulk of the trousers. She sucked in her breath, failed with the fastening and, groping hurriedly, found a safety pin. After a quick experiment she fastened it and demanded the woman's jacket from Revell. It fitted well enough for darkness. Last of all she balanced the hat on her short hair. "Don't know if it'll stay on," she said dubiously, "but I'll try."

"Finished?" Revell asked. "I reckon we've got five, six minutes yet. They'll change the guard 'bout two o'clock."

"What do we do then, wait here?"

"No harm in walkin' past the gate now." Revell nodded to himself in the darkness. "Hang on to my arm. Make it look lovin'."

Amos Grandy snorted.

"All right, so long as you don't go getting ideas," said Linden coldly.

They walked down the center of the roadway clinging together. Grandy stood watching them until they were lost in the darkness.

There was a gas lantern under the central arch of the main gate. It threw a splayed brightness into the rough surface of the roadway, a fan of light that was lost almost as soon as it was clear of the shadows of the central columns of the portico. As they walked toward it they could hear voices under the arches, and the thud of boots, and the sharp metallic thud of a musket butt on the paving.

The light scarcely reached them where they walked in the center of the roadway; there was scarcely enough of it to outline Linden's skirt, yet there must have been sufficient—there was no challenge. They walked past the portico, the long vista of windows stretching on down toward the water's edge; the night was quiet again.

Revell whispered, his face close to Linden's ear: "Main gate's closed —barred most likely. Side wicket's open, two sentries, bunch of men beyond. Listen!"

There was a series of sharp commands, feet crashed on hard paving, gun butts thudded. There was another command, and then the grinding of a heavy gate being pushed back and the long sour creak of hinges.

"Quick. Here!" Revell, his arm round Linden's waist, half dragged her to the porch of one of the small houses across the street. With his arms round her he looked warily up the street toward the main gate. There was another sharp command and the thud of marching feet. A squad of men, tenuously outlined in the gate light, marched out and wheeled down the street parallel with the Marine Barracks.

Revell hissed in Linden's ear: "Patrol! After us?" Common sense came to his aid. "No, wouldn't be after us." The Yard clock began to strike the hour. "Probably goin' to patrol the whole length o' the walls. Start this end. Put your arms round me." He pulled Linden closer. "Eight men and a sergeant." He bent his head, almost crouching over the girl, and kissed her experimentally.

"Do you have to?" she whispered fiercely.

He laughed a little, very sure of himself, and kissed her again. His hand came away from her waist and, moving expertly, slipped up under the light jacket to her breast. She strained away, but he held her prisoned with the other arm and kissed her a third time. The patrol was almost level with them now. With a calm certainty he fumbled with his fingers until he found the buttons of the boy's shirt that she wore and with a practiced ease flipped them open. His hand slid inside.

"Take your hand away!" Linden's voice came suddenly clear in outrage.

He could feel the warmth of the young breast, the subtle smoothness of it, the fierce beat of her heart beneath it. His hand closed.

"Take it—!" Linden wriggled suddenly in a movement that was utterly unexpected. Revell felt the warmth of her face for an instant against his bared wrist. Then she bit him savagely, furiously, like a small animal.

He jerked away from her as he yelped with a sudden pain. "She devil!" he shouted.

From the patrol a voice said: "Smack her on the nose, boy. Women 'n' horses, same thing works with both."

Ignoring him, Linden's voice said hotly: "God ought to've given men breasts. Then perhaps they wouldn't be for everlasting grabbing after ours."

The patrol was past them already. From the last file there was a snort of derisive laughter.

"A-ah, I'm sick of men!" Linden pulled herself away and flung down the three short steps to the sidewalk. "All of you the same." She began to stalk furiously up the street, Revell hurrying behind her, blurting apologies.

A window flung up and a weary voice called, "For Chris'sake, go home!"

The patrol was almost at the water end of the street. Revell hurried until he had caught up with her. He whispered: "Wonderful, Linden, wonderful. I think they'd have taken us in if you hadn't—"

"Wonderful nothing," she said, and hit him expertly across the face. Then, raising her voice, she called desperately, "Jeriel!"

* * *

In the dusty office, crowded with samples of wood, spare saw blades, defective shingles, barrel staves, axes, ax hafts, all the clutter of a lumber business, Cleave occupied the only clean spot—the chair at the ancient desk. In contrast to the confusion about it, the desk was neat, the papers stacked together, spiked on files, or rolled and thrust into the pigeonholes. He looked fastidious in his slightly old-fashioned clothes, sitting up straight at the desk.

Stephen, careless of his uniform, leaned against a stack of sample planks as variegated as the trees of the swamp were variegated. "It's working up fast, sir. They wouldn't have sent Isherwood down if it wasn't working up. I don't know that I ought to tell you this."

"Well, don't!" There was a faint humor in Cleave's voice. "But if it's about the *Merrimac,* it's all through the town this morning. Isherwood's going to have her out in four days. He will too—I've seen him at work before."

Stephen ran a finger round his collar. "Everything gets out—everything!"

"What the devil d'you think," demanded Cleave, "with the night shift coming off work at the time when the women were going to the market?"

"There was a hell of a row in the Yard last night."

"Isherwood's a forceful man."

Stephen considered this for a little before he said: "Lincoln's sent somebody from the State Department to tell Pickens that an attempt will be made to supply Fort Sumter with provisions—"

"Mr. Robert Chew," Cleave proffered the name sardonically. "It's extraordinary how news gets around this town. That can't have been the night shift."

"Are they going to fight?"

Cleave shrugged his shoulders. "They've been breathing so much fire around Charleston lately the gunpowder might go off of its own accord." His tone was bitter. "That's the way wars start—some fool pulls a lanyard."

"If they open fire on Fort Sumter, Lincoln will have to fight."

"I don't know. I don't know. I think he will. I think maybe he's already made up his mind that he has to fight. I think . . ." He was silent, his voice diminishing doubtfully on the last words.

After a long interval Stephen murmured, "What?"

"I think he needs—that they should fire first."

"What do I do?" Stephen asked slowly, more to himself than to Cleave.

Cleave let himself sink back in the chair. The movement seemed to soften his whole aspect. He studied Stephen with a curious compassion. "You've got to make up your own mind. I can't make it up for you. Nobody can."

"I know."

"It looks to me like a three-part problem." Cleave spoke plainly. "The first part is whether Virginia comes first or the Union. It's not any good now saying Virginia's still in the Union. There was another vote at Richmond some time yesterday, a secret vote—sixty to fifty-three it was this time. Still for the Union, but it's getting narrower." He smiled grimly. "Secret! There's no telling what will happen if those fools down at Charleston open fire again. The question you have got to answer for yourself is whether Virginia's bigger than the Union." After another long pause he went on: "In logic I can't see that the part is greater than the whole. Sam and I tried to tell you the other day this town has not always been 100 per cent for Virginia. Your father knew that too."

Stephen nodded. Again there was a long silence.

"Second part of the problem hangs on the first." Cleave's voice was carefully void of all feeling. "Linden is 100 per cent for Virginia—110 per cent, maybe. You've got to shape that one for yourself." He bent down a third finger and Stephen, looking at him, saw that two were already closed against his palm. "Third part's a professional problem. You're a Union officer. All the same you're entitled to resign if you want to—a lot of Southerners have." He waited for a moment, and added dryly: "A lot haven't. I can't help you. It's not any use telling you to ask McCauley; he won't know. There's Captain Farragut. You could ask him. . . ." His eyes fixed on a knothole in the ceiling, and he lay back staring at it as if expecting revelation.

Stephen for no reason at all was jolted suddenly out of his self-absorption. In a tone of surprise, as if it had only now occurred to him, he asked, "What will *you* do?"

"Nothing. I'm a fair hand at doing nothing."

Chapter seven

THE ferry seemed to move with a surprising and unaccustomed speed. It worked its way astern of an English barkentine that was getting her anchor up, and the capstan chantey flooded across. Stephen listened to it critically, as if he were assessing the merit of the English singing. The ferry, getting on her course again, missed by accustomed inches the bows of a tug hurrying down from the Eastern Branch. Again for a while she held her course and then seemed to make a determined effort to run down a small boat rowed by four Negroes. Once more Stephen listened with an appearance of critical assessment to the chorus of shouts. Three men shouted, one man—the bowman—flung back his head, and laughed.

Norfolk waterfront changed from a flat pattern painted across the midday sky to a design of stereoscopic vistas. The buildings of the waterfront, the stores and the warehouses grew taller and taller until they wiped out the dome of the City Hall and the spires of the churches, and the ferry nosed in between the arms of the pier.

Stephen sighed. Nothing was settled, nothing clarified. It was as if his mind were divided into two parts—one part that had watched the English barkentine, that had measured the anchor chantey, that had watched the Negroes; one part that had debated loyalties—and the two parts had at no time come together, and until they came together there could be no clarity.

He crossed Water Street, edging his way between drays and carts, dodging between great piles of cargo, bales of cotton, casks of tobacco, cases and crates of manufactured goods from the North.

He scarcely knew Captain Farragut. Thinking back, he remembered that he had met him perhaps five times in the course of duty. He had never served with him. He was a Southerner—Stephen searched his memory for a minute or two—a Southerner, but not from the Deep

South. Kentucky, was it? No, perhaps it was Tennessee—he could not remember. Farragut's wife was a Portsmouth woman. Again he searched in his memory. Farragut's first wife had been a Portsmouth woman too, hadn't she? Why had Cleave advised him to see Farragut? It had been done without emphasis, negligently almost, an idea thrown out, but Stephen was beginning to know Cleave now, to know his way of approach, to know his unconventional mind.

He crossed up to Main Street. A horse staled close to him, and he leaped aside to save his best uniform trousers. A man driving a surrey checked his mare furiously, and Stephen dodged again. The man shouted cuttingly, "Sailor ashore!" and drove on.

Stephen looked after him, and grinned. The little incident had suddenly brought him back to balance. "All I've got to do," he said to himself, "is to ask."

The house stood back a little from the road. Two white columns supported the cockleshell molding of the tiny porch. The flight of steps was neat, whitened, shipshape, and the brass knocker and the handle of the door were brilliant. He tugged at the bell pull and heard the answering clangor in the basement.

The Negro who opened the door was short and thickset. He blinked slightly at the uniform and held the door wide for Stephen to enter. As Stephen passed him he looked up and asked, "F'the capt'in, suh?"

"Is Captain Farragut in?"

"Eff'n you'll wait, suh."

"My name is Knott."

"Ye', Lootenant, suh."

The narrow hall held two chairs, a half-moon table with a silver tray, a great oval gilt mirror above it, a barometer, and four small silhouettes framed in ebony.

Stephen waited, standing. After a moment the Negro reappeared. He walked in front of his master, giving to his return the air of a processional, a formality. Stephen studied the captain with care. He was square-built, of medium height, clean-shaven, with bushy eyebrows, and his side hair was combed with care and flattened down over the baldness of the dome of the head.

Farragut looked at the far end of the hall a little doubtfully for an instant before he said: "Ah, yes, Knott! I remember you now." The Negro opened a door that led to the drawing room. "What can I do for you? Shall we go in here?" He waved Stephen into the room. The Negro shut the door on them. "Sit down, won't you?"

Hurriedly Stephen selected a chair that would bear his weight, and sat down.

Farragut remained standing, watching him shrewdly. "Well?" he prompted.

"Mr. Cleave suggested that I should see you, sir—Mr. Ashwell Cleave."

"Ash Cleave?" Farragut's manner was ordinary, a shade puzzled.

"I am a Portsmouth man, sir, a Virginian."

"Ah!"

The monosyllable was completely toneless, yet Stephen felt that it held a hostility. He began to defend himself in his mind against the hostility. He searched for convincing words and, as he searched, a sudden riot of bells broke out above them. They rang without rhythm, without logic, without reason—a wild, furious alarm note. For a long minute they hammered against the air and then, because whoever was ringing them lacked skill or practice, they ceased abruptly, and in the silence they could hear other bells farther away, and shouts and distant cheering.

Farragut was silent, watchful, oddly alert, his head a little to one side.

The clangor of the nearby bells broke out again, and Stephen thought that under them he could hear the jangling of the house bells.

The drawing-room door opened again, unceremoniously. Two men burst in.

The leading one said, "They've fired on Fort Sumter!"

The other shouted, "By God, they've done it!"

Without giving Farragut time to answer, the first man went on: "It was folly to send the *Pocahontas*—criminal folly, sir! Abraham Lincoln should be hanged for it."

Farragut lowered his head a little, a truculent gleam in his eye. He asked coldly, his voice cutting across their voices, across the sound of bells, across the predictable growing tensions in the room, "Who fired the first shot?"

"South Carolina," replied the second man. "They had to do it. They were forced."

Two other men came in at the door. They stood motionless, watching Farragut.

"No man," said Farragut, "no man, Jonathan, *has* to fire the first shot."

One of the newcomers said, "There was no option."

Farragut's voice was slow, measured, wholly without emotion. "There was every option. There was the option of ordinary sense. This is a business of fools. The South has no ships, no navy, no bases. It has no factories to make rifles, no arsenals to make guns. War is not just a matter of men, nor yet a matter of battle cries. The South has nothing with which to back its threats."

The second of the newcomers, the man who had not yet spoken, called out harshly, his face set and angry, "You will find it difficult to live here and to express such sentiments, sir."

"Then I can live elsewhere." Farragut's face was calm; there was even the faint mold of a smile about his mouth as he walked slowly over to the fireplace and grasped the bell rope.

The Negro appeared in the doorway as if an invisible thread connected him with the bell pull. He said gently, "Suh?"

"You will present my compliments to Mrs. Farragut and inform her that we shall be leaving Norfolk—at once. I wish her to pack that which she needs for the journey instantly."

"You can't do that!" One of the first two men was scandalized.

"I do not purpose to live where my right to speech is questioned, sir. You gentlemen I trust will excuse me. I have much to do—now." The last word held a faint tinge of irony; there was no shadow of emotion.

Stephen watched the captain with an almost breathless intentness.

The last of the newcomers, the angry man, peered under shaggy eyebrows. "Your brother officers, I believe, sir, will wait upon you."

"They will have to hurry then, sir," replied Farragut coldly.

"If they detain you . . ."

"Who will detain me, sir?" Farragut took a half-step toward the other man. "Mind what I tell you! You fellows will catch the devil before you get through with this business."

The four men went out, angrily. Stephen began to follow them. Farragut stopped him with a gesture.

"You had business with me?"

"I wished to ask your advice, sir."

"About what?"

"About my duty as an officer of the Union Navy, sir. But I have my answer."

"You are a Virginian." Farragut's mind seemed to cast back slowly, almost with difficulty.

"I am, sir. But I would consider it an honor to serve under you."

Suddenly Farragut's reserve broke. "Then you'd better go home and pack your bags, my boy! This town is going to be remarkably excited for the next few days. An intemperate lot . . ."

"I am on Commodore McCauley's staff at the Navy Yard, sir."

"You are, are you? Then tell me, what the devil is McCauley doing? I hear—" He checked himself abruptly. For a moment he stared at Stephen, his eyes keen, then he said, "I should not have asked that question of you." He held out his hand. "I have no doubt but that we shall meet again."

Stephen walked down the street. An elation that he could not define had him in its spell. Bells were still ringing on the outskirts of the city, pealing across the distant water. He could hear the whistles of the tugs and the small steamers. He could hear shouting and the deep and growing overtone of a gathering crowd. And all these things he disregarded. His own path was clear now, his own mind was at peace.

Main Street was packed. A jam of men and boys and an improbably high proportion of women crowded the sidewalks and the road; vehicles, horses, two oxcarts, and an incongruous group of cows were imprisoned in them. As he crossed the street, thrusting his way between the people, a horse reared twenty yards down the road and the crowd opened in a circle about it, shouting and laughing.

He was over Main Street and at the beginning of a crossroad that led down to Water Street when a group of youths shouted: "Navy, Navy. North or South?" He walked on, paying no attention to the shouts. They were repeated. He heard feet running behind him. The nearest voice was almost at his shoulder now. "North or South, North or South?"

For an instant, a fraction of time so small, so immeasurable that he could only recognize it for what it was without assessing it, he felt fear. The same acute, deeply internal fear that he had experienced on the *Star of the West.*

The leader of the group caught up with him. He turned his head and saw the face, vacant, not ill-natured, not even hostile in the proper sense of the word. He stretched out his hand suddenly—the movement was so quick that the youth made no effort to defend himself, no effort to dodge even. His hand closed on the back of the boy's collar, he gave it a half-turn and held him away at arm's length.

The rest of the group stopped abruptly. The boy he held gave a little choked squeal.

Stephen said, "Go play with someone your own size, sonny," and released him.

The boy staggered forward a half-pace and stopped, rubbing his sore neck. "Jeez!" he muttered.

Stephen strode on. There were no more shouts.

The ferry was almost empty. Seth Pritchard, who had been a skipper

on the run since the first steamboats came, left the wheel to his mate
and came over to Stephen. Almost apologetically he said: "Well, we
got to do it now, Knott. Sight of us never wanted it—not nohow. But I
don't see we can fight against the South, and we got to fight one way
or the other."

"Maybe." Stephen frowned, not at the old man but at circumstance.
"Maybe, but they may still find a way out. I don't believe that Lincoln
wants to fight."

"You come across Main Street?" Pritchard looked at him shrewdly.
Stephen nodded.

"Few weeks back Norfolk voted Union."

"I know, but governments make wars, not crowds in the streets."

"What's Jeff Davis got to lose?" The old man's voice was without
illusions. "Democrats is out, can't make no postmasters for the Union.
There's a lot o' pickings in bein' the gov'ment. He'll fight."

"That doesn't make Virginia go in with him."

"No, but that does!" The old man jerked his hand back to the sound
of shouting that followed them across the water above the grumbling
mutter of the ferryboat's engine and the thud of the paddles. "What
d'you suppose they're doing up to Richmond today—sittin' in th'
meetin' house?"

Stephen was silent; there was no obvious answer. They stared together up the crowded water. The English barkentine had disappeared
now, the anchorage was full, and up the Southern Branch the Navy
Yard was almost hidden by the screen of warships at the moorings.

Pritchard said, almost humbly, "What's th' South goin' to do f'r a
navy?"

Stephen shrugged.

"Or f'r a Navy Yard, come to that?"

" 'There's a lot more to war than battle cries,' " Stephen quoted.

The old ferry captain sighed. Again there was a long silence. At last
he said: "Question is, what happens to people like me?" And walked
forward to the cramped pilothouse to take the boat into the ferry slip.

The streets of Portsmouth were empty. Over toward the Court House
there was the deep, excited roar of a crowd. It seemed as if the center
of town had acted as a magnet in the moment of crisis, drawing everything to it.

There was a double guard on the main gate of the Yard when Stephen
came to it. Inside the arches Marines stood handling their muskets
uneasily. There was a contagion of anxiety in the place.

A sergeant called, "Lootenant!" Stephen stopped and the sergeant came up to him, reciting a rote piece that had obviously been recited in vain before. "You Lootenant Knott, sir? If so I got a message for you."

"I'm Lieutenant Knott." Stephen felt a little prickle of uneasiness.

"If you're Lootenant Knott, sir, orders is to go direct to th' *Merrimac,* report to C'mander Alden, sir."

Stephen acknowledged the message. "To Commander Alden." He walked swiftly past the discouraged trees that stood about the flagstaff in front of headquarters and turned at the far end of the second ship house. He could see the upper deck and the masts of the *Merrimac* from there. The main yard was cock-billed; men were using it as a derrick to swing a heavy piece of machinery outboard—it was too far away to see what it was.

As he neared the ship he recognized the figure at the top of the gangway: Isherwood. He stood there in ancient, nondescript work-clothes, wiping his face from time to time with a handful of cotton waste.

As Stephen saluted the deck, Isherwood said acidly, "You've taken your time."

"I was over in Norfolk, sir. Went over"—he added the explanation without quite knowing why—"Went over to see Captain Farragut."

"And what's old Dave going to do? No"—Isherwood held up the hand with the waste in it—"No, don't tell me, I know. Old Dave's a smart man. As Exec of this ship you ought to've been here when the bells started to ring."

"As—as Exec . . . ?"

"Nobody told you?" inquired Isherwood sardonically. "Well, you've been appointed. I appointed you. Commodore McCauley has—I wouldn't say approved, don't wish to burden my soul with a lie—but he's agreed. So's Alden. You will be responsible for everything that happens on board from the main truck to the keelson, from the taffrail to the cap on the flying jib boom. You'd better accept the responsibility; you'll be blamed for everything anyway. Most of all you'll be responsible for seeing I have some sleep, nights. I had none last night. You will oversee everything that happens in the engine room and in the boiler room during the hours of darkness."

"I know nothing of engines, sir."

"You'll learn," said Isherwood caustically. "I admire my sleep. You're young; you don't need it."

"Sir, I mean that I know nothing of the repair of engines."

"Few people do." Isherwood's mouth screwed up into its normal sardonic expression. "If you're in doubt, watch Tom Carr; he's quarterman of the night shift. He's got an expressive face." He looked disapprovingly up the deck. "See that those damned calkers quiet before I go to bed!"

"Commander Alden?"

"The commander"—Isherwood's voice was mocking—"is debating with the commodore the propriety of moving this ship under the masting shears in order to sling her guns aboard. The commodore is being as coy as a young girl at a church sociable."

Stephen looked over the low break of the quarter-deck to the long sweeping emptiness of the port battery. He said slowly, "I see."

"Good," grunted Isherwood ironically. "Now that you've seen, first thing you'd better do is go pack your gear and have it brought aboard. You'll live here."

"On board?" Stephen looked uncertainly at the piles of shavings, the carpenters' workbenches, the lumber, and the dirt.

"In horrible discomfort"—Isherwood's voice was unfeeling—"but at that I fancy it will be better than living amongst your fellow townsmen for the next couple of days."

Stephen shook his head. "I could manage."

"You could, possibly, but we might be deprived of your invaluable services while you recovered from your no-doubt varied injuries in a hospital. Get your gear! That's an order."

Stephen felt a sudden urge of laughter. Instead he asked bluntly, "How did you know that I wasn't going South like the rest of them?"

"Boy, you came round the corner of the ship house like a hound pup that's found a trail by hisself for the first time. Your tail was—perpendicular." Isherwood moved toward the hatch that led down to the engine room, mopping the back of his neck with the cotton waste. The word was repeated as the lean figure disappeared from sight, the accent heavy on the second syllable: "Per-*pen*-dicular."

Stephen went down to the quay again and strode off to get his gear.

All through the afternoon he followed Isherwood, crawling in the oil-saturated spaces beneath the engines, checking over piles of parts that were to him wholly unrelated and altogether improbable. He let himself into the furnace spaces below the boilers and examined brickwork and fire bars. He sprawled over the lagging on top of the boilers, looking for damaged patches. All the while Isherwood kept up an unflagging anathema on the name of the man who designed the engines —he knew a good deal of his private life—and on the name of the builders.

They ate, a dinner brought from the shore, amidst paint pots and carpenters' benches in the desolate wardroom.

Alden arrived in the middle of the meal. His face was heavy and anxious.

Isherwood eyed him without sympathy. "Don't tell me," he barked, waving his right hand. "He's changed his mind."

"It's a madhouse." Alden shook his head as if he were trying to free it of cobwebs. "He discusses everything with everybody and changes his mind after every conversation."

"Drunk?" Isherwood cocked a leering eye.

Alden shook his head. "Not when I left. I didn't see him take a drink all day. It's that he *seems* drunk." He turned to Stephen. "Who's this man Sharp?"

"He's a lieutenant," Stephen began hesitantly. "He's mad South. Talks fast."

"He does! And Breckenham?"

Again Stephen hesitated. "He's a bastard," he replied at last. "Sharp's just crazy, can't think of anything except Virginia. Breckenham's a son of a bitch."

"Somebody's passing every word that's said in McCauley's office out to the Secessionists. Could it be him?"

"It could. I'd lay six months' pay it is."

A workman came in at the open door. "Mist' Carr says he's got th' Number Two air pump clear. Connectin' rod's all to hell. Need's straightenin' or a new one."

Isherwood said: "Get on with it, boy! Your baby." He waved Stephen out of the wardroom and poured himself a man-sized drink. "Won't let you get the guns aboard?" he turned again to Alden.

"Says that his orders are not to create alarm. Moving her under the shears would upset the town."

"What do you think?"

"I think that if the town's upset, the town's upset." Alden's tone was blunt. "He's running out of time."

"Don't give a hoot about him! *We're* running out of time." Isherwood drank, and sat in thoughtful silence.

After a time Alden asked, jerking his head toward the door through which Stephen had passed, "What about him?"

"He'll do. Thinks his way around problems a bit too much. Needs pushin'. Round about midnight I'll appear out of the empty air and push him." He chuckled maliciously.

Alden said abstractedly: "I'll get onto McCauley again about shifting her in the morning. Nothing more I can do tonight."

Down below in the cold darkness of the engine room Stephen crouched over a long flattened piece of steel. Carr explained its defects in a biting voice. It was necessary to decide whether to bluff it through or to place himself in Carr's hands. He knew Carr, had known him to speak to since he was a boy. He interrupted him abruptly. "Can't afford the time for a new one," he said, suddenly sure of himself. "Get it ashore tonight and I'll get onto the machine shop first thing in the morning. It'll straighten."

Carr looked at him with surprise, a faint trace of respect mixed with it. "Right, it's your say."

Half a dozen men were standing round listening.

Stephen looked up and saw them. "This isn't a crap game," he snapped. "Get on with it!"

He knew by the swiftness of the response that he had done the right thing. The tempo of the work seemed to build up even as he listened in the cavernous darkness. Candles and an occasional kerosene lamp served only to accentuate the night. The shadows were enormous and angular and unsteady. The noise was ceaseless.

Even Isherwood's incursion twenty minutes after the midnight break was no more than another noise. His impartial, all-embracing blast only underscored the sense of urgency that already existed in the place. He reappeared twice during the night, but Stephen already had the measure of the gang. The work went on without interruption.

At dawn Isherwood took over again. "Could've been worse," he said by way of greeting. "Grab yourself a couple hours' sleep. You've got a heavy day ahead."

Throughout the Saturday the work went on. Isherwood had the knack of getting the best out of men. He drove, but did not seem to drive. Stephen puzzled over it. With perhaps half a dozen exceptions the men of both gangs were local. If they followed the local trend, 70 per cent of them by now were probably Secessionists. The work on the *Merrimac* was the principal bone of contention in the town, yet they worked hard, harder than any gang he had ever watched in the Yard. He asked Isherwood to explain.

"They're mechanics," Isherwood answered. "No politics in machines —yet."

When he climbed at midnight up the engine-room ladder, bone weary and with his ears aching from noise as the night gang knocked off for Sunday morning, Isherwood was on the deck. Stephen went up to him. The engineer looked out over the Yard. The last of the workmen was clattering down the gangway. Beyond the dim row of gas lamps on the quayside the Yard was dark and silent.

"Quiet enough," said Isherwood softly, all the customary overtones gone from his voice. "Give us three more days and we'll have her away."

"I wonder—" began Stephen.

"You're not paid to wonder," interrupted Isherwood brutally. "You drive the night gang and I'll drive you." He grunted and was silent. Stephen puzzled over the significance of the grunt. After a moment Isherwood went on, "They've sent three delegates to Washington from the Convention."

"What for?" Stephen felt a cold anxiety grip at him.

"To ask Mr. Lincoln his intentions." Isherwood hawked, walked to the side, and spat out into the water. "Can't spit on the deck, front of the first looey," he jeered, and stumped below.

Stephen slept uneasily and woke early. He dressed and began a meticulous inspection of the empty ship. Her emptiness lent her an exaggerated size. He felt strangely small, strangely powerless walking along the cavernous gun decks. Without men the scale of her spaces was inordinate. The hollow sound of her, the echoing of his footsteps accentuated that scale.

As he moved about her he found here and there points that needed attention, work scamped, defects that had been missed, bad painting— little things, little things that would need attention before she was "in all respects ready for sea." But even while he made it he knew that the inspection was futile, that the careful mental notes were pointless, that only one thing mattered: the task of getting the engines turning over so that she could move, move away from the dockside, move out of the Southern Branch, move out of the Elizabeth River, move clear of the smell of tangled loyalties and uncertain treasons—the stench of rebellion.

In Farragut's drawing room he had not faced fully up to this. He acknowledged now to himself that there was no longer even hope. Virginia would go out. The Convention would throw her into the hands of the Confederacy. Perhaps that was not wholly fair—the Convention had tried desperately to keep her out; it was the people who would go into the hands of the Confederacy. He remembered the raw exultation in Norfolk's main street, the deep noise of the crowd outside Portsmouth's Court House, the half-heard talk of the men as they wrestled with jammed gears and rusted valves, with burned-out furnace walls and corroded tubes.

He would have to see Linden as soon as he could contrive it. He could acknowledge, he could understand the tangled impulses that joined and added together and coalesced to make rebellion—but he could not join in them. The whole was still greater than the part. He had to tell her that.

An hour later he saw Alden standing on the gun deck where the morning sun flooded through the opening of an empty port. He walked up to him and saluted.

Alden returned the salute and said tonelessly, "The ship will not be moved under the masting shears." Stephen whistled. "I have attempted to get permission for work to be done today. The commodore"—for the first time Alden allowed a note of criticism to enter his voice—"finds himself unable to agree."

"In that case may I have permission to go ashore, sir?" Even as he finished the sentence Stephen knew that the timing of the request was inappropriate.

Before he could amend it he heard another voice. "Why?"

He jerked round and saw Isherwood in the darkness beyond the sunlight—gaunt, coatless, a towel wrapped round his neck.

"I wish to attend the service at Trinity Church, sir."

"Profoundly religious? Bad conscience? Or a girl?" Isherwood was back in fine sardonic form. "Do we let him go, Alden?"

Alden turned slowly and looked with disapproval at the engineer. Isherwood grinned at him. "He'll come back," he said, as if in answer to an unspoken query. "That is, if his devoted friends will let him. You can't expect to be overwhelmingly popular with the boon companions of your childhood, you know."

"I'll take that risk." Stephen grinned at him. Underneath the crusty façade he could sense a delicate, percipient sympathy.

He remembered the little scene as he walked up the aisle of Trinity Church. The church was crowded. It wanted perhaps three minutes to service time. The harsh tenor bell, the bell that had been recast since the great day when it had cracked telling the river the news of the surrender of Cornwallis, was calling Portsmouth to meet before the Lord; and Portsmouth, splendid in flowered waistcoats and flowered hats, in sprigged muslin, in striped silk, in flounced and swagged and architectured satin, was already sitting before the Lord—waiting.

Stephen felt that it was waiting for him. He heard the buzz of surprise as he entered the church, the rustle of whispering that followed him up the aisle. He watched heads crane round to see what caused the whispering, and heard new whispering begin.

Cleave sat in his usual place four rows from the front on the aisle. Linden sat beside him, between him and Aunt Deborah. As Stephen walked up the aisle, Cleave turned with the others. His eye gleamed. Turning back swiftly, he whispered to Linden and gave her a little push. Aunt Deborah caught the whisper, if not the push. She nudged the child that sat next to her, and the little movement rippled along the bench. Cleave rose as Stephen reached him, and motioned him into the space. Linden looked up and saw him, and her face went scarlet.

Under his breath Cleave murmured as Stephen brushed past him, "You've got nerve."

At once, as if at a signal, the wheezy organ broke into the processional, and the rector entered.

In the noise and scuffling as the congregation rose, he heard Linden's voice, strained, almost frightened: "You shouldn't have come. You shouldn't have come."

As they sat down together his hand brushed against hers. Furiously she snatched hers away.

Through the murmur of the first prayer Cleave, on the other side of him, whispered, "They'll flay you after service."

Stephen sang automatically, making the responses with the habit of long usage. He looked straight ahead, over the hat of old Mrs. Hodges sitting in the seat in front of him. He could see within the limited angle of his vision the flowers on the altar, the color and the richness of the East Window, the gleam of the brass and the silver. All the while he could feel the hostility about him and behind him.

The Reverend Wingfield shared that hostility. Stephen, feeling his thigh against Linden's thigh in the cramped quarters of the bench, missed the text. Perhaps it was not important, perhaps Mr. Wingfield would have preached the same sermon on any text from "In the Beginning" to the last verse of the twenty-second chapter of Revelation. He went up the steps of the pulpit as if there were a flame about him, a burning of belief.

Stephen was held by the crystal sincerity of the voice. This was a man who believed "we will fight not for ourselves but for God and for our country." Wingfield had accepted war, accepted it as a medieval monk accepted a crusade, accepted it with fervor, accepted it without question. He could see nothing but war—holy war, "war as much for religious freedom as for national liberty." The sermon was a call to arms: "that knowledge must nerve us not only to great heroism but incite us to greater holiness of life, that we may be worthy champions in such a conflict."

Stephen could feel the pulse of emotion in the church behind him, the rise and fall of the surge of it. He could feel the answering response in Linden. Twice she tried to draw away from him, but Aunt Deborah was comfortably spread over her share of the bench and there was no escape. Why could he feel nothing himself? Was it some defect in him, some incapacity for ordinary loyalties, some atrophy of normal emotions? Or was it that he belonged more to an outside world than to Portsmouth, that he had forfeited Portsmouth in finding the Union? His thoughts lost themselves in a confusion of religious exhortation and the firm heat of Linden's thigh. Not even the dry skepticism of Cleave on his other side could redress that balance.

The Reverend Wingfield came sonorously to his peroration. He had disposed of the Commissioners from the Convention; he disposed of Lincoln; he unfurled the banner of a holy war. The congregation roared into a last militant hymn, sang it through with a rapt enthusiasm, and chanted the final Amen like a threat.

As Linden brushed past him into the aisle, Stephen put his hand on her arm. "I've *got* to talk to you, Lin!"

She tried to shake herself free, but the throng in the aisle was too close packed for violent movement. In a little group, with Cleave and Aunt Deborah immediately behind them, they moved toward the door. At the back of the church there was a gathering of younger men; Stephen saw Revell at the end of a bench, with two of his close friends. They were waiting, bent forward a little, staring.

Slowly Cleave moved with his family to the end of the aisle, slowly he approached the young men. Even Linden moved in the rhythm of the crowd, surrendered to it. They came level at last. Revell and his friends had risen; they were moving forward as if they proposed to cut into the procession in the aisle. Stephen knew that there was nothing that he could do, no way short of brawling that he could use to stop them.

Then, suddenly, he felt movement on his right-hand side, became aware of Aunt Deborah's hat and Aunt Deborah's bright shawl below his line of vision, and heard Aunt Deborah's voice as she planted herself firmly at the end of the bench. "Revell Jordan, I wish to speak to you."

An instant later they were past the danger spot. He felt Cleave come closer in behind him. In a little swirl of comment and question he and Linden were passed through the crowd and were suddenly alone in the churchyard under the ancient trees and between the ancient stones. He was aware of sun, and freedom, and birds singing, and the warm soft noonday air.

"Linden," he said, "it may be that I won't be able to see you again—I don't know. God knows I want to, but I've got to do what I'm ordered. You know that?" He felt that it was dangerous to pause, dangerous to end on the note of question, but to go on was equally dangerous, to go on was to talk a way into insincerity and worse.

Linden answered: "I don't know. I don't want to know! I know that Commander Page is going South, and Homer Breckenham, and—and Will Sharp—and—oh, *everybody!* Why's it only you?"

"It isn't only me." He was stung to a sudden defensive.

"Who else? Everybody I know is going South. Everybody in this town." She broke off and stared at him for the first time. "Oh, Stephen"—her voice rose, wailing—"why must it be you?"

Out of the corner of his eye he saw men's heads moving along above the old brick wall of the churchyard.

Hurriedly, not knowing what might be about to happen, he said: "Linden, it doesn't matter. None of it matters. I had to tell you that I love you. Even if I don't see you again until it's all over, you've got to know that. You've got to remember it—I love you."

The moving frieze of heads and shoulders above the wall slowed.

Linden looked at him, her face puckered as if she were about to cry. "But why have you got to be the only one?" And then, puzzled, "Love?"

"I'm not. Listen!" He clenched his fists in the tension of his effort to make her understand. "I went to Captain Farragut—"

"And what did he say?"

Stephen searched desperately in his mind for a moment.

Words came clear at last. "The South has no ships, no navy, no bases. It has no factories to make rifles, no arsenals to make guns. War is not just a matter of men, or of battle cries. The South has nothing to back its threats."

"And was that why?" Linden seemed to have reached decision long before he finished speaking; there was disillusion in her voice, something that was terribly like contempt. "Was *that* why? Because the South has no ships, no guns. Because you were afraid." Her mind darted to a fresh point. "Was that why you left Mrs. Prentice's house and went to live in the Yard? Because you were afraid?" She reached back even farther; her hand went up to her mouth. "Stephen, was that why you were so angry after you came back from the *Star of the West*—because—because you were scairt?" She used the colloquial pronunciation of the word with the simplicity that she would have used toward Jeriel.

For some reason that he could not define the word hurt him more than anything that had preceded it. He stretched out both hands to her, and she moved backward with a hummingbird's speed. "Don't touch me!" She almost screamed the words. "Stephen, are you a coward?" Then she turned and flew down the path between the graves toward the gate without waiting for an answer.

Stephen, looking past her to the wall, saw Revell's head and the heads of five others of the younger men. They were watching Linden as she ran. He began to walk down the path toward them. "Might just as well get it over with," he muttered softly.

He had moved perhaps ten paces when he saw Aunt Deborah's hat moving purposefully a little above the line of the wall. He heard her voice, though it was too far away for him to distinguish words. Linden disappeared blindly through the gateway and turned down the sidewalk. The cluster of men's heads began to move, drifting shamefacedly in front of Aunt Deborah.

When he reached the gateway she was waiting for him. "Stephen Knott," she said precisely, her appearance utterly unflurried, "I wish you to escort me home."

He smiled at her in a sudden relief from tension. Nothing very much mattered now. "Aunt Deborah," he murmured gently, "you're a damned brave woman!"

"I will not have you swear in front of me," said Aunt Deborah sharply. "Particularly not on a Sunday, and immediately after service, too."

"I'm sorry," he replied quietly, and meant it.

Revell and the others had disappeared long before they turned up toward the Cleave house. No attempt was made to intercept him on the way back to the Yard. It was as if the whole balloon of personal hostility had been pricked by the hatpins in Aunt Deborah's flowered hat. Stephen went wearily up the long gangway to the deck of the *Merrimac*.

"With your shield or on it?" Isherwood's caustic voice greeted him from the rail. He leaned there, looking hot, in working clothes. "On it, I should say at a guess. All right, eat and change into work clothes. We got a lot to do this afternoon."

Again Stephen lost count of time. With Isherwood he crawled backward and forward through the complex of steel and brass, of timber and iron and brick, checking every detail, inspecting completed work, finding new defects and fresh necessities. Somewhere about midnight the night shift returned, and he harassed them to new speeds, harsher rhythms. Isherwood seemed to be there all the time, driving.

Some time in the course of the Monday, Alden came aboard. He took Isherwood aside and then, before he spoke, beckoned Stephen over to them. "I think you ought to hear this too. Lincoln's called for seventy-five thousand volunteers. Fixed quota from each State."

Isherwood mopped his face with the inevitable waste. Through it he said thickly, "Made up his mind at last."

Alden nodded, his face dark. "The Border States will have to make up their own minds now. It's the end of talk."

"How long have we got?" Isherwood penetrated bluntly to the heart of things.

Stephen spoke for the first time. "Virginia will act according to law," he said with a calm certainty. "Governor Letcher will have to send a formal refusal to the President. The Convention will have to meet. Someone will talk. They won't take a vote before Wednesday—perhaps not even then. You'll get your three days." He stared, broodingly, at Isherwood.

"You could be right, at that." Isherwood, somewhere in the recesses of his mind, made a quick cast-up of the chances.

"North Carolina has seized the arsenals already," interjected Alden.

"Virginia will still do it legally." Stephen's faith was stubborn.

Alden seemed not to hear him. "Washington will have to do something about us now."

"Washington!" Isherwood repeated bitterly. "I reckon what's done will be done by us. Get on with the job, Mr. Knott!"

All through the rest of the day they harried the work gang. They worked in a fever, a brooding, increasing impatience that sometimes provoked explosions of anger among the men. When the night gang came on it was clear that the news was known throughout the town. The tensions grew fiercer, more dangerous. Stephen found himself wondering if the day gang would come aboard in the morning. Isherwood was calmly certain that it would. Once to Stephen's question he snapped: "Course they'll come! The South wants the *Merrimac* ready for sea as much as we do."

"They can't hope to get her." Stephen stared at him incredulously.

"If only Commodore McCauley stood between you and a valuable ship, what would you think?"

Late in the afternoon Sharp sent a message down to the engine room asking Stephen to see him on deck. In the low sunlight Sharp looked clean, unweary, jeeringly superior.

"Commander Page," he said without preamble, "has called a meeting of all Southern officers. He proposes to express to Commodore Paulding our desire"—Sharp's accent had moved out of Virginia into the Deep South—"to be relieved."

"Does he!" Stephen found himself wiping the back of his neck with cotton waste in an unconscious imitation of Isherwood's gesture. "Tell him he can desire what he damned well pleases, but leave me out of it."

"I consider—"

"Consider what you damned well please to! I've got work to do." Stephen turned on his heel and strode over to the companionway.

Behind him he heard Sharp begin, "As a gentleman and a Virginian . . ."

Stephen was gone before the sentence was finished.

Late in the night he leaned over the rail with Isherwood, taking a breather in the cold air. A fresh wind blew down the Branch, carrying a thin sea fog in shreds with it. In the darkness he said: "That bastard Sharp was on board this afternoon with some nonsense about Page and Commodore Paulding. What's Paulding got to do with the Yard?"

"Washington's remembered us," replied Isherwood grimly. "McCauley's got his orders."

"What orders?"

"Let me see if I can remember—'to impose additional care and vigilance in protecting the public property . . .' Or was it 'vigilance and care'? He's to put the *Merrimac*'s armament on board." Isherwood let his eyes stray down the empty spaces of the upper gun deck. "He's to move the *Plymouth,* the *Germantown,* an' the *Dolphin*—what was the phrase? Oh, yes! 'Out of jeopardy.' And he's to defend us 'at any hazard, repelling by force, if necessary, any and all attempts to seize them whether by mob violence, organized effort or any assumed authority.' I remember it—word perfect."

"Is Washington sending troops?"

"They've sent Commodore Paulding. What more could you ask? Hiram Paulding."

"What do we do?"

"Get on with the job," replied Isherwood soberly. "Page gave Paulding a list of the Southern officers who wished to be relieved of duty. Your name wasn't on it."

Stephen grunted and followed Isherwood as the engineer turned away from the rail. At the entrance to the companionway he stopped abruptly. "Something's happening on the *Cumberland!*" he exclaimed.

Both men listened, standing motionless on the dark deck. The sound of whistles and shouting came down the wind, and they could see lanterns moving on the *Cumberland*'s deck. After a moment the shouts subsided and a thin mist hid the lanterns.

Isherwood said, "*Cumberland*'s ordered to defend us. Reckon somebody's feeling defensive."

Chapter eight

REVELL heaved himself up onto the ridge with no effort at all. The length of his legs gave him every advantage. As he reached out for the sill of the window, a heavy stick thumped down on the wood of the sill beside his fingers. Linden's voice said: "Even Jeriel's on'y allowed to try this way after he's thrown ten stones. Get down off that roof, Rev Jordan, or I'll knock you down! Who do you think I am—Lizzie Freeman?"

Revell, more scandalized by the fact that Linden admitted knowledge of Lizzie Freeman—one of the more ornamental of the lighter ladies of the town—than by the stick, gasped, "Linden!"

"Git!" she ordered.

The stick came down again so close to his fingers that he swayed away from the window and stood, precariously balanced, on the roof ridge. Hurriedly he said: "I've got to see you, Lindy. We've got to have your help, we need the boat—"

"Get down to the street," said Linden flatly. "Go get Jeriel, and when you've got him I'll come down and talk."

Ten minutes later she stood in the alley at the back of the houses. Jeriel was there to guarantee respectability.

Revell said: "We got to hurry, Lindy; we lost ten minutes already through this foolishness. We got to have the boat!"

"My boat?"

"No, not the skiff—it's too small. We've got to have your father's boat."

"You can't."

"Lindy, listen!"

"Nobody's allowed to take the *Chula*—even me. I've never been allowed. Not *ever*."

"All the same we've got to."

Ignoring his intensity, she said coldly: "Revell Jordan, this is another of your foolishnesses, like 'capturing' "—she gave the word a full measure of scorn—" 'the Navy Yard.' Why don't you go down to South Ca'lina? You said you would."

Revell stooped, putting his face close to hers, and whispered furiously: "Because there's more I can do here—and better. Listen, Lindy!" He allowed himself a split second of reluctant hesitation before he said: "I'm sorry about that night—I'm real sorry. This isn't for me. This is for the South. We got to have your father's boat—we got to have it *now*." He lowered his voice still more. "They're blockin' the channel between Craney Island an' the Roads tonight. The first boats have started. They're goin' to sink the old lightboats that were lyin' up Paradise Creek."

"Why?"

"To keep the *Merrimac* in. She's damned near ready now."

"Who's doing it?"

"A bunch from Norfolk—Ebbie Rogers, John Amos, Pate Wainwright—a bunch o' them! We got to have boats to take the crews off when they sink. Seth Francis promised his boat but someone run into him. She's got a hole in her side—happened an hour ago. Wasn't another we could get in time."

Linden walked away from him. Over her shoulder she called curtly, "Come on!"

Revell gave a grunt of relief.

Half running, they went through the empty streets, cutting down to the waterfront and the timber yard. The boat was alongside the little jetty in its customary position.

Linden led straight to it wordlessly, lowered herself down the rough ladder, and dropped on the half-deck. To Jeriel, who had said no word at all throughout the proceedings, she snapped: "Find the foresail! It'll be on a rack, starboard side." She began to fumble at the lashings of the mainsail herself.

Revell asked, "What shall I do?" His voice was almost humble.

"Sit. Out of the way."

The boat was old, solid, four times the size of her own skiff. It was three-quarter-decked, with a wide, open cockpit. She had never handled it herself. Cleave or Isaiah, the youngest of the freed men, always sailed it. She was not allowed to take it out: Cleave was absolute about that; it was one of the very few positive rules that he had ever made. She was defying it now, and she knew precisely what that entailed.

Jeriel came up, carrying the heavy bundle of the foresail. Linden went out on the bowsprit and shackled it fast. Feeling uncertainly in the darkness, she found the halyard and shackled the head of the sail. Silently Jeriel passed the sheets.

When that was done she ordered, "Go and clear the mainsail!" The gear was strong, simple. In a matter of moments they had the last of the lashings off. Linden stood motionless for a second, judging the necessities. Fortunately the wind was blowing straight off the little pier. She gave Jeriel quick instructions, ignoring Revell. Then she went aft to the tiller and, fumbling at the after bollard, cast off the stern rope. A moment later, as the boat lay head to wind, she watched the mainsail go creaking up. For two minutes there was a wild slatting of sails, a strange mock-thunder noise in the night stillness, and then she heard Jeriel's voice, "All clear," and felt the boat's head pay off. The loom of the little pierhead disappeared, and suddenly, so suddenly that it was impossible to judge the timing of it, they were lost in the heart of the thin drizzle. There were no lights, there was no land, there was nothing solid—only the drift of rain and the harsh slap of the water under the racing bows.

Revell asked: "Can you see?"

With an impatient indifference she cut him short. "It will clear in a minute. Where did they promise to meet the lightboats?"

"Tanner's Point," replied Revell hastily. "Somewheres near Tanner's Point. There's a place where the channel narrows there."

Jeriel, settled in a corner against the bulkhead, said scornfully, "Take a hell an' all of a lot of lightboats to block that channel!"

Linden said nothing.

The boat went on, divorced from the ordinary world, closed in a small heart of mist. Linden steered by the feel of the wind, by her familiarity with the harbor, by her knowledge of the tide and the run of the currents. Out of these things she made a synthesis of certitude, because of them she knew precisely when she would have to tell them to haul in on the mainsheet and alter course for Hospital Point. She felt that it was not necessary to see, that there was no need of lights or certainties. A strange elation enveloped her, the knowledge that she was giving practical expression to her loyalties.

Revell, peering through the darkness, tried to see her, but her face was hidden.

They were halfway to Hospital Point when Jeriel lifted his head. He said softly, "Boat rowin' somewheres."

Linden listened tensely, brought back out of the exterior world of her imaginings.

Jeriel, with the expertise of a small boy born on the waterfront, muttered, "Navy fashion they're rowin'."

Revell turned sharply. "Where?"

"Shut up!" ordered Linden.

A voice hailed them out of the darkness, upwind of them, hardly more than a few yards away. "What boat is that?"

Instantly, automatically, Linden brought the helm up. The boat's head paid off; she ran downwind like a frightened gull.

Again the voice shouted, a little more distant, a little more insistent: "What boat is that? Come up to us!"

She wondered if she dare slack off the main, and Jeriel, sensing her thought in the darkness, whispered: "Blocks'd creak. They heered our bow wave."

The boat ran on awkwardly.

For the third time the voice shouted—it was far away now, angry with the anger of frustration: "Come up to us or we'll fire!"

"Ain't nothin' to fire at," murmured Jeriel as if to himself. "Not nothin'."

No shot came out of the mist. Slowly, stiffly, Linden brought the boat back on course again. Twice they ran through clear patches in the drizzle, but it was never clear enough to open the lights of the far shore or for them to see back to the boat that had hailed. They were in the full grip of the tide now, moving fast toward the island. Linden was no longer certain of their position. The shock of the challenge, the automatic flight from it, had destroyed the sense of timing that she had built up. Now she knew only that they were in the main stream of the tide, swirling down toward the Roads, moving unnaturally fast with wind and stream together. And she knew that there was nothing else that she could do; but the sense of elation remained with her.

They ran out of the drizzle and the mist off Pinner's Point, but neither she nor Jeriel could place themselves with certainty. They could see clear water ahead of them and, in a ragged break of the cloud, stars and, on the low-lying, almost invisible land, here and there a faint and improbable light.

Jeriel stood now at the break of the half-deck, staring into the darkness ahead. Once he said, "No boats, no Navy boats, anyways." Ten minutes later he said: "Ship at anchor—off to the west a bit. She'll be inside Craney Island."

Linden said nothing.

Revell was out of his element; he knew little of boats. Once he edged up the seat toward Linden, but she said clearly and without emotion, "Keep away from me, Revell Jordan." And something in the night, the darkness, the sound of the wind, and the impalpable emptiness of the water made him accept the order.

It was Jeriel who sighted the dinghy first. He saw the splash of the oars before he saw the dinghy itself. It was perilously low in the water, overloaded with men.

A voice called from her as they rounded into the wind: "You've been the hell of a long while coming. Why in Chris' name couldn't you have been here on time?"

The wild slatting of the canvas drowned Revell's answer.

The dinghy came up astern of them, faltered, fell away, and then came alongside. Men spilled out of her, pouring over the side like a dark wave, trampling the little dinghy under them. There were laughter and shouting and a few curses. The dinghy drifted away waterlogged.

"Wouldn't-a lasted more'n five minutes," said the voice of the man who appeared to be the leader among them. "On'y thing we had to bale with was Abe's hat. Good thing he brought a hat with him. Who's this?"

Revell answered: "Jordan. It's Mist' Rogers, ain't it?"

"Sure it's Mist' Rogers," said the enormous voice. "People know me even in the dark. Who's this?"

The girl said, "Linden Cleave."

"Chris' sake!" exclaimed a voice amongst the group. "What's a girl doin' here?"

And Rogers said: "Lindy Cleave, I know your pap—know you if it comes to that. I seen you over to the yard. What you doin' out here?"

Revell answered for her. "Seth Francis' boat was run into—sunk at her moorings. This was the boat I had to get."

Another voice said: "Long as she floats, don't make no difference to me, and she floats good. Boy, I thought that damned thing was goin' to sink!"

The canvas filled suddenly, and the yard slatted over. The roar of voices was overpowering in the new silence.

Linden called sharply, "D'you want to save the dinghy?"

"Not me, ma'am," Rogers' voice boomed. "Wasn't a good dish anyway. It'll fetch up Seawell's Point somewheres with this wind. Don't care if it don't. We sunk the big one. What does the little un matter?"

"She sunk all right?" asked Revell.

"Slap in the middle of the channel. Don't know about the others. Had enough of a time of it sinkin' her."

Linden held the boat just off the wind. The elation had turned to a violent excitement. She felt an enormous importance, as if she were a part of big events. In a lull of the self-congratulation and boisterousness she asked, "Where do you want me to put you now?"

"We'll put ourselves," replied Rogers with a thunderous cheerfulness. He settled himself down on the seat. "I'll take her now, Miss Lindy."

Linden hesitated and then gave up the tiller. She would not have surrendered it to Revell or to any of her friends, but this deep boisterous voice in the darkness was something out of her experience.

Rogers said: "We'll take ourselves somewheres about Smith's Creek. They'll be watchin' the front, I reckon."

"Navy boat hailed us as we came out." Revell thrust into the talk. "Steam boat?"

"Rowboat," replied Linden. "We didn't see her. There was fog in there."

The deep voice said approvingly, "You got nerve, Lindy Cleave, ain't you?"

She felt that it was an accolade.

Revell asked, "D'you reckon you've blocked the channel?"

"Was what we went for." Rogers' voiced boomed confidently.

Twice as they went in they sighted boats, seeing the dark shapes crossing the shore lights rather than seeing the hulls themselves. They were too far away even to hear shouting. It was close to slack water when they edged into the wide bight between Back Creek and Smith's. Rogers seemed to know exactly where he wanted to go. He handled the boat with a clumsy firmness, knowing what he wanted it to do and mastering it like a man with a balky horse. They drifted in at the last with all sails down, and bumped heavily against the wooden piles. The seven men they had picked out of the dinghy swarmed up and over the piles.

Rogers went last. "Thanks fer the ride, Mis' Cleave. I reckon we won't ferget it." And to Jeriel he said: "You too, sprat. Year or two more an' we could use you proper." He spoke to Revell last of all. "See you, Rev. You better hang on here till mornin'."

Before Revell could answer, Linden said, "We'll work her off when the tide makes a bit."

"Sure, sure," agreed the deep voice, "you can work her off if you want to. Keep away from the Navy! Night, Lindy Cleave."

Chapter nine

"THAT shouting on the *Cumberland* last night, sir . . ."

Isherwood, intent on a slow, reluctant meshing of gearwheels, grunted.

Stephen was not sure whether the grunt was a rejection or a request. He went on cautiously: "The day gang says that the channel was blocked off Tanner's Point last night. The *Cumberland* sent armed boats out to try to stop it."

"And didn't!" Isherwood's grunts translated themselves into intelligible words.

"No, sir, they didn't. Becton says we'll never get her out. They sank a bunch of old lightboats."

Isherwood said: "Toward me a little. No, not as much as that! Don't be in such a damned hurry. Handsomely now. Plenty of water in that channel. Take more'n a couple of old lightboats."

"They say it's blocked, sir." Stephen came back to the main point doggedly.

"If half the things they say around this town . . . Easy now, damn it! I said *easy*."

Stephen stood silent, waiting for the operation to end.

Behind him a voice said, "The boys that did it was picked up by shore boats."

Somebody added, "There was a girl took out one o' them."

Stephen whipped round. "A girl?" He searched the man's face to see if he was mocking him.

The man looked at him, puzzled. "A girl," he repeated. "She took out one o' the shore boats."

"Who was it?"

"Dunno," answered the man without interest. "Some girl."

The gears clashed suddenly into place. Isherwood straightened himself wearily. "All right, make that good. We'll turn 'em over 's afternoon." He looked belligerently at Stephen. "You ever tried to block a channel?" And, as Stephen made no reply, he snapped, "Well, don't talk damn' foolishness." He stumped off down the echoing floor plates.

Already there was an order in the engine room. The loose parts, the separate, incomprehensible sections had grown together in the last twenty-four hours. This was an engine now. It lacked paint, it lacked polish, it lacked the ordered seemliness of use—but it was an engine.

Stephen went through to the boiler room. There was an immense noise here as coal crashed into the bunkers. The place was full of a thin, impalpable dust so that the lanterns glowed red and faintly in the echoing space. Men here were working on the last of the furnace doors. There was some small difficulty. He joined the group, watching intently, and then, because it was clear that they had the root of the problem in hand, he moved away again. Coal dust gritted between his teeth. Somebody thrust a head across the narrow sky opening of the fiddley grating and shouted a question about water, was answered, jeered, and went away apparently satisfied.

Stephen went back to the engine room. Tom Carr, who should have gone off with the night gang, met him with a question about the shaft tunnel. He went with him to inspect a bearing, owlishly and without interest, accepting Carr's information and advice. He returned to the engine room, moving like a planet in an uneasy orbit. Isherwood was damning a dozen men in the hollow, cavernous depths of the crank pit. But already men were cleaning, polishing, lifting away the debris, the broken parts, the discarded, unnoticed rubbish of weeks of labor.

Stephen went back to the boiler room. There was a feverishness about the whole ship now, a last desperate sense of urgency. They were all of them dirty, all of them tired, all of them moving in a strained, remorseless projection of effort.

Alden came into it, looking, in his shore-going uniform, with his neat hair and his washed face, strangely remote, almost hostile.

From the depths of the crank pit, framed in an irregular rhomboid of polished steel, lighted by the uncertain light of a hand lamp, Isherwood called up to him, "What's the old carcass doin' now?"

The thin expression of disapproval that hardly ever left Alden's face deepened. He called back, "Nothing."

"Goin' to move us under the masting shears?" The derision in Isherwood's question was boisterously obvious.

"No," replied Alden flatly.

"What does Mr. Commodore Paulding say?" Again the question was laced with derision.

"He's gone back to Washington." All the gang was listening now. Alden's voice was harsh in the echoing silence.

"We'll still turn 'em over at four o'clock," Isherwood snapped with a note of finality which Alden appeared to accept. He turned and began to climb the ladder back to the upper deck. Behind him he heard Isherwood's voice: "Come on! What are you staring at? Never seen a commander goin' up a ladder before?"

Hours later, days later, weeks later it seemed to Stephen, he stood with Isherwood in the fresh afternoon air. It was cold but the sun shone. The Union flag whipped brilliantly at the Headquarters' masthead. The trees beyond the ship houses were a young green.

Isherwood filled his lungs. He said accusingly, "You never thought we'd do it."

Simply, Stephen answered, "I didn't know you then."

Isherwood grinned. "What you buckin' for—promotion?"

They both laughed.

Isherwood leaned on the rail, and Stephen saw with a sense of shock how tired the man was. The rims of his eyes were red and heavy with exhaustion, his face was strained, a pulse beat in his temple. Yet his voice was round and full as he said, "Give us another hour and she'll be ready." For a single sentence there were no overtones, nothing but the deep satisfaction of a craftsman with his task accomplished. Then a note of self-derision crept in. "Point is—who's she ready for?"

Stephen looked out over the peacefulness of the Yard. Nothing within his view gave the slightest indication of any departure from normality: the Yard was quiet, men moved at a pile of lumber, there was a small cloud of smoke over the tar house, the smokestacks of the foundry drifted a haze above them. Unseen behind the first ship house he could hear a squad of Marines drilling; the voice of the sergeant, refined by distance, had almost a peaceful note about it. Behind him down the river there were ship noises—ordinary, peaceful ship noises —and the bright sun flooded over everything.

Isherwood repeated: "Point is—who? If old Bladder of Lard at headquarters don't make up his mind damn' quick, we're not goin' to get her out, boy!"

"The blockships?"

"Ah, the blockships! Don't bother about blockships," retorted Isherwood. "The block's at the commodore's office. Wish to God somebody'd sink that old fool! All right, don't look so shocked. I'd do it myself if I thought I could get away with it." He sagged wearily against the rail.

Stephen looked at him with concern. "Paulding will let them know in Washington what's happening."

"Paulding!" exclaimed Isherwood scornfully. "I don't like Paulding. Paulding'll be too late anyway. What's goin' to happen will happen tomorrow, this evening, in half an hour's time—God knows." He lifted his head and looked swiftly round the Yard. "It's too quiet, too damn' quiet. Come on! Let's go down and hustle 'em."

At the bottom of the ladder they found Carr. "We need another twenty minutes, sir."

"You can have fifteen," snapped Isherwood.

Carr grinned back at the engineer. "Fifteen and five."

Isherwood laughed. Yet when he went over to stand at the rail of the control platform Stephen could see that the fingers of one hand were clasped tightly, so tightly that the knuckles showed white through the grime of oil and coal dust, and he realized with a sense of shock that Isherwood was strained almost to breaking point.

He sought hastily for something neutral to make into conversation. "Do you go back to Washington after this, sir?"

"Listen! I go back to Philadelphia *in* this. In fifteen minutes those damned engines will turn over. D'you understand that? I need twenty minutes to wash and shave, and then I'm goin' up to see Commodore goddamn McCauley myself."

Isherwood broke off abruptly as a Negro came up to the platform and dumped on the watchkeeper's desk a flask of coffee and a plate of sandwiches wrapped in a damp napkin.

The man said, with an enormous flash of teeth in the half-darkness, "Mist' Carr reckoned you could take you a bite o' food befo' he turns 'em ovuh."

"Now that," said Isherwood gently, "was a sound idea of Mr. Carr's." The Negro laughed and went off. Isherwood turned to Stephen. "That's a good nigger!"

"That's Mr. Porter's Willis."

"Porter, the constructor?"

Stephen, unwrapping the sandwiches, nodded.

"He's a slaveowner?"

"Lot of people are," answered Stephen briskly, pouring out the coffee.

"I don't get it! John Porter's a damned good constructor, he's a damned good designer. What does he want to own slaves for?"

"That"—Stephen seized recklessly at the side issue—"is what you damyankees will never understand. I wouldn't put it that way. The way I look at it, Mr. Porter's Willis owns him."

Isherwood hawked and spat with accuracy into the oily bilges. "Southerners!" he exclaimed scornfully.

"Willis made John Porter buy his wife for him. Cost his eldest daughter a new piano."

"How?"

"Her father couldn't buy both," answered Stephen explicitly. "I was a kid then. I can remember how sour she was about it. Porter nursed him through yellow fever, then he turned round and nursed Porter. He's pigheaded but he's a good nigger. He owns Porter."

"Southerners!" repeated Isherwood still scornfully. Carr came up to the platform. "And here's another. What are you doin' sendin' coffee and sandwiches for a damyankee?"

Carr laughed. "I sent coffee and sandwiches for a damn good engineer. We're ready to go, Mr. Isherwood."

Stephen looked back from the desk to see a group of men stretching up to the great hand-turning wheel.

"All right," said Isherwood softly, "let her go!"

* * *

Stephen closed the door and stood by the wall close to it. No one appeared to notice him. McCauley was sitting at his desk. Isherwood stood across the desk from him, hammering on it. Breckenham leaned over the left-hand end of the desk, Sharp stood close to him, and Page stood away from the desk at the right-hand end. Only five men, yet the room appeared full. The movement, the argument, the atmosphere was that of a crowd—and there was violence in it.

As Stephen shut the door, Isherwood said: "Sir, I repeat—and this is for the record—the engines were turned over at four o'clock this afternoon. The trial was successful in every respect. I have shipped sufficient coal for the passage to Philadelphia. I have on board sufficient firemen and coal passers. Commander Alden is prepared to take the ship to sea as soon as steam is raised. I request permission to light the fires."

Page said, "It would be most injudicious."

Breckenham began to hammer on the desk. "We had your word, sir, that you would not alarm the civilian population."

McCauley ran a weary hand over his forehead. "Gentlemen, gentlemen!"

Suddenly Isherwood's temper snapped. The weary cynicism left his face. He straightened himself. "Commodore McCauley, sir, I insist upon my right to speak to you alone. I request that these gentlemen withdraw."

McCauley said, "They are my staff."

"Sir, if they do not withdraw, *I* withdraw at once and I shall proceed instantly to Washington, there to lay a full report of these proceedings before the Secretary of the Navy."

"You are too hasty, Mr. Isherwood." McCauley repeated the words: "You are too hasty."

"The times demand it," returned Isherwood brutally. "I ask for your decision at once, sir." Some inner compulsion made him pull out a thick, clumsy gold turnip watch. He opened the case with an ostentatious formality. It seemed to hypnotize McCauley. He stared at it, his whole attention concentrated on the watch. He seemed to have forgotten Isherwood with the others. Finally Isherwood put the watch away. "I must ask for your decision now, sir. It is necessary that I leave at once for Washington if you are not prepared to give your permission."

"Gentlemen," said McCauley wearily, "you must go."

"But, sir, we have your word!" Breckenham protested.

To Stephen the commodore was like the wreck of a ship that he had seen once in a heavy gale, swamped now under the crest of a sea, now lifting clear of it; overwhelmed and resilient in a wild alternation.

The old man lifted his head now. "Go! You heard my order. Go!"

Page shrugged, caught the eyes of the two younger men, and, turning, walked toward the door.

McCauley called petulantly, "You too, you too!"

Stephen followed the others.

Outside in the corridor Page demanded, "Is she, in fact, ready for sea?"

Stephen nodded curtly.

Breckenham said: "The Convention met this afternoon. It has voted for secession."

Stephen felt a cold shiver pass through his body. Before he had time to answer, the door opened. The four men crowded at once into the doorway, and Stephen heard McCauley's voice, suddenly full of determination and spirit, say, "I have given orders that the fires shall be lit at dawn."

Isherwood came through the door like an angry wind, scattering them. For a long time, as he and Stephen strode down between the ship houses toward the *Merrimac,* he said nothing, but at the quayside he suddenly snarled: "God sends fools! You'd better sleep tonight, Mr. Knott. I won't guarantee you any sleep after dawn."

"Why was I sent for?"

"He wanted confirmation of the trial, confirmation from *you* after I had given him the facts. Me, the Engineer in Chief! Where's Alden?"

"He left the Yard, sir. I think he crossed to Norfolk."

"Fool!" said Isherwood bluntly. "I think we should take this ship out now."

*   *   *

Through the sighthole in the furnace door Stephen could see the red heart of flame. The heat beat off the steel of the boiler in waves that were almost tactile.

The Irish foreman next to him leaned on his shovel and stared moodily at the gauge glass. "She'll be blowin' off in twenty minutes' time."

The place had order now and a vibrant life, as if the mere application of flame to the oil rags under the furnace had made pregnant this strange dark womb of the ship. He could hear the banging and shouting of the trimmers in the cross-bunker, and the clash and clatter of the feed pumps.

He went out of the boiler room after a little, climbing up to the cool air topside.

Isherwood was still standing where he had left him, leaning over the rails, looking over the dockyard. The first of the sun had fallen across the ship houses and the cupola over the main gate and the Union flag. They had a golden brilliance. He said wryly: "The damned old fool! How is it doin'?"

"Nineteen pounds. Collins says she'll blow off in twenty minutes."

"We've got to catch the next tide. Our time's run out."

Alden came across the deck toward them. "How is it?"

"We could slip in ten minutes' time," answered Isherwood confidently.

"The tide won't serve till the afternoon."

"Then let's slip and lie in the stream," suggested Isherwood.

"We've got to get permission."

"Then for the sweet sake of Jesus Priest let's go and get permission if we have to beat it out of that old fool with a furnace door!"

"Mr. Isherwood!" Alden's voice had a note of reproof.

"Balls!" roared Isherwood. "Balls, Commander Alden! Do you come with me or do I go alone?"

* * *

Two of the Southern faction were in McCauley's office together with the commodore's son. The old man was leaning back in his chair this morning, brooding.

Alden, standing stiffly at attention, disdainful, cold, said, "I request permission to move the *Merrimac* into the stream at once, sir."

McCauley clasped his hands together and regarded them earnestly as if they might reveal to him some answer. At length he replied: "Not yet, Commander Alden, not yet. It is not necessary yet. It is not desirable."

"Why, sir?"

With a sudden flash of spirit McCauley looked up. "Because I say so, Commander Alden." Then, apparently thinking that he had been too positive, he added: "I have still to consider the townspeople, sir— the attitude of the men outside the Yard. I have to weigh these things." He was silent for a long half-minute, then he repeated gently, "Weigh these things."

Isherwood, still hard, said: "Your orders, sir, are to exercise care and vigilance in protecting public property, to put the *Merrimac*'s armament on board, and to move the *Plymouth,* the *Germantown,* and the *Dolphin* out of jeopardy."

"Sir"—McCauley lifted his head, looking like an old lion at bay— "those are my private orders and they are no concern of yours. Your orders were as to the *Merrimac* alone."

Alden said: "Then, sir, I request that we move the *Merrimac* at once under the masting shears so that she may take her armament aboard."

McCauley's head had gone back, but he lifted it a little sidewise to say craftily: "I have to consider the *Germantown* also—she occupies the berth. Moreover, I have to safeguard the Yard, to repel, by force if necessary, mob violence." He repeated the words as if savoring them: "Mob violence." Then abruptly he spread both hands wide. "But I have no troops, gentlemen; I have no troops."

Isherwood almost shouted: "We'll lose the tide again, Commodore!

They've already attempted to block the channel. They'll complete it tonight, sir."

"If you will return later, gentlemen, I will inform you of my decision." The old man pulled himself up in his chair and seized a pen, as if more demanding business claimed his attention.

"What time, sir?" demanded Alden.

"Later"—McCauley waved a petulant hand—"later."

As they went out of the door of the Headquarters building, Mc-Cauley's son caught up with them. "Gentlemen, my father has not slept for five nights."

Isherwood fixed his eye on the boy. "Would it make any difference if he had?" He brushed him aside and stalked on. Half over his shoulder he said to Alden: "You command the ship, Alden. My advice to you is to cast off now."

Alden walked on without replying until they were halfway down between the great sheds. Then he said, "To do that without the sanction of the commodore would be an act of mutiny."

"Balls!" retorted Isherwood.

* * *

Isherwood stared at the gauge glass as if its hot column held some deep inner secret. He stared so long, so fixedly, that Stephen, watching him with an anxious helplessness, felt that the engineer had lost his assurance. Isherwood said at last: "I'll try once more; it's Alden's job, but I'll try. The old fool—the damned soft-brained, frantic fool! Wait here!" He went up the iron ladder heavily.

Stephen, his back against the desk, watched him disappear. The drive, the impetus was gone now. Isherwood's concern had been to get the engines of the *Merrimac* working. They would work now. It was as if purpose and fire had gone out of him. Stephen realized that values differed with each of them. To Isherwood his professional responsibility was ended; all else was the concern of the sailors. He had gone once more to McCauley. After that, Stephen knew, he would wash his hands of it: the responsibility now was Alden's. And to Alden the *Merrimac* without her guns was not a ship of war. He would wait for the guns; he would not make any final decision before he had them.

Collins, the Irish fireman, came up. "She keeps steady." His eyes flickered toward the gauge glass and back. "I was never in her before. They say her engines is hell, always was. We going to move, Lootenant?"

"I don't know," replied Stephen slowly, "I don't know."

Hours later it seemed, but it might have been no more than twenty minutes, Isherwood returned. He came down the ladder slowly, not answering Stephen's shouted question. He walked heavily across the iron grating of the platform. At last, standing close to Stephen and the fireman, he said in a voice that was no more than a rasping whisper, "Draw the fires!"

Collins' head jerked up. "I didn't rightly hear."

"Draw fires!" Isherwood's voice was louder. It rose suddenly to an uncontrolled shout: *"Draw—the—goddam—fires!"* He turned and climbed wearily back up the ladder.

Chapter ten

LINDEN leaned precariously out of the window, the blue shawl swirling up and down in great convolutions of silken brilliance. The head of the column was almost level with her now. A score of children trotted with it, girls walked level beside it. The drum beat out its hard staccato tattoo.

She saw Charlotte Vickery halfway down the length of it on the sidewalk, waving and calling. Rhoda Barret and Prudence Howe and Ernestine Carter sailed along, crinolined and ribboned, in the midst of the running children. None of them had a vast blue silk shawl to wave.

Despite the drumbeat the column marched badly; the men were footsore, leg weary; the handful that were fully uniformed showed up hardly more brilliant than their homespun comrades; a leveling, democratic dust covered them all. It covered too the pathetic deficiencies of their arms—the ancient flintlocks, the duck guns, the squirrel guns, the muskets, the bare half-dozen modern rifles. There was about it a strange, foreboding melancholy, but it was not visible to the girls along the sidewalk, or to Linden waving the silk shawl like a blue banner above their heads.

The men in the leading ranks looked up at it. There were whistles, yells.

A man called: "Com'n down, honey! Ain't no use to us up there."

Behind Choat a man said, "Cap'n, that's Ash Cleave's girl—girl who picked up th' boys from th' blockships."

Captain Choat said, "Give her a cheer, boys."

"Ya-a-a-a-a-ay!"

The girls on the sidewalk looked up, mortified.

Linden spread both arms out. "Ya-a-a-ay!" she called back.

The column went on. The tail of it passed her; it was, after all, very short. The Negro with the fife struck up a marching tune. The column went on to the corner and turned round it into Court Street. It was lost to sight.

One fife, one drum. The pathos was more real than apparent, but the running children could not see it, nor the girls on the sidewalk— nor Linden.

*　　*　　*

Aunt Deborah said acidly, "The Dismal Swamp Rangers."

Linden, disregarding her tone, called back, "They must have marched all the way from Deep Creek."

"What did they want to do that for? Jim Choat could have got wagons enough. All of a piece with the foolishness of the name. Dismal Swamp Rangers—huh!"

"What does a name matter?" Linden's head was still half out of the window, her eyes still bright with excitement. "They're the first company to muster." She heard Cleave's step on the stairs and, running to the door, called, "The companies are coming in!"

Cleave's lack of enthusiasm was apparent as he said, "I've seen Jim Choat."

"There'll be more."

"The Navy still holds the Yard," he said quietly.

"Sixty Marines!"

"General Taliaferro—" she began.

"General Taliaferro's been given a command: he has not been given troops. But even if he had, it wouldn't be the Marines that he'd worry about. It's the guns of the *Cumberland* and the *Pennsylvania*. They could blow the heart out of this town in an hour. If he doesn't know that, the mayor does; I've been talking to him."

"They wouldn't dare!"

"They might," said Cleave gravely. "They might."

*　　*　　*

Commodore Pendergrast moved heavily across to the great stern window. The tide had swung the *Cumberland* so that the window looked straight down the Southern Branch to where the low, irregular skyline of Norfolk blocked the horizon. It was doubtful if he saw water or skyline. His eyes were turned inward, searching his conscience.

He said at last: "I cannot fire upon an undefended town. McCauley has no right to expect that. It would not be an act of war; it would be an act of murder. A man would not wish to die with that on his soul." He waited, as if expecting an answer, but the commander standing against the side table watched him broodingly. After a little Pendergrast went on: "They are our own people. We have eaten with them, drunk with them, danced with them." He beat with his fist against the ledge of the open port. "President Lincoln would not ask it of me. Have you met Lincoln?" He did not wait for an answer this time. "He is a kindly man. He has a warm heart, sir."

There was a long silence.

When the commander spoke, it was reluctantly, as if the words were prised out of him. "Our orders are to defend the Navy Yard, sir."

"The Yard cannot be defended unless I fire into the town."

"Colonel Edelin—"

"Edelin has barely sixty men. It is not possible to defend a mile of wall with sixty Marines. With the seamen he has in the Yard, with parties from the ships, I doubt if he could muster more than three hundred at best. That would leave us with insufficient to man our own guns. They have thousands! Edelin has an agent in the town—I have seen the reports—thousands, and more coming in with every hour. Unless Washington sends troops . . ." His hand drummed on the ledge of the port again. "McCauley should get the ships clear," he said with a sudden energy. "I will not give the order to fire upon an open town."

*   *   *

Revell said: "We could get fifty boys without any trouble—if you need 'em."

Captain Kearns nodded. "It's Mahone's plan. He'll bring in trains on the Norfolk & Petersburg every hour—more, if he can get the locomotives. He'll keep them shuntin' and runnin' up and down all night. The Norfolk companies—some of them, that is—will stand by at the depot to shout, make a big noise, when the trains come in. We shan't get more'n two-three trains here on the Seaboard & Roanoke— ain't got the stock—but they'll run those for us. We've got to have cheerin' at the depot too. It's got to sound like an army, that was Mahone's word: sound like an army. Scare the pants right off that old fool McCauley! They're scared half off already."

"Aren't we goin' to take the Navy Yard, then?" Revell was sensitive about the word "capture" now.

"What with?" asked Kearns simply. "We've got no order from Letcher to muster the companies. Got nothin' except Jim Choat's boys, and they're tuckered out."

"Half of them are drunk!" Revell's tone was censorious.

Kearns laughed. "Wouldn't you be?"

*   *   *

Jeriel said solemnly, subduing an immense interior excitement: "Get fell in! We got to march to the depot."

"Ah, hell!" protested a voice in the darkness.

"Orders," explained Jeriel gravely. "We got to sound like a company. Wisht," he said longingly, "Wisht we had a fife."

Order established itself in the darkness. There were twenty-eight boys in all. Jeriel was by no means the oldest of them but he was invested with authority. Revell had launched him; Revell had said: "You pay attention to Jeriel, he knows what I want you to do. Anyone larkin' —home! See?"

"For-a-a-ard march!" The drummer beside Jeriel picked up the rhythm. Behind him Jeriel could hear shuffling. He called over his shoulder: "Pick it up! Pick it up!"

A breathless discipline enveloped them. They marched, excited, to cheer at the depot, to welcome imaginary companies, nonexistent regiments, invisible armies.

"Scare the pants off'n ole McCauley," murmured Jeriel to himself. He knew the inner meaning of things. He had nothing against Commodore McCauley—only that he was a Yankee. But that was enough.

*   *   *

Commodore McCauley sat upright in his chair. His face was set in a heroic mold, the face of a Roman senator. Between his hands he held a piece of paper, neither fumbling nor fidgeting with it. "I have received a message from Washington. Commodore Paulding will reach us with troops tomorrow—Massachusetts Militia, and a force of Marines."

He smiled suddenly, and Stephen realized that he had not seen the old man smile for weeks, that he had forgotten almost that he could smile. His face had for a moment or two an extraordinary tenderness, a gentleness.

When he spoke again the relief that was clearly flooding him was obvious in his voice. "I have done the right thing. I have not alienated the city. I have not exacerbated the population. All will now be well—all." He was silent for a moment, and then the old nervous trick reasserted itself. He repeated softly: "Militia—Massachusetts Militia," his voice thick and hardly intelligible.

By some inner compulsion Stephen looked over toward the sideboard. The decanter stood in its accustomed place. The cut-glass whisky flask was three-quarters full. He's not drunk, he thought to himself.

"I trust"—Commodore McCauley smoothed out the telegram with careful fingers—"that you will sleep well tonight. You may go."

*　　*　　*

Stephen leaned over the rail at the place where Isherwood had been accustomed to lean. The ship was utterly silent. The coal passers and the firemen had gone ashore or to the *Pennsylvania*. The fires had long since been drawn; the boilers were cold. The ship had died again: she felt dead beneath his feet, inanimate, a corpse. The night was very still; it was warm; there was no wind, and only the confidential rustle and ripple of the rising tide sounded in the dark gut between the ship and the quayside. The stars overhead were brilliant.

In the distance, so far away that he could hardly place it with accuracy, he could hear a train moving up the swamp edge, he guessed, from Suffolk. It would be on the Norfolk & Petersburg; a freight train, no passenger trains at this hour of the night. It came closer and closer.

A duck flighted overhead suddenly, and he forgot the train, listening to the quick beat of wings. His mind went back an undefined distance to the wingbeats over the *Star of the West*. He said to himself, "Could have been Canada geese at that!"

The noise of the locomotive broke across his memories. Somewhere in the same direction, somehow connected with it, he thought that he could hear cheering; and then it died, and the locomotive went on, heading for the bridge. His ears became acutely attuned to it so that when it crossed the bridge he heard at once the change in the note, the harsh, hollow, metallic sound that was superimposed upon it, and then he heard the train pull clear of the bridge and go on, heading for Norfolk, sweeping round in a long, easy curve.

It was time to go below and sleep. McCauley had trusted that he would sleep well tonight. There was no longer cause for anxiety; everything would be all right. As if he had caught the trick from McCauley, he repeated to himself "everything," and grinned in the darkness.

Again the sound of the train caught his attention; again he found himself concentrating on it, listening to the change of emphasis as it passed buildings on the outskirts, ran behind trees that muffled the sound and came out on a note of raucous triumph. He could hear the bell on the locomotive now. She must be going into Norfolk, he thought. It was very faint and yet utterly clear in the stillness. There must be a drift of air, he thought, an imperceptible drift down from the north.

And then across the stillness, over the bell, over even the noise of the locomotive, he heard cheering—real cheering now, prolonged, repeating itself in wave after wave of thin, distant, delicate sound. And he said to himself: What would they cheer for this time of night? Troops coming in? He waited for a little before he said aloud, "Could be."

Far down to the south he heard the noise of another train, very far away, farther than the first had been when he picked it up, but his ears were now more acutely attuned to distant sound: Troops coming in from Richmond.

Chapter eleven

THE corridor was full of men: the handful of the officers of the Yard who remained loyal, the civilian clerks, officers from the *Pennsylvania,* the *Cumberland,* the *Germantown.* The place was a Babel.

As Stephen pressed his way through the crowd toward McCauley's door, a lieutenant he knew from the *Cumberland* asked, "Steve, have you heard anything of the batteries they've emplaced at Berkley?"

Stephen shook his head. "Haven't heard a word. What's all this about?"

"Ordered here," explained the lieutenant.

Beside him an elderly commander said, "Colonel Edelin's agents report that they have brought in five thousand troops during the night."

Another lieutenant broke in excitedly: "I heard the trains; they were running all night. You could hear the cheering over the water."

"I heard it," said Stephen shortly.

An engineer whose name Stephen could not remember called: "That wouldn't matter so much, but they took Fort Norfolk in the night—the Norfolk Militia, it was. Two hundred thousand pounds of powder, ammunition, guns!"

A voice protested, "Weren't no guns to Fort Norfolk."

The engineer's voice growled, "I said guns."

Another voice said: "He's right. There were no guns at Fort Norfolk —powder store—no ammunition neither."

A new voice joined in gloomily: "Local militia've been called up. They was comin' in to town all yesterday."

"Norfolk 'nd Portsmouth combined—that should give 'em another three thousand men, more mebbe," said a newcomer.

Immediately behind him a voice murmured, "Edelin says ain't no chance to hold the Yard, and no sign of the *Pawnee*."

"She's not been signaled. Eight thousand men and powder enough fer an army!"

A door opened suddenly and a voice called, "Silence!" And again, impatiently, "Silence!"

The men nearest the door began to move into McCauley's office. There was a strange indiscipline in the movement, as if all the regulations, the sanctions of naval life had been abruptly abolished.

As Stephen went in with the rest of them he saw McCauley slumped back in his chair at the desk. Pendergrast and Edelin, the Marine colonel, stood on either side of him, their faces lined and full of gloom. Stephen felt that this was only one more of the endless, purposeless conferences of the last three weeks. It was with a sense of shock that he saw McCauley pull himself to his feet.

"I have reached a decision," the old man announced. His voice was full and flexible. "We cannot wait longer for the *Pawnee*. We may be attacked within the hour. I have issued orders that all ships within the area of the Yard, save the *Cumberland,* shall be scuttled immediately."

There was a gasp like a sudden escape of steam, and an immense babble of comment.

Stephen heard himself say in a strained, unnatural voice: "But you can't! Not the *Merrimac*—you can't!"

Pendergrast heard him, he was sure of that, but McCauley made no sign. He was looking straight forward, his immense, shaggy eyebrows hooding his eyes. His whole bearing showed determination, courage, resolution.

To himself Stephen muttered: "My God! He's in another world. He can't have given orders to sink the *Merrimac!*"

* * *

Revell looked over Kearns' shoulder at the end wall. The Stars and Stripes was gone. There was a light patch, curved to the swag of it, on the wallpaper where it had hung.

Kearns said: "I have the orders countersigned by General Taliaferro. Muster at two o'clock in the street outside; we march from here to the Court House. Each man to bring his gun, one blanket, spare clothing according to orders, cooking gear, spare boots." He paused for a moment before adding: "Any ammunition that he can get." Again he paused, looking solemnly, almost sorrowfully, down the length of the table.

"About time too!" Revell's voice was full of eagerness. "Would have been better if we'd had the orders a week ago. We could've taken the Navy Yard any time."

"Fire-eating," said Kearns distantly.

"He's right," Vermillion agreed regretfully. "We should have taken the Yard. If we attack now they'll get the *Merrimac* away. Nuthin' we can do to stop her."

Kearns said: "Had to wait on orders. Your job"—he addressed Revell for the first time—"is to get the sergeants, tell 'em what we've got to do, and leave the men to them. I want two wagons, you know the two we fixed for this. We put the spare gear on them. Hold 'em with a guard in the empty lot up near Trinity! Each man brings food for two days. You got all that?" Again he was silent, looking pensively down the length of the scarred, discolored table.

"We've got no orders to take the Yard?" Revell demanded.

"Look," replied Kearns softly, "you open your mouth too wide and too often. When they want us to attack the Yard we'll get orders 'n' we'll attack, and if we attack we're goin' to lose a lot of men. They've got guns. We . . ." He hesitated, and then abandoned the explanation because it seemed to him unnecessary.

Vermillion said: "I still think we could rush it in twenty minutes. Edelin, he ain't goin' to fight. He's no damn' use anyway! Dozen places we could get over the wall. He can't cover the length of it."

"If they want us to attack the Yard, we'll get orders," repeated Kearns patiently. "If they don't, we won't."

* * *

The boat bumped heavily against the ladder, and Stephen shouted down: "Easy there! Can't you come alongside better'n that?"

The carpenter of the *Cumberland* looked up and said, "Sir," abruptly.

Beside him a voice protested: "Hell's it matter? Ain't we goin' t'sink the goddam ship?"

The carpenter came up the ladder with a squad of six seamen behind him. "Sir, my orders is . . ." he began.

Stephen brushed the words aside. "I know, I know. D'you know where the sea cocks are?"

"I can find 'em." The carpenter's voice was belligerent, as if he were charging against opposition.

Stephen ignored it. An irrational relief filled him: he would not have to show them where the sea cocks were; he would not personally have to take part in this ship murder.

Already the carpenter was moving forward. The men behind him glanced curiously at Stephen, and passed on.

The ship was still full of shipwrights. There were a few mechanics below in the engine room. The riggers were busy working at the fore-mast.

Stephen called the foreman to him. "Get your men together! Tell them to take their tools with them and get ashore."

"Ain't twelve o'clock yet," protested the foreman.

"Never mind," said Stephen quietly. "Get them ashore!"

"What's going on?"

From the fiddley grating a voice floated up: "They're openin' the sea cocks. B'God, they're scuttlin' her!"

The foreman asked: "Is that what they're doing?" The men were gathering round him now. "Is there anything we can do about it?" His voice was earnest, full of regret, uncertain, as if he were looking to Stephen for a lead, looking to him for help.

"Nothing," Stephen answered, "nothing. There's an armed escort with the party. There is nothing you can do."

The foreman looked about him bewildered. The deck was so solid, the water of the Yard was so quiet, so peaceful. The very silence made the thing more monstrous, more overwhelming: there was no more sound, not even from the engine room. The foreman said very slowly: "After all this work, after all this sweat, it don't seem nachrel."

"No," agreed Stephen. "Get your men off now!"

They began to move off unhurriedly, going down the gangway to the quay, wholly unable to understand.

Staring away from them down the quay, Stephen saw a party going aboard the *Germantown*. Somewhere he could hear the sound of axes. The silence was beginning to be overlaid with little noises. Over them, harshly, insistently, the twelve o'clock bell began to ring.

* * *

The crowd was thickest outside the main entrance to the Yard. It reached up and down the roadway outside and it stretched far down Court Street. The great triple doorway under the portico was closed.

Revell, at the back of the crowd, said to the sergeant with him: "We won't get through here. Have to go round the back o' the houses. They've shut the men out—every damn' mother's son o' the work gangs! We ought to've attacked long ago; never was no sense to waitin'. Now we've got no one in the Yard to help us. If we'd hit at them middle of the mornin' or yesterday afternoon, half the work gangs would've come in with us. We could've done it too!"

The sergeant spat. "And what would we have used for ammunition?"

"We had enough," Revell answered angrily. "We had enough! They wouldn't have stood up to us, not with that old figurehead McCauley there."

A voice in the crowd shouted: "Christ! Look at the masting shears!"

The heads turned automatically, as if moved by a single impulse. The great timbers of the masting shears were a landmark for all the Elizabeth, a part of the landscape of Gosport, a part of the background to the lives of all of them there. They had been there since men could remember; they were as permanent, as important, as necessary as the river itself. As men's eyes focused on them, silently, without warning, they began to fall, sweeping down in an immense parabola, the movement growing swifter and swifter until inconceivably, instantly, they disappeared. In the same moment came the sound of an immense crash, a rending, terrible explosion of violence; and over the whole crowd swept a gust of angry sound.

The voice of a carpenter from the Yard, standing next to Revell, shouted across it: "Slap down on the *Germantown*! They must'a' bust her back. Christ, what did they want to do a thing like that for? Bust her back they must'a'—bust her back!"

Again a roar of sound ran through the crowd.

"Mebbe they'd moved her a'ready," suggested the sergeant.

A man answered: "She was there when I came away to eat. Couldn't've shifted her. Wouldn't've had the hands. They bust her back a' right. They must of!"

A small group of men, escorted by four of the town police, came hurrying down Court Street. Revell recognized Murdaugh and William Peters and Sam Watts. He edged his way close to them.

"Mr. Peters," he called, "what's goin' to happen?"

Peters answered: "We've heard that McCauley's going to fire the Yard. With this wind it will burn the town. This is a deputation from the town meeting. He can't do it. He's got to be stopped."

With the speed of thought the news was transmitted through the crowd. Revell could hear over and over again: "*. . . burn the town . . . fire the Yard . . . fire the ships . . . burn the whole goddam town.*"

The deputation was pushing forward now behind the police. Men gave way for them sullenly, grudgingly, seeming to transfer half their anger to the men of the deputation itself.

Revell said to the sergeant: "Better get back, get clear o' this. We got to get the wagons out."

They began to shove back through the crowd up Court Street. At the corner of the block Cleave was standing, watching the crowd, his expression both sad and ironic. They were still ten yards from him when there came the sound of hoofs moving fast, the jingle of harness, and the harsh noise of iron tires on the rough surface. The guns of the Light Artillery came clattering and turned toward the crossroads at the Court House.

Revell began to run toward them, excitement piling upon excitement, and then, seeing Cleave, he slowed down. He called with a welling enthusiasm: "They've turned the guns out, Mr. Cleave! They've turned the guns out! Now we'll see something."

Cleave turned his head back from the little cavalcade that was already diminishing up Court Street. He stared at Revell speculatively for a moment before he spoke. "We'd see more, perhaps, if they had any ammunition."

*   *   *

The *Pawnee* slid swiftly up the harbor. The smoke from her funnel flagged heavily up toward the Norfolk shore. The wind was southerly, too light to hold back the roar of shouting from the Norfolk waterfront.

The men were still closed up at the guns, but the decks were so densely crowded with Marines and troops that it would have been difficult, almost impossible, to fight the ship. Even the quarter-deck was crowded with the officers of the Massachusetts battalion, the Marine officers, the specialists who had been sent with Paulding from Washington. The commodore himself stood a little apart in a cleared space. He stared ahead, resolutely ignoring the sound from the Norfolk shore. To it the wind was bringing now the roar from Portsmouth.

A voice in the crowd of officers said, "They shouted when the *Pocahontas* went out, but they cheered too."

A second voice said, "No cheering now."

There was a brief series of orders, and the *Pawnee* altered course to enter the Southern Branch. Already it was difficult to make out clearly objects in the coming dusk. They moved close in to Portsmouth, very close. The shouting, the cursing, the jeers came over the water with a savage clarity.

Somebody called: "The masting shears have gone, sir!" There was a quick start of acknowledgment through the crowd on the quarter-deck.

"I know." Slowly, almost reluctantly, Paulding took the telescope from under his arm and adjusted it.

Before he had got it to his eye an officer said: "Alden, there's something wrong with the *Merrimac!* She's down by the head."

And another voice called, "Listing too."

A third voice said: "Her lower ports are under water. By God, they've scuttled her!"

The whole ship was full of sound now.

Someone shouted: "Look at the *Germantown!* Look at her masts! Her back's broken—and the *Dolphin!*"

Ironically the moment of realization was underscored with a burst of wild cheering from the *Cumberland,* cheering that was taken up instantly on board the *Pennsylvania,* that drowned out the shouts and curses from the shore, so that the *Pawnee* slid slowly forward toward her berth in a fallacious triumph.

On the ship itself the roar of voices grew. She came alongside with a shuddering jar, but it had no effect on the men. The indiscipline spread and multiplied with the evidence of each fresh wrecking. It was mixed with anger and frustration.

Paulding stood alone, waiting, until the lines were passed. Then he said, "Captain Wilkes, sir." Wilkes stepped forward. "You will see that the Marines are disposed to defend the gates to the best of their power. You will consult with Colonel Edelin. I wish Lieutenant Wise to make an immediate examination of the *Merrimac.* The officers of the *Massachusetts* will get their men ashore as soon as the Marines are clear." He seemed unhurried, sure of himself. Officers were dispatched to a score of tasks; men were detailed off to working parties. There was confident, orderly bustle about the ship. From time to time over the sound and flurry of it came gusts of shouting from outside the Yard.

Paulding was in the middle of a detailed instruction when the officer of the deck said: "Commodore McCauley and Commodore Pendergrast are on the dockside, sir."

Paulding exclaimed, "My God!"

At the rail Alden said, his face lowering, "I did not believe that he ever left his desk."

The old man came up the ladder slowly. The voluminous boat cloak that he wore lifted in the wind, giving him an antique, apocryphal aspect. Paulding met him at the head of the ladder. The two men saluted. McCauley wrapped the cloak round himself with a wide gesture. "You are very late, Commodore Paulding," he said, and before the other could answer he added softly, almost in a whisper, "too late, too late."

"My orders, Commodore McCauley, are to relieve you of responsibility for all ships afloat."

McCauley stared somberly at him. The light of the lantern just behind his head made an aureole of his grey hair under the band of his cap. He brooded over Paulding's words, seeming to examine them minutely. At last he broke the long silence. "Only the *Cumberland* is afloat, sir. You must do your will with her." And then with an angry flash: "I have been superseded. The responsibility now is yours, sir. I have been long in the service of the Navy and now in crisis I am superseded!" He paused and repeated the last word: "Superseded!"

Paulding answered stiffly: "No, sir, I have no orders to supersede you. I have orders only to take command of the ships that are afloat."

"I have sunk the ships," murmured McCauley, and suddenly flung his arms wide, the boat cloak flying open. "It was necessary to sink them. You are too late, too late." With great punctilio he saluted, turned on his heel, and began to stump heavily down the gangway.

Paulding waited until he was out of sight; then he muttered to himself again, "My God!" After a pause he said: "Pendergrast, come to my cabin! You can perhaps explain this." He flung up both arms in a gesture that was almost McCauley's. "I cannot communicate with that man. I cannot understand him. What has happened here? What is the position?"

"McCauley says they have five thousand men ready to attack the Yard, batteries across the Branch in the trees at Berkley. He came to the decision this morning that it was necessary to sink the ships before the mob took the Yard."

"The mob," said Paulding very slowly, "has not taken the Yard. The batteries have not opened fire. Are you sure that they are there?"

They went down the companion ladder to the cabin.

Twenty minutes later Wise came hurrying up the gangway. To the officer of the deck he said, "The commodore—where's he got to?"

"In his cabin with Pendergrast."

Wise went below hurriedly and knocked on the cabin door. He stuffed his cap under his arm and burst in.

Paulding stared at him under the intimidating eyebrows. "Well?" he barked.

"The *Merrimac* has fifteen foot of water in her hold, sir—more. The engine room is flooded. We need divers, sir. We can do nothing to save her without divers."

Pendergrast shook his head. "There are no divers. She is resting on the bottom anyway; the berth is shallow. There is nothing you can do."

Wise waited, forgotten. Paulding and Pendergrast discussed McCauley, their voices low with a deep, controlled passion beneath them.

Captain Wilkes entered the room. "The Marines are posted, sir. There is a vast crowd outside the main gate—two thousand, three thousand, perhaps more. It is not active; it is waiting. The Marine lookout on the bell tower reports that artillery passed up Court Street some hours back. There are small crowds at the other gates. We shall have no trouble holding them for the moment."

A commander came in. "The *Germantown* is wrecked, sir. Her back is broken, her deck crushed amidships. There is twelve feet of water below, sir. The masts have gone."

Pendergrast said, "The *Dolphin,* the *Plymouth*—they'll be full of water by now too."

Paulding walked away from them to the far end of the cabin and stood looking out over the dark water. He said after a long pause: "It is not possible to execute my orders. The ships cannot be moved. It is not my fault." He considered the problem again for a moment. "It is probable that they will attack with the dawn. This ship will tow out the *Cumberland.* For the rest . . ." He stood against the table, drumming on its polished mahogany top with his fingers. "Captain Wilkes, we must burn the Yard!"

*   *   *

The gas lamps lighted the heads of the enormous crowd. They shone pallid and green over the thousands that packed the nearer streets and reached up beyond the corner of the Yard—anxious and silent.

Jeriel made his report to Vermillion: "They're rollin' bar'ls down to the drydock—powder bar'ls, I guess. They bin takin' powder'n' cotton'n' turpentine'n' such onto the ships. They bin carryin' stuff into the ship houses. Reckon they're goin' to fire the whole damn' lot"—he hesitated—"any time now."

"How did you get out?"

"There's a place back o' the rope walks. Takes three to use it."

"You've done a good job." Vermillion paused for a moment and then exclaimed, "Listen!"

There was a sound of singing close by. Other people in the crowd had heard it—heads turned. The singing was irregular, drunken.

"It's in the wing below the main entrance."

Jeriel said succinctly: "Rum store. There was Marines down that end."

"If any of them get drunk . . ." Vermillion murmured softly to himself.

The singing went on. The silent crowd listened.

Jeriel went back to find Linden. She had established herself in a position against the blocked doorway of an old house just beyond the intersection of Court Street. He guessed that she would still be there. In the doorway she was protected from the surging of the crowd and she stood above it, able to see everything. Jeriel wriggled through the densest part of the throng, being cursed and sworn at as he moved. He reached Linden at last. He could see her faintly in the light of the gas lamp at the main entrance.

"Where have you been all this time?" she asked.

"In the Yard," answered Jeriel with pride, "me an' Grandy an' Matty."

Linden bent down and peered at his face. Apparently satisfied that he was telling the truth, she demanded, "What are they doing?"

"Gettin' ready to fire it. Pilin' up powder, cotton, turpentine— ever'thing."

"Are there many of them?"

"Hundreds," replied Jeriel scornfully, "thousands, mebbe—m'litia, Marines, sailors, whole damn' lot!" He paused a minute. "Yard's like an ants' nest."

As he said it, a voice yelled, "Fire!" and at once the crowd roared.

Jeriel jerked round. "The Marine Bar'acks!" His arm darted up. A plume of smoke bellied out from an upper window and, even as his pointing finger found it, there was a little red spurt of flame. "This wind"—Jeriel was awed despite himself—"it'll burn th' whole town."

The sound of the crowd grew thunderous, voice contending against voice. A great surge ran through it like a tidal wave, and Jeriel was forced against the girl. The first roar died and there was a moment of silence, and over it they could hear shouting in the Yard, men running, orders, whistles blowing. The contagion of excitement in the Yard spread out into the crowd: in Court Street at the back men began to run, women at windows in Lincoln Street screamed, a child in the house behind them was crying. Smoke came from a second window in the Marine Barracks and spread almost at once to a third. A naked flame leaped from the roof. Smoke beat down into the crowd, swirls of brilliant sparks hidden in it.

With shouting and the thud of running feet and the clang of iron wheels, the fire engine from the City Hall came clattering up. The crowd blocked it. The engine was half-manned. There was an enormous and intractable confusion. The flames spread with purposive speed. Half the roof was blazing now. The bell tower above the main entrance was hot and red in the flames. The sparks and the smoke began to drive the crowd back up the street away from the water. A fight developed around the engine; then suddenly the crowd broke and let it through. At once, as if its arrival had triggered the fuse, a house on the far side of the street caught fire and in an instant was blazing.

From where Linden stood high above the crowd, the lower part of the street seemed arched with flame. It was possible to see through the flames as through a tunnel to the dark end of the street at the waterside, to see the black, peaceful-flowing water beyond.

The fire was spreading up to the main entrance, searing its way through the wooden building. The crowd swirled back and forth, giving way angrily before the heat. The roar of the flames was heavy now, a deep bourdon of sound. Another house caught, and a woman standing beyond the edge of the crowd screamed on a high, sustained note; and over the main entrance the cupola was suddenly wreathed in upward-soaring flame.

*   *   *

Paulding watched the flickering light intently. From where he stood on the quarter-deck of the *Pawnee* the flames were masked by the vast dark bulk of the ship houses. Behind them the Headquarters building was dark also, and in the three-quarter-mile range of dry dock and mast ponds and engineering shops that stretched up the Southern Branch past the ship there was no apparent life. The gas lights of the Yard shone green and pallid in the darkness.

He shouted angrily: "I can see for myself it's the Marine Barracks! What I must know is who fired it? Who gave the order?"

Edelin replied placatingly, "No order was given, sir."

A voice behind him said, "It could have been the townspeople, sir."

Edelin answered reluctantly, as if honesty were forced out of him: "The men got at the rum store, sir. There is a number drunk. The fire began where they were drinking."

Paulding snorted. "Nothing will be served now by waiting for daylight to fire the rest of the buildings. Get the men on board as swiftly as you may! See that the parties to light the fuses are in position. Get everyone clear of the buildings. Tell the chief engineer to have steam ready within the half-hour, and signal the *Cumberland* to heave short."

Voices answered him in the darkness. Edelin left the quarter-deck. Men moved purposefully in the half-light of the deck lanterns and the flickering glare of the increasing fire. Against it the enormous ship houses stood out starkly—gigantic, slope-sided, many-windowed. The quarter-deck fell utterly silent for a minute, and the noises of the night rushed in upon it. The run of the tide against the timbers of the wharf, the feathering of steam at the funnel, the plunge and splutter and vibration of pumps working, the rush and splash of the condenser water, the sound of oars and boats moving, and the chugging of a side-wheel tug in the Branch—these formed the substructure, the ordered foundation of the wild night noises. Over it all was slashed the confusion of voices from the Yard, the sound of feet running, the distant crackle and crash of the flames, whistles, catcalls, and, beyond everything, the dull, distant roar of the crowd.

Paulding listened to it, cocking his head slightly to one side to use his good ear. Then, not looking for an auditor, his voice terse and harsh, he demanded, "Where is Commodore McCauley?"

"His son is waiting, sir," replied an officer.

"Bring him!"

When they brought McCauley's son to the quarter-deck Paulding was at the after-rail. He turned and barked, "Well?"

"My father is ill, sir." The boy's voice broke suddenly. "He refuses to leave the Headquarters. He says that that is his post and he must remain."

Paulding walked menacingly across the quarter-deck, his head lowered between his shoulders, leaning forward. "Fetch him! Bring him by force if necessary. Tell him that if he stays in the Headquarters building"—his voice dropped an octave—"he will burn. Go with him!"

He turned sharply to two lieutenants. "See that Commodore McCauley comes at once! We have no more time."

Swiftly, hugely, the flames rose. The underside of the low, fleecy cloud was red now. It was possible to see even in the shadow of the great bulk of the ship houses.

A stumbling, irresolute little procession brought McCauley at last to the *Pawnee*. Gasping, disheveled, his hat askew, the old man was bundled unceremoniously up the gangway.

Paulding, on the quarter-deck, made no move to go forward to receive him. As the last man came over the side, he ordered abruptly, "Slip!" Turning his back, he stalked to the rail and stood staring across the water into the dark uncertainty of the Berkley shore. From here he could see the whole length of the fire. The entire range of the buildings was ablaze now, a long, monstrous cube of flame. Its light made easy the passing of the towrope. Already the tug *Yankee* was fast alongside the *Cumberland*. Paulding watched the interchange of signals as the ropes were secured. Finally he lifted one hand, held it level with his head for a second, dropped it suddenly and gave the order, "Slow ahead, sir!"

Underneath them the *Pawnee*'s deck came alive, quivering. Slowly, so slowly that the movement was all but imperceptible, she moved forward. The towrope rose out of the water, splashing, tightened, and twanged like a violin string, sending a brilliant flash of spray above it that took light from the roaring fire. The *Cumberland* came ahead. They moved past the dark hulk of the *Merrimac,* past the wreck of the *Germantown,* past the last of the ship houses, past the enormous, silent bulk of the *Pennsylvania.*

As they drew clear into the open water, Paulding ordered coolly, "Fire the rocket!"

A match flared. There was a small shower of sparks, then with a roar a signal rocket leaped toward the red underbelly of the cloud, made a swift, mocking curve of beauty, and burst.

A strange stillness held the *Pawnee.* No man moved. She was running with the wind. Slowly she reached the speed of it so that she moved in an absolute calm, and, as they watched from her decks, they saw at point after point along the dark, silhouetted shore line a little blaze of fire—a burst of flame on the *Germantown,* a burst of flame on the *Dolphin,* a burst of flame on the *Pennsylvania.* As if in answer the long tiers of windows that rose up the enormous slope of the walls of the ship houses blazed with light.

*   *   *

There was a boat alongside the *Merrimac*.

Wise lighted the slow match and dropped down the rope ladder. "Let go!"

The bowman shoved off.

Another boat lay at the steps of the entrance to the great dry dock. The crew waited in it, taut, full of a silent, unformed anxiety.

Beyond the steps the master's mate of the *Pawnee* rested on one knee. He watched the fire broodingly. Flames were leaping now above the ridge of the ship houses. As he watched, he saw the windows of the ship houses glow with the light of the new fires within. Bending down he lighted the slow matches and then, with a sudden, angry gesture, said, half aloud: "Two thousand pounds of powder—it'd blow stone over half Portsmouth." He watched the slow matches spluttering. "I got friends in Portsmouth," he said to himself softly, "I got a heap o' friends," and he pulled the long black matches away from the trail of powder that led to the charges in the intake of the culvert. He watched the pale light quench itself with a hiss of steam in the shallow water at the bottom of the dock. Then he ran back to the boat. "Shove off!" he called. "Jump!"

A voice asked, "Did you light the matches?"

"I lit the matches," he replied angrily, "I lit the matches."

The boat raced out into the stream.

*   *   *

A voice in the crowd screamed: "The ship houses! They've fired the ship houses!"

The crowd bellowed angrily again. The words "ship houses" became a part of the roar, shaped into it, elevated out of it. At the water's edge a wall of the main building swayed, buckled, and fell with a splash of burning timber and small flames into the street. All the far side of the street was burning now. The crowd had been forced back toward the bridge.

Cleave found Linden splayed against a wall off the street. It was Jeriel who saw him, who led him to her. She stood there with her arms stretched out, her face and body lighted by the harsh, hard red of the flames. She was motionless, her eyes very wide, her face set in lines of horror.

Jeriel said, "Both the ship houses're burnin' now, an' the *Pennsylvania*'s blazin'. Jeez!" He looked past Cleave to where flames raced up the tarred rigging of the old ship, painting her in with swift, brilliant strokes against the night darkness beyond.

Cleave made no move. He was watching the girl. When he spoke his voice was hardly audible above the roar of the crowd. "This is another side of war, Linden."

She made no answer; she hardly seemed to see him. Her eyes were fixed on the flames that leaped in great sweeping tongues, that seemed now to reach right up to the swag of the low clouds.

The smoke cloud lowered on them in a huge, blinding rush of darkness. The wind lifted it, and underneath came a long, continuous spray of sparks like foam whipping off a hurricane sea. The air was full of burned embers, fragments of charred papers, an endless, impalpable dust.

Cleave leaned forward and took her outstretched arm. "We've got to move, Linden. It will blaze up here any minute now."

With Jeriel on the other side of her, they fought their way into the crowd. Again it was falling back—beaten back, beaten by the searing heat and the choking harshness of the smoke. They moved with it down Court Street, down past a mounting block where the Reverend Wingfield stood, calling on God to change the wind. People knelt near him, listening to the high, harsh, confident voice, a voice that was too proud to plead, a voice that commanded. For the most part the mob swept by. It had already the aspect of a refugee crowd: furniture eddied in it in awkward, jerky passage; bedding, personal belongings were carried head-high above it; small children were on men's shoulders or in women's arms.

They were almost at South Street when the wind changed. Linden felt it before the others. She twisted round, pulling herself free from Cleave's grasp. "Look, the smoke is going straight up! The wind's changed."

A woman's voice near her cried: "God's changed it! God's changed it!"

Linden said: "I'm all right now. You needn't hold me. Do you think it was God?"

Cleave smiled at her. "The wind blows one way for one side, one way for the other. I don't think God interferes much."

"It's blowing for the South now!" Linden's voice had a memory of the old triumph.

Cleave said: "Two million feet of lumber in the first ship house and the timbers of the *New York*—been there for twenty years now, drier than an Egyptian coffin—at a guess I'd say the fire is hot enough now to make its own wind without the intervention of God." He stared down the street.

They were far enough back to see the perspective of the fire—the main buildings, the ship houses, the tar houses, the ships alongside the berths, the old seventy-fours in Rotten Row. A mile of wood, of tar, of turpentine and resin and rope was going up in one enormous, conjoined surge of flame.

Horror crept back into Linden's eyes. Her voice hardly more than a whisper, she murmured, "Is Stephen in that?"

But before Cleave could answer there came the thunder of a heavy gun, and the crowd screamed.

2

Thunderhead Rising

Chapter one

A GRAY fine dust covered everything. On the top of the lumber pile it was subtle and neat, except where the last eddies of the wind that had died in the night had engrossed whorls and arabesques of a lighter and feathery white.

The old compositor blew a clear space in it for his elbows. He rested there, watching Cleave as he came wearily up from the boat. His eyes were speculative. "Nice mornin'," he said ironically. "Air's a bit sour."

Cleave grunted.

"Ever see a town with a hangover before?"

Cleave said, with a note as near anger as he ever permitted himself, "I didn't think they'd be such fools."

"Who?"

Cleave stared at him somberly. There was a long pause before he said at last: "Men."

Sam blew at the dust again. After a little he asked in a tone of pure inquiry, as if he had decided to have done with irony, "Anythin' left up there?"

"Little. They sank everything that was afloat except the *United States*—and she's been no use for twenty years. The ship houses are gone and the Marine Barracks."

"An' the rest o' the Yard?"

"There's something standing," Cleave replied. "The sawmill and the foundries. The carpenters' shops looked all right; so did the ordnance building."

"An' the dry dock?"

Cleave looked at him a little puzzled. "Dry dock's undamaged as far as I could see."

"Phoo-o!" The old man filled his cheeks and blew them out. "The South's got herself a Navy Yard then. I thought she'd throw'd it clean away. Foundries, carpenters' shops, dry dock—d'you want more?"

Cleave frowned. "There's no sense to it. If the North wanted to abandon the Yard, they could have burned everything. It didn't want more than a torch. They had time enough. Nobody was attacking them. I can't understand it. I can't see what they were thinking of in Washington—what Abraham Lincoln . . ." His voice trailed away.

Sam asked: "What makes you think Lincoln know'd there *was* a Navy Yard? He's a inland man. Illinois's a long ways away from the sea."

"He's got the Navy Department to advise him."

"Ol' Gran'pappy Welles?"

"It doesn't make sense," repeated Cleave.

"It's war!" The old man spat. "You askin' fer sense in war? More'n that—it's civil war." He stared at Cleave fiercely. "You're sore because you didn't believe it'd ever come to war. Ain't that it? What you goin' to do now, Ash Cleave?"

They stood in silence. A southerly drift of wind brought the acrid, burned-out smell of the Yard to them in a harsh reminder. Far away bugles sounded, and they could hear, thin and crisp, the shouted orders.

At last Cleave answered, "I've been trying to think."

"You'd better make up your mind. Town's made up its mind. Month ago it was one in three for the South. Day before yesterday it was one in two. Ain't nobody shoutin' fer the North today. You kin still git out if you want."

"I can't nor can you—you know that. It's not going to be easy." Cleave looked at him speculatively. "Have you heard that Callaghan's gone?"

The old compositor answered heavily: "I know'd he would, first sign o' trouble. There was a streak in him."

"Where's it going to end, Sam?"

The old man shrugged. "Editor, he sent fer th' Book o' Genesis 's mornin'. '. . . and lo the smoke of the country went up as the smoke of a furnace.' "

"Where do *you* think it's going to end?"

"I never heerd of any country that won a civil war."

Cleave nodded grimly. "The country always loses." He looked up. "Morning, Lin. I didn't think you'd wake till noon."

The girl came slowly toward them, her feet scuffing in the drifted ash between the lumber piles. Her face was gray as the ash, and she moved slackly, as if the spirit had gone out of her.

The old compositor spoke without turning round. "So you got home last night! Last I saw o' you I thought you'd jined the army permanent."

Linden said, not looking at her father, "I didn't think it would be like this."

"Nor'd your father," observed Sam softly.

Her eyes lifted to her father's face and she searched it anxiously, looking for some kind of help.

But his eyes were indrawn, focused on other things. He said moodily, catching at words out of a distant past: "War's not all flags and drums, Linden. I've said that before."

There was a long silence with each of the three thinking, separately, sundered.

Linden broke it at last. "We should have taken the Yard—we should have taken it a week ago. It wouldn't have made any difference. We'd have got it then. They were fools!"

The old man said lazily: "Your father thought they was fools too, only he thought the fools was in Washington. What you gripin' about, Linden? You got a Navy Yard." He looked over to the right where the wisps of smoke still rose leisurely into the clear morning air. "You got yourself a nice flagpole and a flag atop o' it." Cleave and the girl turned with him. A little air plucked at the blue Virginia flag and lifted it clear of the tall flagstaff. "What you goin' to do with it?"

Linden wheeled on him. "I hate you when you talk like that! We'll use it. There's something left. We'll build ships. We'll *make* a navy."

Cleave watched her, anxiety in his eyes. "You've got to see realities, Linden. Even if there is enough of the Yard left to build ships, they'll put a blockade on this river that will hold it tighter than a leg iron."

"We'll build ships strong enough to break the blockade. We've got timber"—her eyes widened suddenly as she looked across toward the Yard—"we've got guns—we've got men."

"North's got Baltimore, Philadelphia, New York, Boston—all the New England coast." The old man's voice had a calculated aggravation. "You goin' to outbuild all of them with one beat-up Navy Yard?"

The girl turned on him, whitely angry. "We've hoisted our flag over it. There isn't *anything* Virginia can't do."

"How long do you think that'll fly over it?"

"It'll be there when we've smashed the North."

"Give it five days." Sam's voice was placid now.

"Five days—what do you mean?"

"Have the Confederate flag up there in five days. You didn't think this was goin' to be a Virginia war, did you? Come five days you goin' to have Jeff Davis and Alec Stevens in Richmond—Governor Letcher, he'll sing pretty small then."

"At least"—the girl's voice rose still higher—"at least it'll be government of gentlemen!"

"South'n gen'lemen," said the old man tonelessly.

Cleave watched him with his eyes narrowed. The girl was being led deliberately toward something; Sam was like an aged eagle, waiting to pounce, his eyes malevolent.

"Southern gentlemen," echoed the girl defiantly.

"Yup." The old man snapped his jaws, and Cleave knew that the trap had closed. "Take Memminger now"—Sam drawled out the name —"he was a orphan boy, German at that, Lutheran; he's got the Treasury. Take Slidell—his pa, he was a tallow chandler. Take Benjamin—he's Attorney General; he was throwed out of his school takin' money that belonged to somebody else. Take Mallory—you got to be specially interested in Mallory, he's goin' to have the say-so in the Navy Yard. His ma, she ran a boardinghouse at Key West. He was a newspaper man at the start, wrote some o' the damndest drivel I ever did read—yet."

"Jefferson Davis—"

"Right, take Jeffy Davis! Name's properly David—his granpappy was ol' Owen David, come over from Wales, laborin' man. Jeffy Davis, he's a plantation owner—only it ain't his plantation. Still belongs to his brother Joe. That's why Varina Howell, she hates Joe. Ain't much to choose between Jefferson Davis and Abe Lincoln. They was both Kentucky boys, both of them born in about the same sort o' cabin, in about the same sort of way."

Linden turned on him, her eyes enormous and near to tears. "I hate you! I hate you!"

Cleave could see now where the old man had been moving. He said softly, "I'm not a gentleman if it comes to that, Lin."

The girl turned to him blindly. "I hate you too."

"Your trouble, Lindy Cleave"—Sam's voice was a little sharper— "your trouble was your father never skelped your bottom enough when you was little. Now he reckons you're too big to skelp." He ran his eyes slowly over the girl's body. "You got a nice bottom, Lindy. Wouldn't mind skelpin' it myself."

"You're not a gentleman, that's for certain!"

"Sure," agreed the old man, "sure, I had me more fun that way."

There was a silence. The girl stood still, facing them, wordless, drained momentarily of enthusiasm and of anger. Overhead, gulls called, and far away there was the everlasting bugle.

At last Linden said, "It doesn't matter where a man was born."

"A South'n gen'leman, he's born on a South'n plantation," said Sam lazily. "You ask one!"

Jeriel came down the alleyway between the lumber like a gray ghost. He looked from one to the other of the three faces, said softly, "Mornin'," and slumped to the ground with his back to the timber and his face to the sun.

After another long silence Linden asked, "What's happening?"

"Nothin'," Jeriel replied, "nothin'—jus' talk. Ever'body—they jus' talk."

Cleave caught Sam's eye and exchanged a gleam of self-mockery.

"What were they firing at last night?" Linden asked.

"Weren't firin'. Some Yankee fool left the guns o' the *United States* loaded."

Jeriel scrabbled with his toes on the ash-covered sawdust. He made patterns, examining their intricacies, rubbed them out and made fresh patterns. At length he said: "National Greys, they stayin' in the Navy Yard. Rest o' the companies, they're marchin' to the Navy Hospital. Goin' to build them a batt'ry on Hospital Point 'gainst the *Pawnee*'s comin' back." He paused and waited for the information to sink in. Then he addressed himself more directly to Linden. "Thought mebbe you'd want the boat."

"Yes, I want the boat. You don't know how bad I want the boat." Life and energy seemed to flow back into the girl. " 'Bye, Father—'bye, Uncle Sam. I'll be back before dark." There was a challenge implied, a defiance.

She did not wait for an answer, but went down toward the jetty with a little insolence of movement. Jeriel followed her like a small gray dog.

Sam said: "I don't know it wouldn't be best to beat her at that. You got something on your hands, Ash Cleave."

"The young have to work out their own salvation." He watched her as she dropped, graceful and taut, into the boat. "She'll beat herself in her own time."

"You won't beat her, you could try beatin' young Jeriel," suggested Sam dryly.

"No"—Cleave shook his head—"Jeriel saves her from her worst mistakes. There's a lot in that boy, Sam."

"There's a hell o' a lot too much in most boys," growled the old man and, turning, began to stump up the path through the lumber.

*   *   *

The cotton bales were hot in the young summer sun. The girl lay indolent and catlike, watching the flash of the spades.

Farther up the bank they were unloading new mounds of cotton. The coarse sacking was dark and stained in the brilliance of the sun, but the white cotton that expanded out through the holes had a matching brilliance. Downriver the cotton bales were already a rampart. It followed a design; a thing of bastions and embrasures, planned, plotted. Men were working in the gun pits, stripped to the waist, shorn of the colored finery of their coats. Some of them had wide-brimmed hats, some of them had kepis, all of them worked with an immense gusto. Earth rose out of the nascent gun pits. Brick, gravel, broken paving stone rumbled down into them to make a platform for the guns. Horses snorted, oxen moved with a heavy patience.

In the distance, above the clamor of men's voices, above the rumble of wheels and the clatter of the spades, she heard girls' laughter. She turned over onto her stomach, propped her chin on her paralleled forearms, and searched. They were standing, four of them, in the shade of the live oak trees in front of the hospital, framed by the ten great columns of the portico. Even the trees seemed to be set to show off the brilliance of the pink and pale green dresses, the bell of the skirts. They carried parasols. Linden snorted.

Men stopped at the group, collected round it, were shouted at by the sergeants, and moved away. More men collected. More laughter. Linden frowned. The new group was shouted away.

Linden lay still, watching. The sun felt hot on her bottom. She said half aloud and half angrily, "That old Sam!" and wriggled.

Jos Butt came up behind her and leaned against the bale. He was breathing with the hard rasp of exhaustion. "Lindy Cleave, you lie still as a cat. What's your mouse?"

She murmured, motionless, "Them."

Butt followed the line of her head until his eyes focused on the girls. Yet another group of young bare-chested men was just being shouted away. He grinned. "Ain't got no notion of tactics. Right out in the open like that! You got to learn to use cover." He laughed and waited, getting his breath back.

He was sick, Linden knew that; had no business to be here, had no business to muster with the company. To Linden there was a special glory in this.

After a few minutes he went back to his shovel.

Linden lay still, watching. There were long periods now when the four girls stood uncourted. The parasols drooped. Linden laughed to herself. Presently she heard a scrunch of gravel. The bale moved slightly in an intimation of arrival.

She felt a hand on the small of her back, stroking gently. Without turning she said: "Don't do that, Rev!"

He said easily, "Honey."

She accepted the caress in the word, too preoccupied to move, too indolent with the sun—too excited with war—too filled with superiority over four silly girls who stood twirling their silly parasols.

Another sergeant shouted another group of men away.

"All the good they'll do, they'd be better back home scraping lint," observed Linden.

Revell's hand slid down from her back and found the curves of her buttocks, molding them, pressing her down warmly into the warm softness of the cotton, sensuous—sensual.

For a brief moment she yielded to it. It was as if she accepted it as part of war's tangible excitements. Then she twisted, switching from the cat in indolence to the cat in anger. As she twisted, her hand found the handle of Revell's spade. She snatched at it and swung it in a sweeping, scythelike movement. "Do that again, I'll hit you!"

He leaped back, laughing. "You wouldn't strike a gallant soldier of Virginia," he mocked her from a safe distance.

"I would," she retorted. "You and that old Sam!" Anger died, and she sank back on the bale again.

Revell returned cautiously, but he kept his hands to himself. He too watched the girls. "Charlotte Vickery," he murmured after a while, "Eleanor Mallet—can't see who the next one is, not with that bonnet."

"Mellie Brent," Linden said sleepily. "She thinks a might of her complexion."

"Fourth one's a stranger."

"Yes."

They watched in silence. Presently Linden's eye was caught by a different uniform—a naval uniform, that of an officer. He was moving slowly down the line of half-formed redoubts, an Army sergeant with him. They had a measuring line. Now and then the sergeant stooped to put pegs into the hard earth. Occasionally they broke away to set off angles.

Linden jerked her head toward him. "Who's he?"

"Commander McKintosh. He's layin' out the battery—Navy man, knows about big guns."

"You don't." There was an edge to Linden's voice.

"We can learn." Revell drifted away, going slowly back to his gun pit.

Linden heard him greeted with laughter and ribald comment.

McKintosh came closer and closer. She could see his face now; she remembered him at the Porters' house and once with her father. She waited till he was directly level with her, stooping at a new peg, then she said from above him: "Commander McKintosh, is it true Mr. Mallory's mother kept a boardinghouse at Key West?"

McKintosh straightened himself with a jerk, almost dislodging his naval cap. "What the hell? What are you doing here? This isn't a place for a girl. What about Stephen Mallory?"

Linden regarded him with interest. She thought: He disconcerts easy.

Up at the corner of the hospital building there was an outburst of cheering. They could see men running. There was noise, the thunder of hoofs on the gravel; then fresh cheering as a gun team came round the roadway at a crazy speed, the horses wild with the shouting, and the men running beside them.

"Damned fools!" McKintosh was standing straight, his shoulders back, his head held forward, eager.

Jeriel came running from the nearest gun pit. He was shouting: "The guns is coming! The guns is coming!"

McKintosh said, "The first of them." His voice was full of a proud satisfaction. "Now we're ready for that damned *Pawnee!*"

On all the gun pits the men were standing now, on the ramparts, on the piled earth, on the wagons that had brought the bricks and the stones and the timber. They were cheering, waving their caps, throwing them in the air. The gun horses turned wildly round the corner at the center of the great portico and surged down toward the river.

Linden said, "Mallory. *Did* his mother . . . ?"

McKintosh answered her without turning. "How should I know? My God, girl! Yes, come to think of it, I heard something once. Yes, I guess she kept a boardinghouse all right."

With a final delirious swoop the gun team cut across the ground toward the northernmost gun pit. There was a last wild burst of cheering and over it one high shrill "Yi-i-i-ie!"

Linden, on her knees, her eyes glistening, said, "I don't care."

McKintosh began to walk toward the gun. He walked slowly, stiffly, full of pride.

When all the excitement had died down, when the horses had been unhitched and had gone back up the path and out of sight, when the men had returned reluctantly to their own gun pits and the hoarse sergeants had dropped their voices, when the four girls had disappeared, neglected, McKintosh came back to his line of pegs.

Linden, lying flat on the bale of cotton, watched him come, her chin propped up on her hands. It was possible now to ask the question that she had wanted to ask all the time. She said quietly, "Commander Mc-Kintosh, what happened to Stephen Knott?"

McKintosh stooped down to pull out an old peg. "Knott," he replied testily, "Knott, he's gone North—he's for the Union."

"But what happened to him?"

"How should I know? Went out with the *Pawnee,* I heard."

"He wasn't left—in the Yard?"

"Nobody was left in the Yard." McKintosh straightened himself angrily. "Nobody except two damned fools who got themselves cut off by the fire. We've sent 'em to Richmond."

"And Stephen Knott wasn't one of them?"

"I've told you, girl!" McKintosh glowered at her. "Get down off that bale and hold the end of this line. That damned sergeant's disappeared."

Linden heard herself say as she slipped off the bale, "I'm glad."

Chapter two

ISHERWOOD'S room at the Washington Navy Yard was simple, direct, and untidy like the man. Isherwood himself was sitting at a desk littered with drawings. He glowered over them at Stephen. "So you kept the faith," he said mordantly.

"Did you think I wouldn't?"

"These days I bet on no man. You finished with Gideon Welles?"

Stephen thought back to the long interview in the office of the Secretary of the Navy—the preposterous look of the man, with his enormous beard and his wig, and his huge craggy face and small, shrewd, intelligent eyes. "He told me to report to you," said Stephen. "I asked him for a seagoing appointment. He said he hadn't got one."

"*I* asked him for you," said Isherwood placidly, "soon as I heard you'd come in. What did Uncle Gideon want you for?"

"To talk about Portsmouth and McCauley and the state of the Yard."

"Always talkin' to junior officers!" Isherwood's whole attitude was disapproving. Then almost reluctantly he added: "Gets what he wants all the same. Franklin Buchanan, he says if you was to put Uncle Gideon's wig on a figurehead, you'd get about the same results. He's wrong. For all Welles looks like Noah, he's a smart man." Isherwood got up from his chair and reached for his hat. "We'll go get us a bite to eat. I'll not talk in here. Talkin's safer in the fresh air. I think Stephen Mallory's got a listenin' tube laid onto this office."

They went out into the street. There were no soldiers—there had been no soldiers since he arrived in Washington three hours ago; there were only bugles very far away—but the street was full of traffic: carriages and farm carts, barouches and buggies, even an oxcart or two, moving in a confusion, an excitement. There seemed to be flags everywhere; or perhaps it was only that in the last days at Portsmouth there had been no flags, only the one lonely banner on the high staff of the Navy Yard.

Isherwood said, "I asked for you but I don't want you around the office and I don't want you at the Navy Yard—not till tomorrow, day after, perhaps."

Stephen knew that he was meant to ask a question. "Why?"

"Because Captain Franklin Buchanan's goin' South." Isherwood gave the news no more expression than he would have given to a comment on the weather.

Stephen caught his breath with a sharp intake. "Buchanan—good God! He's about the best we have."

"He's no good to us," said Isherwood succinctly. "Let him go! He'll take half the officers of the Yard with him." He looked round with the old sardonic glint in his eyes at Stephen. "You've walked yourself into something, ain't you?"

"But Buchanan's from Maryland! I'm sure of that." Stephen disregarded the personal implication.

"Sure he's from Maryland and he thinks Maryland's going South with him. It may at that. Baltimore's playing hell." Irony and flippancy suddenly deserted Isherwood. Somberly he went on: "Civil war's a thing on its own. We're in a bad way in Washington. You'd better know just how bad. We've got a handful of troops and a few companies of volunteers, and Scott reckons it'll take best part of three months to get the Army back—Buchanan's gov'ment scattered it right down the frontier, fighting Injuns. Baltimore's refused to let troops pass through the city, and the bridges are down. That means we're cut off from the north. A good many of the best of the Army officers've gone South. Bob Lee's gone—did you know that? Beauregard's got ten thousand men, and he reckons he won a victory at Fort Sumter. He's hot on victory—he thinks he can march to Washington and take it." Isherwood was silent for perhaps five paces. "I think he can too. This place is rotten. You can't tell friend from enemy. The sooner Frank Buchanan goes, the better." He looked sideways again, wryly, at Stephen. "D'you still reckon you did right to come?"

Stephen nodded. "It hasn't changed me any. It can't be all as bad as that."

"No," agreed Isherwood heavily, "I'd forgotten the President's guard, the Frontier Guard. It's sleeping on the carpet in the Blue Room—you'll see it. Other thing we've got on our side is that things'll be just as bad with Jeff Davis—I'm counting on that. I've got to, I've got to have time. President's slapped a blockade on the South, and I reckon he's right. Uncle Gideon don't. He don't want it called a blockade, I don't know why—he'll chop lawyer's logic all day, give him a chance. Whatever it's called it means the same thing—you got to have ships to have a blockade. I reckon we've got forty ships, but they're all round the world—Pacific, Europe, down in the Caribbean. We want ships and we want 'em now. We've got to buy 'em or borrow 'em or beg 'em, and we've got to patch up everything there is in the yards that'll float and send it out to sea. That's what you've got to do. You've got to chase work gangs. You've done it before and you'll do it again—and you'll do it till you drop."

"Are we going to build?"

Isherwood snorted. "We've got no time to build. We've got to get out what we've got now."

Through the apparent brusqueness Stephen sensed the engineer's fundamental courage.

They had reached the open space on the forward slope of Capitol Hill now. Blocks of marble, stacks of timber and builders' materials littered it. It had something of the air of an ancient European city, a ruin. Between the blocks of marble a long distance away Stephen saw two men walking, one of them very tall, wearing a very tall stovepipe hat and a long black coat that flapped. He walked with a curious unrhythmic motion, long shambling strides that lifted the loose frame up and down.

"Looks like a black heron goin' down between the stumps to find a frog," said Isherwood softly. "That's the President. We've got him on our side too. You'll hear things about him in Washington. You can start by not believing 'em. If he's still in the White House end of three months, he'll be a great President." Again he walked in silence while Stephen's eyes followed the two distant figures until they disappeared behind a clump of trees. "Thing is—do we get through the next three months?"

Chapter three

THE water was clear. There were days, inexplicable days, on the Southern Branch when the water was like crystal, when neither wind nor tide stirred up the mud and it was possible to see right down to the bottom, to see old junk mud-crusted lying on the river floor, to see fish moving, to see age-sodden snags spread out like improbable monsters on the bed of the channel.

The boat slid slowly up the river along the frontage of the Navy Yard, moving with the tide, its sails listless in the listless air.

Linden, lying sprawled across the thwart with one hand lazy on the tiller, squinted up. "Morning, Mr. Porter! I haven't seen you in a long time. Where's Martha?"

The constructor stepped one dangerous pace to the side over the charred ruin of the hull and peered down. "It's Linden Cleave. I didn't see you first. She's down with her sister at Cahaba. I think she's well."

Jeriel, lying on his back in the bows of the boat with his legs hung wide apart over the for'ard thwart, asked, "Where's Cahaba, Mr. Porter?"

"Down on the Alabama River." Porter turned again to Linden. "I thought it would be quieter for her there."

Linden digested this while the boat crept imperceptibly by. Porter stood looking down on her. "What are you going to do with the *Merrimac*, Mr. Porter?"

"She's in the way," replied the constructor, more as if he were thinking aloud than answering her question. "We need the berth."

Jeriel demanded, "You goin' to rebuild her?"

Porter pursed his lips and shook his head very slowly. "She's not worth rebuilding. Better to start from the bottom up with something that's worth while. We'll have all we can do to handle that in a little."

"Are you going to move her?" asked the girl.

"Baker's got the job"—Porter had the engaging habit of talking to the young as if he were talking to equals—"the Wrecking Company. Shouldn't be a big job. She's solid enough below the fire line. They sank her with the sea cocks—close them up and she'll pump out at low water."

"And then tow her up on the mud?"

Porter shook his head. "She's got engines. We need engines badly— anything that will turn over. We'll put her in the dry dock and whip them out of her."

Jeriel said cynically, "My uncle, he said they was a run-down coffee mill."

Good-humoredly, Porter answered, "We're going to need even coffee mills." A freak of the tide speeded them up and they were halfway down the length of the ruin before he spoke again, but his words came clear and distinct over the still water. "There's no end to what we need."

*   *   *

The boat came foaming up to the wreck of the old schooner that lay half up the beach at Pinner's Point. It had been Linden's own private landing place since the company moved from the Hospital battery. Jeriel smothered the foresail with one hand, whipped round with the automatic ease of practice, and dropped the mainsail.

The lookout in the little sandbagged post on the riverbank grinned at her—he was an old friend. "Lindy Cleave, you'll catch it if Major Harrison sees you."

"I can fix George Harrison," she said calmly. "Where's Rev?"

"Should be at Number 3 gun. He's got the duty. You'll prob'ly find him on his butt. Jeez, can he sleep!"

Linden walked over the bank to the battery without comment.

Jeriel stayed behind. "You don't do so bad yourself, Jim Riddick. Reckon you was asleep when we come up—wasn't, you oughta hollered us."

Revell was not asleep. With three of the gun crew he was playing cards under the shade of a tarpaulin that spread from the wall of the gun pit to the tail end of the enormous, shiny barrel of the Dahlgren gun. "Lindy, I told you you weren't to come without you got permission! The major—"

"I can fix George Harrison," she said again. "This all you've got to do—sit and play poker?"

One of the other men squinted at her against the bright light of the afternoon sky. "Aw, Lindy, what else is there? Ain't nobody comin' up this river, not this war."

And Revell added, "Not after what happened to the *Monticello.*"

"Nothing happened to the *Monticello!*" There was an edge to Linden's voice. Her mind went back to her own tremors on the quiet morning when the *Monticello* had come over from Fortress Monroe to probe the unfinished batteries.

"She went away, didn't she?" demanded one of the men.

"She came back two days later," said Revell, "and she went away again—nobody hit in the batteries, nobody hit on the beach. She's not goin' to come far enough up the river for us to fire on her."

Linden moved in under the shade and sat down. "Then the sooner they move all of you out to where you can fight, the better!"

"We started as fightin' soldiers," said another voice, "now we're fortress 'tillery. I reckon it's more comfortable."

"Any news in the town, Lindy?" asked Revell.

"Big news," she answered scornfully. "Miss Virginia Handy, she's made up a committee."

"Ginny Handy—she's got a committee? What for?"

Linden sat with her arms round her drawn-up knees and her chin dropped on them. She stared balefully round the group. "Miss Virginia Handy is about to sew a silken banner for you heroes."

"Jee-sus!" exclaimed the fourth member of the gun's crew, who had not spoken.

They were all silent, examining the possibilities.

"Ginny'd do a damn sight better," said one of the men, "if she'd come down and do somethin' about my socks."

"Miss Virginia Handy," returned Linden caustically, "only does fine needlework."

"You're sore you ain't on the committee, Lindy."

Linden gave him a baleful look.

Revell grunted. "All right, so we get a silk flag. Any more news in the town?"

"They're going to raise the *Merrimac,*" she said.

"Why?"

"What good'll that do?"

"She ain't no use to nobody."

"They ain't goin' to try to rebuild her, Lindy?" Revell asked.

She shook her head.

One of the other men said: "I seed her Sunday mornin', we went into the Yard. She was a mess." He thought a minute and then added, "Boy, she was a mess!"

The fourth member of the group spoke again. "That won't win no war."

*   *   *

The old compositor was stumping down the street, muttering to himself. Nobody had ever been able to discover what he talked to himself about, but the habit was a part of the corpus of the town.

Cleave caught up with him. "Evening, Sam. I hear they're going to lift the *Merrimac*."

"What for?"

"According to Porter, because they want the berth."

"They got more berths than they'll ever be able to fill," the old man snarled. "She sticks up like a sore thumb at low water. You don't think they're goin' to try to rebuild her?"

"Porter says not."

"Be a nice fat timber contract for you, supposin' they was," said the old man slyly, looking sideways at Cleave.

"But they're not," answered Cleave good-humoredly.

The old man tried the direct approach. "Ash, what you goin' to do when they do come to you to buy timber?"

"Sell," replied Cleave bluntly. "What else can I do?"

"My, my!" Sam shook his head. "Make a fat profit providing war materials for the side you don't back!"

"What else can I do?" repeated Cleave, shrugging his shoulders. "I've thought it all out, Sam. I'll sell. If I refused, they'd close me down. Somebody—the Confederate Government perhaps—would take over the yard. What good would that do? I've got to keep on here and I've got to live."

"And make a fair profit."

"And make a fair profit." Cleave suddenly grinned at the old man. "It's no good you trying to rile me, Sam. I won't take a war profit out of them; I'll take a business profit, and they'll get the wood at business speed. I won't let them down but I won't rush the job—when and if it comes."

"Makes sense," agreed Sam—"that's if anythin' makes sense in war."

They walked slowly in a companionable silence. The town, out of

Main Street, had fallen back into a peacetime calm. There were a few more men in uniform, a few more flags in gardens. It was very quiet; even the distant bugles seemed to have faded into silence.

At length Sam said: "Wouldn't do any good if they was to rebuild her. The Yankees, they've got three ships lyin' off Fortress Monroe now. She wouldn't ever get out the river. South's goin' to feel the blockade one o' these days, Ash. It's goin' to pinch bad."

*   *   *

In the humid darkness of the May night it was impossible to see Isherwood's face. His voice seemed disembodied. He asked: "Well, what of it? The *Merrimac* was burned to the water's edge. They won't be able to use her for anythin', short of rebuilding her from the bottom up."

"Her engines . . ." Stephen put in the words tentatively.

Isherwood snorted, an enormous disgusting noise between a sneeze and an eructation. "Engines? Damn it, Stephen Knott! You know more about her engines than anybody except me and the fool that built 'em. They've been under water now for six weeks. The Elizabeth River's good and muddy. What use d'you think her engines'll be to them or to anybody else? I reckon all it means is Page is tidying up now he's been given charge of the Yard. He always was an old woman—fussy bastard!"

"The report said that Porter was responsible. It was Porter that gave the contract to the Baker Wrecking Company."

"Could be. Is the agent reliable?"

"As spies go."

"Porter's no fool." Isherwood whistled gently but tunelessly. "Could be that he wants it for somethin', but I wouldn't think so. Burned to the water's edge—"

"She wasn't!" Stephen protested. "She'd sunk more than twelve feet when she was fired. She was on the bottom, and the tide must have put the fire out round about dawn. There's more of her left than you think."

"Still don't see what he can do with her." Isherwood shook his head in the darkness. "Better to build a new ship; cheaper too, if it comes to that. Fire's bound to have ate down places, always does. You get any other news with the report?"

"Bit more stuff about the batteries. Estimate of the number of troops."

"No, I didn't mean that. Any news about your girl?"

"Our agent in Portsmouth is not commissioned to gather personal news for me," replied Stephen stiffly.

Isherwood began to laugh in the dark. "Then you don't know how to use the service!" He turned off, whistling "The Girl I Left Behind Me." He was perhaps twenty feet away when he called back, "Even Porter won't be able to do anythin' with the *Merrimac*."

Chapter four

THE tiny, wizened man on the box glared down at Porter with a proud malignity. He was far past the age when he could still get down to help his fares with their bags.

Porter said: "Morning, Asa. D'you think the old mare'll live to reach the depot?"

The little man cackled. "She'll live if I lives. When I die, she dies. When she dies, I die. I'm feelin' good this mornin'."

Porter settled himself in the hack. Asa, or possibly the horse, waited until he was settled and then started very slowly down the street. Mrs. Porter went into the house.

Asa said over his shoulder, leaving the route to the mare, "Goin' to Richmond to get some go into this war?"

"How did you know I was going to Richmond?"

"Where else?" demanded Asa. He stroked a little pointed beard with the satisfaction that comes from inside knowledge. "You and Mr. Williamson both—goin' to Richmond to see Stephen Mallory. Reckon he's goin' to try to do somethin' 'bout the war if Ma'rs Robert won't."

"How did you know Mr. Williamson was going?"

"Sent his nigger round to tell me for to fetch him for the depot same as you did."

"And?"

"Told him the mare only goes to the depot once for one train on account of she's nigh as old as I am." Asa cackled again.

"I reckon he'll get there," said Porter solemnly.

"Steve Mallory's the fightin' kind."

"How d'you know?"

"Fit with him in the Seminole War," replied the old man proudly.

It was clear that he had been leading up to this. "He had a longboat. Saw him two-three times."

"The same Stephen Mallory?"

"The same. 'Bout time you stirred up somethin' in this war. Town's losin' interest."

"What d'you mean?"

"Isn't much of a war whichever way you looks at it. Abe Lincoln ain't doen much about it—no more's Jeff Davis. The boys from this town is sittin' on they butts playin' poker in the sun and drinkin' in the cool of the evenin', and the girls is hangin' around. Wisht there'd been this kinda war when I was a boy!"

The old mare turned the corner of her own accord. Theoretically she trotted, but the forward motion was that of a quiet walk.

Porter was used to Asa—everybody was. "It'll liven up when they get ready."

"Huh!" snorted old Asa. "They thought it was goin' to liven up when the Rip Raps battery opened fire on Seawell's Point t'other day. Can't say as I noticed it. Did you? Even the women's gettin' tired. Ain't no fun scrapin' lint if you don't get no wounds to put it on!"

"Nonsense!" retorted Porter explosively.

"Ain't nonsense. Best fun a woman gets out of a war's havin' a man helpless on her hands. Do what she wants with him then. No fightin'—nobody's helpless."

Porter laughed. "You're a scandalous old man."

"You don't believe me, you ask your Mis' Porter how many's turnin' up to bandage parties now and how many turned up week after the fire. I tell you this town ain't got no interest in it any more. Fire's wore off."

Williamson was already at the depot. He came forward as the hack drew up and took from Porter a box and then a traveling bag. "I had to get Jim to drive me down," he said. "This old scoundrel wouldn't come."

Old Asa stroked his beard with complacency.

The train was almost empty. It pulled out on time, moving slowly through the town.

Williamson traveled fussily. He tried two corner seats and replaced two bags and Porter's box twice before he was satisfied. Finally he settled.

Porter watched him with a quiet amusement. When he judged the engineer was ready, he said: "Old Asa says the town's lost interest in the war. He could be right at that. He says the young men are sitting on their hunkers playing cards."

Williamson nodded. "I judge this war's becoming a social occasion. There's been more fightin' between the Marion Rifles and that dam' old hen Colonel Pryor than anywheres else."

"What does Steve Mallory want you for?" asked Porter.

"Nothing in the orders." Williamson frowned a little. " 'Be available at my office first thing tomorrow.' What are your orders?"

"Report to *him* first thing." Porter smiled ruminatively. "Gives him a feeling of power. You're an engineer, I'm a constructor—at a long guess I'd say he's made up his mind to build a ship."

"He's been fussin' about it since we came to Richmond, he and Brooke."

"That's John Brooke, isn't it?"

"John M. Brooke. You ever worked with him?"

Porter shook his head. "I've seen him."

"Uppish young man," said Williamson. "Reckons he knows more about guns than Dahlgren."

"Does he?"

"No." The two men grinned at each other. "As of now," Williamson went on, "he's crazy about an ironclad. He draws ideas with a pencil and shows them to the Secretary. They had your master carpenter up last week; Brooke wanted him to draw a design for a ship."

"Joe Pierce told me." Porter nodded.

The train had pulled out of the shanty town now. The firm ground was giving way to swamp. Dark, stagnant patches of water showed between the naked, eroded stumps of old timber to the east of the line.

"All the same he's right." Porter was evidently referring to Mallory. "His report to the Naval Affairs Committee was sound. It's no use building wooden ships—that way we'll never catch up with the North. 'Inequality of numbers' "—he was obviously quoting—" 'can be compensated for by invulnerability.' He's got something there!"

"Where," asked Williamson skeptically, "is he going to get the iron?"

"He'll get it if we push with him."

Williamson looked at him with the quizzical smile of old friendship. "You've always been crazy about ironclads yourself, haven't you?"

*   *   *

Porter ran his eye over the dusty and undistinguished façade. The letters "Mechanics Institute" were fading, the paint peeled off a little by time. The Confederate Navy Department was housed on the second floor. It's no palace, he thought. It seemed to him to reflect somehow the desperate needs of the Navy of the South.

There was a door with a sign marked "Messengers," but the room was empty. A big notice said: "Persons are notified not to enter any of the offices without addressing the messengers. Positively no persons, on or without business, will be received in the offices after three o'clock P.M. Gentlemen will please read the signs on the doors."

Porter studied it carefully. He said to himself: "I would have put the last sentence first." A messenger came up behind him. "The Secretary of the Navy"—Porter consulted an elaborate watch—"at ten o'clock." It lacked two minutes to the hour.

"Sir," said the messenger, and led him down the short, grimy corridor.

Mallory rose in his chair to greet him. The fringe of beard under his chin seemed longer than Porter remembered. The square, bucolic, farmer's face was friendly.

Porter thought, He's pleased about something.

Mallory said: "Sit down, Mr. Porter. I think we are getting somewhere."

It was as though there had been no interval since his discussion with Mallory in Montgomery two months before.

Mallory continued: "I propose to go ahead with an ironclad ship. I have President Davis's sanction. It's the only way I can see out of our dilemma." He paused for a few minutes. The slightly bulging eyes were fixed on him. "You have theories, Mr. Porter."

Porter said, "I have a design, Mr. Secretary."

Mallory put the tips of his fingers together and looked over the small "V" of his thumbs. "You have more than a design, Mr. Porter— you have a model." Porter started. Mallory waved one hand negligently. "All right, all right, Parks told me."

"Commodore Parks approached me in May, sir. He wished to purchase vessels for North Carolina to use in the Sounds."

Mallory nodded benignantly. "And you showed him a model."

"I did, sir."

"He was impressed, and ordered a number of vessels of the type to be constructed."

"He was instructed to prepare a bill for the North Carolina legislature to order such vessels, sir."

Mallory grinned at him. "I stand corrected." Then, as if he were tired of fencing, he said bluntly: "And that model is there." He dropped his eyes to the box on the floor beside Porter's chair.

Porter nodded. "I made the original drawings when I was in Pittsburg in '46, sir. I adjusted them at the end of April of this year and in the beginning of May to suit our capacity to build, and I had a model constructed in the Yard."

"All right, man," said Mallory impatiently. "Open it, open it!" Porter stooped down and fiddled with the string for a moment. Mallory held out a knife. "Cut it!"

The knot came undone and Porter opened the box. The model was of wood, unpainted. It was flat bottomed. Its sides rose at an ugly, awkward angle from the bottom and met a sloping superstructure that ended in a narrow, level deck. Halfway up the slope the sides of the superstructure were pierced for gun ports. It fined away to the bows in a hideous angularity. The stern was square and uncompromising. The whole thing had a barge-like ugliness. There was no curve, no vestige of grace or beauty.

"My God!" exclaimed Mallory. Porter stiffened. The uncertain contours of the Secretary's face creased in a sudden smile. "All right, all right, I'm not going to offend you! But even you wouldn't call it beautiful—would you?"

"Sir, I had no concern with beauty when I drew the designs. I was concerned only with strength."

Mallory nodded. "First consideration," he agreed. "Why do the sides slope like that?"

"Above the waterline they slope so that shot will ricochet from them. They give a glancing effect."

"And below?"

"Because that's the easiest hull form we can build—the quickest—with our resources."

Once more Mallory nodded. He turned the model round and then with his finger poked clumsily at one gun port after another. "Fourteen guns?"

"No, sir, six."

"Fourteen gun ports?" said Mallory quickly.

"I have planned her for pivot guns, sir. Four in the center line will fire through ports on either side. The bow gun will fire through the three ports in the line of the shield for'ard, the stern gun the same."

"And you could armor her sufficiently to withstand shot?"

"To withstand anything that the North has at the moment, sir." He hesitated, then added, "If we can get the iron."

"You will get the iron." Mallory turned the model round again, holding it out at arm's length so that he could look at its squat, strong profile. Again the shadow of a grimace showed on his face. At last he said: "I can't make the decision alone. I'm not technically equipped. You will meet with Mr. Williamson and Lieutenant Brooke at your earliest convenience and consider this matter in detail. Lieutenant Brooke has ideas of his own. If you cannot present an agreed report to me, you will present two reports. It must be done at once." There was a hint of dismissal in the voice. Porter began to get to his feet. "Leave this with me." Mallory was staring at the model on the desk. "No, it's not beautiful."

Porter said: "Mr. Secretary, may I make a suggestion?"

"You may." Mallory kept his eyes on the model as if he were fascinated by its ugliness.

"The Navy of the South needs engines and it needs iron more than anything else. Ships we can build—we've got the timber, we've got the workmen, we've got the yards. In the whole South there is not one firm that has built engines. I doubt if there are two rolling mills that can turn out plate."

"And you suggest?"

"That we buy them abroad, sir—and at once, before the blockade closes on us."

Mallory sat silent for a full minute. At length he began to drum with his fingers on the sloping side of the model. "We took over one ship only from the United States Navy, the *Fulton*—you know the extent of her usefulness. I sent agents in March to Baltimore, to Philadelphia, to New York, to Canada—we got little enough from that. I have sent Bulloch and James North to England with instructions to attempt to purchase the *Gloire* from the French. Ships would be better than plate or engines."

"If they were good ships, sir. I don't know enough about the *Gloire,* I know only that she has weaknesses. We *must* have engines if we are to build, sir."

"We're still negotiating with the East India Company for their steam fleet—you know that, of course—but their price will not be below ten million dollars for the ten ships. We could cover it with forty thousand bales of cotton, but the President's policy is to hold the cotton."

With a little gesture of both hands Porter intimated a vision of riches. "Ten million dollars! Sir, you could buy engines enough, iron enough, to build a fleet of your own."

"President Davis"—Mallory spoke slowly and distinctly, still not looking at Porter but keeping his eyes fixed on the model—"President Davis believes that with cotton the South can force the support of England. He plans for a short war."

*   *   *

The office was small and desperately in need of paper and paint. Brooke's desk stood across a corner. It had an accumulation of documents on it, an air of busyness. The atmosphere of the office was that from it great affairs were conducted with great difficulty.

Porter smiled tolerantly at Brooke.

Williamson, sitting back in a threadbare armchair, asked, "Wouldn't it help if we had the model?"

Brooke said, "I've sent a messenger for it."

The door opened and a messenger came in with the box and put it on Brooke's table. As the man went out, Brooke took the model from its resting place. At once his nose wrinkled.

Porter said: "All right, it's ugly. The Secretary thinks it's ugly. I'm prepared to admit it's ugly—but it will float and it will do the job."

Brooke smoothed out his face. "I wouldn't care to go to sea in it."

"It's not meant for the sea," Porter assured him patiently. "It's meant for smooth water—for the Chesapeake. It draws eleven feet, it's a hundred and fifty feet long on deck, and it has a beam of forty feet. It's designed for seven knots—should do eight. We could build it at Portsmouth now with what we've got there if we could get the iron."

He unrolled a sheaf of plans. Methodically they began to discuss them. Porter found a side table and cleared it brusquely of an accumulation of books. The plans were spread and the three men stood round them, arguing each point as it emerged. A curious excitement seized them. It was not shown in any increase in the tempo of the conversation or in any raising of the pitch of voices, but there was a tension in their discussion that lifted the whole affair out of departmental debate. Hour after hour the argument went on. Hour after hour Porter made his defense or explained small amendments.

It was Williamson who said at last, "It can't be done in a hurry."

"The Secretary wants—" began Porter.

Williamson broke in scornfully: "Steve Mallory will have to learn to want! It will take us twelve months to build engines powerful enough to move her."

"I've asked him to buy engines from Europe."

"Still take the best part of twelve months," Williamson maintained, pulling at the end of his nose. "Couldn't be done in less"—he repeated the irritating gesture—"unless perhaps"—his voice was hesitant, as if he were trying to search his memory—"unless we could use some of the machinery from the *Merrimac.*"

Porter flung both his hands wide in an enormously enlarged version of the gesture that he had used in Mallory's office. "Why couldn't we use it all? I can adapt this model to the *Merrimac* and use her own machinery in her."

"The *Merrimac*," Brooke reminded him sharply, "is a wreck."

Porter shook his head. "She's sound under the fire line; I've surveyed her. Her engines were never sound."

"Even an unsound engine is better than none," said Williamson. "Isherwood overhauled them in April."

"They've had six weeks under water since then," Brooke protested, "and the best part of a month lying in the open."

"Ben Isherwood did a good job on them," said Williamson. "I think they'll run."

"You may be right at that," Brooke admitted.

Porter let out a long-pent explosion of breath.

*   *   *

Mallory regarded them with an oddly distant look. He paid no attention to the paper in his hand. "You have come to your conclusions with extraordinary speed."

Porter smiled at him. "Your instructions were to make all possible haste, Mr. Secretary."

Mallory grinned. His eyes moved slowly from man to man. His face seemed even more amorphous than ordinarily. At last he dropped his eyes to the paper and read: " 'Sir—In obedience to your order we have carefully examined and considered the various plans and propositions for constructing a shot proof steam battery, and respectfully report that, in our opinion, the steam frigate Merrimac, which is . . .' The *Merrimac!*" Mallory looked up from the paper, glaring. His forehead was creased into a multitude of angry wrinkles. "The *Merrimac* is a wreck!"

"Sir," said Porter softly, "the *Merrimac* has been so burned that she is useless for rebuilding as a frigate—but she is not a wreck. I have surveyed her. She was resting on the bottom when she was fired. The flames were checked by the water."

"Why did you not report that?" demanded Mallory.

The constructor allowed himself one tiny moment of triumph before he murmured, "I did, sir."

Mallory turned indignantly to his secretary who sat behind him. "I have not seen that report!"

"Filed it, sir."

Mallory began, "Your passion for files . . ." and allowed his voice to die away. His eyes dropped to the paper. "'. . . which is in such condition from the effect of fire as to be useless for any other purpose without incurring a heavy expense in her rebuilding, can be made an efficient vessel of that character, mounting ten heavy guns; two pivot guns, and eight broadside guns of her original battery, and for the further consideration that we cannot procure a suitable engine and boilers for any other vessel without building them, which would occupy too much time, it would appear that this is our only chance to get a suitable vessel in a short time. The bottom of the hull, boilers and heavy and costly parts of the engine, being but little injured, reduce the cost of construction to about one-third the amount which would be required to construct such a vessel anew.'" He repeated the words "one-third the amount" and looked up. He read on in silence for a moment, then asked, "How long will it take to prepare a detailed estimate?"

"I will require to measure her," replied Porter, "and to draft new plans to adapt the shield of the model to her size and capacity."

"How long will it take?" demanded Mallory impatiently. "Two months? Six weeks? A month?"

"I hope, sir," Porter answered formally, "to be able to present plans to the Department within fourteen days."

Chapter five

THE water was clear. This was another of the strange, inexplicable days when the water in the Southern Branch was like crystal. Porter was leaning over the rail of the gates of the dry dock. Linden watched him with a lively interest as the dinghy crept closer and closer to the wall. Her memory reached back to the day in May when she had watched the constructor as he moved somberly over the charred wreckage of the *Merrimac.* Jeriel lay sprawled in his favorite place in the bows.

She asked, "What's he doing, Jeri?"

"Thinkin'," replied the boy instantly.

"Yes, but what's he thinking about? He's looking over the *Merrimac.* Last time we came this way he was looking over the *Merrimac.* Are they going to do something with her?"

"She's a wreck." Jeriel dipped his hat with finality over his eyes.

Linden eased the tiller a little. The boat crept almost imperceptibly into the jaws of the dry dock. When she judged it was close enough she called up, "Mr. Porter!"

The constructor whirled round and glared down, interrupted in a moment of intense concentration.

"Are you going to use the *Merrimac,* Mr. Porter?"

He moved over to the outer rail, rested his hands on it and stood looking down at her. "I told you before, Linden, we've got to use everything we have."

"Just the engines, Mr. Porter?" His face was impassive, expressionless, and she went on uncomfortably: "You can't use her for anything else, can you? She's a wreck."

"Wrecks have their uses. You'll find a bit of wind out in the Branch, Linden."

*   *   *

Williamson grunted. After a long interval the words came clear. "The iron—that's going to be your trouble. The iron. There's timber enough in what's left of the lumber stacks and in the town to build anything you like, but there's no iron. You want plates, you want big plates, you want thick plates. There's nothing that can roll 'em. I can make her engines run." He wiped his hands of the filth of charcoal and grease and rust. "Hey, hey, she's a mess! But I can make 'em run. You can build the ship you want and you can get the guns, but where're you goin' to get the iron?"

"We'll get it," Porter answered quietly. "I've talked to Joe Anderson of the Tredegar Works. He reckons he can roll it. They'll have to adjust the mill that they use for railroad iron, but he says he can do it."

Williamson shook his head. "You're goin' to need an awful lot of iron, John—an awful lot of iron."

"We'll get it." Porter repeated the words with a quiet confidence.

"How long is it goin' to take you to work out your figures?"

"I've done a rough cast," replied Porter slowly. "I calculate that on a depth of twenty-one feet I'll have fifty tons of displacement to spare. She'll float."

"I hope she will," said Williamson bluntly. "I'd hate to see another lot of good work on those engines spoiled."

*　　*　　*

Jeriel said furiously: "I won't sit down comfortable for a week! Ten he gave me with the end of a rope. I tol' you it wasn't no good in the daytime!"

Linden smothered the beginning of a laugh. "I thought there wouldn't be anybody around. It's no distance from the end of the rope walk to the dry dock."

"It's best part of two hun'r'd fifty yards, an' that's two hun'r'd twenty-five yards too much. I wasn't clear o' the shadow before he got me. Next time they catch me, he says, they put me in the brig."

"At night you would have seen nothing." Linden's voice was reflective.

"Daytime I ain't seen nothin'," protested Jeriel tartly. He fingered his bottom with caution. "My ass's like a new-ploughed 'bacca field."

"I'm sorry, Jeri. I didn't think you'd be caught. I've got to try now."

"If Schisano gets you, you go quiet. He gave me an extra three for hitting him in the guts."

"You didn't tell me that!" Again Linden suppressed a laugh.

"I had to hit him jus' once."

"We've still got to find out what they're going to use the *Merrimac* for," she said soberly. "I can't find anybody that knows."

*　　*　　*

The master carpenter said: "We can do it all right but we haven't got the timber. Lost a lot in the fire. It's the heart pine that's goin' to give you trouble. You want twenty-inch section and a good length. We ain't got it in the Yard. You'll have to go outside. You want an awful lot of it."

"We've got to have it. Where will I find it outside?" Porter asked.

"Ash Cleave's got a mort of it back o' the sawmill. Don't know if he'll sell it, though—he's no friend o' the South."

"I can deal with Ash Cleave. If you reckon he's got enough of it, that's all I want to know."

"He's got enough." Pierce nodded. "He's got a stack o' grown oak knees too that we can use for the deckin' for'ard. Goin' to need nigh as much timber as you'd want for a new ship, Mr. Porter."

"We'll save six months using her hull and the engines. Six months is six months."

"Mr. Mallory says the war's goin' to be over in six months," said Pierce tonelessly.

"Did you ever know a politician who couldn't see what he wanted in the future?" Porter's voice was soft and speculative.

"No, can't say I did."

* * *

Linden looked morosely at the boy. "Wouldn't let me go past the Headquarters building. I told them I wanted to see Mr. Porter, and they said Mr. Porter was busy."

Jeriel laughed aloud unfeelingly. "Least you didn't get your bottom tanned!"

"They wouldn't dare." Linden lifted her head a little. "I can't find anybody who knows. I've asked everybody I can think of. He's been out there every day for a week, looking her over, measuring, poking around in the bottom of the dock, looking at guns, fingering, calculating, drawing, and nobody knows what it's all about—nobody!"

"My uncle says he reckons they're goin' to build her up again."

"If they were, they would have said. It would take 'em a year to do it." She shook her head. "No, it's something else. I can't think what." Her eyes were alive, intense. "If Martha were here I'd ask her to ask her father."

"She's down in Alabama." Jeriel's tone was final.

"It wouldn't be any use asking Mrs. Porter. She never knows anything about what he's doing. Mr. Williamson's been there with him. D'you know anybody who knows Mr. Williamson?"

Jeriel shook his head. "My uncle, but he don't know him that well."

"Mellie Brent goes to his house."

"Her!" snorted Jeriel with a proper scorn.

"If I have to ask her, I'll ask her." Linden looked out beyond the boy, her eyes glinting.

* * *

Porter walked silently on the soft sawdust carpeting in front of the mill. He took Cleave a little by surprise. "Ash," he said, "I want to talk to you."

Cleave nodded. They walked down toward the little pier together.

Porter said: "I need that heart pine you've got back of the mill and I need those grown oak knees. Are you willing to sell?"

Cleave put his head on one side and looked at the constructor with amusement. "Did you think I wouldn't sell, John?"

"You aren't with us—that's your business; no reason why you should be if you can't see it our way."

"No, I'm not with you, but I'm not going to argue it."

"I didn't come to argue. I came for timber. Will you sell?"

"I'll sell."

Porter jerked his head up and looked Cleave full in the eyes again. "I'm glad of that, Ash. We'd have had to close down on you if you couldn't see your way clear to it."

"I know." Cleave grinned. "That's why I'll sell."

"You can fix your own price—in reason."

"You can have it at the price it was in my books on April 18th."

Porter shook his head. "There's no call to do that, Ash. You can take a fair wartime profit."

"That's my price. I don't aim to make money out of this fight."

"You'll have to pay more to replace it."

"I'll take the chance. I'm not in this war."

"I don't understand you, Ash! Yes, I think I do. How much of the heart pine have you got?"

"Let's go and see."

They turned up toward the mill again.

"Some of it will come out under twenty-inch—we can use that too—but it's the twenty-inch I want. You don't ask me what I want it for, Ash."

"That's your business." Cleave smiled again.

"I'm going to rebuild the *Merrimac*," said Porter with a sudden rush of words. "There won't be any secret to it in a week's time. You can't keep anything secret in this town. Everybody knows everything."

"Linden doesn't." Cleave allowed himself a little humor. "She's been pestering the life out of the Yard one way and another."

"I know!" Porter smiled warmly. "If Linden doesn't know, I guess it's still a secret. I'm not going to rebuild her as a ship. I'm going to make her into a battery, an armored battery." Porter hesitated, thinking back to Mallory's reaction. "She won't be beautiful but she's going to be strong. We've got to break the blockade."

"You'll never do that. The Yankees will build and build and build. Sinking a few of them's not going to do any good. The South's going to lose this war on the sea."

They came to the end of the lumber piles. Porter looked at the clean, honest ends of the logs. "That's good timber. You're wrong, Ash, you're wrong! They can outbuild us one way but we can outbuild them another. 'Inequality of numbers' "—the quotation was firm in his mind —" 'can be compensated for by invulnerability.' "

"How," asked Cleave, "would you define invulnerability, John?"

*   *   *

"She has the temperament of a squirrel," said Aunt Deborah. Cleave looked at her admiringly. It was not often that his sister displayed such percipience. "She pops up and down"—she paused, hunting for a suitable simile—"as if she was collecting nuts for the winter. I'm getting too old to follow her. I thought I was catchin' up when she fell quiet beginning of the month; now she's way up top of the tree again. I can't keep pace, Ash!"

"Don't try," answered Cleave comfortably. "Squirrels can look after themselves."

"Squirrels can be shot with a gun!" Aunt Deborah shut her eyes. "Soldiers have guns."

Cleave looked at his sister in surprise. If she meant what he thought she meant, he was astonished. If she didn't, he was equally astonished.

"The last few days," Aunt Deborah went on, "she's been like a squirrel that smells the snow comin'."

Cleave nodded. "I know—and I know what the snow is."

"She's your daughter," said Aunt Deborah darkly.

"Do any of us know our daughters?" asked Cleave.

She looked at him balefully.

"D'you think Father did?" Cleave prodded his point home.

Aunt Deborah became absorbed in her work. Cleave watched quietly. She was fitting the sleeve in a gray shirt. Aunt Deborah had informed the women of her acquaintance at the very start of things that she would sew nothing for Confederate soldiers. She was prepared, however, to make clothing for the sons of her friends. "They're local boys," she had said, "not Confederate soldiers."

Linden came in much later. She dropped wearily into a chair. Her eyes were dark and her whole body drooped, yet there was a definite elation behind it, an assurance that belied the weariness.

Cleave asked, "What's the trouble?"

"Nothing."

"Sold a lot of timber today," said Cleave with a careful lack of emphasis.

"Did you?" Clearly Linden did not take it in.

"Every last foot of my yellow pine."

"You won't find it easy to get more."

"I sold the grown oak knees too. Ship timber."

Linden came suddenly upright. "Yellow pine you could sell for houses, but what are you selling ship timber for?"

Cleave ignored the question. "Good seasoned wood it was too. Most of it came from way upstate, up against the mountains."

Linden was bolt upright in her chair now. All the fatigue was gone from her as she realized the significance of Cleave's information. "Who did you sell it to, Father?"

"John Porter."

"John Porter!" She was out of the chair and on her knees at the side of her father's chair. "John Porter—what did he want it for? You sold it to the Confederate Navy?"

"Yard's still under the Virginia Navy."

"It doesn't signify! It doesn't signify! What did Mr. Porter want it for?"

"The *Merrimac*."

"I knew it! I knew it! What's he going to do with her—rebuild her?" Cleave nodded. "But it will take a year!" Linden's voice rose.

"He's not going to rebuild her as a frigate. He's going to make her into a battery, an armored battery."

"An ironclad?" Her hands came together in a clasp so tight that Cleave could see her knuckles shining white through the skin. "An *iron*clad!"

*   *   *

Isherwood flipped the paper across the table. "If you haven't seen it, you'd better read it. They're going to rebuild the *Merrimac* as an ironclad."

"Good God!" Stephen jerked himself out of the chair and snatched the agent's report from the desk. "*Can* they?"

"Porter's doin' it," replied Isherwood. "He's always hankered after buildin' an ironclad."

"He's a good man," said Stephen soberly.

"Sure he's a good man."

Stephen's mind went back to the great uprush of flame against the blazing background of the ship houses. He could still see the yards and the rigging, the halyards and the masts, each of them a many-armed cross of brilliance. "There can't be enough of her left to make a ship out of!"

"I'd back John Porter's knowledge of ships against yours." Isherwood's tone was brittle.

Stephen made a little gesture of surrender. "Has the Secretary seen it?"

"Noah sees everything." What name he gave to the Secretary of the Navy depended on Isherwood's mood: if he called him "Noah" he was feeling well disposed, if he called him "Uncle Gideon" he was friendly; on occasion he called him "that damned pragmatical Yankee news-paper editor." "Noah's sending a dove to Congress tomorrow."

"The request for an Ironclad Board?"

"The same. You are about to see the fruit of your endeavors. I don't know if you've been long enough in Washington to know the meaning of the word 'about.' This is what will happen. Senator Hall will get hold of it, Senator Hall will talk. Then Senator Hall will find something to criticize. Senator Hall's got to justify his existence—he bolted when he heard that Beauregard was heading for Washington; now he's come back and he's got to shout loud. When the senator's finished with it, the House of Representatives will get down to it. When everybody's chewed it over, it will go to the White House and it will lie on Nicolay's desk for a week, and then it will lie on the President's desk for another week. Maybe we'll get a decision in December. Maybe we won't. There's more ways of fighting a war than at the end of a gun."

"December! They'll be six months ahead of us by then."

"Maybe they will, maybe they won't. Steve Mallory has his troubles too."

"But if we only get a Board in December . . ."

Isherwood looked at him tolerantly. "Oh, maybe it won't be as bad as that! Maybe it will be the end of November."

*   *   *

John Porter stood on the granite coping of the dry dock looking down at the long, black shape of the ship below. The clean lines of the *Merrimac* were lost in a chaos of burned plank and driven ash. Here and there white timbers, rain-washed, stood out of the ruin of fire. In places, about the hatches to the engine room, about the entrance to the lower holds, were bleak clearings.

He said: "Good! Clear up the burned wood, clean up the wreckage, get down to the sound timber, and we'll take another look at her."

Pierce, the master carpenter, answered, "Right, we'll make a start."

Overhead a gull, wheeling lazily in the first hot upward currents of the morning, called, and out over the Southern Branch another, im-patient, answered it.

Chapter six

ULYSSES HOGAN'S voice went up in pitch to a wail. "I can't, Linden —I dassen't! Editor took the hide off me last week. You had best part of a column 'n' a half then. He said—"

Sam looked up from his composing stick. " 'I will not have you using the columns of this newspaper to further your private amours,' " he quoted with malicious accuracy.

Linden had the grace to blush; it was a very slight blush, gone almost before her cheeks had colored. She had also the guile to turn it to advantage. "Did he say that, really?"

Though he could not see her face, Sam knew that she was staring enormous-eyed at Ulysses. He snorted.

Ulysses turned uneasily toward him and turned back to Linden like a frog fascinated by a moccasin.

Linden said: "I'm not asking you to do it for me, Ulysses. It's for the South. It's for the *Merrimac.*" There was sufficient helplessness in her voice to stab at an unprotected heart. The assistant editor's heart was unprotected.

Sam watched him from inside his own indurated shell.

"We might manage just a short paragraph—" Ulysses felt Linden's eyes on him again and changed it hurriedly—"or—or two on page four."

"Not on page four," Sam corrected him.

"Why?"

"Frame's locked."

"Oh, Ulysses!"

Ulysses was very young. Heartlessly, Sam watched him squirm. There was an actual, physical undulation of his body. "Lindy . . ." he began.

"I've nobody else to ask." She injected a world of shameless dependence into her voice.

Ulysses capitulated with a rush. "I'll put it on the main page," he said, the words tumbling. "Editor, he may throw it out, but I'll put it there."

Linden moved forward, put a hand on his shoulder and, reaching up, kissed him, high on the cheek and modestly close to the ear.

"Ah, Lindy!" he murmured confusedly.

"You goin' to be late for the judge's meetin'." The old man came to his rescue.

"Holy God!" Ulysses stared open-mouthed at Linden for half a second and turned, stammering apologies.

Sam put down the stick and rested his elbows against the long spreading type case. "Lindy Cleave," he said softly, "ain't you got no conscience at all?"

"None."

"I don't know how you do it." He shook his head ruminantly. "You dress to cover your nakedness—not even your poor aunt could say more. Half the time you're out with men you wear pants. You don't dance with them. You don't flirt with them. I never heerd of you writin' a little note excep' to ask Jeriel why the hell he wasn't where you wanted him to be. And yet you twist 'em round your finger."

She grinned at him, and he threw back his head, and laughed.

But when she spoke she spoke soberly and with restraint. "Sam, what I do I do for the South—and for the *Merrimac*."

"Began long before the *Merrimac*."

"I didn't bother before that, hardly at all. I've got to make them do things—there's so much to be done. The *Merrimac*'s ours, Sam."

He looked at her sardonically. "Not mine, I'm nootral."

"She belongs to Portsmouth. You're a Portsmouth man."

"She belongs to the Confed'rit Gov'ment. Jeff Davis'll foot the bill."

"You're wrong!" she flared. "She's ours. Anybody else would have left her to rot on the mud. Mr. Porter was the only one to see it. He was the man who made it possible. He's a Portsmouth man. He's a great man. His idea's so new nobody knows how good it is yet—"

"John Porter's got ideas," agreed Sam slowly. "Don't know that any good ever comes of them. Like when he sold his piano to buy a wife for that no account nigger Willis."

"He didn't sell it," contradicted Linden calmly. "He used the money he'd set aside to buy one, and Willis was married already. He did it to save her being sold south. And they're still happy."

"Huh!" He stared at her under the shaggy eyebrows. "John Porter dreams. He's dreamin' now."

"I don't think he is." The girl outfaced him stubbornly. "And if he isn't, we've got a chance to do something—something great. Can you think of any other way we could break the blockade?"

"Is this contraption goin' to break the blockade?" His scorn was palpable.

"At least it's going to try." She spoke somberly.

The old man for an instant saw into her soul, into its fervor and its faith—into its fear. He picked up the composing stick again, and his hand flickered out for the type. For perhaps two minutes he worked with speed and concentration while the girl stood silent. He had no way to comfort her, no help for her loneliness.

He said at last, accusingly, "You still got the kids playin' hell on the sidewalk, front of the Whitehurst House?"

"How did you know I set them to it?"

"Lindy Cleave"—he looked up from the type—"I've knowed you for a long time."

Primly she said: "Mr. Whitehurst has very kindly agreed to let us have the hall for the cartridge bag parties and as a depot for flannel petticoats and such. Do you wish me to go into exact details?" The laughter had come back into her eyes.

" 'N you've called off your hellions. That's Tammany Hall tactics, Lindy. Ain't you above using Yankee methods?"

"I'll use any methods at all to get money for the Gunboat Fund."

"So I've noticed," he acknowledged dryly. "Ain't nothing you won't offer. One o' these days one o' the hot-blooded young men in this town's goin' to come for payment."

"I can look after myself."

"Yeah," he snorted, "that's what I'm afraid of. Number of girls I've heard say that, that couldn't, would keep a midwife goin' full time."

She grinned at him wickedly.

"You've raised more hell in this town since you started this dam' fund, and you've got more young men fetchin' an' carryin' for you than is safe for any girl."

"Fund's making money," she said airily, and came and stood beside him, squinting sideways and trying to read the lines of type as they built up. "Uncle Sam"—unconsciously and dangerously her voice took on a faint note of wheedling—"will you help Ulysses to get it on the front page tomorrow?"

So swiftly that her eyes did not even catch the motion, the old man's hand flashed forward in a stinging blow that caught her on the rump and jerked her into the open space between the two fonts.

She wheeled even as she regained her balance, her face white and for an instant set with anger. Then suddenly it relaxed. With a faint suspicion of a grin she said, "Any other man in Portsmouth'd done that, I'd have slapped his face."

"Any other girl in Portsmouth, I wouldn't'a' done it. Don't you try that on me again, Lindy Cleave! Next time I'll see my hand's been in the printer's ink before I skelp you."

She rubbed her bottom ruefully. "I won't. You're a sour-tempered old beast—but I love you, Uncle Sam."

He threw back his head again, and laughed.

He was still laughing when the editor came in through the street door. He said acidly: "Glad somebody's got something to laugh about. Lindy Cleave, what are you after? Ulysses!" He shouted the name with a strong undercurrent of suspicion.

Sam looked at him sideways. "Judge Crampton called a meetin'."

"Well, he's safe, then! What's it this time, Linden?"

Directly and simply the girl answered: "Some of the men think it's time they started to do extra work on the *Merrimac*. They're ready to work nights till eight o'clock. They think it's time she speeded up."

Sam's jaw dropped a little as he watched her. There was no trace of wheedling, no hint of sex. She was as direct and as clear as a man. He waited for the editor to explode.

There was a long silence before he heard the editor say, his voice abstracted, "Yes, it's time she speeded up."

"If you could give them a lead—it would help with the rest. . . ."

The editor nodded soberly. "Yes, I think we could give a lead." He crossed the composing room to his office and stood for a moment with the door open. Over his shoulder he said, "Thanks, Linden." He went in and shut the door.

She studied the closed door soberly. After a pause she said: "I thought he'd tell me to mind my own business. I'm scared of him when he's polite like that." She wheeled on the old compositor. "Why did he take it that way?" she demanded.

He shrugged his shoulders.

Acutely she asked, "Does he know something?" And then, as the old man's response hesitated, added, "Do *you* know something, Uncle Sam?" There was no coquetry now, only the same uncompromising honesty with which she had faced the editor.

The old man hesitated, then he groped in his hip pocket, found a clipping and pulled it out. He held it between finger and thumb, folded. Linden took it.

In the center of the clipping was an advertisement, an official Union Navy Department advertisement, dated from Washington. It was ringed in blue pencil. She studied it for a minute, frowning, then she read aloud:

"'. . . offers from parties for construction of one or more ironclad steam vessels of war . . . to be rigged with two masts, with wire rope standing rigging.'" She read on in silence. Finally she said aloud: "'. . . specifications by September the third . . .'" She stared at the old man wordlessly.

"You must'a' known they'd do it, Lindy—sooner or later they was bound to do it."

"I knew," she said briefly, and began calculating advantage. "We've had a month already. They won't have plans, specifications, anything before September the third. Even then they'll talk about it and argue. We'll have three months' clear start—three months at least. And we've got the hull—and the engines. . . ."

He saw that her eyes were shining, that she was caught up in the challenge.

"It'll be a race, one of the greatest races in—in history." Again she paused and then said, ending the matter, "We'll win it!"

"They've got foundries, Linden, and yards, and factories, and men—"

She dismissed the warning. "You weren't going to show it to me, Uncle Sam?"

"Hadn't made up my mind."

"But why?"

He looked at her with a slow, sweet smile that had no trace of irascibility in it. "Mebbe I'm fond of you, Lindy."

Chapter seven

THE deep note of the whistle of a tugboat on the Hudson flowed in at the open window like the preliminary chord of an immense solemnity of orchestration. The man on the piano stool moved uneasily, as if the sound sent memories coursing in his mind. He waited until it had died away. Then he surveyed the three fingers that remained on his right hand with a curious, almost feminine particularity, and adjusted the plaster that protected a split nail on the middle finger. Finally, he picked up his pen and began to make a fair copy of the letter.

To His Excellency ABRAHAM LINCOLN, President of the United
States.

New York, August 29, 1861.

Sir: The writer, having introduced the present system of naval pro-
pulsion and constructed the first screw ship of war, now offers to
construct a vessel for the destruction of the rebel fleet at Norfolk
and for scouring the Southern waters and inlets of all craft protected
by rebel batteries.

He raised his head, his face grave, contemplating the immensity of
his offer. The neat, precise draughtsman's hand was faultless. He read
the sentence through, looked at the rough copy, and began to add a
fresh sentence to the effect that he claimed no reward, sought no advantages. He informed the President of the success of his caloric engine.
Then he went on:

Attachment to the Union alone impels me to offer my services at
this fearful crisis—my life if need be—in the great cause which
Providence has called you to defend. Please look carefully at the
enclosed plans and you will find that the means I propose to employ
are very simple—so simple, indeed, that within ten weeks after commencing the structure I would engage to be ready to take up position
under the rebel guns at Norfolk, and so efficient, too, I trust, that
within a few hours the stolen ships would be sunk and the harbor
purged of traitors.

The letter flowed on and on. The neat hand retained its neatness.

. . . due weight, I respectfully submit, should be given to the circumstance that its projector possess practical and constructive skill
shared by no engineer now living.

He frowned a little over the phrasing. At least it was a fair summation
of his own capacities. He was quite certain that there was no engineer
living to match his genius. He explained his background, his military
education, his skill in artillery. Again his eye ran over the rough copy.
The sentence that he had already drafted pointing out that he was at-
tributing these statements to the necessity to prove his ability would
cover him, he calculated, against any charge of vanity. Slowly he came
to the final paragraph:

I cannot conclude without respectfully calling your attention to
the now well-established fact that steel-clad vessels cannot be ar-

rested in their course by land batteries, and that hence our great city is quite at the mercy of such intruders and may at any moment be laid in ruins. . . .

He rounded off the final paragraph and added the subscription:

. . . with profound respect, your obedient servant

J. ERICSSON.

The deep, booming note of the tug whistle sounded again. She must, he thought, be working a ship into her berth at one of the wharves a little down the river from the end of Beach Street.

The roadway below the window became suddenly full of the sound of hoofs and the creaking of wheels and the shouts of the driver as a heavy dray came up the slope from the river. Once again he waited with a solemn patience for the noise to subside. A question was forming itself in his mind: Would it be safe to send the plans through the mails?

When the last of the clatter had died away he added a postscript:

At the moment of putting this communication under envelope it occurs to me finally that it is unsafe to trust the plans to the mails. . . . Should you decide to put the work in hand, if my plan meets your own approbation, please telegraph and within forty-eight hours the writer will report himself at the White House.

Methodically, somberly, he read the letter through again. When he had finished, he nodded as if across the desk there were some visible assistant, but it was himself that he addressed in silence: "I will not deal with the bureaus. It is for the President to decide."

*   *   *

Slowly, gently, Cleave pulled in the ugly horse. The wheels came to rest with a slight shirr against the coarse sand of the track. He said softly, "Look!" The deer crossed the track thirty yards ahead of them, stepping delicately over the wheel ruts. The buck led. Between him and the doe a half-grown fawn, sun-dappled and with its underbelly made almost luminous by the light reflected off the sand, stopped abruptly on the far side of the rut, threw up its head in pretended terror and then, with a humorous, idiot gesture, bucked upward like a spring released, landed with all four feet meticulously together on the green strip between the ruts, bounced up again and landed in triumphant safety on the farther side. The doe watched it tolerantly before she crossed herself. They disappeared without apparent movement, absorbed between breath and breath in the green of the underbrush.

Linden watched with her lips parted. They could not be her deer—this was another part of the swamp—but the memory was the same. Aloud she said to her father, "It seems a long time ago."

"What does?"

"The deer—the deer that Jeri and I watched."

He nodded with the ghost of a smile.

"A lot's happened since then." She turned her eyes inward on herself. "I think I've grown older."

"We tend to age," said Cleave with tolerance. There was a little pause, then he lifted his head questingly. "What would that be?"

Very faint, very far away, there was a sound like fingers tapping on taut parchment. He sought for the direction. It was hard to be certain; the sound was tenuous, beyond the horizon—he could not even guess how far beyond it—somewhere to the southeast.

The girl said, "Woodpeckers?"

He made an almost imperceptible gesture with his head in contradiction.

The sound came again, moving in a rustle to a dry, ghostly crescendo, and faded once more.

"Guns," Cleave murmured, straining his ears.

"Guns!" Linden repeated the word breathlessly. "It couldn't be guns! There's nothing down there. It would be this side." She jerked her head back toward the Chesapeake.

Cleave shook his head. "They've been expecting trouble along the Sounds. It could be Roanoke." He listened. "Couldn't be Hatteras—it's too far, must be all of a hundred miles from here." He paused again. The silence was absolute. "There's no wind," he said reflectively, "just a drift of air from the southeast. Gun shots would carry a long way over the Sounds. Perhaps it *could* be Hatteras. Listen!"

The fingers were tapping again beyond the horizon.

Close to them in a swamp maple a cardinal began to sing in cascades of triple notes, drowning the sound of the guns.

Linden tried to listen to them under the flood of song. Finally she clapped her hands and called, "Shush, you redbird!" With a whirr of wings the cardinal launched itself out of the tree and flew like a rocket down the way that the deer had gone. As the whisper of the wings died, the sounds beyond the horizon came clear again—clear and sinister.

Cleave woke the mare and they moved forward. "Nothing we can do about it. There's no way of telling from this distance. It had to come sooner or later."

"Why?" The girl's voice was troubled.

Cleave, his voice dispassionate, answered: "The South can't be strong everywhere, Linden. North's bound to feel out the weak points and hit at them. From what I've heard, Jeff Davis doesn't take much interest in the Sounds."

With an awkward agreement she said: "The boys have been saying that. Ned Kearns was down at Elizabeth City a while back. He said that on Roanoke Island they were expecting an attack in August—but that was weeks ago."

"It's still August," Cleave reminded her grimly—"the twenty-ninth."

She was beginning to recover herself. "They'll hold out. Even if they did get into the Sounds, they couldn't do anything. They'd still have to fight their way onto the shore. There's a lot between the Sounds and Portsmouth."

"If they get into the Sounds," Cleave pointed out prosaically, "they'll cut off a lot of blockade running for a start, and they'll stop all the traffic through the Sounds. And if they ever get to worrying about the *Merrimac,* they'll be in a position to attack from both sides at once."

Linden lifted her head defiantly. "We'll finish the *Merrimac* long before they can do that. Once she's finished, they won't be able to attack."

Cleave pulled in the mare again. For a minute or two they sat in absolute quiet. There was no sound over the horizon, no redbird sang. As he touched Beauty into reluctant life, he muttered, "Whatever it was seems to be over now."

They drove in silence—personal silence. It was as if the swamp noises had ceased for a brief purpose—to let them hear the delicate, elusive finger tappings to the southeast. Now they returned to their ordinary level: frogs croaked; water birds took off from the stagnant pools, clattering with feet and wings; birds sang in the trees; a deer barked somewhere. There were unidentifiable, vague, irritable animal noises.

Against the background of them Linden asked, "Why do you hate the South?"

Cleave turned and looked at her. "I don't hate the South. I just think that it's wrong."

"Why?"

"Slavery, for one thing."

"We've lived with slavery for hundreds of years."

"*We* haven't. Perhaps slavery isn't as bad as some people make out—I don't know. Sometimes I try to think what I would feel like if

I were a slave, but it isn't easy—perhaps it isn't possible. I know what they tell me they feel."

She looked at him awkwardly, puzzled. "I've never seen a slave whipped, not in Norfolk."

"It isn't whipping, Lin. There are worse things."

"Such as—"

He was silent for a moment, trying to formulate his ideas. At last he answered: "Virginia isn't in the main a slave-using State any longer. It used to be but it isn't now. It's a slave-breeding State. We had the slaves early and we used them—we used them to kill the soil. We took too much out of it. Tobacco burns, and there isn't anything left, so we took to breeding slaves for the rest of the South. This is a slave-exporting State. D'you like that?"

She flushed momentarily. With a courageous honesty she said: "No, I don't like it, put that way. But that isn't all of it—that isn't the whole of it. The South's the South. You hate Virginia."

"No," he repeated, shaking his head. "I don't hate Virginia. I'm a Virginian."

"I've heard you say you hate the Fall Line Towns."

He turned on her in a sudden fury. She could not parallel it, she could not remember when he had last given himself to anger in this way. "The Fall Line Towns wouldn't take us when the yellow fever hit. We were Virginians too, but they wouldn't take us. I never told you. They wouldn't take you, they wouldn't take your mother—and your mother died because of the Fall Line Towns. Don't talk to me about loving Virginia! I'm a Virginian, I live in my own country. But I haven't got to like everything about it. I haven't got to say that it's right when I know that it's wrong. I haven't got to say that it's sane when I know it's mad!"

Linden sat tensed, gathered into herself, frightened.

For a long time they drove through the swamp noises, the sound of Beauty's hoofs soft on the green of the middle strip, the wheels swishing and grating through the sand. Birds sang triumphantly. She remembered the bird that had drowned out the sound, almost even the memory of the distant cannon. She put out a hand timidly and touched him. "I'm sorry—I didn't know."

Again there was a long pause and again she broke it. "I'm truly sorry, but I can't help loving the South—everything, the birds and the sun and the water and the songs and the flowers and—even the smell of the swamp. I can't help it, I can't help it! I've got to do what I do."

Cleave had recovered himself. His voice was gentle again, and equable. "We've all of us got to do what we think right. I've not stopped you. Sometime perhaps you'll see it another way."

Almost brokenly she whispered, "I'll not stop loving you."

*   *   *

Isherwood held up the paper with an air of triumph. "Surrendered—both the forts at Hatteras Inlet!" He put the duplicate of the message down on the desk. "We're in Pamlico Sound now. Isn't a thing to stop us getting into the Albemarle. Once we're in the Albemarle isn't a thing to stop us getting into Currituck. Once we're in Currituck we're in the back door to Norfolk. They'd better get the *Merrimac* ready for sea."

Stephen wrinkled his nose. "I wouldn't like to lead an attack through the Dismal Swamp."

"That," said Isherwood with a hint of malice, "is the Army's job." He abandoned the subject. "Ironclad Committee wants a qualified assistant."

"Does that mean I've got to go?"

"It does not. You ain't qualified," answered Isherwood shortly. "They can sort out the results of their advertisements for themselves. Every damned crank in the Union has sent in plans and specifications. The desks are piled with them—the floor too. Tell me"—he glared at Stephen as if he had had some part in this—"why does every damned fool who's once seen the sea from the top of a mountain think he can design a ship?"

Stephen shrugged. "Won't need more than a glance at the first paragraph to throw out 75 per cent of them."

"That still leaves 25 per cent. Maybe there's a dozen worth the looking at," said Isherwood, "and Great Grandfather Joe to consider them." He was abruptly savage. "The way I see it, it's a race between the Army at Hatteras Inlet and Commodore Joseph Smith. Fifty-two years in the Navy of the United States, and not picked up a grain of sense in all that time! Paulding's the one man with any brain on that Commission. He'll sort 'em."

"Davis?"

"He's a bastard. Worse, he's a stupid bastard."

"What's the best of the stuff you've seen?"

Isherwood lay back in his chair, staring up at the ceiling, the first two fingers of one hand tapping on the arm of his chair. "Pook's design —S. H. Pook. I reckon we could make something of it. Maybe it isn't the answer, but it's a sound bit of work. There was one other had something in it that I saw. God!" He shook his head as if trying to free himself from intangible cobwebs. "Float 'em on barrels, build 'em on rafts, run 'em under water on the sea bottom, on wheels—they've put in plans for everything except one with wings. Maybe there's one of those too—I just didn't see."

Cautiously Stephen asked, "Ericsson put in a plan to the Committee?"

To his surprise, Isherwood was not drawn. He merely answered thoughtfully: "No, he hasn't. I can't think why."

Emboldened, Stephen asked, "You hate his guts?"

Isherwood shook his head slightly. "No, I don't hate his guts. He just makes me mad. His mouth's bigger than a furnace door. Every time he opens it he's done something better than somebody else. I remember the *Princeton*."

Stephen wrinkled his forehead. "Wasn't his gun!"

"It was a gun Stockton built 'cording to Ericsson's ideas. He could have stopped it. You can't blow up the Secretary of State and the Secretary of the Navy in one explosion without some comeback. Stockton was a crazy fool, but Ericsson could have stopped him."

"The Court of Inquiry cleared Stockton."

"Courts of Inquiry!" Isherwood spat into a well-filled sand container next to his desk. "Ericsson said he'd never come to Washington again after the *Princeton*. He's come plenty, but he doesn't come to this bureau. Since the *Iron Witch* went sour on him he's been in and out of the Treasury like a dollar bill. He talked Walker into a passel of business with the revenue cutters. Last time he wanted business he sent Delameter up. He's got an interest in Delameter's foundry. Delameter's been trying to knife me fer the last three years." He rubbed his hands over his chest with a sudden humorous gesture. "Ain't got no wounds yet."

Chapter eight

CORNELIUS BUSHNELL crossed the road in a series of short sharp rushes that were somehow typical of the man, dodging between a carriage with two ladies in it, a dray with beer, and a little cavalcade of officers on horseback. At the entrance to Willard's he almost collided with a heavily built man.

He said, "Your pardon, Mr. Delameter, sir."

They stepped out of each other's way, and Delameter said, "I did not know that you were in Washington, Bushnell?" The statement was phrased in the tone of a query.

Bushnell answered, "I am forced to spend more time almost in Washington than in New York."

"Indeed." There was a slight frostiness in Delameter's manner.

Defensively, Bushnell added at once, "We have secured the contract for the building of the *Galena*."

Delameter looked at him ponderously. "I must offer you my congratulations."

"Would you join me in a glass, sir?"

The other man half shook his head. "I was about to make my way to the Treasury . . ." He changed his mind. "I should be delighted, Mr. Bushnell."

Over the drink Bushnell said, "It is not without its responsibilities, sir."

"A new era," Delameter raised his glass.

"Exactly!" Bushnell's tone was suddenly dry. "A new era, and precious few rules to go by. I have had a disturbing discussion with the Navy Yard."

"With Mr. Isherwood?" Delameter pronounced the name with distaste.

Bushnell shook his head. "No, not Isherwood. Cashwell and a commander named Perrick."

"Cashwell I have met. Perrick I do not know."

"They say that the design is unstable, sir; that the amount of iron that Pook plans for her armor will sink the ship." His forehead creased.

Delameter, watching him with a heavy shrewdness, asked, "And what do you think?"

"I don't know." Bushnell looked up at him with a disarming frankness. "I have not built an armored ship before—nobody in this country has." With a ghost of a smile he added: "Not even Stephens. There are no calculations that are of service; there is no experience to draw upon. We—We must grope in the dark."

Delameter unbent, dropping something of his pomposity. "And you have little time for experiment."

"Sir, we have *no* time for experiment."

"You have news of the *Merrimac?*"

"She progresses—rapidly, I understand." Bushnell suddenly held up both hands in a passionate gesture. "If I knew one engineer who could check the figures for me—but who in the whole of the North has the experience?"

Delameter said, "One man only."

Bushnell lifted his head, asking the question without words.

"John Ericsson."

Bushnell frowned. "I have not the honor of his acquaintance, but I understand that he will have no dealings with the Bureau of Construction."

"He has been infamously treated, Mr. Bushnell—infamously! He is a great genius, the greatest engineer in the United States—the greatest in the world, perhaps. He could check your figures for you. I know of no one else."

"Would he?" Bushnell's tone was dubious.

"John Ericsson is a patriot, Mr. Bushnell. I can answer for him that he would sink his differences in such a situation."

Bushnell sat silent for a moment, watching his glass.

Ericsson's quarreling with the Navy Department was common knowledge in the business. He murmured at last, "He put in no design himself to the Ironclad Committee."

With the solemnity of a disciple speaking of a major prophet, Delameter said, "He wrote personally to the President—in his own hand."

"And Lincoln refused it?"

"It was ignored, Mr. Bushnell, it was ignored." He finished his drink ceremonially.

"And you still think I ought to go to him?"

"I have said, Mr. Bushnell, that Mr. Ericsson is a patriot, and I believe that you have great need for haste."

*   *   *

Cleave stared down from the rim of the dry dock, gauging the progress of the work. The *Merrimac* was complete in outline now. Forward the sides had been cut away to a level that seemed extraordinarily low, far below—if his judgment were correct—the point of the original waterline. The new superstructure was complete, a vast, sloping deckhouse that was no kin to anything that perhaps had ever floated, with the possible exception, thought Cleave, of Noah's Ark. He could not see clear to the stern, but from where he stood it seemed to him that she was not yet decked there.

Porter said: "She's all right up this end. It's aft that we had the trouble. I need between twenty and thirty more live-oak knees, Ash Cleave."

Cleave shook his head. "You've cleaned me out."

"That was two months ago. What have you got in since then?"

"Nothing."

"You mean you won't help?"

"If I had live-oak knees in the yard, I'd sell you live-oak knees," replied Cleave. "I told you that last time. But I won't go out of my way to help your troubles, John."

Porter smiled faintly. "You've got a bold tongue, Ash. One of these days it'll make trouble for you."

"It's only you, John," said Cleave simply. "I'll speak my mind to you—I always have. When I had the timber in the yard and you wanted it, I let you have it. You couldn't testify otherwise, not in any court."

Porter nodded grimly. "I couldn't, but I need the knees."

They were silent while the derrick swung, inching its load infinitely slowly over to the sloping afterend of the enormous deckhouse.

Porter said at last: "We're trying the first of the iron. We can't afford to wait on the timber, but we need it badly, Ash. Where can I get it?"

Cleave shrugged. "I don't know. They've cut up a lot of good timber for fool jobs on the batteries and such. It could be that there isn't any left in Portsmouth. Norfolk either, for that matter. I've had no call for it, so I haven't looked. What I've got I'll sell you."

"Stubborn as a mule," declared Porter heavily. "I've got to finish this ship, Ash, and I've got to finish her quickly! I don't like this thing over at the Hatteras forts. They'll take Roanoke next."

In a cascade of shouts the long iron strip was manhandled slowly into place. Men working at the bottom of the dock looked up.

Cleave said, "She won't be beautiful, John."

The constructor nodded equably.

"I'll go farther—she's going to be damned ugly. Will she float?"

"She'll float," Porter answered. "We've got to make do with what we've got. It isn't much, you know that. Ash, I mean it; you'd better keep your mouth shut round the town. There's—There's some fanatical people about these days."

"I think it's a fool war, and there are fanatics on both sides. What are you fighting for, John Porter? Don't talk to me about States' rights!"

"I'm fighting for Virginia," replied Porter soberly.

"I'm not fighting for anybody. You leave me alone, I'll leave you alone."

Porter's eyes searched his face. "Where will I get knees?" he asked again.

"You could try Petersburg, but I misdoubt it would do you any good."

"If you won't handle big timber, what do you propose to keep the Yard going with?"

"Shingles," snapped Cleave. "You try to build an ironclad with shingles!"

Porter laughed outright, a rare thing with him. "I had to ask you, Ash," he said when the gust was over. "It was an order."

"Get after that damned Yankee Cleave and dig the stuff out of him!" Cleave imitated the manner and the tone of Commodore French Forrest. "I thought it was something like that."

The derrick swung away from the ship, its slings dangling. On the bottom of the dock a man flung his head back and began to shout a long request. It was answered by somebody on the ship. More men appeared. There was a thunderous, echoing hammering. Smoke ballooned up from a forge on the keelblocks. Cleave had an impression of frenetic energy.

Porter's face had a quiet pride in it.

For a while they watched the progress of the work. Another long strip of iron was lifted and swung outward and landed with elaborate care. There was a fresh chorus of shouting. When it died, Porter said: "I've never known men to work like them. There's an enthusiasm . . ."

"You always could make men work, John."

Earnestly the constructor shook his head. "No"—he shook it again almost angrily—"it's not that. They want to work; they know what they're trying to do; they know that the country's behind them. Have you seen the request to be allowed to work overtime?"

"I'm not shown documents like that, John."

With a curious delicacy Porter said, "Your daughter was behind much of that, Ash."

"I know." Cleave's voice was expressionless.

"She's helped us a lot—as much, I think, as any woman could. She's a good girl, Ash. I'd like you to know that I admire you."

"You, John? Why?"

Porter hesitated, then he said tentatively, as if he were searching for unaccustomed words: "Because she's 100 per cent and more for the South, and you are what you are, and you're friends—still."

"Old Sam says I ought to beat her."

"You won't." Porter's voice was warm. "But *I* might, if I were in your place."

"The young have a right to their own opinions," said Cleave. "They have to live their own lives."

* * *

Improbably, the grass had already grown upon the ramparts. Linden lay on a cushion of it, in the lee of the bank out of the searching wind. It was hot in the shelter. Jeriel sat against a stump of timber, picking his teeth with a blade. Revell leaned back on his elbows, standing more or less upright, scuffing his feet through it.

Linden continued with the commination. "You haven't shaved for four days," she said evenly and acidly. "You aren't overly clean. It could be that you haven't washed for four days either. You've grown lazy as an overfed hound dog, Revell Jordan. This whole battery's running to seed. You haven't any of you done an honest day's work since you finished the earthworks."

He shrugged his shoulders lazily while Jeriel squinted up at him, closing one eye against the sun. "Ain't a thing to do, Lindy."

"You were going to make lieutenant by August." She squinted up at him in turn. "August's gone!" she snapped with finality.

"Ain't no promotion for sittin' behind a gun that you don't fire."

"Then shift to the Rifle Patriots."

"Ah, hell, Lindy!"

"You'd be in Portsmouth. You could get leave nights when you were off duty——" She had an uneasy memory of old Sam; her cheeks flushed a little, but no one noticed.

Jeriel said softly: "Old man Forrest, he told Cap'n Etheredge he'd had a letter from the Yankees sayin' they'd give a million dollars to anybody who'd put a light to th' *Merrimac*."

Linden protested in a fruitless attempt to put the record straight: "He said he'd had a letter *saying* that the Yankees said——"

"Same thin'." Jeriel selected another grass blade.

A squadron of five gulls, maneuvering against the hot wind, found the updraft from the glacis of the battery and soared for an instant, controlled and superb.

Jeriel's murmur overtopped the silence again. "They could shet in yo' eye easy as look at you, Rev."

"Shut up, Jeriel! Revell, you'd be much better off with the Rifle Patriots. You'd have a chance of promotion at least. You'd have something to do. And you'd be in the town, not 'way out here on the beaches. I'd talk to Jetson Jett for you."

"That's a fool name," said Revell. "What's the matter with you, Lindy? Why's this so important all of a sudden?"

"Ever since the Yankees took the Hatteras forts they've been getting worse at the Yard. I can't find out things. Mr. Porter tells me what he wants to tell me—and that's not enough. I want to know more!"

" 'N you want me to find it out."

"They beat my ass if I go in the Yard." Jeriel was just stating a fact, not complaining.

"I'll think about it." Revell fenced for time.

With a quaint lilt in her voice Linden said: "You'll not think about it, Rev. You'll just put off thinking about it. You'll make up your mind here and now!"

He sat down beside her and put out a hand and started rubbing her shoulder. His hand was hard and it hurt a little. He squeezed the curve of the flesh, gripping with his fingers. "Would I see you sometimes—nights, Lindy?"

She remembered Sam's words exactly: "One o' these days one o' the hot-blooded young men in this town's goin' to come for payment." Revell was one of the hot-blooded young men. She said absently, keeping all significance out of the words, "I'm around."

Revell's hand began to search, slipping down under her shoulder. She made it as difficult as she could without being obvious. This was the crucial point now. She heard Jeriel get up; she could not move to see what he was doing because that would have freed the way to her breast. It could not be that he was being delicate—Jeriel was hardly that delicate. Perhaps he thought she needed time, scope, freedom to work out her play. She didn't. She needed him—there. Revell's hand was forcing itself beneath her arm. If she checked him abruptly, he would sulk; if she slapped his face, he would refuse to make the change. It was as simple as that. She lay and endured, wondering how to end it. Damn old Sam! The hand levered her shoulder up. From the position in which she lay on her stomach, in the angle of the rampart, it was impossible to put more than a dead weight of resistance on it. Then, raucously across the soughing of the wind, she heard the roar of the sergeant's voice. "Get th' hell out o' the gun pit, Jeriel! Rev Jordan, I tol' you to keep that Chris'-forsaken boy outa the gun pits. I'll take you up before the capt'n."

"God damn!" Revell climbed up from the ground. "Jeriel, I've told you eleventy hunder' times—"

With a swift motion Linden swung herself off the ground and added her voice to the tumult. "Jeri," she called, "Come out of there! You know that you oughtn't—"

His head appeared over the top of the ramparts. His eye caught Linden's, and there was the ghost of a wink in it.

"Go down and get the boat ready," she ordered. "We're due home." Then, as he turned away, she said to Revell, "Are you going to come?"

He knew that the moment of decision had arrived. There seemed no other way. She hardly ever came out to the battery now; he scarcely saw her. If he were billeted with the Rifle Patriots, he would be in the town. If he had leave at nights . . . He said abruptly, "Yes."

"Aa-ah!" She let out a deep breath of satisfaction. "Thank you, Rev."

In the distance Jeriel was bending over the boat. They could hear his voice—he was singing a new Army song that had just become popular:

> *"I got à gal*
> *In Cumberland Gap.*
> *She's got a babby*
> *That calls me Pap."*

There was a note of profound derision in his voice.

Linden, looking up into the wind and the blue water and the wave ripples that fanned through the grass with the gusts, began to laugh.

Chapter nine

BUSHNELL walked, as always, apprehensively. He was apprehensive now about Ericsson's opinion. If Ericsson condemned the *Galena* on the specifications that he had given him—and to himself Bushnell admitted that it was wholly possible that he would condemn the *Galena*—would he be justified in asking for a cancellation of the contract? On the other hand, would Ericsson necessarily be right? He had only Delameter's word for that. It had against it a score of opinions garnered last night in a hurried canvass at the club—each opinion worse than the last. Ericsson was a man of failure.

Bushnell crossed Moore Street anxiously and walked on, deep

in thought. Ericsson's first flame engine, much publicized, much trumpeted, was a failure. Ericsson withdrew the "Novelty" in the contest with the Englishman Stephenson for the steam locomotive. The caloric engine was a failure—at least for large plants. His brows wrinkled still further as though the point were of a more than academic importance. Two of the men at the club had condemned it out of hand; three had offered vague and diffident support. Did Ericsson really invent the screw propeller? Opinion seemed to be about equally divided. He had made no money out of it anyway. Six at the club had argued the *Princeton* disaster. Whatever it was, wherever the blame lay, the gun had blown up, the Secretary of State and the Secretary of the Navy had been killed, and Congress had never paid Ericsson for his work. The *Massachusetts* had had a first success, but in the end the engines had been taken out of her. The *Iron Witch*—Bushnell remembered the *Iron Witch;* he had won money betting against her. The *Ericsson,* the ship that the inventor had named after' himself—Bushnell tried to remember O'Neill's precise words: "I could forgive the ship capsizin' even in New York Harbor, I could that. But b'Jesus, I couldn't forgive what he wrote after! D'you know what he called her? 'The finest and strongest ship perhaps ever built.' And she capsized in the harbor—in the harbor, m'boy!"

Bushnell came to the corner of Beach Street and turned down it apprehensively.

The old, shrunken Irishwoman who looked after Ericsson and guarded him, some said, like a house dog, opened the door grudgingly. "It's you," she said, and let him in.

Ericsson was seated on the piano stool, raised on a rough wooden box to give him height. He was crouched over the drawing board. Without looking up he said: "Sit down for a minute, sir. I shall, if you will permit me, finish this small matter."

Bushnell sat down in an uncomfortable chair. He had time to study the austerities of the room. A long table next to his own chair was covered with books and papers, drawings and diagrams. Ericsson sat at another plain table with a drawing board on it and a small fretted rack beyond him that held instruments and inks and pencils. There was a desk that had an air of little use standing to the left across from the window. It had rounded ends, and marquetry outlining the drawers and along the sides. Otherwise the room was undecorated, a workroom dedicated to a single purpose.

After perhaps a minute and a half Ericsson straightened himself stiffly. He turned round on the piano stool. "Good day to you, Mr. Bushnell," he said, and sat staring in a potent silence.

Bushnell had time to permit his memory to race back over the long list of failures and to remember, almost with a sense of shock, that each man in turn had declared: "And yet he's a genius—there's no doubt about that—he's a genius."

The man opposite him gave an impression of immense size. He was broad, his shoulders were powerful. His head had a superb sculptural quality, a composition of wide, deep-etched planes, enormous strong curves and hollows. His hair had receded a long way over the domed forehead. On either side it fell, massing heavily over the ears. Dark, iron-gray whiskers matched it, covering the sides of his cheek and throat. His upper lip and chin were shaved. The mouth was wide and determined. The eyes had more than a touch of choler. It was the head of an arrogant, brilliant man who believed utterly in himself.

He said without preamble, "She will easily carry the load you propose."

For a reason that he could not explain even to himself, Bushnell felt a quite disproportionate elation. But there was still his second question; he had the impression that Ericsson was waiting for it to be repeated. "But will she be vulnerable, sir?"

"She will stand a six-inch shot at a respectable distance." The engineer slid down from the piano stool and stood square and granitic. It was apparent that the business was complete.

Bushnell said: "I am most grateful to you, sir. I have an explicit confidence in your judgment."

The big Swede seemed to thaw. He did not smile, but there was a relaxation of his facial muscles. He bowed very slightly, and it was as if a statue has acknowledged a courtesy. Then he said, with something that in another man might almost have passed for humility: "Mr. Bushnell, have you time at your disposal—now—to examine the plan of a floating battery, which I believe to be absolutely impregnable to the heaviest shot or shell?"

Bushnell jerked up out of his chair in surprise. "Good God, Mr. Ericsson, for three months I have lived with nothing else in my mind! I have examined a half-hundred plans. I have talked with designers and inventors and engineers." He stretched out a finger with unconscious drama. "In all that time this is all that I have found."

With a diffidence that sat oddly on him, Ericsson appeared to hesitate. Then he walked ponderously across the room and stretched up to a high shelf and took from it a box coated with a soft gray dust. He lowered it, looked at it doubtfully, suspiciously, and then blew at the dust and watched the resultant cloud with sadness. Finally he placed it on the table and opened it.

"Sir, the Russians are the hereditary enemies of my native land." Ericsson peered down into the open box, and his fingers disturbed a small sheaf of papers. He took these out and laid them on the table. "In September of the year 1854, France being at war with Russia, I sent to the Emperor of the French the design and model of a floating battery which I conceived could destroy by itself the whole fleet of Russia."

As if he were under a hypnotic influence, Bushnell moved to the table and peered down into the box. Through the hesitant screen of Ericsson's fingers he could see that it held a model of wood or of cardboard. From his height it was impossible to guess at its shape and purpose. Impelled by something outside himself, Bushnell asked, "The emperor rejected it?" And, as he spoke the words, he thought: Another failure.

Delicately from the box Ericsson withdrew a single fold of paper, heavy and embossed with a crown. He opened it and read:

> The Emperor has himself examined with the greatest care the new system of naval attack which you have submitted to him. His Majesty directs me to have the honour of informing you that he has found your ideas very ingenious and worthy of the celebrated name of their author; but the Emperor thinks that the result to be obtained would not be proportionate to the expenses or to the small number of guns which could be brought into use.

Ericsson folded the paper again. "The emperor rejected it then," he said with a heavy bitterness. "The President of the United States, Mr. Bushnell, has rejected it now." His hands dipped suddenly into the box, the fingers curved under the object in it and lifted up the model.

Bushnell saw what looked to him like a raft superimposed upon a shallow boatlike hull. It had, at what he took to be the stern end, a propeller and a rudder. On the raft itself was what looked like a circular deckhouse. In it it had two elliptical gun ports from each of which the muzzle of a gun protruded.

"It is my theory," said the big Swede—and his words held in them the spirit of absolute conviction—"that the principal desideratum in a fighting ship is that she should offer the smallest possible target to her enemy. It is essential that, as in the *Princeton,* her engines should be below the level of the water and therefore immune to the enemy's fire; that she should have no projections above the water other than are essential to house her guns. Their number, sir, is of no importance provided that they are impregnable. This, sir, is a revolving turret."

With an extreme delicacy, surprising in fingers as strong and purposeful as his, Ericsson took the turret between forefinger and thumb and revolved it slowly in a circle so that the muzzles of the guns swept round from bow to stern in a great semicircle, and continued the sweep about the other side of the ship and back to the bows again. "The turret is designed to be built of a thickness of nine inches of steel. It could be built, if necessity arose, of twelve. No gun on earth, sir—not even my own gun—could penetrate twelve inches of steel. Moreover, the shots will not hit upon a flat surface; they will glance off the curve of it. There is nothing else for an enemy to hit except the flat of the armored deck."

"It would float?"

Distantly Ericsson answered: "I have designed it to float. It will draw with full load—eleven feet of water. Its purpose is to be used inside harbors and in shallow estuaries, but it will make sea voyages with safety, Mr. Bushnell." He became technical, describing the propelling machinery, the size of the propeller demanded by it, the machinery for turning the turret, the shape and purpose of the raftlike upper section. The habitual tone of sadness left his deep, heavy voice and enthusiasm replaced it—eagerness and an absolute certainty. At times his accent became guttural, the vowels broadening, flattening in a reversion to his native Swedish. At times an English accent made its way to the surface.

He spoke with a direct lucidity so that Bushnell could follow the original and intricate technical details. He felt himself carried along on the flood of the man's words, caught in his enthusiasms, dedicated instantly and completely to his banner. He believed in this strange construction, this leap into the future. He believed in this man.

"Wooden ships," said Ericsson with a somber, scathing condemnation, "are as anachronistic as the mammoth."

Bushnell knew that he was right.

*   *   *

Gideon Welles still wore his wig. His beard was as biblical as ever, but against the background of his Hartford home the man seemed softened, more approachable, more human. He brushed aside Bushnell's anxious apologies for the intrusion. He knew his Bushnell.

He rumbled, the words seeming to come from deep down in his protuberant stomach: "Matters of vital urgency, Mr. Bushnell—what are they?" His head shot forward as if worked with a spring. "You have found that the *Galena* will not float?"

"The *Galena* will float, Mr. Secretary." Bushnell contradicted him with a remarkable access of courage. "She will float and she will withstand shot; I have an absolute assurance of that. I have to report to you a matter of an infinitely greater significance. I have seen the design for a ship"—he paused, with unconscious dramatic effect—"the design for a ship which in my belief would sink the *Galena* with ease."

Welles stared at him from under shaggy eyebrows. Finally, after a prolonged silence, he permitted himself a single deflationary word, "Indeed."

Bushnell's enthusiasm lent him temerity. "I will go farther than that, Mr. Secretary, sir. She will sink any ship in commission or under construction for any navy in the world."

"Including the *Merrimac?*" Welles darted the question at him like an old lion with its claws unexpectedly extended.

"Including the *Merrimac.*" Bushnell answered him bluntly.

Welles' shrewd eyes traveled over him. Bushnell often had enthusiasms but this was something beyond any previous experience of the man. He was too timid ordinarily to stretch his neck out for the ax. Cautiously the Secretary asked, "How large and how costly is this paragon?"

"Sir," replied Bushnell with a simple dignity that for the first time revealed the whole man, "she is neither large nor costly. She could be built swiftly—I believe within a hundred days—and I would be prepared to undertake her construction myself."

Welles pounced again. "Whose is the design?"

"John Ericsson's."

"Ericsson!" Welles was startled into a rare profanity. "A damned difficult man."

"A man of many failures." Bushnell conceded the point at once. "But this, sir, I believe will be a triumph."

Welles accepted the statement without comment. Abruptly he said, "Show me the plans!"

* * *

"The Secretary has authorized me"—Bushnell was a shade pompous among his equals—"to approach you gentlemen and propose a consortium."

"All right." Winslow's voice was brusque. "I don't want to know what Uncle Gideon said. What we've got to do is to convince the Committee. Have you brought the plans?"

Bushnell fumbled in his case and produced a sheaf of papers. He held them clutched in his hand. "I would prefer, before I show them to you, to explain briefly Mr. Ericsson's subaquatic theory."

"My God!" exclaimed Winslow. "All right, if you must."

Griswold leaned back in the only comfortable chair in the office and watched the interplay of emotion between the two men with an unconcealed amusement. Bushnell invariably irritated Winslow; there were always difficulties; but in the end they worked together surprisingly well, each supplying something that the other lacked.

As Bushnell hesitated, Winslow said impatiently: "Come on, Cornelius, come on for God's sake! What *is* a subaquatic theory?"

"It is Mr. Ericsson's theory that an armored fighting ship should present the minimum target to the enemy, that its structure should be raftlike, with the deck armored so that shot would glance from it, and that it should carry a small number of guns—preferably two only—in a turret so thick as to be impregnable."

Winslow put his head on one side. "Put like that, Cornelius, it sounds like sense." The hostility and impatience were gone. "But if you have only two guns—" he checked for a moment—"how does he place them? One on each side?"

"The two guns are in parallel," replied Bushnell. "The turret revolves with them. It is Mr. Ericsson's theory that his armored ship would choose the angle from which it proposed to attack the enemy, would approach at superior speed on a line on which the enemy's guns could not bear, would select its point of aim, fire, revolve its turret to protect the reloading of the guns while it withdrew, and attack again from another angle of choice."

Griswold said, "Sounds remarkably like sense to me."

Bushnell spread out the plans with a flourish. Then, bending down, he lifted out the model.

"Christ Almighty!" exclaimed Winslow. "That's a hell of a contraption."

For an hour and a half they wrangled, fighting over the details of the conception.

It was Griswold who ended the debate. Wearily he said: "All right, let me talk! It all comes to this: we can't any of the three of us pronounce on a thing like this. Either we trust Ericsson"—he looked from one to the other grimly—"or we don't. There's no more to it than that."

Bushnell said promptly, "I do."

Griswold nodded, "Me too."

Winslow grunted ungraciously, "Guess I'll have to."

"Magnificent," said Griswold ironically. "If we're all agreed, we've got to decide on a plan of campaign. If Great-Granddaddy Smith sees that model naked, he'll have an apoplectic stroke. Paulding we might be able to argue into it. Davis will turn down anything as a matter of principle; he has up to now and he'll go on doing it."

Winslow grunted again. "Pressure. We've got to put pressure on the Committee."

"How?" Bushnell looked worried.

"We could start with Seward," replied Winslow.

"Smith's the oldest serving officer in the Navy. He don't give a damn for Secretaries of State. We could start with the President and we'll end with him. There ain't nobody else that Smith would take notice of. Seward can give us a letter to the President."

"Will he?"

Bushnell smiled for the first time in the discussion. "Mr. Welles said that if we considered invoking the aid of Mr. Seward, it would not be necessary for us to stress *his* interest."

Griswold flung himself back in the chair and slapped his thigh, laughing. "The damned old fox!"

*   *   *

Winslow said to the bellboy, "Two bottles of bourbon, one of rye, and a bucket of ice!" He waited until the door closed, then he stretched himself and began to laugh. "Trouble is, nobody ever believes the way a nation conducts its affairs. If we're right, this thing will win the war. If we're wrong, it could lose it. And the Committee agrees to look at it because Abraham Lincoln tells an anecdote." He flung himself down in the armchair, draped one long leg over the arm of it, contriving somehow to make himself look disjointed, ungainly, inordinately tall. He lifted his hands as though he held something in them, the fingers separated widely. He twisted the invisible object one way and another; held it up, down, sideways—even as the President had held the model of Ericsson's ironclad. His head followed the model as he turned it, leaning awkwardly, ludicrously. In a voice that mimicked with a complete fidelity Lincoln's diffident, hesitant tone, he said: " 'All I have to say is what the girl said when she stuck her foot into the stocking. It strikes me there's something in it!' " In his own voice he said coarsely, "Damme, I need a drink!"

Griswold watched him coldly. "You'd do fine in vaudeville. Can you think of any other way we could have got that old fool Smith persuaded?"

Winslow snapped at him, "By a direct order."

"And Smith would have washed his hands of it—that's what he wanted! He'd have said the President ordered it; and nobody would have questioned it, nobody would have examined it. Any fool"—Griswold was deliberately insulting—"can imitate Lincoln, but Lincoln's a damned clever man. Smith's got to take account of it now and he can't turn it down without reason. He'll have to account to the President, else."

Bushnell said: "I think you are correct, John. I do not think that the President is convinced—not certainly on our side—or he would have ordered it. But I think he believes precisely what he said: that there is something in it. He wants it considered. Smith has called a meeting for tomorrow."

"Davis is the man I'm scared of," said Winslow. "He's a sour bastard."

"Believes in nothing." Griswold nodded. "He's the man you've got to look out for, Bushnell. Paulding's got an open mind. Smith will follow the President. Davis won't."

The bellboy came in with the drinks.

Over the tinkle of the glasses Winslow said, "It would have helped if Uncle Gideon had been there."

"It wouldn't," contradicted Griswold rudely. "The Committee's been set up. The Committee's got to do the considering. He'd only have made Davis madder still—Paulding too, maybe."

"He will be back from Hartford by tomorrow evening," said Bushnell soberly. "I am sure that he will help us."

"We're going to need it," snapped Griswold, pouring himself out a stiff half-tumbler of bourbon and filling the glass with ice. "We're sure as hell going to need it."

*   *   *

"Mr. Secretary"—Bushnell was crouched in the chair across the desk from Welles, the picture of supplication—"Mr. Secretary, I am in despair. Commodore Smith I have persuaded, though since the President left the Navy Office yesterday I believe every officer in the department has been to him to talk of Ericsson's past failures. Sir"— once again the innate dignity of the little man pierced through—"they were not failures. Mr. Ericsson is ahead of his time. It is inevitable that he should meet with difficulties. Commodore Paulding, I think, sir, is reasonable. I have talked to them both. I have explained. They are willing to build a trial vessel if Captain Davis will join with them. They see the necessities, sir. To Captain Davis I am unable to talk. He does not purpose to listen to me, sir. He has rejected the plan out of hand."

Welles looked at him benevolently. "What did he say?"

"He handed the model to me, Mr. Secretary, and he said: 'Take it away—take it away! Take the little thing home and worship it, it won't be idolatry. It's in the image of nothing in the heaven above or on the earth beneath or in the waters under the earth.' "

"Ah!" Gideon Welles put his fingers together without even the ghost of a smile. After a time he asked, "And what do you propose to do?"

"Mr. Ericsson," said Bushnell firmly, "must come to Washington and plead the cause for himself. I am not able. I am not worthy of it."

Welles looked benevolently at him again. "I would not go so far as to say that, Mr. Bushnell, but I think that Mr. Ericsson would be advised to attend. If you believe that you can induce him to come, I will meet you both here in this office."

Miserably Bushnell said: "Mr. Secretary, I do not know that I will be able to induce him to come. His views about the Bureaus . . ."

"I am aware of his views as to the Department." Welles' expression was remote. "Nevertheless it is necessary that he should come. I would suggest, Mr. Bushnell, that you inform him that the climate of opinion is favorable but that only he can lend to the subject the essential conviction."

Bushnell looked up at him wide-eyed.

"I will endeavor," said Welles, rising, "to secure that favorable climate."

* * *

Stephen stood with his back to the wall, watching intently. His hands rested against the warm plaster. He was wholly in the dark as to the reason for his presence in the room. Commodore Smith had snapped the order without even a suggestion of explanation.

Smith sat now at the center of the long mahogany table. Commodore Paulding sat at his right hand, Captain Davis at his left. Davis looked ill-tempered and acrimonious. The table in front of him was clear, not even a pad of paper on it. Paulding had a small pile of notes, Smith a thin book.

Ericsson came in with the messenger, his jaw forward, his whole bearing confident and aggressive. The short man who followed him, Stephen knew, must be Bushnell.

He's scared, Stephen thought.

There was a little buzz through the room. The secretaries at Stephen's end exchanged quick confidences. The place had the air of a court-martial; a palpable hostility filled it.

Smith greeted the inventor. To Stephen there seemed something shamefaced in his manner. "Will you be seated, Mr. Ericsson?" The big Swede sat down heavily. Smith went on at once hurriedly, too hurriedly: "I regret—that is to say, this Committee regrets—that it is unable to recommend—that we are unable, that is, to place an order for the construction of an ironclad war vessel according to the plans submitted to us by yourself."

Stephen saw the engineer's head snap up. He missed the first fleeting expression, but, as Ericsson turned to look at Bushnell beside him, he saw that the Swede's face was black with fury and at the same time full of a bewildered pain. Davis was staring out the window. Paulding looked straight ahead of him. Only Smith watched Ericsson from the Board table.

There was a brief, pregnant silence.

Ericsson thumped both hands down on the arms of his chair. He turned away from Bushnell and half rose. Then he sat back again with a gesture that reminded Stephen of an old lion freeing its mane. He began, his voice harsh with the harsh conflict of emotions: "I understood—" He checked himself. With an extraordinary speed he appeared to master his emotion. When he spoke again his voice was cool and direct. "Is it permitted to me to ask the Board's reasons?"

Davis made an irritable, negative gesture, but Smith, watching the engineer, replied: "It is permitted, Mr. Ericsson. In the judgment of this Committee the weight of iron in the superstructure of your vessel, and particularly the weight contained in the gun turret, must affect the inherent stability of the vessel. In the opinion of its members this Committee considers that it would be impossible for your vessel to survive in a seaway. At an inclination of more than fifteen degrees—"

Leisurely and with a supreme confidence Ericsson rose from his chair. He stood with his feet wide apart, staring down at Smith. The chairman of the Committee bit off his sentence.

Ericsson said: "Since it is apparent that the Committee is in complete ignorance of the laws determining stability, it is obvious that it is incumbent upon me to offer it an explanation."

Stephen saw Davis turn angrily and begin a protest, but Smith stopped him.

"If you will consider first the beam of the vessel of my design in relation to its length . . ." Ericsson disregarded utterly the captain; he addressed himself to Smith and Paulding, moving his eyes from one to the other slowly. His voice was loud but he spoke with care—coolly, reasonably, marshaling his sentences with a direct and brilliant logic. He reduced the masses of the ship to their constituent elements, he dissected the effects of leverage. He showed—his fingers drawing diagrams in the empty air—the action of the turret in relation to the movement of the ship.

Stephen listened with a constrained fascination. The secretaries who had come to scoff listened with him. The whole room was caught in the fire and the lucidity of the man's words.

Patiently, simply, with an almost spiritual intensity, Ericsson hammered out his theories. He produced analogous examples. His comparisons were simple, clear, understandable, and practical. And all the time he stood with his feet eighteen inches apart, square as a wall, defiant as a rock in a high sea.

Even Davis began to listen, to concentrate, to comprehend.

The big Swede ended abruptly: "That, gentlemen, is the theory of stability." He sat down, but before Smith could answer him he added, "After what I have said, I deem it your duty to the country to give me an order to build the vessel before I leave this room."

The secretary nearest to Stephen let out a faint, thin whistle of shock. Stephen watched Smith.

The old man passed a hand across his eyes. He sat for a long moment shuttered by it. When he spoke again his tone was wholly different. There were in it respect and admiration. "Mr. Ericsson, I have to thank you for a most clear and cogent thesis. We shall need time to consider it again. Could we trespass upon your good will by asking you to meet us again at one o'clock?"

Ericsson got up with heavy dignity. "I will be here."

* * *

Stephen squeezed into the Secretary's room in the wake of the others. Welles was leaning across his desk shaking Ericsson's hand. Above the noise and the bustle he could hear little. He did hear Ericsson's voice boom out "two hundred and seventy-five thousand dollars," and took that to be a contractual price. Somebody repeated the phrase "a hundred days." Then Welles got to his feet and there was a silence.

Welles said: "Commodore Smith, do you recommend that a contract be entered into between the Department and Captain Ericsson for the construction of his vessel?"

Smith nodded and said firmly, "Yes."

Welles turned to Paulding. "Commodore Paulding, do you so recommend?"

Paulding answered, "Yes, sir."

He turned slowly, almost malevolently, to Davis. "Captain Davis?"

Davis hesitated, and then said, "Yes."

Welles turned for the last time to Ericsson. "Captain Ericsson, the rebels have worked four months already on the *Merrimac*. The need for haste is desperate. I charge you to use all possible speed. You will begin to order your materials upon your return to New York tomorrow. A contract will follow. You have promised that you would complete your vessel in a hundred days. This is the fourteenth day of September!"

Chapter ten

"I UNDERSTAND," said Commodore Smith in his slow, tired voice, "that Mr. Pinkerton was a railroad detective. It was not to be expected that he or the men that he employs would have a knowledge of ships."

The old man was getting at somebody higher up—that much was obvious to Stephen. So far as he knew, Welles had not employed Pinkerton. It must have been Scott's responsibility, or perhaps McClellan's;—more probably McClellan's. He watched Isherwood push a small sheaf of reports across the untidy desk.

Isherwood said, "These are valueless."

"The requirement," said Smith, " is for a man with an intimate knowledge of Portsmouth and the Navy Yard, and a special knowledge of the *Merrimac* and her engines." He kept his eyes fixed on the sheaf of papers.

Stephen felt a chill along his spine. This was the reason he had been ordered to attend the conference: they wanted him to go to Portsmouth; they wanted him to spy on the progress of the *Merrimac!*

"A knowledge of the first date upon which they could hope to float her must determine our policy toward the rate of building which Mr. Ericsson uses with his ship."

Isherwood said, "It must determine also the size and the disposition of Commodore Goldsborough's forces in Hampton Roads."

"Goldsborough," said Smith testily, "can wait upon events. It is the long-term view of their potentiality that is presently of importance to us."

Still neither man looked at Stephen. He thought bitterly: This is why Isherwood wouldn't tell me anything about it! He sat silent, waiting for the next move.

Smith lifted the papers and went through the motions of reading them. When he looked up it was with a suddenness that made Stephen's cold spine tingle. There was a chill glare in his old blue eyes. "You have the necessary qualifications, Mr. Knott. Are you prepared to undertake the investigation?"

Stephen knew that they had expected him to volunteer. He resented the way in which Isherwood had, in a sense, tricked him into this. He was aware that both men were momentarily hostile toward him. Well, he was hostile toward them. Soberly he answered: "If I am ordered to make the attempt, I will make it to the best of my ability, but I think that the commodore should understand that I was bred in Portsmouth, that I spent a considerable part of my recent Service career there, and that I am known. Portsmouth is a small town, sir. I must be known to every man, woman, and child."

Isherwood grunted. "That has been considered. It is our opinion that the advantage of your familiarity with the area is sufficient to outweigh the obvious dangers. The plan is that you will be landed at a point of your selection close to the end of Lincoln Street at dusk immediately after the cessation of work for the day. This coincides, owing to the hours of extra work now being performed, with the arrival of the evening train from Richmond. You will enter the Yard as an officer from the Navy Department at Richmond to make a specific investigation in the engine room of the *Merrimac*. According to these reports"—he reached over the desk and tapped the papers that were still in the commodore's hand—"it is customary for three or four men—gang foremen and the like—to remain behind after the guard has carried out a search of the hull, to measure up work done during the day and to prepare estimates for the morning. I have here a list of the men most likely still to be aboard. If any of them are well known to you, it might"—he accented the word deliberately—"influence our decision."

Stephen knew why Isherwood was angry. He knew that Isherwood had presented him to Smith as a willing protégé. He knew also that

with this list Isherwood was offering him, reluctantly perhaps, a way
out. He read down the seven names carefully, searching his memory
with each of them. Oddly enough, only one of them was familiar:
Southey Rew, he was a machinist—a foreman machinist by now, probably. Did Rew know him sufficiently well for it to be a danger? He
looked directly at Isherwood for the first time, and was surprised to see
something that looked like sympathy in the engineer's eyes.

Stephen said: "Southey Rew—he was with the gang for two days
after you came. Then he was shifted to the *Germantown*."

Isherwood searched his memory in turn. "Tall man, with an under-
slung jaw?"

Stephen nodded.

"The ship is very badly lighted, according to the Pinkerton man."

"He went aboard?"

"No," replied Isherwood with disgust in his voice, "he stood outside the main gate, and guessed."

"How do I get up the river?" asked Stephen, and he was aware that
both men were now looking at him intently.

Isherwood answered softly: "That has been arranged. There'll be no
difficulty in getting through the Harbor Guard in daylight. There may
be a Yard patrol in the Eastern Branch that will have to be dodged at
the end, but that's all that directly concerns you."

Stephen drew a breath. "I'll try it."

*   *   *

The younger of the two oystermen said, "She's on time, barring four-
five minutes." He watched the smoke between the houses with a judicious eye. "Boat patrol ain't come out yet. We'll put you ashore like you
said, between Baker's yard and the boat shed." He put the helm down
and brought the boat round. She heeled lazily to the light evening wind
and stood across the tide.

Stephen felt a high tension growing within him. It was not so dark
as he had hoped—or perhaps it was that his eyes were strained to an
abnormal acuity. The tide was stronger in the middle of the channel,
and the boat began to move crabwise down the Branch with it.

The oysterman said, "Come up, you old bastard!" and brought her
closer to the wind.

Stephen searched until he defined the limits of the Cleave yard. The
stacks of lumber were smaller than he had remembered them, but a big
new pile of shingles gleamed whitely in the dusk. Cleave's boat was at

the ramshackle pier, and he thought that he could see Linden's skiff inshore of it. He was aware of a welling of emotion.

The train reached the waterfront, curving into the depot with a fuss of steam and whistling, the sound of the bell made mellow and ecclesiastical across the water. The air seemed to fill with noises.

Stephen said, "All right, take her in when you can!"

In the bow the other oysterman called, "There's th' patrol boat now, crabbin' over to t'other shore like always."

The man at the tiller grunted: "Ain't no call to worry 'bout her. You'll be up to the houses afore she comes this side again."

The light left the water suddenly as they came into the evening shadow of the boathouses and the buildings on the bank. The boat's keel grated on a slope of rubbish, and Stephen jumped ashore.

*   *   *

The sentry at the main gate called the sergeant, and the sergeant read the pass that Isherwood had given him and said: "Lootenant Vickery from Richmond. Okay, Lootenant."

Stephen had never seen the man before—he was certain of that. Casually he asked, "There'll still be somebody aboard the *Merrimac?*"

"Bound to be," replied the sergeant indifferently.

The sentry on the inside of the gate challenged a man coming from the Yard and demanded the reply for the night.

The man said, "Mobjack," and Stephen knew that he had acquired the countersign. Isherwood had said, "Hang about any main gate three minutes and you'll get the challenge and reply." He would have to tell Isherwood that he'd been right.

He walked away from the main gate, striding confidently toward the dry dock. Isherwood had said it would be easy, but this was too easy. Isherwood had said: "Imagine you're a Southern officer wantin' to see somethin' in the Washington Navy Yard—as if there was anything worth seeing! All you'd have to do is show a pass at the main gate. *Is* there anything else?" And Stephen, sitting back on his chair in Isherwood's office, had considered the security of the Washington Yard, and said, "No."

He approached the dry dock with the confidence of old knowledge. He was certain, though the Pinkerton man's report had omitted the fact, that the gangway to the ship would be opposite the point where the road came from the head of the timber dock to the edge of the granite slabs of the dry-dock basin. He knew it from an ancient appreciation of senior officers' convenience. There would be a sentry at the head of it. There would probably be a sentry at either side of the caisson bridgeway. They were unimportant—he had the password for the night and he still had his pass. It was the Pinkerton man's specimen of the pass in use that had determined the whole affair. Yet he walked stiffly, feeling the short hairs on the nape of his neck standing as if charged with electricity.

The Yard was utterly silent. He could hear nothing, not even voices, as he walked between the echoing sheds, only the sound of his own footfalls, brisk and determined. He came out beyond the last of the sheds. The evening wind had fallen clear away now; the air was utterly still. He could see, as he had known he would see, the glow of the lantern at the gangway. He walked toward it with assurance—all the while feeling the goose pimples on the back of his neck and down his spine.

The sentry challenged him. Stephen gave the reply, and was passed, and went up the gangway. It led to the upper deck of the enormous sloping deckhouse that the Pinkerton man had described. It was impossible to see the clear outline of the ship nor could he pause to try to determine it in the darkness, but he could see and judge roughly the size of the deckhouse in relation to the length of the ship and he could see below him the plain unbroken surface of the new decking of the bow. Making quick calculations, and with the gooseflesh creeping farther and farther down his body, he reached the upper deck and the light of another lantern set at the head of another ladder that this time led below. He kept close to the lantern so that the light would shine against his legs, but there was no one on the deck, and he went down it.

His knowledge of the old *Merrimac* was of no help to him now. This was a new, strange shape grafted upon her. He could see nothing except the faint glow of a third lantern at the foot of the ladder and the almost indiscernible outline of the nearer gun ports. His feet touched a wooden deck, and at once a voice so close, so apparently threatening that he jerked an arm up to protect himself, demanded, "Who are you?"

"Vickery," he snapped out, "Lootenant Vickery. Department of Steam Engineering, Richmond."

Isherwood had said: "Richmond—remember you come from Richmond. Use it every time. They'll hate higher Headquarters like hell—everybody does—but they're scared of it."

The voice snorted, "Engineers' Department!" seemed to consider something, and then said, "Ugh."

Stephen asked with an abrupt authority, "Is Southey Rew aboard?"

The voice replied: "He's gorn. John Cain's down in the engine room."

Stephen felt a flooding relief. Cain he did not know, could not even recall the name. He snapped, "He'll have to do then." He had to impose himself now on this invisible man. Brusquely he went on: "Better take the lantern and light the way to the engine room. This deck's badly cluttered."

For the first time he saw the other man as he shuffled forward and stopped indignantly, muttering.

The engine-room hatch was far down the cavernous darkness of the interior. He stumbled once to justify the lantern. There was more light in the engine room; he could see that when he came to the head of the ladder in the hatch. Three or four lanterns were burning, and he went down the ladder with a sudden sense of familiarity, a swift return of knowledge.

The man who had been his guide called down: "John! Here's a officer from Richmond—wanted to see Rew."

A man came shambling round the cylinder housing, wiping his hands with cotton. At the same time Stephen's guide shambled away.

The newcomer said—there was neither greeting nor friendliness in his tone—"What would it be you was wanting with Rew?"

In the face of that tone he had to take a chance, the chance that Williamson would be in Richmond. Perhaps it was not so gigantic a hazard. Certainly Williamson had more than enough to keep him occupied in Richmond. "Mr. Williamson wants the condensers examined," replied Stephen.

Isherwood had said: "If you've got to be specific, make it the condensers. They was just about falling down when we tinkered with them."

"Again?" the new man asked wearily.

"Again!" snapped Stephen firmly. "The last report was wholly unsatisfactory."

The other man spat. "Wasn't nothing more than a bit of rust." His voice was surly. "If Williamson'd come down for hisself and look, maybe we'd get on a bit better. Ain't the condensers that's the trouble. It's the boilers. Take three months, the way we're workin', to get them straight." He came up close to Stephen and suddenly held up the lantern that he carried. "Ain't you Steve Knott—Lootenant Knott?"

All the gooseflesh, all the chill that had crept into Stephen's spine since this attempt had first been outlined, came together in a cold climax of fear. Now he knew that he would have to kill the man. He began to search his mind for a method. He had to think of silence and speed and secrecy. He had to give at once an answer that would accord with these necessities. He was astonished at the calmness of his voice as he said, "Yes, that's right—Knott."

The man looked at him doubtfully. "I heerd you went North." He cleared his throat again, and spat. "In the *Pawnee,* I heerd."

Stephen kept his voice equable, quiet. "Yes, that's right. My orders were to go North. Virginia wasn't in the war then."

The other man seemed confused. His voice was tired. "And then you came South?"

Suddenly Stephen knew that it would not be necessary to kill him. There was a way out, a better way perhaps. He answered with a humorous inflection: "Well, I'm here, ain't I? What's the trouble with the boilers, barring the tubes? We've heard about the tubes. And there was a bum firedoor on Number 2, wasn't it?"

"You folk in Richmond don't hear nothing." The other man let his voice fall away. "You don't read the goddam reports."

Stephen knew that he had won. He snapped back at the man: "We read them, but the folk down here don't say what they want or what they mean! I'll talk to Rew in the morning. Way you sound you'd be better in bed yourself."

"Chris'!" said the other man ungraciously, yawning. "I'm beat."

Stephen found his way to the foot of the ladder and went up it. The first man—he decided that there were only two of them on board—had left the lantern at the hatchway. He picked his own way to the deck ladder. He had almost reached it when from somewhere far away in the darkness he heard the first man calling, "Mr. Vickery, Mr. Vickery!" And with a cold desolation he knew that he had failed: the voice would carry throughout this echoing and silent ship.

The next moment his head emerged into the warm darkness of the deck. He moved as swiftly as he could without making a noise. Almost at once he was at the head of the ladder to the shore. He went down it lightly, rapidly, and the sentry grunted at him, not bothering to challenge. When he was sure that he was out of the sentry's range of vision, he began to move as fast as he could without actually running, keeping on the balls of his feet so that the sound of panicked footfalls would not echo in the silence of the Yard. His ears waited the alarm of shouts from the *Merrimac's* deck; his back waited the sentry's bullet—its chill, its gooseflesh justified and made reasonable.

He reached the dark shelter of the buildings without noise behind him, and desperately, illogically, he began to hope. Perhaps the second man was too tired to hear the shouted name, perhaps his brain was too slow, too disconnected to make the association. Perhaps the echoes of those dark and cavernous interiors distorted it beyond danger. He was coming to the head of the timber dock now—was halfway along it— then, thin and far away in the darkness behind him, he heard a voice calling.

In his memory he measured the distance to the main gate. Out of his knowledge of the Yard he tried to decide if there would be other sentries before he reached it. He could remember one on the way in, but that proved nothing. He moved faster still, impossibly balanced between the need for silence and the need of speed. His calf muscles hurt; his breath was beginning to labor. Common sense asserted itself, and he remembered that it would be dangerous to appear breathless at the main gate. Despairingly, he slowed down again.

Then suddenly he was through the gate, the challenge and response dealt with, the scrutiny of the sergeant, the opening of the wicket. He heard the door clang behind him, and knew that he had still a chance of freedom.

At once it was necessary to make a decision. He could go straight forward from the gate, cross the bridge over the creek, and find a hiding-place in the town. He could make an attempt to reach the skiff that had been left for him. He could turn up the street and try for shelter in the outskirts of the town. For the first he needed time—time to get down the stretch of open roadway to the arch of the bridge and across it. There was no cover, no cover at all from the guns of the sentries of the main guard. It was improbable, of course, that they would hit him in the fitful light of the widely spaced gas lamps, but the shooting would bring out every soul in town; and there would be no escape from that. For the second he would need time—the waterfront would be the first place that they would search.

He chose the third instantly and, as he ran, he heard shouting behind him in the Yard and knew that he had chosen correctly. There was an alley thirty yards up the street between two of the houses. He knew it from ancient hunts and hidings. He was transported back to his boy-hood, when his gang had run from other gangs or pursued its rivals. He began to search desperately in the darkness. There should have been a street light here. The place was unfamiliar, empty, desolate; and he realized almost with panic that the houses were gone, burned out per-haps in the big fire. As he heard the main gate crash open, he found the ghost of the alley and plunged down it, sobbing for breath. There was cover in the heaped rubble and the debris, and he began to move with an immense caution, abandoning speed.

From the gate he could hear the heavy crash of Army boots, men running, shouting—somewhere in the Yard a whistle blowing. He wondered if there were an alarm bell. The sounds came up the street, feet running hard—a patrol, he guessed—but the main noise was still down the road, going toward the water, going out toward the bridge. It would take time to organize a search, but the Yard was like a wasps' nest outraged.

He waited for the first urgency of it to die a little, and then carefully, methodically, he began to make his way west along the alleyways behind the houses. Presently he found himself in ground that he recognized, beyond the area of the fire.

*   *   *

He had to get back to the water. It would be impossible now to use his landing place and the boat that had been left for him. But he still had to get back to the water. The whole area between the creek and the Yard would be stiff with soldiers. It would be impossible to use the nearer streets. He remembered a secret way that he had sometimes used as a boy close to the head of the creek by the small bridge. There would be a guard on the bridge, but it was very dark. He started to make his way toward it. This was what Smith had meant when he said an intimate knowledge of Portsmouth was essential. The route was a boy's route—difficult, as he remembered it—and there was a chance that it might be built up or grown over or otherwise impassable, but he had to take it.

Oddly enough, it was completely simple, offering no difficulty at all; even the obstacles were smaller than he had remembered. The three men on the bridge banging the butts of their muskets on the wooden decking were of no importance whatever. In fifteen minutes he was on Elm Street.

He was almost at the corner of South and Elm when he saw that there were soldiers beyond him, down near County Street. At the same moment he heard pounding feet coming up South Street. He turned and doubled back.

People were coming out of their doors now. He heard a man's voice bellowing: "Anybody sees Stephen Knott, shout! Anybody sees Stephen Knott dressed as a navy lootenant, shout!"

At once, instantly, as if the voice had released a trigger, he heard a small boy scream: "There he is! There he is!"

He ran blindly back toward the bridge, remembering the thud of the muskets. He heard more voices. He heard his own name shouted as he ran. He saw a man he knew in the light of an open doorway and a girl that he had danced with suddenly illumined under a street lamp. A horror took him. These were his friends, these were the people that he had lived with, the people that he had loved; and they were shouting his name now like hounds in cry, snarling his name, baying it against the night stillness. He could hear feet behind him, doors slamming open and window sashes thrown up, and always his own name penetrating all other sounds.

Another boyhood memory rescued him. Even as the horror of their enmity enveloped him, the terrible knowledge that he could expect at any instant to be shot by a bullet from the gun of a boy he had gone to school with, or felled by a blow from the father of a friend, he remembered a tiny cul-de-sac and another alley between houses, an alley that was blocked by a door he had climbed as a child and been beaten for, and would climb again.

He was over it before the accumulating noise had reached as far as his cul-de-sac. He went over it silently, aware, with a sudden hope, of his strength. He dropped on the other side of it, disturbed a vagrant cat, took off his shoes, and padded silently into the wilderness of yards and stables behind the houses of South Street.

He knew what he would have to do now, and a fresh excitement that was both hope and apprehension took him. He would make his way to Ash Cleave, and Cleave would hide him and help him.

Horses stomped in the stables. A dog barked twice and then was silent. Every inch of this dark wilderness he knew. The flight had become innocent. He had gone back in time: Ash Cleave had helped him when he was a boy.

He found Mullin in silence and without difficulty. Somewhere beyond him the chase had swept on and lost itself in the night darkness.

Mullin was sitting at a table poring over a newspaper. He showed no surprise, no sign of shock. He said only, "Mist' Stephen, I thought yo' was in the No'th."

"The patrols are after me." Stephen knew that the word would convey a particular meaning to the old man. "I've got to speak to Mr. Cleave."

"I think Mist' Cleave is in the house."

"Ask him to come out here," Stephen said urgently. "If he isn't, find him." He looked searchingly at the old man and then added gently, "Please."

The old man nodded, folding his paper with an intolerable slowness.

"Sho', Mist' Stephen, sho'." He went to the door and at the door he turned. "Would yo' want to see Mis' Linden?"

Stephen shook his head. "No," he answered with a pang.

"Then yo'd best blow out th' lamp."

* * *

He huddled in the comforting darkness of sanctuary. He was trembling all over, as if in the early stages of a fever. His legs hurt and his feet. His heart was pounding more from fright than from exhaustion. Mullin at least would help him. Would Cleave? He was forlornly aware that in this last hour he had forfeited his birthright; that his friends were now his enemies. He sat contemplating the tragedy at the heart of civil war.

Cleave came to the door softly. In a low voice he asked, "Is it you, Stephen?"

"Yes, it's me." And with a humility before something that he could not fully understand he asked, "Would you like me to go?" Involuntarily he scraped the chair back a little, waiting.

Cleave came in and shut the door. "No," he said, still softly, and then almost irrelevantly: "We heard the noise, the shouting, but we could not, of course, know that it *was* you."

"They've got patrols in all the streets now."

"I expect so. It's a primeval instinct, taking after something on the run: an animal, a slave, a man. Why?"

Stephen shook his head. "I don't know—instinct?"

"No." Cleave's voice made no alteration in level. "No, I meant: why are *you* on the run?"

"I'm a Union man," replied Stephen grimly. "I went into the Navy Yard to find out something."

"The *Merrimac?*"

"Yes," answered Stephen reluctantly, "the *Merrimac.*"

"We'll have to get you away," said Cleave.

Abruptly, Stephen felt relaxed and safe and full of hope.

Cleave went on: "It won't be easy. They'll search this house, of course—they're bound to. We need five minutes, perhaps six. There are certain arrangements to be made, but fortunately . . ." He let the word trail in the air. After a moment's thought he asked: "Did you know, Stephen, that we—old Sam and I—are responsible for what some people call the 'underground railroad' out of here?"

Stephen hesitated for an instant before he said: "No, but I wonder if you will believe me if I say that I always thought you could be."

Cleave murmured, "Thank you."

Again there was silence. Over it Stephen could hear Mullin's voice talking to a horse, and the grating of wheels on the cobbles of the coachhouse and the creak of harness leather.

He felt a need to justify himself, as if he owed an explanation to the man who stood across from him. He said: "I was ordered to do it. I had no choice. It is important to us that we should know when the *Merrimac* will be ready."

"Of course." The voice was noncommittal.

"When *will* she be ready? You would know, I think."

Cleave's voice was unaltered as he replied: "If I knew, I would not tell you, Stephen. I will not help either side in this. What I have to do I have to do, but I cannot help in this fratricide."

"And yet you will help me?"

"I will help any man in flight from the inhumanity of man."

There was another silence.

Cleave spoke across it. "You won't be able to see Linden, Steve."

"No," Stephen said sadly. "I think I knew I wouldn't be able."

"I'm sorry, Stephen."

Mullin came back into the room. "I reckon she's ready, Mist' Ash. Ain't goin' to be easy to get him into the carriage box. He's a big man."

Cleave, his voice suddenly at ease, said, "He'll have to squeeze, then." And to Stephen: "We use the brougham sometimes at night to collect my sister Deborah when she is out visiting. It will not attract attention."

*   *   *

Cleave settled himself over the paper. He had taken his coat off and put on his glasses. He would have liked to put on his slippers, but he was not sure there was time. He sat patiently waiting, and because the circumstances were, in a sense, not without precedent, he waited quietly, actually reading the paper.

Ulysses Hogan had some story about worm in the timbers of the *Merrimac*. It was like all Ulysses' prose—highfalutin and impassioned. There was a grain of truth in it—he knew that, of course—but he wondered why Porter had allowed the story. The constructor, he knew, could keep Ulysses in check. Perhaps—he allowed himself the ghost of a chuckle—Richmond wanted it to appear for purposes of deceit. There was an irony in that at the present moment.

The racket at the front door neither startled nor disturbed him. He went to it slowly. "Just fast enough to reach it before they use their rifle butts," he said to himself. He opened it in the middle of a new attack on the knocker.

Revell still had his hand on it as Cleave pulled the door wide. He had half expected that it would be Revell—Revell with a brand-new sergeant's stripes and a patrol behind him down the steps.

Revell faced him angrily, as if he had expected someone else, or perhaps nobody. He shouted: "Steve Knott's loose somewheres about here. He's been spyin' in the Navy Yard. My orders are to search this house."

Cleave opened the door the rest of the way and stood a little to one side. "You've got orders to show?"

With an ugly arrogance Revell slapped the butt of his gun. "This is my orders!"

Cleave shrugged tolerantly.

"If I'd seen him in the Yard, I'd have shot him like a dog."

"I have no doubt." Cleave nodded his head. "You're wasting time, aren't you? Hadn't you better bring your patrol in and search?"

For an instant Revell looked deflated. Then he answered, with a belated attempt at civility, "I'm sorry, Mist' Cleave, but I got my orders." He shouted back down the passage at the men, and five of them came trooping in. He said, very much the sergeant, his voice blustering: "Edmonds and Murden, you get out to the stables. There's an old nigger named Mullin there. Make him talk! Ritter, you go with them. Randolph and Detrick, you go up to the rooms at the top."

As he began to stamp up the stairs himself, Cleave said equably: "You won't find Mullin. He's out."

Revell turned and glared down suspiciously over the banisters.

In the same instant Linden came in through the front door like a gust of wind. "What's this about Stephen Knott? What are they shouting about him?" She looked up with surprise and saw Revell and the other men on the stairs. "Revell Jordan, what do you think you're doing?" she demanded.

His voice was arrogant again, large and dramatic. "I'll get that bastard! I'd have shot him if I'd seen him in the Yard. I got to search this house, Lindy. First place in Portsmouth he'd come to."

With a white fury she faced him from the foot of the stairs. "Where are you going to search for him—under my bed?" She paused. "*In* my bed? You're a fool, Revell Jordan. You're crazy. All right, go on up!" She turned and looked at her father.

He was watching the scene with his habitual air of amused tolerance.

Revell bellowed, "Go on up!" to the two men, and came down the stairs. "If you say he's not up there, Lindy, we won't."

Between her teeth she said, "Do what you damn' please, Revell Jordan."

The man Ritter came back from the yard. "No one there. No nigger neither."

Linden glanced fleetingly at her father.

"Is there a horse there?" demanded Revell.

"No horse."

Cleave explained gently: "Mullin has taken my sister's brougham to collect her. I have only one horse."

Again Linden glanced at her father.

For an instant Revell stood irresolute. Then he shouted: "Ah, hell—come down from up top there! The wood yard's the likelier place. We should'a' gone there first." He turned with a sort of threatening politeness to Cleave. "You got any objections, Mist' Cleave?"

Scathingly gentle, Cleave replied: "You know your way there, Jordan. You've played there often enough."

Linden, her voice hard and angry, said: "I'll come with you, Rev Jordan. You're li'ble to make a fool of yourself."

Cleave walked to the front door behind the last of them and stood in the half-darkness at the head of the steps, watching until they had reached the corner. Then he went back to the drawing room and, pulling out his watch, began to make a calculation of the possibilities.

*   *   *

The darkness in the yard was absolute. Off Crawford Street there were no street lights. Out on the water of the Branch there were the lanterns of a ship at moorings and here and there the glimmer of boat lights, but they did no more than point the blackness.

Revell growled angrily, "We ought to have more than the one lantern."

Linden, in the darkness, said, "You could have borrowed half a dozen at the house if you hadn't been so full of yourself."

They were stumbling along the path. One of the men sniggered, and Revell snarled at him.

"I'll call Isaiah Brown for you. He sleeps in back of the office." Linden shouted at the top of her voice: "Isaiah! Sergeant Jordan wants to search the yard. He needs a lantern."

"Damn it, Linden!" Revell swore at her. "You want to let ever'body know?"

"Everybody knows already," she retorted savagely, "the noise we made coming in. You're a hell of a sergeant, Rev Jordan!"

Two of the men sniggered this time.

The door of the little shack behind the office opened and made a cube of warm light in the darkness.

Isaiah Brown came out with a skillet in his hand. They could see the steam rising from it. He called out: "Is that you, Mis' Lindy? Mind how yo' come! There's a lot small bits an' ends by the side o' the track there."

They went up sheeplike, and the Negro stood waiting for them. He was young and tall and athletic. He had an air of bottomless patience. "What was it yo' called 'bout a lantern, Mis' Lindy?"

"I need another lantern to make a search." Revell thrust himself into the exchange, but his voice had lost something of its authority.

The Negro peered down at him. "Sho', Mist' Revell. I got three-four lanterns. Be better with one each." He turned and went into the room. A smell of cooking hung in the air.

Linden heard feet running lightly on the path behind them and, as the men heard and turned, Jeriel came into the glow of the light from the door. Unaccountably, and without being able to explain it to herself, she felt her heart sink. "Jeri, what are you doing here?"

"I come," he answered, as if that were explanation enough.

She stood motionless, aware in a brief instant of time that she had to think now. Before she had not thought, she had only been angry, she had undergone emotion, she had taken an active part. Was it Stephen— Stephen, who had held her in his arms, who had kissed her, who had protected her when she was little and teased her, and loved her—she knew that he loved her. Stephen had gone North. Stephen was in Washington. Stephen had nothing to do with her or with her loyalties.

Was Stephen here?

She heard herself say, "Are you sure it was Stephen Knott?"

The men were clustered round the door, waiting for the lanterns.

Isaiah moved with a deliberate, careful slowness, filling, adjusting, lighting.

Revell exclaimed: "Good Christ, course it was Stephen Knott! John Cain reckernized him. Admitted he was Stephen Knott. Gave some other name at the gate—Vickers, Vickery, somethin'. If I'd a seen him—"

She interrupted harshly: "I know—you'd have shot him." And all the men laughed.

Revell said, "Blast your hide, get those lanterns out!"

Obsequiously Isaiah Brown answered: "Yes, sir, boss. Yes, sir." And the light in the last lantern went out and had to be relit.

At last they were armed with lanterns, spread in a line of search. Linden knew that she would have put two men first of all on the rickety jetty, but Revell was a fool. They searched uncertainly, without proper directive, not knowing what they were meant to do.

Murden found the hide. It was carpeted with shavings. There was a tin plate in it and a candle on the plate and a single blanket. He found it, pulling the short butt ends of timber from the end of the stack. He shouted, and the others gathered round. Linden stood back, her lips parted a little, her heart beating furiously. They held the muzzles of their guns to the opening in the stack while the last of the ends were pulled away. She knew now that she had to save Stephen. Whether he had spied on the *Merrimac* or no, she had to save him.

Even as the men dropped to their knees, their fingers on the triggers, and Murden flashed his lantern into the hole, she heard a rustle behind her, and the ghost of a voice said, "Bless you, Lindy," and was gone. Jeriel was pressed against her. She felt him start but he did not turn. Neither did she.

Revell was bellowing: "We got the bastard! God damn it, this was his hideout!"

Murden said across the shouting: "Empty. Ain't nobody here." He disappeared into the hole, and they heard his voice come back muffled, "Candle ain't been lit."

Revell was bellowing for Isaiah. The tall Negro was standing close to him, his back against a stack of shingles. Revell said: "This is a hide-out. How you goin' to explain this? How you goin' to?"

Isaiah laughed softly. "Yes, sir, boss, that's Eben's hideout. Times when his wife throw him out, he sleeps thar. Eats with me. Mist' Cleave doan like him to sleep in th' shack."

In a fury of suspicion Revell turned to Linden. "Did you know about this?"

She answered obliquely, "Everybody knows about Eben's wife."

Murden had come out of the hole. "Ain't nobody been there tonight anyways. Place stinks o' nigger."

"All right!" shouted Revell. "All right, get on with it. Get down to the water."

Linden carried the lantern that Isaiah had given her, holding it high, swinging it from side to side, knowing that the light would shine in the eyes of the searchers. When, with Jeriel close behind her, she reached the base of the rickety pier there was no sign of the small boat that belonged to the *Chula*. Ordinarily it lay above the high-water mark. She stood on the decking of the pier, moving the lantern from right to left. Well down the Branch, close in under the dark, uncertain shadows of the bank, she thought she saw a dark shape moving but she could not be sure.

*   *   *

Much later, walking wearily back up South Street, Jeriel took the lantern from her. The patrol had been formed up and was marching back to the main gate now. She could hear Revell's voice, angry, baffled, but still arrogant, diminishing in the distance. People remained in knots at the street corners or clustered on the steps and the porches.

Jeriel said, as they crossed Court Street: "He'd know how to use the little dinghy. He's used her before."

And Linden, emotionally exhausted, thought: How do I handle this?

Chapter eleven

THE Secretary of the Navy sat as if he were his own memorial carved carelessly out of rough sandstone. The hair of his beard and his wig looked incongruous on that chiseled exterior. He said bluntly, "Your task was to ascertain the earliest *date* at which the *Merrimac* could be ready again for sea."

Isherwood shot a covert glance of humorous sympathy at Stephen.

Stephen cleared his throat and waited a little—Isherwood had given him a warning: "Don't hurry your answers." When he spoke he spoke slowly. "Mr. Secretary, it is not possible to give a date with accuracy."

"May I ask why?" Welles allowed himself a ponderous sarcasm.

"Because, sir, the date depends in the final analysis upon factors outside the control of those who are responsible for her construction at Portsmouth."

Welles nodded with something near approval; he had a weakness for the well-turned phrase. "Would you be so kind as to explain?"

Again Stephen took his time. "Mr. Secretary, if the *Merrimac* were in a Northern Navy yard she could be complete by the end of the month if you, sir, judged it desirable. At Portsmouth they lack facilities which are present at, say, New York. But that is perhaps of no great importance. The worst of their delays is caused by lack of iron. They depend sir, upon the Tredegar Works for their iron. It comes in narrow strips, a few bars at a time, two inches thick, about four inches wide. The Tredegar Works has other tasks, sir; the calls upon it are urgent. Moreover, Mr. Anderson, the president of the Tredegar, has entered the Confederate Army."

"With the rank of brigadier," Isherwood interposed softly.

"And her engines?"

"So far as I could judge in the brief time I was able to spend in the engine room, her engines are in much the same state as when we left them—no better, no worse. The effects of the water and the mud are not apparent. They have been cleaned and repainted. The boilers are unsatisfactory: they might need two months' work upon them—on the other hand, they might not. It is the iron that matters, Mr. Secretary."

"Can you not make a"—Welles' precise mind boggled at the use of the word "guess"; he substituted—"an estimate?"

"Sir," Stephen replied after proper cogitation, "I can make nothing more than a guess. My guess would be that she cannot be completed in less than three months. I feel it is more probable that it will take four."

Welles relaxed. More to himself than to the two men he murmured: "Three months. That will bring us to the middle of January. Ericsson has committed himself to building his battery in a hundred days. . . ." He paused as though expecting a response before he went on: "We still have a chance. He must fulfill his undertaking." The keen eyes focused slowly on Stephen. "Mr. Knott, you will proceed to New York as soon as your formal report upon the *Merrimac* is complete. You will observe the progress of the work at Mr. Rowland's yard; you will report on it at suitable intervals. You will use every effort to ensure that Mr. Ericsson's estimate of time is adhered to. Good day to you, sir." Almost reluctantly he added: "And thank you."

Outside the door Stephen said hotly: "If he thinks I'm going to spy on Ericsson"—he looked suspiciously at Isherwood—"if you do too, you're damn well mistaken!"

*   *   *

She sat on the end of the jetty with her legs dangling. The cold wind caught at the hem of her dress and lifted it in billowing immodesty. Angrily she pulled it down. Revell watched with a sour frustration.

"He was at your house—I'll swear that!" he blurted out. "That black bastard Mullin won't say nuthin'. But Knott was *there!* He came from your house to the yard—there was that hide place—I don't believe that goddam story about it being a place for Eben when he's had a spat with his wife. He took the li'l' dinghy an' he got clear away in her. Stands to reason your father must of helped him."

Linden glared at him. "You talk like a fool, Rev Jordan, and you think like a fool. He made straight for the yard because he had good cause to know there was always a boat there. You've good cause to know too. What would you have done? If the little boat hadn't been there, he'd have taken my boat, and then you'd have said *I'd* been helping him. You make me sick."

He continued to watch her morosely. After an interval she said, "New load of iron came from Richmond today."

"That stinkin' ship!" He glowered. "Don't you ever think of nothin' excep' that stinkin' ship? Lindy, ain't we ever goin' to do anythin'? You won't marry me—I've asked three times." His face became flushed and hot. "If you won't marry me, will you"—he sought fearfully for a delicate phrase—"will you let me come into your bed with you? Once, Lindy, jes' once!"

With a dangerous awareness of strength Linden said: "Don't talk that way, Rev. I won't let you come near me if you do. And don't go talking about my father the way you talked to me."

"I've a mind to—" he began.

"Rev Jordan!" Her voice was scandalized as she recognized the hint of blackmail. "You talk like that and I'll make Captain Etheredge bust you. I'll make him give you every bit of dirt comes up for the whole company. I'll make him . . ."

"You talk," he growled doubtfully. "He's the captain."

With an infinite, calculated cruelty she added, "I'll let Captain Etheredge sleep with me if he won't do it else."

*　　*　　*

"Sir," asked Ericsson with a chilly politeness, "are you a mathematician?"

Stephen shook his head doubtfully. "I had the ordinary training in mathematics and in navigation that is required of a naval officer, sir."

"Then you are of no service to me." The big Swede plowed on through the grimy snow, heading inflexibly toward the small forest of steel ribs and unfinished plating, of derricks and winches and piles of snow-encrusted metal. He wore an air of determination like a garment.

Stephen nodded in complete agreement. "I was not sent here to assist you as a mathematician, Mr. Ericsson," he explained evenly. "I was sent to assist you as a naval officer. My orders are to render you every service that lies in my power."

Ericsson snorted. "A trained engineer would have been more use!"

Stephen nodded good-humoredly. "I daresay he would, but I heard you talk before the Ironclad Board, Mr. Ericsson, and I would not judge, sir, that you had a great need of help in that direction."

Ericsson snorted again, but the snort had lost much of its roughness. After a long interval of silent striding he said, "I shall work you hard, sir." And Stephen knew that he had won.

He watched the engineer as closely as he could, as closely as was safe, while he picked his way through the oddly shaped piles of metal, girders, and plates, made more dangerous by uncertain drifts of early snow. This was a man. At Washington he had succumbed to Ericsson's genius. Already, in the brief hour since he had arrived at the Greenpoint Yard at Brooklyn, he was aware of the man's ruthlessness, his drive, his obsession with the task at hand. The conviction of certainty shone out of him.

They stood at the side of the long slipway. The gaunt, uncompromising shape had little relation to anything that Stephen knew as a ship. It was angular and graceless, but Ericsson said, with for the first time something that was gentle in his tone: "She will make a name for herself, sir. She will set a new fashion in war. I am not afraid of John Porter. If you are correct about his difficulties"—he broke off and contemplated Stephen as if he were only just aware of him—"if you are correct, we have time in hand, sir."

*   *   *

"Mr. Mallory's letter—it is dated November 3rd—is positive." Commodore Forrest tapped the closely written sheet as if to call it to witness for itself. "Lenthall has condemned this floating battery of Ericsson's out of hand."

Williamson snorted. "If I hadn't believed in it before, I would now! When did Lenthall ever get the rights of anything?"

"None the less, he has had the opportunity of considering the plans and examining the calculations. He says that it is beyond possibility that it will float."

"Then it *will* float!" Williamson asserted.

Commodore French Forrest looked inquiringly at the chief constructor. "Mr. Porter?"

"The Navy of the United States was divided, as I know you are aware, sir, into those who believed in Stockton and those who believed in Ericsson. It was a sharp cleavage. John Lenthall belonged to the first group, sir."

Forrest nodded. "He did. What are your own views?"

"In the absence of any specifications, of even any reliable description, it is impossible to have views." Porter's voice was cautious. "I think, however, that Ericsson is a great engineer. I know that he is a man of enormous ingenuity and great energy."

"And?"

Porter made a rounded gesture with one hand as if to suggest completeness. "He has the resources of the New York yards; he has shipwrights and engineers by the hundred; he has the foundries of Baltimore and Philadelphia and Troy and a score of other cities if need be. I fear him, sir, and I fear his ship."

"He has the capacity to build what engines he likes"—Williamson nodded in impatient agreement—"allied to the ability to design them."

"It resolves itself into a question of time." Porter put the position simply. "We have had the advantages of an early start. If Mr. Mallory's report is accurate, we had three months of work before Ericsson laid the keel of his ship."

"And we have thrown it away!" said Williamson angrily. "We're trying to do too many damn things at once—the *Arkinsaw* and the *Tennessee,* the *Louisiana* and the *Mississippi*—there ain't enough iron to go round! Mallory knows that, but he won't do anything. What did you get last week, Porter—twenty bars? May have been thirty. Tredegar Works have got half their men working on the shaft for the *Louisiana.* You won't get more this week—nor the next. If there was a man in the talking house at Richmond, the Secretary of the Navy'd be impeached."

Forrest said in an oblique reproof. "It isn't only Stephen Mallory, Mr. Williamson—"

"All right, the Pres'dent too then! Jeffy Davis don't know the hull of a ship from a molasses bar'l."

*   *   *

"Everett is a fool," declared Ericsson bluntly. He held up the letter. "This is dated December 5th. Commodore Smith writes: 'I saw Mr. Everett today, who says your turret will not be ready to leave his shop short of *thirty days.* I beg of you to push up the work. I shall demand heavy forfeiture for delay over the stipulated time of completion. You have only *thirty-nine days left!*' "

Griswold snapped like a starved dog: "Damned old woman!"

Bushnell said: "We have made it as clear as we may possibly do that unless we receive our money it is impossible to pay for more night gangs. The work *cannot* be accelerated."

Griswold snapped again: "Thirty-seven thousand five hundred dollars so far—that's all we've prised out of the old bastard. How much have we spent, Bushnell?"

"It is difficult to be precise, but we should have had a second payment by now at least. I would estimate that we have spent $140,000."

Ericsson's eyes came into focus again. It was as if the man had come physically back into the little shed. "The money is of no importance. It is important that Everett should have gone to him. It is disloyal of Everett. Of the Navy Department I expect nothing"—he hammered suddenly against the wall, and the shed shook—"nothing! But of those who work with me I expect loyalty. This old man"—he held up the letter again, and the tone of his voice savagely demolished Smith's pretensions—"knows nothing, can imagine nothing. Every day he writes me. One day he worries about stability. The next day there will not be enough fresh air for the crew. The third day she cannot float. The fourth day the turret will not turn." He wheeled with a darting movement of his head to Stephen. "Do the officers of your Navy have nothing else to do? Is there so little work for them in Washington that they must spend their whole time writing letters that would be foolish from a child"—again he waved the letter angrily in the air—"from an imbecile?"

Stephen waited. He was used to Ericsson's outbursts; there was no way of dealing with them until his indignation had exhausted itself. He could not defend Commodore Smith and he would not make the attempt. It was more than clear to him now that there was a cabal against the ship in Washington, headed, he guessed, by Lenthall, with Davis supporting him. No one in Washington believed in the battery. They worked here in New York in an enveloping enthusiasm. Paulding supported them. But outside New York the thing was a joke: "Ericsson's Folly," they were beginning to call it—"Ericsson's Folly."

*   *   *

Ulysses bowed the chief constructor in as if he were a candidate for President. "This way, Mr. Porter. Mind the step, Mr. Porter."

Linden, flattened against the wall behind the type fonts, stifled an inward laughter.

The editor came out of his door, holding up the thin magazine. "This will shake you, John. This is a full description of the Ericsson Battery."

Porter said gently: "If that is the issue of November 16th—"

"It is not!" interrupted the editor with the self-satisfaction of one who brings bad tidings. "It's the issue of November 23rd, and it's a different kettle of fish."

Porter held out his hand wordlessly. "I would not have thought that even the *Scientific American* would be so indiscreet." His poise deserted him and he began to read with avidity. Presently he held the paper away from him at arm's length and then brought it back again, and said aloud, evidently reading: " 'The contract bears date 5th October and stipulates that within one hundred days the entire structure must be ready for active service.' " He looked up at the editor. "One hundred *days,*" he repeated with a little whistling intake of breath.

Old Sam, leaning in his dark apron with his belly against the lower case, said: "January 12th. You goin' to have your ship ready by then, John Porter?"

Porter disregarded him and went on reading aloud: " 'In view of the magnitude of the work to be performed this condition would appear almost impossible to comply with and calls for considerable diligence on the part of the constructor. Another stipulation is that the trial of the efficiency of the battery must be made under the guns of the enemy's batteries at the shortest ranges.' " He looked up a second time with his face puckered in thought. "Only Ericsson would have accepted a clause like that—only Ericsson." Again he read: " 'The structure consists of three principal parts, viz., a shallow decked vessel with perpendicular sides, dead flat bottom and pointed ends. Under this shallow vessel a second and deeper vessel is attached with raking stem and stern, perfectly flat bottom and sides inclined at an angle of 51° to the vertical line.' "

"Explain it," ordered the editor impatiently. "Explain it! It sounds like nothing I have ever imagined even in dreams."

"Wait! This is written with authority. No one but Ericsson could have written it; it has his style." Porter read on, silently now. Occasionally a phrase emerged: " 'A hundred and seventy-four feet in length . . . only eighteen inches above water . . . bulwark plated with iron six inches thick . . . turret nine feet high . . . eight consecutive rings each one inch thick . . .' "

He went on for a long time until again the editor urged: "Explain it, John!"

At length the constructor looked up. "Sam, give me a sheet of paper!" He took a big soft drawing pencil from his pocket. "I think"—he spoke more to himself than to the others—"I think it means something like this," and he began to draw. In quick, graphic strokes the picture of a raft grew—a flat thing with pointed ends mounted above a simple boat-shaped hull. On it was a round tower nine feet high from which two guns showed, dark and formidable.

They crowded round him as he drew, Linden slipping out from her hiding place to look over old Sam's shoulder.

Porter said: "I don't know. It's too new. I don't know—but it could be that he is right. I must have time to think it over. Our guns could scarcely hit her here"—his pencil followed the sweeping curve of the sides—"our shot would bound off her deck. The turret—nine inches thick. . . . We could not hope to penetrate the turret. And he will build it in a hundred days, a hundred days from October 4th."

"Can he?" demanded the editor.

"He can," answered Porter somberly. "I know John Ericsson."

Sam said, "You won't be ready by January 12th."

Porter was silent a moment. "He will still have to run his trials. There will be difficulties—there must be—it is too new. She will still have to steam here from New York. We will have perhaps till the end of January. If we could get the iron, we would be ready for her then. It is lack of iron that cripples us."

Linden's eyes went from one face to the other: Porter's absorbed, the editor's doubtful, Ulysses' uncomprehending, Sam's blank and neutral.

The editor said, "If they would tear up the tracks of the Portsmouth & Weldon . . ."

"You got to get a railroad pres'dent to agree to that. Ever know'd a railroad pres'dent to agree to anythin'?" demanded Sam.

Porter murmured softly, "We've *got* to get the iron."

*   *   *

Out of the sleet and bluster of the January night that closed Fortress Monroe like a forest of spreading trees, the man lumbered in. He stood facing the Northern general, half defiant, half fearful. He was breathing heavily, unsteadily. One eye was half closed and swollen, and there was a great red bruise on his chin. He said, his voice between arrogance and anxiety, "Your men mussed me up some, General."

"I am sorry," General Wool answered. "They have had much trouble with fishermen from Norfolk running the blockade."

"I ain't a fisherman"—the man's attitude was hardening—"I'm a shipwright." He offered the trade as if it were a justification. "They didn't oughter done it."

"I am sorry," Wool repeated, "it was a mistake. We will endeavor to compensate for it. You have news, I am told, of the *Merrimac*."

"I got news," replied the man arrogantly, and stopped.

Wool waited. He looked old, tired, uninterested.

The man watched him calculatingly, as if he wanted to fix a price but did not yet dare to do so.

Wool said indirectly: "The Norfolk papers say her hull's rotten, that she's got the worm."

"Crap!" commented the shipwright bluntly. "She didn't have no more worm than any other Navy ship's got. What there was Porter cut out. There was a bit of it aft. He was hung up there a little. She's a'right. Ain't nothin' wrong with her engines neither—no more'n there was before anyways."

Wool leaned forward slowly. "What *is* your news?"

Again the man looked as if he would like to ask a price, hesitated, and lost the opportunity. "They're 'bout ready to let the water into the dock any day now. She's strong—two layers of iron. Ain't nothin' here that'll hold her. All these wooden ships . . ." His nostrils flared suddenly.

"When d'you think they'll float her?"

"Any day now—any day. They was talkin' of We'nesday next week. You got to do somethin' 'bout her."

Wool nodded gently, his head repeating the motion over and over again like a Chinese toy. Finally he asked in a thin voice, "Will she float?"

Angrily the man replied: "Don't you believe what you see in th' Norfolk papers! She'll float."

Wool shrugged his shoulders. "There have been so many reports."

"She'll float!" The man almost shouted at him. "Cap'n Fairfax, he's got sense—*he* says she'll float." He calmed down again. "Ain't no reason why she shouldn't, come to think of it. Porter ain't a fool."

Wool pushed his head forward again slowly. "Why did you come over?"

"I ain't a Southerner," replied the man sullenly. "My folks come from Vermont when I was 'bout ten year old." He hawked and used a spittoon. "They make me sick. If'n you Yankees take Roanoke, won't be anythin' of them left in a month. I reckoned I'd git."

Wool said censoriously, "You've been drinking."

"Sure I been drinkin'." The man's voice was a snarl. "Would you try to get through your own itchy-trigger-fingered bastards sober?"

* * *

Linden sat crouched at the point where the lumber pile joined the rusty stack of unused metal. Her gray dress was inconspicuous, merging into the background. She looked unfeminine, pathetic, implausibly helpless. Jeriel crouched on the ground with his back against her legs. They sat wholly still.

Porter had said: "You keep out of the way. Don't get in Commodore Forrest's line of sight! He'll have you out of the Yard else. He doesn't want any women or any ceremony."

Linden remembered his face as she had asked: "Why? It's the great day for the *Merrimac*. It's the great day for you. There ought to be ceremony, there ought to be flags, there ought to be bands!"

And Porter had muttered quietly, so quietly that it was almost as if he were speaking to himself, "He doesn't think that she'll float."

She watched him now. Forrest was down near the far end of the dry dock. Captain Fairfax stood with Porter.

She watched Lee, the executive officer of the Yard, go up to them. She heard his voice above the murmur of men's voices, the hammering, the banging, the clank of metal. Lee's deep, hail-fore-tops'l voice was clear. "Do you really think she will float, Mr. Porter?"

She saw Porter nod gently. He was always gentle; she wondered how he sustained his gentleness in the face of stupidities like Lee's.

The men were crowding closer to the basin now. The guards round it had a parade look, a useless air. Revell was inspecting them one by one, ostentatiously. He was still wearing his sergeant's stripes.

Fairfax asked Porter a question. She could not hear his words nor could she hear Porter's reply, but she saw him nod again.

Lee bellowed, "Open the valves!" And for a little there was an absolute silence.

The day was cold and exquisitely clear. The air had a wine sparkle. Her mind went back to that January day a year ago—earlier than this it was, she could not remember the exact day—dates were unimportant. She could remember only the quality of the air, the vibrant light in the swamp, the character of the stillness, and the grace and the beauty of the deer. She looked down for a moment at Jeriel, wondering if he too remembered. In a quick transposition of image she saw the *Merrimac* as the younger deer: it had to be the younger deer, it *had* to be the victor. And in the obscurities, the undergrowth, of the North, the other deer lurked: the *Monitor.* The name had reached Portsmouth now, the name that was the essence of the arrogance of Ericsson.

The water swirled into the dock, a brown stream, frothed and flecked with bubbles, lifting the rubbish of the bottom of the dock with it: ends of timber and broken planks, shavings and bark and paper.

The old deer was the *Monitor,* the young deer the *Merrimac.* Who was the doe?

She watched the water swirling farther and farther up the granite sets of the bottom.

The doe was Virginia! It was as simple as that.

The men crowded still closer to the edge of the dock, surrounding the sentries.

Revell strode up and saw Linden and Jeriel. He was on speaking terms again. He demanded importantly: "How did you get here? Commodore said there wasn't to be no women."

"We came," answered Linden shortly.

And Jeriel, not looking up, his eyes fascinated by the coils and arabesques of the currents in the water, muttered: "Mr. Porter, he said: 'Least we can do is to let you see it. You two've done more'n anybody else in this town fer th' *Merrimac*'."

"Sure," said Revell patronizingly. "You've done a lot."

Jeriel, his voice still absent but with the suspicion of a trap in it, asked, "Is she goin' to float?"

"Cap'n Lee"—Revell became pompous again—"he don't think she's got a chance. Cap'n Fairfax, he does. Commodore Forrest, he don't know either way." He swaggered off toward the next sentry. Over his shoulder he flung back negligently, "Mebbe she will, mebbe she won't."

Linden made no attempt at answer. She sat silent and still, her eyes riveted on the bows of the ship far below her, on the enormous iron wedge of the ram.

The water had reached the end of the dock and was banking up in a froth of brown and yellow and white.

Jeriel said distantly: "My pa, he had a house dog like that once." Both of them watched the water for a long time, and then Jeriel added, "He shot him after."

The little group of senior officers, the head shipwrights, the engineers moved forward in a body to the edge of the dock and stood staring down. The ship lay immobile, dead-looking. Rust showed here and there on the painted iron of the armor, and her funnel had patches of rust on it. She had an unkempt and careless appearance, but under it was the somber certainty of strength.

The water began to climb the sides of the dock.

It moved with a stealth, as if it had no responsibility toward the immense weight of the structure in the womb of the granite. The froth and the bubbles were held against the far end of the dock, Linden's end, by the stream of the current. The surface was smooth now, a glassy smoothness that renewed itself always as the upward currents swept to the top and rounded themselves off and flattened themselves and engulfed themselves again in an endless ceremony of eddies.

Linden measured progress by the tiers of the granite blocks that lined the basin. Almost imperceptibly the flood rose to the lines of jointure and swallowed them, and crept inexorably toward the level of the next. There had been noise with the first rush but that was gone now, and the voices of the men had fallen too; they stood waiting.

Movement in the group of officers pulled Linden's eyes at last from the water. She saw Porter and three men walk forward to the gangway and move down it to the foredeck of the ship. The sound of their footfalls and the creak of the gangway were loud in the silence. Instantly about them grew an uprising of voices that lasted until long after Porter had taken up a position at the bows.

It died again then, and the water crept up and up and up—and everybody waited. Even the wheeling seagulls were silent. Once a tug hooted far down the Branch off Norfolk. A locomotive bell rang and was silenced. Somewhere in the Yard was the noise of horses' hoofs, and that in turn died away. Only the upward-creeping water seemed alive in all that stillness.

It rose to the ram, stealthily swallowing it, and still the *Merrimac* was a dark inert weight, portentous as a half-tide rock.

Linden heard Jeriel whisper, "Jeez, why don't she float?"

A tension held them all, binding them into immobility. Only the water moved, making its curves and its patterns, borrowing glancing blues from the sky.

Suddenly, with the hesitant, incredible movement of a great tree falling, a prop on the port side that stretched to the wall of the dock fell to the water, and a splash of brown flecked through with white bubbles rose in the sunlight and took brilliance from it. At once a prop on the other side of the ship fell away.

Over the stillness that followed the dying whisper of the splash they heard Porter's voice, utterly calm: "She's afloat."

Chapter twelve

THE rain was cold. It fell in thin irritable trails that blotted out the houses on the island of Manhattan. The harsh outline of the New York shore was softened temporarily in its drift. There was little wind. If it had blown as hard as the pessimists had prophesied, they would have had to postpone the launching.

Ericsson was carrying out a final inspection. It was unnecessary—he had inspected everything already—but Stephen knew that compulsions moved the man that were not shared by others.

There was a dense crowd round the slipway: the workmen, the men from the neighboring yards, the men from the shipyard office, even a sprinkling of women—wives and girl clerks. Small boys climbed up the derricks and the staging that paralleled the next ship on the slips, and clustered on the roof lines of the sheds like wet starlings, bedraggled and jaunty.

The betting had become the jest of the whole affair, the cream of the whole jest.

An old voice croaked, "Fifty to one she don't float!"

As ten voices accepted the offer, another man shouted, "You ain't got fifty cents to pay out if you lose."

The old voice cackled high and shrill, senile and hilarious.

Ericsson's Folly.

The air was full of an indefinable hostility, a jeering incomprehension; unbelief propagated and spread. For a moment it seemed to Stephen that no one anywhere believed except the big powerful Swede who walked tapping and stooping and peering under the dark, new-painted hull, and perhaps Greene standing beside him, and himself.

He said to Greene, "All crowds are crazy."

A man near them turned and said, his voice educated and ironic: "Are you so damned sure yourself? In my opinion she'll go down the ways all right, but Ericsson will spend the next three months picking her out of the mud on the bottom of the harbor. She'll dive straight in."

Stephen asked coldly: "Will you back that opinion with fifty dollars?" He could not afford fifty dollars. He had laid out all the money he could spare in bets already, forced to it by the endless, nagging challenge of unbelief.

"Done!" replied the man.

Greene said, "I'll have fifty dollars of that too."

Ericsson came stooping out from under the bottom of the *Monitor* for the last time. "We will go aboard, gentlemen." Turning, he began to climb the single ladder that led to her deck.

Stephen watched it sag and give under the engineer's weight. He waited until Griswold and Bushnell had followed Ericsson to the deck. He let Greene go forward; Greene had been appointed first lieutenant —it was his place to lead. Then he turned and with an affectation of courtesy said to the man with whom they had placed the bets, "Would you care to join me, sir?" and nodded toward the ladder.

Bitingly the man answered, "I'll live out my life my own way."

Stephen went up the ladder in his turn.

Ericsson selected his position with care, as if he found some particular virtue in the featureless point of the wide flat armored deck he chose. He stood there in his familiar stance, and Stephen's thoughts went back for a fleeting moment to the morning in front of the Ironclad Board, Ericsson's feet well apart, his body firm, only the iron head slowly moving from one side to the other. When he was ready he said to the master shipwright, "Does the tide serve?"

The shipwright replied, "As much as we need, Mr. Ericsson."

"You can let her go." The words were simple; there was no vainglory in them.

Stephen saw the master shipwright cross the deck to the edge and bellow down. He heard the immediate crash of the hammers below them as the blocks were knocked clear. He thought that he discerned a faint moment of hesitation, an infinitely brief resistance, and then the *Monitor* began to move, to slide, to rush, at last to hurtle down the ways toward the water. It was as if in this single sentient moment the mass of iron and timber, of engines and guns had come to life, as if a soul of motion, a spirit of energy had entered into it; and even as he thought this she hit the water. An enormous cloud of spray, dull and angry-looking in the gray light, flashed up on either side. A wave lifted above her and climbed for a brief, agonizing moment up her deck. Then it was all over, the deck rose clear through it, the water sluiced away, and the ship floated on an even keel, solid, strong, buoyant.

On the shore there was an absolute silence, a silence compounded of wonder and astonishment; and then the cheers began. He could see the hats tossed into the air, the handkerchiefs, the hands waving. The small boys on the roof ridges were standing up, flapping like fledgling crows. The small boys on the cranes were hanging desperately with one hand and waving with the other. The sound came out to the *Monitor* and enveloped them, and Ericsson stood motionless, his feet rock-firm, eighteen inches apart, and at last allowed a quiet smile to soften the dour, harsh molding of his mouth.

*   *   *

Aunt Deborah used the rocking chair as a weapon. If she turned it sidewise, she was indifferent. If she used it obliquely, she was oblique. If she turned it straight toward the person she addressed, she was direct. It was oblique now.

She said obliquely, "Are you ever going to be more than a part of a ship, Linden?"

Linden was instantly on the defensive. "What do you mean, Aunt Deborah?"

"A woman, for instance."

Patiently Linden explained: "There's all my life to be a woman but there's a war now. I've got to help, I've got to do what I can."

"Fund raisings, bazaars, sales of work, cartridge bags, plays."

Linden fell into the trap. "That's woman's work," she protested.

"But you do it a man's way," Aunt Deborah cut back, turning the rocking chair with a quick, sidewise thrust.

Linden knew precisely what she meant. "It works quicker." She nodded toward her father's chair. "He said that he was pleased that I was getting along better with the other girls. . . ."

"Your father," said Aunt Deborah dismissively, "is a man. He doesn't see things. You're just using the other girls. They ain't goin' to love you for it."

Linden grinned engagingly. "They're foolish, just plain foolish." Then, as Aunt Deborah did not respond, she added in explanation, "Like hens."

"And botherin' Captain Etheredge and Mr. Porter and gettin' in and out of the Yard, is that woman's work?"

Linden grinned again, knowing that Aunt Deborah had been waiting for the moment to pounce.

"Stayin' out half the night with Revell Jordan!"

"And Jeriel," said Linden.

"Another year and Jeriel won't be safe either."

Linden's mouth opened as it always did when Aunt Deborah abandoned her mask for a moment. There was no answer to this.

Cleave came up the South Street pavement. It was a rare February day, a morning so still, so ready in its acceptance of the warmth of a young sun that it was like spring come early. No trains moved. There was no traffic in the streets; no hoofs of horses, no grating of wheels sounded. The children were in school and there was no shouting. There was not even, now that the *Merrimac* was in the water, the distant sound of riveting from the Navy Yard.

They recognized Cleave's footsteps from a long way off. They both knew the sound, and loved it.

He came to them at last. "There was nothing to do in the yard. There's little enough in the way of timber to be got anyway." He sat down in his chair, and when he had settled himself, the whole world was silent again. As if it were waiting.

Linden heard it first—the thin, tenuous tapping on the horizon, the sound that they had heard four months ago in the great clearing of the swamp. She jerked herself upright in her chair.

Aunt Deborah opened her mouth to speak, but no sound came.

Cleave listened for a moment. He said gently at last, "Your wood-pecker's nearer this time, Linden."

Her face had gone white. "It'll be Roanoke."

They listened again to the mutter of distant guns.

Cleave nodded. "Yes, it'll be Roanoke. That's where Goldsborough was heading when he cleared out of the Roads a month ago."

"If he takes Roanoke Island . . ." Linden's eyes were hooded.

"If he takes Roanoke Island," said Cleave, "John Porter had better get the *Merrimac* to sea. He won't have much chance after."

They were silent again, and across the silence the ghostly tapping of the guns went on, rising and falling.

It sounded, Cleave thought, astonishingly like a woodpecker.

*   *   *

The low, lazy beat of the engines slowed, ceased, and became silent. The *Monitor* made a curious little backward movement as the thrust of the propeller against the mooring ropes fell away to nothing.

Stimers, the chief engineer, said: "It isn't right. I don't know what it is, but it isn't right. I don't think we can find out any more along-side. I think it'll show up when we get her away from the dock."

Griswold grunted: "Washington is going to be damned angry if there are any more postponements."

Stephen watched him broodingly.

"Washington's got the diarrhea since they floated the *Merrimac*.

It's my guess Smith spends three-quarters of his day on the heads. He writes his letters from there. Ericsson show you the last one? 'Let us have the test as *soon as possible,* for that ship will be a troublesome customer to our vessels in Hampton Roads.' He's been a bit more civil since we told him that he couldn't have her till we were paid according to the contract."

"At least," Stephen thrust into the conversation, "we've got the Assistant Secretary on our side."

Griswold turned on him waspishly. "Fox waited long enough. Winslow talked to him the best part of two days early last month before he could get him to help. He's like the rest of them—waited to see if she'd float before he jumped. Now he's gone the other way."

"What do you mean?" asked Stimers.

"Ericsson got a note from him: 'Can your *Monitor* sail for the Gulf of Mexico by the 12th inst.?' "

"He's crazy," said Stimers shortly.

"Everybody in Washington's crazy. Fox, he's got a maggot in his insides about the Gulf. Rest of Washington's scared about Hampton Roads."

Stimers grunted. "Stands to reason. Burnside's got Roanoke Island and he's all set to cut across to Norfolk. They've got to get the *Merrimac* out before that happens, so Washington's scared. We ain't ready. Don't look as if we're goin' to be—with the crosshead squealing like a stuck pig. *I'd* be scared if I was in one of Goldsborough's wooden coffins."

Griswold turned again to Stephen. "How long will it take Burnside to get through? You're a Portsmouth man."

Stephen shook his head. "No telling. Either he's got to come through the Dismal Swamp or he's got to come round it. Each way they can hold him for a long time if they've got troops and guns. If they haven't, he could be there in four days."

Griswold looked him slowly up and down with a glint of contempt in his eye. "The trouble with you, Lieutenant Knott," he said coldly, "is you're too damned judicious."

*   *   *

" 'You are hereby detached from the office of "Orders and Detail" and will proceed to Norfolk and report to Flag Officer Forrest for the naval defense of the James River. You will hoist your flag on the *Virginia (Merrimac)* . . .' " Forrest looked up at the man across the desk from him.

Franklin Buchanan sat bolt upright in the chair. The wings of his collar sprang out on either side of the stubborn jaw. The mouth even in repose had an angry arrogance. The bold hooked nose pointed that arrogance.

Forrest said: "Time he made up his mind what he's going to call her. You can't signal a ship: '*Virginia* brackets *Merrimac.*'"

Buchanan's voice was humorless as he said, "I have no doubt that she will be properly called the *Virginia.*"

Forrest allowed himself a faint grin. "I have no doubt that everyone in this town will go on calling her the *Merrimac* to the end of her days." With superstitious haste he added, "May that be a long time away!"

"Amen," said Buchanan.

"'The *Virginia,*'" Forrest read on, "'is a novelty in naval construction, is untried, and her powers unknown, and the Department will not give specific orders as to her attack on the enemy.'" Forrest looked up, and this time he allowed the grin to spread. "Stephen Mallory's learning sense," he observed expansively. "Six months ago he would have been specific. God, how specific he would have been!" He read again: "'Her powers as a ram are very formidable, and it is hoped that you will be able to test them. Like the bayonet charge of infantry, this mode of attack will commend itself to you in the present scarcity of ammunition.' There's sense of a sort in that. Be better if he saw that you got the ammunition, though." Forrest's eyes concentrated on the orders again. "'Could you pass Old Point and make a dashing cruise on the Potomac as far as Washington, its effect upon the public mind would be important to the cause.'" Forrest let out a great expulsion of breath. "Franklin, you've been with him a lot lately. I haven't seen him in a month. Does he *really* believe she could do that? It's back to the old Mallory—all the way back, and more."

Buchanan shook his head. "I cannot say that I know what the Secretary thinks. No man knows that except himself. These are my orders. I shall carry them out to the limits of my power."

Forrest accepted the evasion. "You'll do that, Franklin, I know. I'm glad he chose you. It won't be easy, but if any man can get what we need out of the *Merrimac,* you are that man." He put down the orders on the desk and picked up another small sheaf of papers. "I've made arrangements for the commissioning ceremony"—he looked abstractedly at the date—"February 24th. We should have most of the crew together by then. Thirty men were on their way from Magruder's army last night. The local men are ready for you now. I doubt if there's a full crew, though—Magruder's a hard man to convince." He smiled suddenly and charmingly. "I'll wish you luck now, Franklin. You'll be needing it."

*   *   *

Stephen held up the *Tribune*. "Paper says that they commissioned the *Merrimac* the 24th."

"That's fair enough," said Greene. "We commissioned the 25th. One day in it, we've caught 'em up. They've still got to run trials with that thing."

"What are *we* doing now?" asked Stephen.

"Runnin' a trial. And it don't sound too good."

Both men listened, their heads slightly cocked. It was difficult to be certain of engine sounds on the deck. What came up the berth-deck hatch was distorted and full of unrelated echoes. None the less it was possible to discern harsh overtones in the beat and run of the engines.

"Stimers said it would show once we got outside if it was anything at all." Stephen listened again.

They were out of the East River now, past Governors Island and heading into the Upper Bay. The water was yellow and unreflecting. Boats moved in it, coming up the harbor with the young tide, their sails dull in the leaden light. The cloud hung very low.

Greene said: "Hope to Christ nothin' does go wrong! John Ericsson's on the prod."

A side-wheeler came close, crossing their bows, and they heard a bellowing from the squat, heavily armored cube of the wheelhouse.

"He's on the prod," said Stephen in agreement.

They crept on down the bay, the adverse tide making their movement appear slower than in fact it was. There was no question now that there was trouble with the engines. Gulls wheeled behind them and moved away disdainfully, finding only a barren swirl of foam in their wake.

From the top of the turret it was possible to view the whole ship in one quick sweep of the eyes. She moved squatteringly like an ancient duck, frighteningly low on the water, pushing the yellows of the bay on either side of her curious flat nose. Now and then a little wave climbed lazily over the bows, trailed aft, and spilled away. She seemed contemptuous of them, quivering only to the uncertain beat of the engines.

"I wonder what in hell she looks like from outside?" asked Greene.

"Tin can on a shingle," said Stephen caustically.

"Listen!"

The beat of the engines now carried a shrill upward wail at every stroke. The wail grew, became more shrill, more insistent. The ship began to come round in a staggering, uncertain circle. It was obvious something was desperately wrong. She was in a tight turn now, heeling over just a little so that the small waves slapped onto the edge of the starboard side of the deck. Without more warning there was a loud grind of metal, then a moment of complete silence, and at once, after that, steam blowing off in a long, shuddering roar.

Above the roar Greene said grimly: "Stimers was right. I've an idea we're going to be too late for the *Merrimac*."

* * *

Revell glowered at her from his place amidships in the skiff—he was always angry these days. "Mr. Ramsey said, far as I can remember it: 'A more ill-contrived and unreliable pair of engines than the *Merrimac*'s could be found only in the U.S. Navy.' " He took a delight in hurting her. As she did not respond, he went on: "Ramsey ought to know. Hell, he's her chief engineer! He's got to try to work the damn' thing."

Linden said calmly, "You're always picking." Then, dismissing the subject: "I know all about her engines. They'll work." She was supremely confident.

"What good d'you think seein' her now's goin' to do to you?"

"Nothing," she answered, still calmly. "I just like to look at her once in a while to see that she's still there. You didn't want to go anywhere else. Tide's wrong for the lower harbor anyway, and the Harbor Guards think they own it now. I'm going to talk to Captain Young."

"Lindy Cleave, one o' these days somebody's goin' to chop you! You think you *own* the *Merrimac*, you think you own *Portsmouth*"— he became almost incoherent—"you think you own *Virginia!*"

Linden began to enjoy herself. "Why do you come sailing with me if you hate me that much? Why are you always sitting around on our steps?"

He groaned. "Lindy Cleave, you're a bitch!"

Jeriel's knees—he was lying in his favorite place in the bows— quivered, but he lay still.

The expletive seemed to relieve Revell a little. He said with almost a touch of his ordinary vainglory, "I could get any other girl in Portsmouth."

Linden giggled. To Revell it was the first feminine thing that she had done in his presence for months. "Lucy Anne Watts?" she asked.

"She ain't got the parts," replied Revell with an angry crudeness. He tried a simple, direct approach. "I want you."

Deliberately she slacked off the main sheet, letting the creak of the blocks answer him. They were coming up level with the stern of the *Merrimac* now. The strange nightmare of a ship floated ponderously on the still of the evening water. The Confederate flag was brilliant on the portentous hull.

A sentry on the wall of the dock shouted at them, and Revell exerted himself enough to peer round the foot of the sail and shout back. The man's voice across the water came back, "Okay, Sarge."

Jeriel, up in the bows, again laughed silently to himself, and Revell scowled at him.

He said bitingly: "You don't think she's ever goin' to go to sea? They spend all day fightin' over her—Porter and that fool Brooke, Williamson and Cap'n Buchanan—all four o' them and old Forrest. The second boiler's on the bum again and one o' the pivot guns won't train proper. And they fight, fight, fight and nothin' gets done."

Serenely Linden answered, "She'll go out when she has to go out."

"She needed to go out six months back!" Revell was crushingly triumphant. "Last report from New York says th' *Monitor*'s workin' out in the harbor. It took a whiles to come through, that report. Mebbe this thing's too late already."

"She'll go when she has to," said Linden again.

"She has to go *now*." The stubbornness in his tone had an ugly, frightening quality. He was using the *Merrimac* to hurt her deliberately, and the timbre of his voice had vicious overtones of pleasure.

*   *   *

The *Monitor* lay quite silent on the silent water. Silver winter mist encircled her so that she seemed to float in a brief circle of visible sea that had no positive boundaries but merged imperceptibly into the mist. It was not a plain silver: it had alloys, tones, gradations; it was subtle and cold and beautiful. The tug showed in it vaguely, its shape hardly more than a thickening of the mist.

Stephen crawled out of the manhole of the turret and stood disconsolate on the top of it. The signaler followed him out and began to light the flare. It burned uncertainly. At night it would have been spectacular; this silver light robbed it of four-fifths of its brilliance, but eventually the tug saw it and lit an answering flare.

The signaler appeared immoderately satisfied. He said, his voice eager, "Them bastards don't keep a lookout ordinary." And more directly to Stephen, "Rudder jammed up, sir?"

"She won't steer," answered Stephen shortly.

"D'you think she'll ever steer?" The man looked down disparagingly at the flat, low expanse of the bows; then, as Stephen made no answer, he went on, "Don't look to me as if she's got the shape."

Furiously Stephen turned on him. "God damn it! What do you know? Your job's to send signals. The crowd of you down there's got nothing to do but pick holes. Stop it or the lot of you'll be up before the captain!" He knew he was being unfair, but he was suffering from an accumulated load of failure, frustration, and a desperate anxiety.

The man said, unabashed, "Johnny Atkins run last night."

"He'll be back," said Stephen.

"He won't. Took the ship's cat with him. He was set on that cat."

A head thrust through the manhole and called to him, and Stephen went below. He passed through the turret and down into the space that held the training engine and, incongruously, the galley stove. The cooks were busy over a meal; the place had the odors of a bad eating house. It was ill lighted, and swirling with the smoke of burning fats.

Ericsson was in the captain's cabin, sitting in the one padded arm-chair the place afforded. On the round table was spread a sheaf of drawings. As Stephen came in he was storming at Worden, the *Monitor*'s hastily appointed captain. "I thought that he was too stupid to make a blunder. I should have measured it before she was launched." His finger was tapping the drawing of the balanced rudder. "There is too much for'ard of the rudder post. My eye told me but I did not check it. It is in that degree my fault, but he was a fool." He looked up sharply at Stephen. "Where have you been?"

Stephen knew how to deal with him now. He answered evenly, "Signaling the tug to come in and give us a line."

"It is the rudder," said the Swede furiously. "You have already reported the rudder to Washington?"

"It was clear that it was not satisfactory at the first trial, sir."

"It is I who should decide whether it is satisfactory or not," Ericsson barked at him.

"My instructions, which came from Washington last night, sir, were that the ship was to be dry-docked and a new rudder designed and put in if it failed again today."

Ericsson lumbered up out of the chair and smashed down both fists on the round table. "The *Monitor* is mine, and I say it shall not be done!" Again the fists crashed down.

Worden looked on in astonishment. He was not yet used to the engineer's gusty furies.

Two of the sheets of plans swirled to the floor.

"Put in a new rudder! They would waste a month doing that; I will make her steer satisfactorily in three days." He glared at Stephen again. "See that the towline is passed at once, and tell the tug to take us in as fast as she can!"

Stephen glanced automatically at Worden, and Worden nodded imperceptibly.

As he passed through the wardroom he saw Greene. "Three more days," said the first lieutenant. "We haven't got it. We're too late."

*   *   *

"Read it!" ordered Buchanan tensely. "Read it!" The hand that held the letter shook. "Mallory's mad—mad! Does he listen to nothing? Does he never read reports? Does he take in nothing? Read it! Go on, read it!"

Commodore Forrest took the letter from the shaking hand. He settled himself back in his chair and looked at the superscription. The letter was dated that morning—March 7—from the Confederate Navy Department at Richmond and it was signed, he could see, by Mallory.

"I submit for your consideration the attack of New York by the *Virginia*. Can the *Virginia* steam to New York and attack and burn the city? She can, I doubt not, pass Old Point safely, and, in good weather and a smooth sea, could doubtless go to New York. Once in the bay, she could shell and burn the city and the shipping. Such an event would eclipse all the glories of the combats of the sea, would place every man in it pre-eminently high and would strike a blow from which the enemy could never recover. Peace would inevitably follow. Bankers would withdraw their capital from the city. The Navy Yard and its magazines and all the lower part of the city would be destroyed, and such an event, by a single ship, would do more to achieve our immediate independence than would the results of many campaigns."

Forrest gave a brief, low whistle.

"It was bad enough when he wanted me to go to Washington," Buchanan fumed, "but New York! *New York!* God's name, I don't know that she will get down the river in safety. All I know is that she will float in a dock basin. Williamson will not answer for her engines. The only thing that he will say is that he's done everything that a human being can do. I don't know how she'll stand to gunfire. I don't know how she'll steer. And he wants me to take her to New York!"

Forrest said quietly: "You'll have to fight a battle in Hampton Roads first. You'll know by the end of that."

Bitterly Buchanan agreed: "I'll know." He walked silently up and down the length of the cabin while Forrest watched him. "I have not even a full crew," he broke out again after a little. "I've had to complete the manning of my guns with artillerymen—artillerymen, Commodore! And they won't take orders from me—they've got to have their own officers with them, by God, sir! Was ever a ship so manned?"

Equably Forrest said: "Still, they're aboard and they're good men, Franklin. Richmond was quick and sensible about that, at least."

"I have taken one more man—I found we needed one—a sergeant from the ship's guard, the Norfolk County Rifle Patriots, I believe, sir." Buchanan was too angry to use the advantages of friendship.

"I will make that right with Captain Etheredge," said Forrest.

"He at least had the dignity not to make conditions."

"You have all your ammunition aboard?"

"All that there is." The bitterness was heavy again in Buchanan's voice. "I am to batter New York to the ground and destroy the Navy Yard and chase the bankers out—and I have ammunition enough for barely one day's battle. He is mad, mad!"

"There will be more powder on the 10th, according to my advices, and more shot not later than the 13th."

Buchanan came to a sudden stop in front of Forrest. "Commodore, sir," he announced formally, "I have given orders for the priming of the engines. The fires were lit an hour ago. I will sail with the morning."

Forrest rose from his chair and put the letter on the table. Then he held out his hand. "God go with you," he said very quietly. "I came aboard to tell you that, according to a signal I have received from Richmond, the *Monitor* sailed from New York at dawn yesterday."

Chapter thirteen

GRISWOLD was drunk. His manner was little altered from its norm: he held himself straight, his eyes were steady, even the hand that moved incessantly on the stem of his glass betrayed nothing. The drink showed only in the increased acridness of his voice, in the bite of his questions as he baited Stephen. "What you mean adds up to this: Either she will be a good sea boat and float all the way to the Chesapeake or she'll be a bad sea boat and sink. Mr. Lootenant Knott, d'you ever make up your goddam mind about anything?"

Stephen was aware of Ericsson's eyes on him. Worden was sitting next to Ericsson; he also was watching, missing nothing. Stephen answered, "You asked me for a balanced view, Mr. Griswold."

"And I got it!" retorted Griswold savagely. "It may be white but, on the other hand, it might perhaps be black. You're a judgmatic bastard, Mr. Lootenant Knott!"

Stephen saw Worden's head jerk up. The great black spade beard accentuated the movement. The trivial quarrel had developed suddenly into something much more important. He had been brought to a declaration of faith, he knew that. He said: "Mr. Griswold, my orders are to return to Washington upon completion of the *Monitor*. I take it completion means the moment the orders are given for her to sail."

He was aware in a shift of Ericsson's glance, by the movement of Worden's beard, that he had failed them—that they required something more of him.

Griswold snapped contemptuously, "Orders!"

Suddenly Stephen knew what he had to do: he had to make his declaration, to announce his faith. With a sense of shock he realized that both Ericsson and Worden had unacknowledged doubts about him. Nothing less would satisfy them or, perhaps, he thought, comfort them. For Griswold he had no concern; he disliked Griswold. And Griswold was drunk. All of them, except perhaps Ericsson, had had too much liquor. Griswold's rudeness was of no importance.

Stephen said: "I must return to Washington, but I can see no reason why I should not return to Washington in the *Monitor*." He half turned and looked at Paulding, who sat beyond Winslow to the right of him.

Paulding grunted, "I don't know that I have the authority."

Ericsson said angrily: "I have. Do not forget, Commodore Paulding, that the *Monitor* is still mine. For ninety days until the fulfillment of this iniquitous contract she is still mine. The Navy Department considered it necessary that I should have a naval officer attached to me while she was being built by me. I consider that it is necessary that I should have a naval officer attached to the ship while she is being tested by the Navy Department."

Stephen bowed with an odd formality and let his eyes move on to

Worden's. "Lieutenant Worden," he asked stiffly, "have I your permission?"

Worden's eye glinted; he too disliked Griswold. "Glad to have you, Knott."

Winslow began to talk, overrunning Griswold's slow attempt to resume the argument.

Stephen sat still, considering Worden. He had never served with him before. Worden was five years his senior. His appointment as captain of the *Monitor* had taken everybody in New York by surprise. Oddly enough, Stephen had seen little of him in the last weeks of the completion of the *Monitor,* and that little had been mostly at times of crisis: at the moments of the engine breakdowns, of the failure of the rudder, of the trouble with the guns, in arguments over crew, ammunition, and the weight of the powder charges. None the less, he decided, he liked the man, liked even his short, salty temper. He wondered if he had made his decision to please Worden or to please Ericsson; and even as he wondered he knew that he had made it for neither man; he had made it for himself. He had made it because he was afraid of being afraid.

The *Monitor* could not be a good sea boat, he knew that.

They had stopped calling her "Ericsson's Folly." They were now calling her "Ericsson's Coffin Ship."

*   *   *

The dawn was cold and reluctant. Again the cloud hung low above the low ridge of Manhattan Island, and the houses along its skyline were squat, irregular, and seemed to shiver in the unwelcoming hour. The East River, ruffled by the dawn wind, was dark and leaden under the line of the houses, but there was no weight in the ruffling, no threat of a sea outside the harbor. From where he stood Stephen could see the *Currituck* juggling her paddles to stem the tide. The *Sachem* was to meet them down the harbor past Governors Island after they had completed the formalities at the Navy Yard.

The tug, the *Seth Low,* was alongside. She towered over them. It was extraordinary, for she was, after all, no more than a tug. She stood high, her sides, gigantic in the half-light, accentuating the low, raft-like freeboard of the *Monitor.*

Ericsson came up out of the turret hatchway for the last time. He lowered himself down the vertical ladder that clung close against the turret wall, breathing heavily. Worden followed him.

On the deck Ericsson beckoned to Stephen. Gruffly he said: "You have been helpful. I would be glad to work with you again."

Stephen knew that the words were a reward commensurate with his efforts. He had come to love this man in spite of his irascibility and his vanities. He held out his hand. "It has been a privilege to work under you, sir. I shall remember it all my life."

"If naval officers ever remember!" retorted Ericsson, caustic to the end, and strode off the ship. At the quayside he turned and, in his deep, booming voice said: "Even if the rebel fleet hides under the stolen guns at Norfolk, you can split it into matches in half an hour." The shout was addressed to Worden, but it was meant, obviously, for the whole ship's company.

Worden's great black spade beard lifted with the faint wind as he raised his hand in acknowledgment. Then, with the Swede watching them, rocklike on the quayside, his feet wide apart, Worden turned to the master of the tug. From his place in the bow Greene took up the orders. The two ships began to move slowly out into the young ebb tide. The *Currituck* let out a long blare on her whistle, and the *Seth Low* answered it. There was no demonstration along the shore; there were no spectators—no one except Ericsson, a handful of people from the Yard, and a small boy with a dog, wide-eyed and astonished in the early light.

They went down the East River with the tide.

Worden stood for a moment on the deck beside Stephen. "It was worth waiting for the wind to fall. We've a good day for a beginning. There won't be a ripple."

*   *   *

Greene closed his telescope with three sharp, incisive clicks. "Barnegat Light." His voice was definite. He consulted a small pocket compass. Then he stooped over the open hatch of the conning tower and shouted down: "Report to the pilothouse—Barnegat Light bearing south by west, as near as I can make it." He straightened himself again. "How the devil they expect a compass to work in an iron box . . ."

Stephen watched the faint pricking of the light against the dark of the horizon. The night was clear enough to show the towline when it dropped to the surface of the water and rose again, lifting with it a white fall of spray. The *Seth Low* loomed high against the sea edge at the end of it. The noise of her paddles came over the water, sometimes only a rustle, sometimes a beating roar like the sound of an angry rapid. The line between the tug and the *Monitor* seemed to divide the world into two halves: one half, to port, was utter darkness; the other, to starboard, was full of light—the deck lights of the *Sachem* and the red of her port light, the lights of the *Currituck* a little astern of her, and far beyond them, pale as drowning stars, faint lights along the Jersey shore.

Greene said: "We must be making best part of seven knots. We had Sandy Hook abeam around four o'clock. She's standing up to it."

"He said she would." Stephen kept his eyes on the winking lights ahead.

Greene grunted and then said aloud, "You think a hell of a lot of Ericsson, don't you?"

"I think he's a great man," replied Stephen simply.

"Goes for me too. This ship's different. Even when she moves she's different." Greene turned and tried to see Stephen's face in the darkness. "Was that why you came? You had no call to come."

"Yes, I had to come. There was too much talk."

"Coffin ship?" Greene's voice ended on a note of derisive interrogation. Stephen said nothing. After a little Greene spoke again. "Mare's-tails at sunset."

"I've seen mare's-tails of an evening often enough and no wind followed."

"We all have!" The derisive note was back in Greene's voice.

*   *   *

Stimers woke him. Stephen felt the bruise of the engineer's fingers on his shoulder. He said: "Daylight and the wind's making." His face looked curiously concerned, yet when Stephen asked, "How's she taking it?" he answered sharply, "She's a good sea boat."

Stephen dropped his feet out of the bunk and stood up. There was little motion. The narrow cabin was full of noises: the rustle of the sea underscoring the beat of the pumping engines and the throb of the blowers, and over that the deeper note of the main engine. Above the conjoined noises there came suddenly a long, shuddering groan. Stephen exclaimed, "Christ, what's that?"

Stimers snapped back: "You sleep like a log in a swamp! That damned contraption's been howling like a screech owl best part of an hour since the wind started. You're wanted in the pilothouse." He stomped out of the cabin.

Stephen reached up for a heavy jersey to pull on over his shirt and remembered suddenly that this was the *Monitor*. No one in the *Monitor* went on deck. No one on the *Monitor* was in the open. He grinned at his reflection in the tiny inadequate mirror, pulled on his uniform coat, and moved out into the wardroom.

The lamp in its gimbals swung a little, or seemed to swing, with the motion of the ship. Keeler, the paymaster, was asleep, sprawled half across the table, his head clear of the intended pillow of his arms. Logue, the surgeon, was next to him; he was awake, but his eyes were closed. The deep shuddering moan came again from the forward part of the ship.

Logue said, his eyes still closed: "That's Ericsson's patent hawsehole. If you didn't know Ericsson, you'd say it was the soul of a ship in torment." He jerked his head toward the paymaster. "He sleeps through it. My own soul isn't clean enough."

Stephen laughed and went on, feeling his way in the uncertain, flickering lights for the foot of the pilothouse ladder.

It was wet. The deck below it was wet; water dripped down in a cold freshness. As his shoulders thrust up into the pilothouse, Worden, close beside the hatch, said, precisely as if he were continuing an interrupted conversation: "It's inevitable, of course, that the water will come in with the slightest head sea. We must have the damned slits uncovered if we're to steer at all." A shower of stinging spray punctuated the sentence. "Won't be fun if the sea makes, will it, Frederickson?"

"No, sir," replied the stolid master's mate at the wheel.

Stephen said nothing.

"Pilothouse ought to have been on top of the turret," Worden's voice went on, unheated, dispassionate, clear. "Told him so. Said he knew but there wasn't anything he could do about it. What do you say, Knott?"

"It couldn't be done in the time," Stephen answered, watching the bright divided bar of light between the ponderous blocks of armor that framed the pilothouse. "He made drawings, but it couldn't be done."

"Should have come to sea with us," said Worden crisply. "Taught him a thing or two. All shipbuilders should be taken to sea in their own ships. All constructors . . ."

Stephen felt the deck give abruptly below him. It was a different motion from anything he had felt before. In the fractional second that followed it he remembered Stimers saying that she was a good sea boat. Then, without warning, the light of the slit was cut off. For a moment he saw the water, like an ingot of translucent green, squared to the shape of the slit, luminous. Then it hit. Frederickson was knocked away from the wheel, Worden was jerked back against the bulkhead,

Stephen himself was knocked against the captain. He was soaked, they were all soaked. The place was suddenly a maelstrom of spray and broken water.

"See what I mean?" came Worden's voice in Stephen's ear. "No fun at all. You all right, Frederickson?"

Frederickson was back at the wheel already. His voice was no longer so stolid as he said, "Yes, sir."

A dart of spray came through.

Worden disregarded it. He said carefully to Stephen: "Want you to get up to the turret. They tell me it's spewing the oakum out of the deck ring. See what you can do. And tell Greene to do something about that damned noise."

"Sir," said Stephen, and dropped down the wet ladder. The deck was swimming below it.

The surgeon's eyes opened for an instant as he passed through the wardroom again. "You're wet," said Logue reprovingly.

On the berth deck men were working with buckets and mops. Water was coming down through the hatch.

Stocking, the bosun's mate, called needlessly, "Water's beginning to come in, sir."

Stimers was in the turret. He shouted irritably: "It's coming in between the Chris-forsaken ring and the shield—can't get at it." He looked angrily at Stephen, as if in some way he were responsible. "That crackpot idea at the Navy Yard—wedge it up and calk it with oakum! Oakum must have gone."

Again the ship plunged through the horrible falling motion that had preceded the flooding of the pilothouse. They could hear, despite the muffling steel, the crash of water against the turret and the hiss and suck as it spurted in below the ponderous cincture of the armor.

Stephen said, "She doesn't like it."

"There's a gale blowing."

Stephen said hurriedly, "We'd better get up on deck and see what it is." He was overwhelmed with a sense of confinement, with the knowledge that above him was the open sky and the wind, and that here in this iron box there was only still air and half-darkness and the sound of water. He began to climb the ladder to the turret hatch.

Water came over the hatch as he opened it in a great arc of brilliant spray. He thrust his shoulders through. The sea was racing aft over the flatness of the deck. The sun had risen and the day was brilliant, cold, and clear. There was no gale—only a short, steep sea, a shoalwater sea.

Stimers came up behind him, followed by Stocking. The deck was clear now. They dropped down the ladder. It was difficult to see under the edge of the armor in the shallow channel of the deck ring; they could find only wisps of fiber, indeterminate ends of the calking. There were areas that seemed to be empty. Stephen was stooping to examine one of these when a third sea came aboard. Stocking was still on the ladder. Stimers jumped for the lower rungs. Stephen half turned, saw the sea, and spread-eagled himself against the turret face. He felt it give with a heavy slowness as the ship dropped at the bows, and then the water crashed against him. He felt his hands scrabbling for the rivet heads, heard the roar and fury as the water swept past his ears; and then it was over and the deck was clear again. He went back up the ladder with the water streaming off him.

To Stimers, on the roof of the turret, he said: "She's grinding the oakum every time the ship drops her head, spewing it out when the seas hit her. They sweep aft like a battering ram—nothing to stop them."

Stimers answered, hurriedly defensive: "He planned it that way. He used to watch the timber rafts when he was a kid. They took everything that came, and the pilothouse rode through it all."

Greene had his head and shoulders through the hatchway now. "*They* were made of timber."

Stimers snorted.

Greene went on: " 'Tisn't a gale; why, it's no more'n a fresh breeze!"

Stimers pointed to the *Currituck*. "Look how *she's* rolling!"

Behind him Stocking said, "The ol' *Currituck,* she'd roll in a dry dock."

An hour later Stephen reported to Worden. There appeared to be no way to stop the flow of water under the turret, but the pumps were dealing with it. The berth deck was wet and uncomfortable, but there was no apparent danger.

Worden asked: "Is the wind freshening? You can't tell in here. It whistles through that damned slit every whichway. Only thing we can judge by—the sea's coming through more often."

"It's freshening," replied Stephen shortly.

Two hours later Newton, the assistant engineer, came forward. "Been tryin' to get you on the voice pipe. Water's comin' in through the air blowers. We goin' to have trouble. Can you stop her till the wind drops?"

Worden answered curtly: "No, it's an onshore wind. We'll slow if we have to."

"Better slow then," said Newton bluntly.

"If we have to."

There was no hot food; the galley under the turret was flooded out.

At noon Stephen went aft. The cooks were working disconsolately with hard biscuit and preserved meat. The galley floor was awash. Water dripped at a dozen places. The machinery that turned the turret was being drowned. The air was used up and foul: the smells of old cooking, burning coal, and oil were all compounded.

One of the junior engineers called to him as he passed: "Ventilation's on the bum. The belts have come off the blowers."

He thrust his head into the boiler room. The narrow alleyway was full of fumes, gas, and smoke. It was barely possible to see across it. The lamps flickered, red and faint. At once he was assailed by voices. Hands and Campbell were both shouting at once—shouting for the surgeon. Their voices in the confined space hammered at his ears. He was aware suddenly that the main engines were dead; there was no beat, no vibration.

Hands came close to him. He shouted: "Stimers is out—out like a candle. Somebody get the doctor!"

Stephen thrust through to the engine room. Stimers was being carried out. Newton was shouting beyond them. On a half-word his voice ceased. There were more cries. Stephen pushed in between the engines. Newton was lying across a grating, his body partly supported by hot pipes. Two men were heaving at him. Stephen went to help them, and they got the engineer down to the level and began to pull him hurriedly through the boiler-room alleyway. Stephen's eyes were burning and tortured, the reek of gas in his lungs. He began to cough; the men were coughing too. They slithered on the greasy plating, half dragging Newton, his heels bumping on the ridges of the plates, and finally they reached the space below the turret. The pumps here were silent too. They almost tossed Newton through the elliptical doorway in the bulkhead. Many hands took him on the far side.

"Get him up into the turret!" Stephen ordered.

Many voices said: "Yes, sir . . . Yes . . . Logue's up in the turret with Mr. Stimers. . . . Get him up into the turret! . . . Get him up!"

Stephen followed the engineer's unconscious body into the turret space, helped awkwardly and unnecessarily by what seemed a multitude.

Logue had already gone up to the roof of the turret. Stephen heard the surgeon calling impatiently: "Bring him up to the air! God damn it, he's got to breathe, don't he? There's no air down there now—not a breath that's fit . . ."

On the roof of the turret one of the men said: "They were trying to get the blowers going. There wasn't draft enough for the boilers.

They was blowing back—hot gas. Christ, I never breathed anything like it! Mr. Stimers, he went out just like you'd blow a candle."

Hands said, "The hand pumps can't hope to hold the water."

Stephen looked out over the sea. It was not an angry sea; it was a sea of small waves. It would have been a friendly sea from the side of a three-decker, or even perhaps from the quarter-deck of a frigate. He dropped down the ladder into the turret. Water from a sea that he had not acknowledged slapped over the turret and poured down the open hatchway after him. Men clutched his legs as he came down.

He heard voices: "Is she goin' to sink, Lootenant? . . . How we goin' to get out o' here? . . . She's a goddam 'Coffin Ship' all right! . . . What we goin' to do, Lootenant?"

He shouted at them furiously, his voice blazing with an anger that was directed more against himself than against them: "Quiet, you fools! Pipe down!" And then more loudly, more savagely: "Shut up! She's not going to sink. It's no more than a hard breeze up there. We'll get the blowers working again."

He went down into the training-engine space below. The cooks assailed him; some of the men held cloths against their noses. "Is she goin' to sink, Mr. Knott? Is she goin' to sink?"

Storming and shouting, he made his way against the tide of men to the pilothouse.

Worden's voice greeted him at once, calm, conversational. "There's too much noise among the men, Mr. Knott. What's the situation?"

Stephen said: "The blowers have failed. Steam's down to less than five pounds. The pumps have stopped."

"The wind?"

"Moderate, sir. There's a short, steep sea. I think that we're crossing a shoal patch."

Worden said coolly: "We are. The wind will moderate at sunset."

"I hope so."

Worden's tone was composed and certain. "It will moderate. If it doesn't, we'll heave to." He raised his voice. "Get the Worthington pumps manned, Mr. Greene!"

And Stephen heard Greene's prompt response below him, as if he had been awaiting the order, "Ay, ay, sir."

*   *   *

The wind dropped at sunset. The men laboring at the hand pumps greeted the news with a ragged cheer. They could hear below them the slosh of the water in the bottom of the ship. They could feel her altered, uncertain motion. They worked in short spells, going up under orders to the turret top for fresh air. At nine o'clock the engine-room crew, sobbing for breath in the foul air of the boiler room, got the fires to draw again. Hands and Campbell had at last got the belts on the air blowers. Slowly, reluctantly, the air cleared. Smoke and steam and gas and foulness blew out of the compartments. The ship seemed to come alive again under their feet; the main pumps started up, and the exhausted men collapsed in cursing heaps beside the Worthingtons.

A little after eleven o'clock the cooks got coffee made, and men drank and laughed and clapped each other on the shoulder, and a babel of sound began in the berth deck.

"She come through it all right, the old bitch."

"I said she'd swim."

"The hell you said! You said we'd sink."

"She ain't no bloody sea boat."

"She's a goddam canal barge."

"She rides all right."

"She rides like a half-tide rock."

"We come through all right, didn't we? What you belly-achin' about?"

At precisely two minutes after midnight a low, soft moan like that of a cow separated from its calf came up again through the patent hawse-hole.

Worden was in his cabin. Stephen was leaning against the lintel of the door.

Worden, in his composed, conversational voice said: "Chincoteague shoals." His eyes held Stephen's, and Stephen thought that in them he could see a wealth of fears, a concentration of anxieties, and he knew for a moment the terrible responsibility of command. Worden went on, "It might be that it would have paid us better to head out to sea." His eyes remained fixed on Stephen's. After a long pause he added: "Lose us a lot of time, though. I don't think we've got any time left to lose."

The hawsepipe groaned again.

Worden rose and began to pull on a wet oilskin. "Is Stimers on his feet yet?"

"He looks as if he were at the end of a ten-day jag."

Worden nodded. "I want you in the turret. We may have to signal suddenly." He went forward to the pilothouse.

At seven minutes past one the wheel jammed. Webber's shout could be heard through half the ship. It could not be heard, however, as far as the turret. Stephen, sitting with his back against one of the gun carriages, felt abruptly an altered motion. He went up the ladder to the hatch with a first intimation of disaster. In the night darkness it took him a long minute to focus properly. He could see the stars overhead first and then the lights of the ships in company. There was nothing ahead of them, nothing at all where the *Seth Low* should have been. Almost unwillingly he searched her out and found her stern lights abeam of them. It was difficult to believe: it had no rational explanation. He felt the slap of another sea, this time broadside on to them, and knew from the feel of the wind and the angle of the sea that they had yawed widely out on the end of the tow and that there was only one possible explanation: the steering had broken down.

A heavy sea broke over them from broadside on, and then savagely the nose of the ship was dragged round and she began a wild, incalculable sweep to starboard. He heard men on the turret top behind him and voices in the turret. The night lost order and rule and discipline. The ship became a chaos.

Again the blowers failed. Again the water crept up into the ash pits. Again the steam and the hot gas and the sulfur smells spread through the ship. Slowly the pumps died. The ship filled with new sounds, new water noises, new shouting, and the clatter of hurrying feet. Men came up in relays, and crouched gasping and sobbing for breath in the cold wet windiness of the night. They went below, and others took their places. And always the ship yawed wildly from side to side, heeling with the impetus of her movement, swept endlessly, remorselessly, brutally by the chop—helpless and impotent.

At twelve minutes to five Greene clawed his way, cursing, up the ladders, shouldering the men aside. On the turret top he shouted into the darkness: "Knott! Stephen Knott! Where the hell are you?" And, as Stephen answered him, he called: "Captain's orders: burn a red Coston light, Mr. Knott!" When he had identified Stephen, he clawed his way close in the shrieking darkness and said: "She won't float above an hour. The Worthington pumps are jammed." Then after a pause, very softly, so that Stephen could scarcely hear it, "We're sinking."

3

Storm Center

Chapter one

JERIEL sat hunched against the wall with his head sunk between arms that rested on his bony kneecaps. It was impossible to tell whether he was asleep or awake.

Old Sam yawned. His voice growled as he said: "Four A.M., Lindy. You oughter been home hours back."

"I've got to wait, Uncle Sam."

"I'm scairt," admitted Sam candidly.

She bubbled with laughter. "Of my father?"

"I ain't scairt of Ash Cleave. Your Aunt Deborah I can soft talk." He pointed with his pipestem at the crouched figure of the boy. "I'm scairt of his ma."

Jeriel did not lift his head. "She don't know I'm out—never does. Vernie Grant's takin' an all-fired time." There was a little silence and, as nobody seemed disposed to challenge the remark, he added, "Mebbe he's found a girl." And as that produced no response, he said, after another pause, "Mebbe it's jest he's been shot."

The old compositor began to calculate. "Hickory's the first place he could pick up anythin' certain. If the Yankees have come up past Currituck, they'd know it there for sure. Ain't twenty miles to Hickory; he could be here any minute. If they're *in* Hickory, he's been shot— an' you an' John Porter better get that fancy ship o' yours away, Lindy!" He drew on his pipe for a little. Then he leaned forward confidentially over the stone, his elbows black on the ink-marked metal. "Reckon the editor's howlin' up th' wrong tree."

Linden shook her head stubbornly. "There were three gunboats, and they were seen in the deep water north of Currituck."

"There was two boats seen west o' Elizabeth City day before yesterday." The old man hawked and found the spittoon with the precision

240

of years. "Even Ulysses, he didn't claim it was more'n a reconnaissance in strength." He chewed the phrase over, relishing it.

Linden said, "That was a feint," and then hesitated uncertainly, realizing that old Sam would relish that phrase too. She went on hurriedly: "They want us to think they're going to come up through Elizabeth City again so we'll shift what men we've got there."

"But they ain't," agreed Sam. "They're just goin' to peck away—peck, peck, peck like a bird in a plum tree. An' one o' these days they'll come in blam—somewheres where you're not lookin', for all you talk like a full general. You go home, Lindy Cleave, an' get some sleep. You got t'keep th' roses in your cheeks." He allowed his voice a full measure of irony.

Linden made no reply.

They sat quiet, the minutes ticking by on the big wall clock of the composing room. The two other compositors and the colored boy were fast asleep. The silence became enormous, portentous, as if the whole weight of the precarious affairs of Portsmouth were crushing them down. The enemy was moving up the Sounds now, probing up and up in the rear of the railroad tracks, behind the Dismal Swamp, up into Currituck Sound. Linden knew from the personal, intimate gossip of the camps how little the Confederate Army had to stand against the enemy, how wide the area that it had to cover, how broad the Northern Army's lines of attack.

For weeks now—ever since Roanoke and Elizabeth City had fallen —the tension had been growing. It was visible in the streets, in the faces of the women, in the uncertainties of the Yard, in the growing shortage of food and goods in the shops. For the first time since the burning of the Navy Yard the war had moved in on them. Before, there had been nothing except the occasional venturesome gunboat dropping a shell on the batteries to stir up a futile exchange of idiocies, and the long gun on the Rip Raps fort lobbing a shell across the wind-ruffled water. Now it had the feel of a hand on the throat in the darkness. It held all the seeds of unreasoning terror.

It was Jeriel who heard the footsteps. He lifted his head suddenly from between his knees. "Here he is!"

"Then he's walked the twenty miles from Hickory." Sam's ponderous sarcasm filled the room. "Ain't brought no horse with him anyways, 'less he's carryin' it."

The feet came nearer, hurrying up the sidewalk. Revell came in, not Vernon Grant.

Linden exclaimed almost angrily, "It's you!"

He said, "Linden, I had to see you."

"At four o'clock in the morning?"

"I had to—it was my only chance. I climbed up the back roof."

Sam leered at him. "Lot o' bright young men's been cut off in their prime fallin' off roofs in the dark." He paused, then added, "With a charge o' buckshot in them."

Jeriel put his head back between his knees and sniggered.

Revell ignored the old man. "Lindy, I've got to talk to you. Come on outside!"

"It's warm in here. You can talk."

"No," he answered her, fiercely demanding, "you got to come outside! I got to talk to you alone!"

Frostily calm, she said: "I'm not coming anywhere for you to paw me around, Rev Jordan. I'm tired of being pawed."

Jeriel raised his head and stared at Revell, and one of the other compositors, wakened by the commotion, sat up and laughed.

Revell flushed angrily. With instinctive drama he said, "I come to say goodbye, Lindy."

She got up with a quick eagerness. "Goodbye? Revell Jordan, where are you going? What's happened?"

He moved toward the door, wordlessly, and Linden followed him.

As it closed, the old compositor turned to Jeriel. "See? Curiosity gets 'em every time. Any woman. Works better'n liquor."

Outside, Revell put his arms round Linden. The gesture was masterful; he was sure of his ground now.

Linden, protected by a thick dress and a winter overcoat, submitted. "Where are you going, Rev?"

"I've volunteered for the *Merrimac*." His voice was full of arrogance and self-esteem, but she overlooked this. She twisted herself round, flung her arms round his neck, and kissed him passionately. His own arms tightened, crushing her against himself. "Ah, Lindy, Lindy! I did it for you." He felt the returning grip of her arms slacken a little, but was not percipient enough to examine the cause. "They need another man"—his voice was boastful now—"'a good man,' Captain Buchanan said, 'a good man who can handle guns.' I said if they wanted a good man I was ready. I knew you'd want it that way, Lindy."

"I want it that way." And all the while Linden knew that he should have done it for Virginia, not for her—that that was the way she really wanted it. She knew somehow that this was not real, that somewhere it was dishonest.

Urgently he murmured against her ear: "Come on down to the wood
yard, Lindy. It's quiet there, we can talk. We got to talk, Lindy"—
with a quick, splurging pathos he ended—"before I go."

It might be false, it might be real. She was caught in the moment's
emotion. The words had a special significance in these times, they had
connotations of sorrow and endings. Goodbye had different meanings
in peace and war.

"I was the one Cap'n Buchanan picked," he said importantly and
impatiently before she had time to act on her hesitations. "I knew you
would want it." He kissed her again and she returned his kiss, but without the earlier fire. He had thrown away an opportunity, but he did not
know it. "Come on, let's go!" He urged her forward.

In the darkness behind them the door of the composing room opened
and let out a red-gold light and closed again.

He said passionately: "Ah, come, Lindy, come!" not knowing that it
was already too late.

In the darkness on the porch of the newspaper office somebody
whistled—a long, low, derisive whistle.

"One o' these days I'll break that damn' boy's neck!" exclaimed
Revell furiously.

"Don't talk like that, Revell; I can't come to the wood yard—you
know I can't. You know you wouldn't want it, after. Ah, Revell, don't
ask it—don't! I'll see you in the morning."

With an elaborately somber gesture he said: "In the morning'll be
too late, Lindy. Too late . . ."

"You're not going—"

"We lit the fires three hours back, Lindy. We're goin' out this
mornin'—to fight."

The door behind them opened again, let out its flood of light, and
closed. In the silence that followed the short, sharp slam she kissed him
once more—kissed him in a return of the earlier passion, clinging to
him, part of him. She was immensely, immeasurably moved. Her heart
was pounding; she felt strong and weak at the same time. Barriers were
down, inhibitions no longer had existence.

Then the light of the composing room flooded the street a third
time, and old Sam's voice boomed out across its passionate silences.
"Is that true what you say, Rev Jordan—is th' *Merrimac* goin' to sail
in th' mornin'? Are you sure of it? By dam, this'll make a better special
than if the Yankees had *took* Currituck! Lindy Cleave, come in here!
You gotter help. Boy, go get Ulysses Hogan! Jeriel, you wake up the
editor! Rev, what time does Buchanan aim to sail?"

A window flung up and a voice called, "Is the *Merrimac* goin' to sail?"

Another window flung up.

A door flew open.

Chapter two

THE bows of the *Sachem* reared above the laboring *Monitor* like the roof of a house lifting in a hurricane. The bowsprit made a wide ragged circle against the brilliant stars. Then it plunged down suddenly with an immense roaring of water on either side, and Greene said angrily, "Dammit, he'll sink us!"

Neither Stephen nor he himself saw any incongruity in this. They had room only for an exhausted anger. The *Sachem* was turning now, her port paddle still, her starboard paddle thrashing above the noise of the wind and the endless, unceasing crash of the seas. She moved past them, slowly, rolling and plunging simultaneously. Broken water streamed from her.

A voice bellowed through the megaphone: "Wind's steady, but we're less'n a mile from the edge of the shoals. If you can hang on . . ."

A man crouched at Stephen's feet on the overcrowded, heaving turret top gasped: "Christ, no! How can we hang onto this?"

The *Monitor* lurched violently. There was a sickening dead feeling at the end of the lurch, as if something held her, some invisible hand that was reluctant to loose its grip. Stephen lost his balance and fell into the heaving mass of men and hit out blindly in an effort to regain his balance. Men held him round the legs.

A voice said, "Shove your hand on my shoulder, Lootenant."

Another said, "Let's get the hell out o' this!"

Greene was still standing. Stephen saw him in the faint light cup his hands to his mouth and bellow: "We'll hang on. But you'd better have your boats ready."

The trumpet voice came back: "Less'n a mile."

A sea crashed over them. It was threaded with gleaming sparks of phosphorescence, so that for a moment Stephen had the illusion that they had turned upside down and were looking at the stars streaming past. Then it cleared, leaving throbbing brilliances on men's clothes, on their faces, on their hair.

The *Monitor* yawed wildly away from the *Sachem*. The towrope stretched bar-taut in the darkness, holding them to the tug as if they were a loose-jointed, articulated part of her. Water crashed over them again, but Stephen had a wild, hopeful feeling that it was not so heavy this time, that there was not the same angry viciousness in it.

He got back on his feet. There was a sudden commotion among the men, different from the heaving, animal movement that followed slowly on the movements of the ship. Stephen heard a voice say: "The cap'n— make room for the cap'n! This way, Cap'n. Put your hand here— your foot now." They were lifting Worden into the dark chaos, handling him up, deriving a sense of importance from his presence.

"Where the hell's the *Sachem?*" he demanded.

"She closed us, sir. Said we were less'n a mile from the end of the shoals—could we hang on."

"You said . . . ?"

"I said 'Yes,' sir," answered Greene proudly.

A sea broke over them again.

Chapter three

THE crowd blocked Court Street outside Trinity Church. The square, uncompromising tower lifted over it like a lighthouse. People had flooded into the churchyard round the ancient graves. The long, shallow pediment of the east end seemed to cover them like tired wings. Linden could hear the organ, hear the deep, beating notes of it throbbing out the air of a psalm. She heard over the hushed and silent heads the opening words: "Blessed be the Lord my strength, which teacheth my hands to war, and my fingers to fight."

A woman close to her took up the words: "My goodness, and my fortress; my high tower, and my deliverer; my shield, and he in whom I trust; who subdueth my people under me."

The whole crowd was singing now, calling up out of memory the ancient words, swept by a deep and passionate fervor. "Lord, what is man, that thou takest knowledge of him! or the son of man, that thou makest account of him!

"Man is like to vanity: his days are as a shadow that passeth away. . . ."

From inside the church came the rich bass of men's voices; through the wide-open doors a diapason of deep, full notes. Linden felt the tears streaming down her face. There was in this dark singing a profound emotion. All the officers of the *Merrimac,* she knew, were in the church; Jeriel had brought the news to her. Porter was there and Williamson and Jim Meads and a score of the men who had worked on her, and French Forrest and Captain Lee and Captain Fairfax and the officers of the Yard, and their wives, and the men who had helped and their wives, and the mayor and the people—the people of Portsmouth, for this was their ship, this was the thing they had done for the war, the thing they had done for Virginia.

The psalm moved thunderously to its close, a deep, smoldering passion behind the words, a dark awareness: "Lord, what is man, that thou takest knowledge of him . . ."

She heard above the silence the voice of Mr. Wingfield, earnest, self-righteous, calling down the Lord's fire, calling down the help of God.

Next to her a woman cried, with a hot, revivalist fervor: "The Lord will hear! The Lord will help!"

Through blinding tears Linden said, "It would help a lot more if he called on Mr. Mallory for ammunition," and, turning, fought her way out of the crowd.

Behind her she could hear the indignant chorus of voices: "Linden Cleave! . . . Linden Cleave! . . . That girl! . . . Lindy Cleave!"

*   *   *

The quay was crowded. All work in the Yard had stopped. Every man who could had come to the wharf. There were women there, and the officers of the Yard, and Marines, and seamen off duty, and people from the town and children—small boys had climbed on points of vantage. The crowd was full of shouting and laughter. It had an effervescent excitement.

The *Beaufort* was slipping her lines.

Jim McCarrick went to the edge of the stringpiece and bellowed across to her as the water widened: "Charlie, bring a Yankee master's mate back with you so that I can be exchanged for him!"

In the crowd voices took up the story. "Jim, he was captured a

'Lizabeth City. . . . He was sent back on parole. . . . He cain't fight again 'less he's exchanged. Hey, Jim, you don't want to go back fightin'. Ain't you got no sense at all?"

A midshipman on the *Beaufort* shouted back, "We'll get one for you, Jim!"

The gap widened and became open water.

The crowd surged toward the *Raleigh*'s berth. There was an exhilarating interchange of instruction, of crude, earthy humor. In turn she too slipped her ropes and stood out into the Branch.

The crowd flooded back to the *Merrimac*. The big ship had singled up her lines. Now, as they watched, shouting across the open space between the ship and the edge of the quay, men finished plastering the last of the slush and the grease down the ribbed sides of her armoring. Workmen came hurrying ashore, carrying their tools with them. From somewhere inside her, somewhere on the level of the gun deck, there came the sound of continuous hammering. Orders and counterorders were shouted: instructions to workmen still on the ship, requests to people ashore. Seamen hurried backward and forward up and down the single gangway. Through all the froth and excitement the *Merrimac* shone in the morning sun, black and formidable, and the battle flags lifted and fell and lifted again above her.

Buchanan came up onto the gratings of the upper deck. Before he was fully visible the crowd recognized him and began to cheer. He turned toward the quay and acknowledged it with a full salute. There was a kind of pageantry in the moment. Catesby Jones came up and joined his captain, and the crowd cheered again. Two pilots added themselves to the group, and the crowds cheered them too.

The atmosphere of the yard had become charged with an electric energy. In a thunder of cheering Buchanan passed an order to Catesby Jones, and the lieutenant bellowed it through a speaking trumpet. The gangway came down with a run and crashed on the quay. The stern ropes splashed in the water and were hauled ashore. The bow ropes came home. There was a brown-white flurry of broken water at the *Merrimac*'s stern and, with the tug hauling at her bow, she moved slowly away from the wharf. Above the noise of the cheering a ship's whistle blew and another joined it and was followed by another and another, until the air of the Branch was quivering with thunderous organ notes. In the Yard a bell began to ring furiously, and a bell in Gosport church answered it. The bells of Trinity sounded, and were joined by bells from across the water. In an enormous fugue, whose harmonies were made of human voices and steam whistles, of bells, and the sound of paddle-wheels and the cries of the startled gulls, the *Merrimac* went out to war.

*   *   *

Sam rested his elbows on the familiar timber. Over the roar of the steam whistles and the clang of the bells he said evenly: "She's sailed. Don't know as I ever thought she would. How many false alarms we had, Ash?" He did not bother to turn his head toward the Navy Yard.

Cleave had climbed a little up the pile to get a clear view. "She's sailed. She was bound to sail sometime, Sam. There's a point where all work comes to test. You can't avoid it in a man or in a ship."

"And if the test don't work?"

Cleave stepped down from the ledge on which he had been standing. "If it fails, it fails." He knew that Sam was thinking of Linden. Without bothering to acknowledge it in words, he continued: "She's built everything on this, everything she's ever done for the war, everything in a sense that she's ever thought about it. It's a part of her now." Very softly so that the words were hardly audible above the continuing blare of the whistles, he added, "I don't know what she'll do if the *Merrimac* fails."

Dryly the old man said: "If I was her father, I'd worry a sight more about what she'll do if the *Merrimac* wins!"

Cleave shook his head as if freeing himself of something irritating and unimportant. "That doesn't matter."

"Way she was last night, I'd say it mattered a lot. I reckon that boy Jeriel saved you a peck o' trouble round about four o'clock this morning."

Cleave shook his head again. "It's of no importance."

"Most fathers set a bit more store by their girls' virginity."

Cleave turned to look at him. "Does it matter? She'll lose it now or she'll lose it later. It's what may happen to her herself if this thing fails. Look!" He pointed to the boat sheds beyond the lumber yard. Clear of them the black and rounded end of the *Merrimac*'s armored housing slid with a slow, inexorable movement into view. They could see the dark openings of the gun ports and the rounded muzzles of the guns, the knot of men standing on her gratings, the great central smoke-stack joined at last to the black column of smoke that had lifted for hours above the clustered buildings of the Yard.

Reluctantly Sam turned his head at last. For a long time he watched wordlessly while the bells clamored and the air trembled with the shudder of the whistles. He said at length: "God damn it! If that isn't the ugliest thing I ever seen float on water . . ."

"Nobody'll worry about her looks if she smashes the wooden ships out of Hampton Roads," observed Cleave grimly. "She's floating, she moves, and it looks as if she'll steer. Sam, if that thing does what Franklin Buchanan says she'll do, it will stretch this war out another year—at least!"

The old compositor grunted. "You lose either way, Ash Cleave. You don't want her to win, and you reckon if she loses she'll break Linden's heart—and there ain't nothin' you can do about it either way."

"Nothing, but I wish it wasn't Revell Jordan."

"Mebbe," said Sam meditatively, "if the *Merrimac* sinks, he'll drown. He's aboard of her."

"I know."

* * *

Commodore Buchanan stood out alone on the grating that formed the deck of the armored house. He had found the pilothouse cramped, the view limited. He had the sailing-ship captain's need for a free view of the sky. Catesby Jones stood two paces behind him. A signaler stood with him, and a brace of messengers and three senior officers, with Ramsey, the engineer, to the right of them, making a solid triangle based on the companion hatch.

Buchanan, his eyes fixed on the channel down past the point of Craney Island, spoke into the faint, gentle wind of their passage. "Mr. Ramsey, your engines appear to be turning steadily. Are you content with them?"

Ramsey answered: "Sir, nobody would be content with those engines —not ever—but they are doing more than I'd hoped for."

"Do you consider that you need a further trial, Mr. Ramsey?"

"We've ten miles to go to the Roads, sir. That will be trial enough."

Buchanan abandoned the interrogation. For a long time he was quiet.

The water was clear ahead of the ship—the obstructions had been removed from the center of the channel when the *Germantown* was placed in position as guard ship. This was the real mouth of the Elizabeth. After this, harbor ended.

They were almost up to the batteries on Craney Point before he spoke again. "Mr. Ramsey?"

Ramsey, who had been hovering in half-doubt as to whether he were still wanted, stiffened and said, "Sir?"

"Mr. Ramsey, what would happen to your engines and boilers if there should be a collision?"

"They are braced tight, sir. No collision could budge them." Ramsey waited.

Again Buchanan was silent for a long time. They could see men of the batteries on Craney Island standing on the glacis, cheering. The low, level flat of the island had a crest of people. The buildings, the magazines, the shelters, the guns themselves were crowded with men cheering and waving.

Buchanan said: "The *Cumberland* has the new rifled guns, the only ones in their whole fleet we have cause to fear. The moment we are in the Roads I propose to steer directly for her, and ram."

*   *   *

"Sir," said the lookout of the *Roanoke,* "the smoke's closer now by a mile."

The officer of the watch growled, with a gesture of irritation, "I'm watching it." He looked down the vast curve of the northern shore of Hampton Roads with an instinctive caution. Far away in the distance, over against the point of Newport News, the *Cumberland* lay silent, undisturbed. Through his telescope he could see that the crew's washing festooned her lower rigging. The *Congress,* closer in between the Middle Ground and the houses at Newport News, had no washing hung out, but she too lay silent and undisturbed. The *Minnesota,* four cable lengths from the *Roanoke* herself, had a Saturday somnolence.

The lookout said: "It's got to be a ship, sir. Ain't nothin' else'd make smoke like that that moved."

The officer of the watch grunted. "All right then, so it's a ship! They're forever running gunboats down to Seawell's Point. Or mebbe it's another guard ship like the *Germantown* that was trouble enough when she came down. Ain't nothin' we can do to 'em under the batteries."

The lookout persisted. "Reckon I can see a smokestack."

An elderly lieutenant, lying at length in a chair, demanded, "Have you got to jabber all the afternoon?"

The officer of the watch snapped back, "Supposin' it's that Thing comin' down the river?"

"Ah, hell! Do I get to read my paper in peace?"

The lookout, not moving his eye from the telescope that he steadied against the shrouds, said: "It's a damn great smokestack, sir."

The officer of the watch leveled his telescope toward the smoke. "All right, it's a smokestack! Still it's a gunboat."

The lookout stood silenced. At length he muttered stubbornly: "Captain's standin' orders, he's to be told 'bout anythin' moves in the Elizabeth."

"Captain's sitting on the court-martial," said the officer of the watch with a brusque finality. "I'm not goin' to get my ass ate out."

"Ah, Christ!" The elderly lieutenant folded his paper with an almost formal anger and climbed up out of the chair. "There's no place you can get any peace in this damned ship!"

The officer of the deck moved his shoulders uneasily, as if shrugging something away. He repeated the words as if he had only just heard them: "It's a damn great smokestack."

The lookout called: "There's a ship ahead of it! I can see her masts. Two ships! There's another astern of the stack!"

The officer of the deck said, "There are no masts on the ship with the smokestack."

The lookout allowed excitement to enter his voice. "By the holy God, sir, it's the *Merrimac* come out!"

A midshipman hurried over.

The officer of the deck exclaimed, "It *could* be the *Merrimac!*"

Another officer came running.

The officer of the deck ordered, "Get aloft and watch her!" He began to move, galvanized into a furious activity. He went down the steep companionway on his heels, landed with a thud on the deck below, and made his way swiftly to the wardroom where the court-martial was in progress.

John Marston, the captain of the *Roanoke,* sat at the center of the long table. Captain Radford, the captain of the *Cumberland,* sat at his right hand. The room was full of officers. Marston looked up, furious at the interruption.

The officer of the deck said, "Sir." And there was a pregnant moment of absolute silence.

Marston began, "This court-martial is in session—"

The officer of the deck interrupted with a desperate urgency: "The *Merrimac* is heading down the Elizabeth River, sir."

Radford said, "Is she, by God?"

Marston said, softly and dangerously, "You had better be right."

Without an order given, without words, the court-martial disintegrated. Two officers close to the door slid out of the room. The structure of the assembly lost cohesion.

Radford said: "Sir, I'm a long way from my own ship. If the *Merrimac* . . ."

Marston sat back in his chair, drumming his fingers on the polished mahogany. Angrily he said, "This court will adjourn for fifteen minutes to investigate this situation."

As Marston reached the open deck above him and opened his telescope, the long black mass of the *Merrimac* slid slowly out from behind the screen of the land and stood clear against the waters.

In the same instant, there was a flash from the Old Point Comfort shore and the hard, sharp crack of a signal gun on the bastion of Fortress Monroe.

John Marston said softly between his teeth: "Beat to quarters, Mr. Gilphead! Beat to quarters!"

*   *   *

The sound of the bells was muted. It had a silver and a lovely tone. The sound of the whistles was muted also, softened by distance.

Linden looked over toward the *Merrimac*. Astern of the ironclad in the deep water of the channel was an incredible procession of ships. Everything that could put to sea in the Elizabeth River seemed to be thrusting out through the narrows past Craney Island. Instinctively Linden headed the skiff westward over the shallows of the Craney Flats. It drifted now, barely ghosting through the still and brilliant water.

Jeriel looked back at the deep-water channel. "That bunch'll be in trouble when the shootin' starts."

Linden answered abstractedly, "Maybe." She was trying to figure out the shape of this battle.

Hampton Roads was a long, irregular triangle of water. The Portsmouth shore from Pig Point to Craney Island made the base of it; Hampton Creek was the apex; and the James River ran its deep channel dog-legged through it to reach the Chesapeake at Old Point Comfort. From Newport News to Fortress Monroe was enemy coast. The bight of the Roads was filled with shipping. Coasters and transports, brigs and schooners, steamers and tugs crowded the shoal water along Hampton Flats. At the western extremity, off Newport News, lay the *Congress* and the *Cumberland* to cover the passage up the James River. To the eastward lay the rest of the blockading fleet in the Chesapeake, outside the high red walls of Fortress Monroe.

The Rip Raps battery lay athwart the entrance. If the *Merrimac* attempted to break out into the Chesapeake, she would have to run the gauntlet of its rifled guns and the heavy artillery of the fortress. Old Sam had said, "Franklin Buchanan'd be cuttin' his own throat."

It was an enormous arena, but the battle would take place, Linden knew, in the deep water. The *Merrimac* drew too much to attempt the shallows, and the deep water was bisected by the long shoal of the Middle Ground.

She found that she could remember every word the old man had said, every inflection of his voice: " 'Divide your enemy and defeat him in detail.' He don't have to do no dividin'; Goldsborough's done it for him. It don't make sense to me. All Franklin Buchanan's got to do with the *Merrimac* is to get her up to Newport News an' pick off the *Congress* an' the *Cumberland*." Perhaps old Sam was right.

Jeriel's eye was caught by a flash on the walls of the fortress. He saw a plume of smoke rise, grow, and hang for a little before it drifted in the light air. He said abruptly, "They've fired a gun!"

A long time afterward the sound of it came to them, sharp and brief and ominous.

Chapter four

FROM the poop of the *Roanoke* the smoke of the gun was brilliant for an instant in the light of the afternoon sun. Then it was gone as utterly as the echoes that lost themselves in the stamp of the bare feet of running men. Bugles blared, drums thudded, gun carriages rumbled.

Above the chaos of sound and movement Marston said, his voice unhurried: "In my judgment she is making a trial run. I do not estimate that she will venture beyond the range of the guns of Seawell's Point. None the less I cannot rest the fate of the blockade upon a supposition. We will put Commodore Goldsborough's plan into action, gentlemen. If she continues her present course, the *Congress* and the *Cumberland* and the batteries of Newport News will hold her. The *Minnesota*, this ship, and the *St. Lawrence* will place themselves between her and her return to the Elizabeth, and bring her between a cross fire that must inevitably shatter her, iron or no."

There was a ripple of enthusiasm that was almost a cheer.

Marston, his telescope to his eye, continued: "She's a remarkably ugly thing, gentlemen. In my experience of the sea an ugly ship is never a good ship."

A voice said, "She looks like the roof of a barn floating down the Mississippi on a flood."

Marston turned to the captain of the *Cumberland*. "I could wish you were aboard your ship, Captain Radford."

"By God, so could I! Captain Marston, may I ask—"

"I have no tug to help you, sir." For the first time Marston took his eye from the telescope. He bowed faintly. "The *Zouave* is with your ship. The *Dragon* will tow us into action. The *Young America* must bring in the *St. Lawrence*. The *Minnesota*—"

"My boat will take an hour, sir—more in this wind. In God's name . . ."

"With a good horse you could make it along the beach in half the time." The Army officer who had attended the court-martial stepped toward Radford.

"Sir"—Radford bowed quickly, like a marionette—"will you supply me with a horse?"

"You shall have my own, Captain. It will be an honor to send a naval officer into battle on a blood mare."

Marston said harshly, "Mr. Gilphead, signal the *Minnesota* to slip without delay."

Heads turned to the *Minnesota,* lying half a mile beyond them in the Chesapeake. Steam plumed from her black smokestack, carving white swathes across the darkness of the smoke.

Marston said angrily: "She has her orders, she knows what to do. There must be *no* waiting!"

Across his words came a cry from the signalman, "*Minnesota*'s slipped, sir."

"Good." Marston's relief was manifest. "Mr. Gilphead, tell the engine room to blow steam from the smokestack valves. There is no need to let the enemy become aware that our engines are useless. Is the tug here yet?"

"Tug's coming, Capt'n," said a midshipman.

*   *   *

The *Beaufort* swept by and began to diminish in a dramatic perspective with the *Merrimac,* the Confederate colors bright at her masthead. The *Raleigh* came up, took a sheer toward the skiff and then, as if mindful of the shallow water, held on her course again.

An officer came to her side with a speaking trumpet. He shouted through it, his voice metallic and resonant: "Miss Cleave, take that boat back into the river! Head across the shallows to the other shore boats. There will be danger here within the minute!"

Linden took off the soft hat that she had long ago stolen from her father and that she wore sometimes as a protection against the sun. She waved it as she would have waved a hound dog on to the kill. "Go in and give them tessy, Jim Alexander! Particular tessy!"

Like a punctuation mark a single gunshot cut across the last of her words. For a moment Linden stared incredulously toward the northern shore, looking for the gun smoke.

"That damyankee tug! Sounds like a duck gun." Jeriel grinned at her, wide-eyed. He had a rare feeling of weightlessness. They were both of them uplifted in excitement so that ordinary things were magnified, so that the familiar was incredible and the impossible was within their grasp.

The *Raleigh* swept churning past. From her stern an old man shouted, needing no trumpet: "Take that dam' thing in, Lindy! I'll larrup you else, moment I get back."

"Beat the hell out of them, Keziah! Beat the hell!" And then, only a degree more softly, to Jeriel she said: "Why did I have to be a girl, Jeriel? Why did I have to be a girl?"

In the same moment the sharp thunder of heavy guns drowned out speech.

She jerked her head back. This new firing was astern of the skiff on her altered course—rifled guns from the Southern batteries, shooting across the Roads.

Over against the northern shore the transports, the coasters, the store ships were slipping their moorings in a panic of white sails and black smoke. Already twenty, perhaps thirty of them were heading desperately for the narrows, scurrying to get past the Rip Raps and Fortress Monroe before the storm burst. Opposite them, contrapuntal, she could see the warships moving in past the red walls of the fortress: the *Minnesota,* her jibs and foresail brilliant in the splendor of the sun with a great black flag of smoke above them; the *Roanoke* astern of her, a confusion of tug and ship, of steam and smoke and sails. As Linden watched, the *Minnesota*'s guns fired in answer to the batteries and, as the white smoke whipped clear of the frigate, she saw, still more brilliant, the fountains of the Southern shell splashes lift from the water close to the Northern ship.

Jeriel was standing up in the bows. The skiff was wildly unsteady. He was shouting: "Rip Raps're firin' too! Holy Jesus, we're slap in the middle of the battle!"

Linden called, brought for an instant to sanity. "Sit, Jeriel! You'll have us over."

A high fountain of spray lifted from the water close to the bell buoy—she guessed that it was a wild shot from the Rip Raps' heavy guns or perhaps from the gun of the tug that had fired the first shot. A fence of smaller plumes grew like white poplars on the shallow water off Seawell's spit. The batteries thundered again. Gulls rose wheeling into the air, their screams sharp against the rumbling explosions.

Jeriel said: "Lookit!" and pointed. "Lookit th' bastids in the channel! They're scairt, the goddam lot of them."

The regatta-like fleet of small craft that had come downriver from Norfolk astern of the *Merrimac* was turning tail, streaming desperately back up the channel toward Craney Island, heading out of range over the inner shallows of the Craney Flats.

Linden, remote and unaffected by the panic of the distant boats, said: "We're a long way from the Rip Raps and we're out of the line from the ships to Seawell's Point. We'll go into the shallows a bit ourselves and take the sail off her and drift with the tide." She paused while the shock of another salvo beat against her eardrums. Then she added primly, as if trying to put a curb on her enthusiasm, "At least we'll see the fight."

"Give me that glass, Lindy! Give me that glass!" Jeriel stretched out a hand impatiently for the telescope. "She's hit!" He focused on the *Minnesota*. Half her mainsail hung shredded from the yard.

*   *   *

Catesby Jones saluted with angular stiffness. "The men are assembled, sir." There seemed to be no conventional expression that he could use for this curious gathering on the iron gratings high above the real decks of the ship. Buchanan made no answer, and Jones added, "Lieutenant Minor reports that the *Minnesota* appears to have been hit by the guns of the batteries, sir."

Buchanan turned his eyes slowly from the *Congress*. "That is satisfactory news, sir. I will speak to the men."

For a moment he allowed his eyes to run over the irregular ranks. There was an air of motley in them. Some of the men were in normal naval uniform, some wore the soldier's gray; there were two men in Zouave trousers; the gunners, for the most part, were stripped to the waist. For a reason not apparent even to himself, Buchanan took off his hat. The wind ruffled the fine gray hair so that it stood up in plumes on either side of the great bald dome of his head. He looked magnificent with the sun across his face, stressing its strong planes. Even the sour, irascible mouth was strong in this light of battle.

He barked, his voice sonorous: "You are now to face the enemy. You shall have no reason to complain of not fighting at close quarters. Remember, you fight for your homes and your country. You see those ships?" Suddenly, and with an intense dramatic fire, he wheeled and pointed to the *Congress* and the *Cumberland.* "You must sink them! I need not ask you to do it. I know you will do it." He looked broodingly at them for an instant, then he wheeled back to his lookout. "Mr. Jones, dismiss the men!" And, as Catesby Jones acknowledged the order, he turned to the gunnery lieutenant, Simms. "Mr. Simms, we will open fire with the seven-inch rifle on the *Congress* at a thousand yards. Pass the orders!"

*   *   *

The gun deck of the *Congress* was silent, motionless, frozen in tension in the moment before the order. Even the crying of the men who had been wounded by the first ranging shots from the *Merrimac* was hushed. The single whiplash command tore through the silence like the blade of a sword: "Fire!" The guns crashed, the smoke whipped back. The gun deck was fogged, impenetrable for a minute. Then the faint cross wind that blew through the gun ports drifted the smoke across to the disengaged side. Men, as they ran out the sponges, took time to look at the monstrous, irrational ugliness of the *Merrimac.* They saw their shot glance off her side, overleap her, rebound from her. It was outside belief. They had fired a broadside at short range. The Southern ship was a bare three hundred yards away. With the earlier ranging shots the angle of her armor might have been expected to make the difference. But this was beyond the experience of man. A derisive voice, remembering his captain's speech, shouted: ". . . the great Southern bugaboo, got up to fright us out of our wits." And, as the man shouted, the side of the *Merrimac* flamed. An answering voice had time only to call, "I'm frit," in a mock terror that was more than half genuine before the ship reeled under the shock of the hits.

Three shells struck at the level of the gun deck. They brought with them shrieks and cursing, and the splash and the scent of blood. They brought light with them in great ragged holes that opened in the sides of the *Congress.* They brought terror with them—terror that wiped out laughter.

The black cube of the *Merrimac* passed on, inhuman, metal.

*   *   *

Linden had the telescope. The skiff drifted on the calm water, moving slowly with the slowing tide. Astern of them the Southern batteries were silent at last. The *Minnesota* had long passed out of the narrow sector in which she had been within range of the rifled guns on Seawell's Point; the *Roanoke* had just cleared it—she had stopped her own fire. The two ships moved softly, almost stealthily, the white of their foam hardly visible at the distance, the smoke of their funnels lazy above them.

Linden said: "I can't make out . . . the *Merrimac*'s not firing; she's passed the *Congress*. Just the one broadside and she's gone by."

"Headin' for the *Cumberland*." Jeriel had an absolute certainty. There were no mysteries for him. Whatever happened was right. He had a perfect faith in victory.

"The *Congress*'s the smaller ship."

"Got rifle guns," said Jeriel out of his immense and particular fund of knowledge. "Ol' man Buchanan's goin' t'knock her out firs', then he'll come back and beat up the big one. He's got no cause to worry; ever'thing bounces off th' *Merrimac*—ever' *goddam thing*. Hey—hey!" He let out a long breath that was like a sigh.

It was impossible now to tell whose shells were falling. The *Cumberland* was firing at long range. The shore batteries at Newport News were firing. The *Congress* was firing—only a few of her guns now, but still firing. The small craft were still fleeting across the shoals; store ships and fodder ships, coasters and horse transports, keeping as far as they could from the Seawell's guns.

In the focal area about the *Merrimac* shells splashed directly into the water, sending up high, straight columns of glistening spray. Shells ricocheted at strange, unlikely angles and plowed through the water. Shells rebounded from her armor and fell with hardly more than a splash into the bright surface. Smoke drifted in from the ships toward the shore in dense masses that suddenly broke and vanished.

Through the smoke and the brightness the *Merrimac* moved on in ugly majesty—invulnerable.

*   *   *

"No sign of the captain's boat, sir." The midshipman looked at Morris, the *Cumberland*'s executive officer, with an exaggerated respect. He allowed himself to wonder what it felt like to take command in the moment that action was forced upon the ship.

Morris said steadily: "Very good. Get along to Mr. Alcott on the gun deck."

The gunner sweated over the elevating screw, naked to the waist; his face, his chest already blackened with powder smoke.

Alcott, the master gunner, clawed at the bar. "Can't see where y'r buggerin' shells hit—all them guns firin' from the goddam batteries. Get it up, Sullivan! The hell you think you' doin'? Get it up! She's closer by half a cable." He squinted through the gun port at the *Merrimac*.

The Southern ship was end on, a blunt-angled striation of iron, a misbegotten, truncated triangle of metal surmounted by a thick, clumsy smokestack that had already two great holes in it. The black plume of her smoke was ragged now: it belched out at three places, the plumes swirling together again. It made no apparent difference to the ship. She came slowly on.

To Alcott it seemed that she moved wholly indifferent to everything in the world outside herself. "God blast her!" he cried. "She ain't human. Ready—fire!"

A flame leaped simultaneously in the center of the black triangle, and the bow swivel of the *Merrimac* crashed. A shot splintered through the bulwarks of the *Cumberland,* and burst. Men dropped on the still-unblooded deck. There were calls for the surgeon. Fire leaped in a red fury.

The *Cumberland*'s guns blazed again. Her men could see their own shells rebounding now. There was a terror inherent in the sight. The men who served the guns were grim.

And still the *Merrimac* came slowly on. Once she slewed out of line, opening up the foremost of her side ports, caught in a swirl of the tide. As she swung, a shell from a broadside of the *Cumberland* hit in the opening, a red flower bloomed in a hard, brief passion. Thereafter that gun was silent.

And still the ship came on.

She grew with her movement. She loomed against the distant glistening sea. She became tall, the triangle broad, the smokestack gigantic. Deliberately now she swung over to starboard and opened up the other broadside and, when the guns bore, fired. The shock of the salvo lifted the *Cumberland* and left her quivering. At the guns they could smell the smoke of a deep fire. The decks were ugly with shrieks: the air was full of pain. Through it the surgeon and his aids moved helpless in the shock and reverberation.

"She will ram us level with the foremast," said Morris slowly, his voice still steady. "We shall have our chance then."

"How?" demanded a voice in bitter doubt.

"Call away your boarding party, Mr. Blake." Morris's voice had a ring of steel. "Stand by to board!"

The *Merrimac* became a triangle again, a triangle with its apex truncated by the narrow limits of the pilothouse. The bow gun fired. She swung once more, this time opening her starboard broadside. Four guns fired. On the gun deck of the *Cumberland* Sullivan fell and lay silent. Alcott fell and lay cursing. The surgeon was working over a heap of flesh ten yards away and could not come. In a little, Alcott was still.

The black triangle came closer. It floated on a petticoat of broken foam, a surge of mocking delicacy. All above the foam was incomprehensible. In the last moment the *Merrimac* achieved a brief burst of speed. She wiped out the horizon from the men who lay bleeding by the open bulwarks; she assumed a monstrous fury.

In the silence before she struck a single voice cried: "We can't stop her! We can't stop her!"

She rammed the *Cumberland* just level with the fore chains. The Northern ship rolled with the shock, giving before she broke to it. There was a terrible shriek of shattered timbers, a screech of metal, the cries of men. It was no longer possible in the moment of impact to distinguish the animate from the inanimate, the men from the ships. Then the *Cumberland* rolled back, dying.

*   *   *

At the forward end of the *Merrimac*'s gun deck men were flung to their knees, jerked across the guns, pounded against the wooden backing of the armor by the shock. Dinwiddie Phillips, the surgeon, kneeling over a man wounded when the gun on the starboard side was smashed, was flung across his patient, his probe jerked across the scarred and filthy deck.

Revell was flung against the backing timbers. He fell crouched on his knees and elbows in the angle of the shield. He felt the upward lift as the *Cumberland* rolled and took the *Merrimac* with her. He felt the give as she returned and the downward plunge as the *Cumberland* rolled back against the ram. The water, borne forward by the last frenetic rush of the Southern ship, recoiled from the *Cumberland,* swept back, and came in through the for'ard ports. He knew suddenly that he was afraid; and one part of his mind acknowledged the fact, astonished, while another part screamed out in terror and his voice screamed with it: "We're goin' down with the *Cumberland!* For Chris' sake, let's get out!" And the first half of his mind watched him still crouched there, unable to command his muscles to lift him up.

Simms' voice somewhere in the dark confusion of the gun deck roared: "What bloody soldier shouted that? Shut your goddam mouth or I'll shoot you! We're not sinking!" An insane glee took him for an instant. "They can't touch us! Pivot gun ready?" He waited briefly for the affirmation. "Fire!"

Cahill, the gun captain, jerked at the lanyard. The gun exploded in noise and flame and smoke. The recoil mechanism shrieked. Cahill, watching through the port, saw in the brief second before smoke clouded his vision a hole open in the side of the *Cumberland* level with his eyes and barely thirty feet away. Through the hole he saw an instant glimpse of the interior of the ship, and of men broken, and fire and destruction. Then smoke wiped it out.

Dunbar, the sponger, leaped into the port. At once he fell, half his body out of the ship, a musket bullet through him.

The first half of Revell's brain impelled him forward. He made a dive and caught Dunbar's legs before the body slipped down into the water. The other members of the gun crew helped him. They pulled the body back through the opening.

Lieutenant Wood had come forward. He slapped Revell on the shoulder. "Good man!"

Somebody in the darkness sniggered.

The sinking *Cumberland*'s guns fired again, and in the *Merrimac*'s citadel they felt the shock, and then it was gone and there was nothing more. A howitzer shell from the shore batteries hit against the forepart of the shield, and again they felt the shock and nothing more.

The first half of Revell's brain impelled him to call in echo of Simms' voice, "They can't touch us!" And again in the dark security of the gun deck a man sniggered.

*   *   *

The *Minnesota*, still two miles short of the fight, dragged for a minute, checked, and stopped with a heavy lurch to starboard. Water rushed past her in a new-made wave, creaming beyond her bows.

Van Brunt's face drained of blood. He dropped his telescope and snarled at the pilot: "God's teeth! You've put us aground!"

The pilot snatched at the engine telegraph and rang "Stop!" The throb of the engines ceased before the bell. Steam began to blow off in a screaming, tearing whiteness.

Above it Van Brunt was shouting: "Full astern! Get your boats away, Mr. Elbrick. Get a kedge anchor ready immediately. We must get clear of this mud—by God, we must get clear of this mud! The *Cumberland*'s sinking. Signal for a tug, Mr. Jackson!"

The pilot said, "I've never known the Roads this shallow."

The white fury came back to Van Brunt. "You are an incompetent scoundrel, sir. Damme, you are a traitor! This is the midst of a battle. We must save the *Congress*—by God, we must! Get the kedge over!"

The vibration as the engines went astern shook the anger from his voice. He ran to the side. An enormous upflooding of mud stained the green surface in sweeping convolutions. It flooded along the side of the ship, moving with the still-flowing tide.

"No good!" said Van Brunt in a soft, slow agony. He wheeled round. "Signal the *Roanoke*—inform her. We must have tugs—we must have more tugs. We *must* get off! The *Congress* cannot fight her alone. The *Merrimac* is a monstrous thing."

*   *   *

The messenger held himself upright by a visible exertion of will. He said thickly, but with a careful respect, to Morris, "Cap'n, sir—carpenter reports we're done for." Then, quite slowly, in a macabre, mechanical sequence, his knees gave and he slumped to the deck, squatted for a second on his heels, folded head first toward the deck, and rolled over.

"Take him away!" ordered Morris sharply. "If the *Minnesota* gets to us in time, she can take us in to the shoal water."

A voice beside him said: "Sir, the *Minnesota*'s in trouble. She's blowing off steam and she's putting a boat in the water. I believe she's aground."

So softly that not even the nearest man could hear him, Morris murmured, "Then we are finished. We cannot last above a quarter of an hour."

On the gun deck the *Cumberland*'s guns roared, immersed in their task of answering the implacable metal of the ironclad. The deck was a shambles: timber from the splintered bulwarks was scattered about it; rigging had fallen away and hung in derisive festoons; the boats on the starboard side were shattered. The boats . . .

It was intolerably difficult to think swiftly amidst the chaos and the ruin, but the boats reminded Morris. Through his speaking trumpet he bellowed: "Man the launch; get a line to our stern and tow us round!

Get it across to the schooner there. It's the top of the tide, the beginning of slack water. Tow her round! Bring the port-side guns to action!"

He stood silent, slackly, staring at the greased sides of the armored citadel of the *Merrimac*. At last he shook his head slowly. "A boarding party would have no chance," he murmured to himself, "no ghost of a chance." Aloud he said, "Get your boarding party back to the guns, Mr. Waterman!"

He knew that it was too late, that everything was too late. The muscles of his feet told him; the truth lay in the slant of the deck.

Another salvo from the *Merrimac* hacked through below them—four guns, four balls, four adjutants of death. The deck was sloping faster now. The *Cumberland* was heeling to starboard, her masts, her yards out of alignment against the impeccable blue of the sky. He looked up at the still-flying flag.

The boat was manned: he could see the men strained at the bending oars; he knew that they could not move the weight of her. The tide was still running, and the ship was too heavy for them. The water, the inrushing, unstanchable water of the hole that the *Merrimac* had smashed, was too heavy for the ship.

Morris said, almost conversationally, wholly without emphasis, looking up at the flag as he spoke, "All save who can!" And the officers about him took up the words as a shout.

Men began to run across the broken decks, men dropped from the bulwarks, men clambered over the rails. They carried their wounded with them; boats were filled with bloodied men. Shore boats came off, outfacing the splashes of the shells. Deep in the dark spaces of the ship the water roared. Men were penned in the powder rooms and drowned, screaming. Men were swept into air locks that formed as the angle of the ship increased, penned in darkness and incomprehensibility, and died there.

The *Cumberland* sank suddenly, without more warning than the crash of a breaking bulkhead. She slid down at the end of her anchor cable, head to tide, her bowsprit pointing out toward the narrows and the sea, her flags still brilliant, still immaculate in their color, still gay in courage.

*   *   *

The mare pecked, went down on one knee, struggled up again and moved forward slowly. Savagely Radford dug in the unfamiliar spurs. The mare was too far gone to answer them as she had answered at first. She struggled on, near fetlock-deep in the soft patches of the sand.

He beat her furiously. It made no difference. She moved slower and slower, and at last, without warning, she rolled over to one side and lay still, pinning him down by one leg. He fought angrily to free himself, and men came running. When they lifted him clear at last, the mare was dead.

The old man who knelt at her head rose, uncoiling an unexpected and surprising height. He had a white beard, beautifully trimmed, his dress was that of a gentleman. "Sir, you have ridden a good mare to death."

"I had to get here," protested Radford. "I had to get here!"

The old man said: "You have done a monstrous thing, sir. Who are you?"

"I am"—Radford made a little open gesture with his hands, "I was —the captain of the *Cumberland*."

*   *   *

Linden said, deeply moved, "She's sunk." Presently she added, "All her men . . ."

Jeriel growled, "She was a Boston ship." Fascinated, he stared through the telescope at the three mastheads that still showed darkly above the water, the flags whipping from them. Softly he began to sing:

> "*I got a gal*
> *In Cumberland Gap.*
> *She's got a babby*
> *That calls me Pap.*"

After a brief pause he said, "*Congress* nex'."

The *Merrimac* was still heading up the river. The shore batteries were blazing on her and her own guns answered them. She moved in a cloud of brown and white smoke, and the white plumes of the shots that fell beyond her reached up against the leaden color of the smoke.

Jeriel turned from her to watch the *Congress* again. He could see men on her foreyard. The topsails were dropped in the brails and sheeted home. The foresail came down and filled with the wind. A tug surged up alongside her.

"Why don' the *Merrimac* turn?" demanded the boy fiercely. "Why don' she turn? *Congress,* she's goin' t'get away!"

They heard the new guns to the west of them, not far away, firing from the Southern shore.

"Pig Point bat'ry." Jeriel was unenthusiastic. "What d'they think they'll hit?"

Linden turned reluctantly from the *Merrimac* and found the shell splashes. "They're firing at the *Minnesota*."

"She's on the Middle Groun'." Jeriel wrinkled his nose. "They ain't got the range."

They watched, absorbed. Outside this duel over the bright water, the sound of the *Merrimac*'s guns was distant now. The firing from the Northern batteries was ragged.

"Why don' the *Merrimac* turn?" the boy asked again after a long wait.

Linden took the glass from him and focused on the *Congress*. Finally she snapped out: "The *Congress* is aground! I've watched her, and she hasn't moved in three minutes."

"They've done it a purpose," Jeriel said instantly, "so that she won't sink." Then, more slowly: "First bit o' sense they've had. The *Merrimac*'s comin' back."

Chapter five

"THE western battery has not fired a gun the last eight minutes," said Catesby Jones. "Shall we record it silenced, sir?"

Buchanan looked at him, almost benevolent, his acid mouth twisted in a wide smile. He said paternally, "Wait till we've passed it again, my boy—wait!"

Catesby Jones frowned slightly; he had no sense of humor. "By observation two guns are dismounted in Number Two battery and one in Number Three, sir. The ship at the wharf beyond Number Two battery is on fire and sinking. The transport lying to the northeast of the wharf has sunk. The boat party from the *Beaufort* has cut out the schooner and is bringing her off."

"Good," said Buchanan without particular emphasis, "good." He kept his eyes fixed on the approaching gunboats of the James River squadron; the ships from Richmond had kept their rendezvous. "Tucker is bringing down his vessels with dash, sir—with great dash." He turned to his executive officer abruptly, his eyes piercing. "The *Cumberland* fought with much gallantry, sir. I fear she will have lost a great many of her men. What is the position in relation to the *Congress*, Mr. Jones?"

"She slipped her cables in the last minutes of the *Cumberland*'s sinking, sir. They have run her aground as close as they could bring her to the eastern batteries."

"How does she lie, Mr. Jones?"

"Heading in to the land, sir, with her stern to the deep water."

Buchanan clasped his hands together with a macabre gesture of satisfaction. "With her stern to the deep water, Mr. Jones—that is an error, a very grievous error."

Catesby Jones stared at him, not able to fathom Buchanan's thought processes. The coolness, he sensed, was on the surface; underneath Old Frank was effervescent with a high triumph.

Buchanan turned to Parrish, the senior pilot. "Mr. Parrish, I think we have water enough to essay a turn."

Parrish looked across at the other pilot. "It is as wide, Captain, as we'll find it for a long way."

"Then we will turn, Mr. Parrish, and go back upon our course."

*   *   *

Jeriel said, "It's quiet." The air was utterly still. The water had glazed over, reflecting the simple beauty of the spring sky. The skiff hung suspended in it. "Too quiet," he added uneasily.

Linden did not answer him. She was lost in the silence. She had thought of battle in terms of noise and violence. It was difficult to understand this long peacefulness. Somewhere in it there was a pattern and a purpose, but she could not discover them.

Jeriel searched in the canvas carrying bag for the food that he had cajoled from Jacinta. He offered it first to Linden, but she was too enclosed in her own thoughts to notice.

He was still eating when he saw the small ships begin to move. He watched intently until he was certain of what was happening. The *Beaufort* and the *Raleigh* were edging in toward the stern of the stranded *Congress*. When he was sure of that, he turned and watched the *Merrimac* again. He calculated that she must be almost within range of the westernmost of the Newport News batteries. Even as he settled it in his mind, the *Beaufort* opened fire. He saw a puff of smoke from her bow gun. A long while afterward the silence of the afternoon broke with the slow, heavy reverberation of the shot. Methodically, the two small ships began to pound the Northern frigate. Three minutes later the *Merrimac* opened fire again on the shore batteries. The water was full of noise now, and a little wind sprang up and sent dark patterns of ripples over it, as if it were trembling under the violence of the guns.

*   *   *

"Ragged!" observed Flag Officer Buchanan. "Army gunners!" he added after a long while, with a thin, nostril-curling contempt.

Catesby Jones, standing next to him, with his head and shoulders just above the level of the gratings, said: "Half their guns must be out of action, sir, by now."

"Half their men," declared Buchanan contemptuously, "must be hiding in shelters. Pusillanimous, sir, pusillanimous! If Magruder had been ready to thrust, we would have held Newport News by nightfall." Very softly he added a single word—Catesby Jones thought that the word was "Army." He turned his head away from the batteries at last and looked down toward the stranded frigate.

The *Congress* loomed enormous with the upreaching of her masts and yards and the white of her topsail hanging slack in the brails. The two gunboats were like dogs baiting a bull.

Buchanan said: "Mr. Parrish, we will make a sweep round and come up toward her stern. How closely can we approach her?"

Again Parrish consulted one of the other pilots by eye; he was nervously unsure of himself. "A half-mile certainly, sir—perhaps a quarter of a mile. She has grounded on the edge of Newport bar."

Buchanan watched him closely. After a moment he turned. "We will close to two hundred yards, Mr. Jones."

Parrish made a faint squawk of protest.

Buchanan turned back to the batteries.

In a slow, lazy curve the *Merrimac* began to head toward the Northern ship. Now and then she dragged behind her a swirl of yellow mud. The pilots watched it anxiously, more frightened of the mud than of the enemy. The James River ships came scurrying down, their paddles making an undertone to the hard impact of the noise of the guns. They swept round clear of the *Merrimac* to avoid fouling the range.

Buchanan watched them. The gun deck beneath him was loud with orders and counterorders, the clash and clatter as rammers and spongers were thrown down on the deck, the thud of shot dumped at the muzzle of the guns, the rumble of the carriages. Punctuating it and regimenting the uproar was the terrible crash of the broadsides.

The bow gun fired independently, immersed in the destruction of the *Congress*. Behind it the shrill shouts of the powder passers were like a threnody.

To starboard the *Patrick Henry* of the James River ships came into action, her light guns almost falsetto against the deep bass of the *Merrimac*.

*   *   *

Lieutenant Joseph Smith, son of Commodore Smith of the Ironclad Committee, captain of the *Congress,* said hopelessly: "We can expect nothing of the *Minnesota.* She will be the next to go. It looks as if we can expect nothing of the *Roanoke.*" His eyes clouded as he watched the flagship making a wide turn in retreat a mile and a half below the stranded *Minnesota.* Smoke belched from the smokestack of the *Dragon,* and from a second and smaller ship lashed alongside the *Roanoke* steam rose impotently. He staggered slightly as half a broadside from the *Patrick Henry* hacked through the hull beneath him. "How many dead have we?"

The executive officer, Lieutenant Pendergrast, looked at him somberly. "We cannot tell, sir—eighty, perhaps a hundred. The gun deck is a ruin of broken timbers and overturned gun carriages."

"There is no *Monitor,*" said Smith with an infinite sadness, and in the next instant spun round and fell, slashed across with blood and broken flesh.

The word went through the ship like wind through a forest: "Captain's dead. Captain's killed."

Every man thought: Me next?

The man who caught Smith as he fell looked up. "Ain't nothin' the doctor can do."

Pendergrast, kneeling a little to one side, said, "None the less, we must have the surgeon."

The surgeon came. He said at once: "Take him below! No, there's no point in that. Put him in the shelter of the break of the poop."

A messenger came running. "Forepeak's afire, Lootenant!"

The surgeon said to the exec: "*You*'re captain now."

Pendergrast stood silent while the man panted beside him, blood running down across his face from a deep cut in his scalp, his skin blackened, his clothes scorched. But at last he said, almost with despair, "My God, I'm in command!" Then he called, "Mr. McClintock, get a fire party to the forepeak!" At once another concentration of fire from the Southern vessels hacked through the ship below him.

The surgeon had gone, the deck about him was almost bare; only the bodies of dead men lay close to the wheel. Pendergrast said aloud to the emptiness, "How many guns will bear?" and knowing that the answer would be at the most two, went down to the gun deck.

In a shambles of smoke, in air thick with the rotten-nut smell of gunpowder, in a chaos of shouting and screams and groaning, he found that there were no longer even two guns bearing. The gun on the port quarter had been dismounted. He shouted to the gun captain, "What happened, Barron?"

The man answered: "Hit us with the last salvo, sir—hit us on the muzzle. It won't fire again."

The starboard-quarter gun fired, and a Southern shell came whistling in through the fantastic ruin of the stern, sang past them, and burst somewhere far up ahead in the black chaos of the gun deck.

The exec forced his way back to the ladder through shouting men and came up into the exquisite, almost tangible coolness of the late afternoon air. McClintock was back on the poop. He said, "Mr. McClintock, we have no alternative but to surrender."

McClintock answered, "We're on fire in three places, sir."

Heavily, brokenly, Pendergrast said: "You will haul down our colors, sir. Cease fire!"

*   *   *

The silence was absolute. To Linden it had an oppressive quality, as if something were waiting to break through it, something to flower in terror or in triumph, and in that instant through the telescope she saw the Stars and Stripes lowered slowly through the ruin of spars and broken rigging from the mizzen masthead of the *Congress*.

Jeriel saw it without the aid of a telescope, his eyes sharpened by excitement. He shouted: "By damn', she's surrendered! Stars 'n' Stripes is down. She's surrendered—she's finished!" His voice croaked across the silence.

A gull, half asleep on the water twenty yards from them, took off in a tumult of beating wings, and the blue ripples raced out across the water.

"Two of 'em—two of 'em, and the little uns up to Newport News! An' the *Minnesota*, she's stuck on the mud—she's stuck—she's stuck!" The words became a chant.

His words rekindled in Linden her early feelings of elation, and she began to shout with him: "She's stuck on the mud! She's stuck on the mud!" Suddenly she broke off and began to sing "The Bonny Blue Flag."

Jeriel joined in, croaking. They forgot the words, they broke the tune, they laughed, they lost the rhythm and found it, and laughed again. They were drunk with excitement, alone by themselves in the silence, with nothing for company but the gulls and the knowledge of victory. Everything had come to flowering—all the work that they had done, all the efforts that they had made, all the schemes, all the venturing had come to triumph. The *Merrimac* had won. The *Roanoke* was scuttling back to the shelter of the guns of Fortress Monroe. Only the *St. Lawrence* was creeping, slowly, reluctantly, dubiously, forward. And the *Minnesota* was stuck on the mud—stuck on the mud—stuck on the mud.

Jeriel stopped first. With a burning sense of loss he said: "They wouldn't take me as a powder passer, they wouldn't take me! I was too young, they said."

Linden answered him: "They wouldn't take me as anything, not as anything. I was a girl, they said."

They both laughed at each other jeeringly, full of the knowledge that they had earned the right to share in this victory in spite of everyone.

Eventually they quieted down. The *Beaufort* and the *Raleigh* were moving in to the silent *Congress*. They watched the *Beaufort* come alongside her. After a brief wait the *Beaufort* moved away from the Northern ship and, turning, sped back to the *Merrimac*. She hovered alongside the ironclad for a minute or two, and went back again. Evidently she was transferring messengers, orders.

Linden, reaching forward in time, asked, "What will she do when she's smashed the *Minnesota*?"

"Fight her way out into the Chesapeake."

Doubtfully she said, "Past the Rip Raps and Fortress Monroe?"

Jeriel shouted back: "Ain't anythin' she cain't do—ain't *anythin'*!" The guns crashed again.

*   *   *

Buchanan stormed up onto the open grating. "By God, sir, it's treachery—nothing less! Open fire on the shore batteries, Mr. Wood, at once! Instantly! Damm their black hearts, it's treachery! They've fired on a flag of truce."

Catesby Jones said: "Not the batteries, sir. It's a troop of field guns along the beach and the tug *Zouave*. They've come into position these last three minutes."

Buchanan stood there, shaking his fist against the shore. The *Merrimac*'s broadside crashed below him at last, and his view of the beaches was cut off by the smoke.

The *Beaufort* and the *Raleigh* were pulling away from the *Congress* now, their side wheels threshing.

"I see no flames on that ship," bellowed Buchanan, beside himself. "I see no flames, sir! They have not fulfilled my orders. I ordered her burned. Will nobody burn that ship for me?"

Lieutenant Minor, standing on the companion ladder with his head and shoulders above the gratings, called back, "If I've your leave to take the *Teaser,* I'll burn her, sir."

"Take anything you damn well please"—Old Frank was in a frenzy of rage now—"but burn her!"

Another broadside roared out against the batteries. Again the smoke whipped over them and they stood for a brief while blinded in its acrid smother. When it cleared, the *Teaser* was halfway between the two ships. The field pieces on the beach that had opened fire on the transfer of the wounded had fallen silent now with no near target. While they watched her from the grating of the *Merrimac,* the *Teaser* went in and in. She was fifty yards from the *Congress* when the field guns opened again, hitting her squarely amidships with the third shot.

Almost screaming with fury, Buchanan shouted, "Bring me a carbine!" He reached down and took the weapon as it was passed to him and, as he straightened himself, he ordered: "Open fire on the *Congress* with hot shot, Mr. Jones, as soon as it can be done! That ship will burn." He waited while the orders were shouted down the companionway, and, turning, sought for a target on the beach, put up the carbine, and fired.

In the same moment he spun round and dropped to the gratings with a Minié ball through his thigh.

From the head of the ladder a shout went down: "Dr. Phillips! Send for Dr. Phillips!"

A voice came up through the gratings: "Old Frank's hit!"

*   *   *

The gun captain lay flat on his back in the ruin of the gun deck of the *Congress.* The first round from the hot-shot gun of the *Merrimac* had come in through the only section of the stern that was still whole. A black fragment of wood beginning to burn had knocked him down, and the starboard-quarter gun, hit for the second time, had lifted and fallen again, pinning him under it. He lay half conscious, held by the upper arm under the distorted iron. He could smell burning.

He felt no pain, but he was puzzled by the smell. It brought to him the memory of a trail herd. He was a Western man; he should not have volunteered for the Navy, he should not even have been a gunner in the Army; he should have gone to war with the cavalry; his life had been lived with horses. The burning smell was like beef roasting in the still ember-scented air of evening. He could hear the bellowing of steers around him; he could hear the boys talking to them, soothing them.

Once he'd lain out all night, his leg broken and pinned under a dead horse. It was like that now, only then there had been no fire. He could remember quite clearly: the night had been very cold—it was in October.

The smell was stronger. It was not quite like beef roasting; there was another smell to it, a richer smell.

He felt better now. There was still no pain, but it was impossible for him to lift himself. With an immense and desperately sustained effort he moved onto his side and lifted his head enough to see over the cannon—to see what was burning.

It was his hand.

It seemed reasonable enough that it should be his hand. The fingers were splayed out and dark with the near heat of the flames. They ran with hot fat like a thick-cut steak. The flesh on the back of his hand was browned and rich-looking, and a section of it was split and white bone showed.

The flame licked closer and a little light of it seemed to dance separately above his fingers. It seemed unimportant. Only when another tongue reached out and fired his hair did he begin to scream.

No one answered his screams. There was no one else left alive and able to move aboard the *Congress*.

*   *   *

The *Beaufort* came roaring up toward the skiff, the white water threshing from her paddles like chaff in a high wind. She slowed a little before she reached them.

Lieutenant Parker was on the paddle box with a speaking trumpet in his hand. "Linden Cleave," he bellowed, his face red with excitement and triumph, "get into the shoal water before you get hurt! The battle ain't ended. There'll be shells from the *Minnesota* here in a little. Get in with the other boats! You're a clear mile out beyond the next of 'em."

"We've won," she shouted back deliriously, utterly ignoring the warning. "We've won!"

Parker abandoned the pretense of admonition. He shouted back excitedly: "*Cumberland* and the *Congress* gone, *Minnesota* next. I've got forty Yankee prisoners on board, and wounded. We even got a master's mate for Jim McCarrick!" He went back to the wheel.

From the deck below, a score of voices shouted at her. She saw the Yankee prisoners; they looked shocked, incredulous. A dozen men pointed them out.

Jeriel was standing up and swinging his hat round and round and cheering, and the men cheered with him.

Somewhere somebody began to sing the Yankee minstrel song that had become the battle hymn of the Confederate Army,

> *"I wish I was in Dixie . . ."*

and the deep bass voices came pounding in:

> *"Hooray! Hooray!"*

Linden began to sing, and Jeriel with her:

> *"In Dixie Land, I'll took my stand,*
> *To live and die in Dixie. . . ."*

The *Beaufort* swept past, and the song traveled across the water, not dying but only changing its strength as it went. A song of victory, a chant of praise, a *Te Deum*.

Above it all the gulls swirled like snowflakes in a rising squall.

Chapter six

FROM the turret top of the *Monitor* Stodder watched the dark tower of the lighthouse slide slowly across the field of his telescope. He judged its position with an exactitude that was wholly unnecessary. When he made the report the relief in his voice was deep, but he said simply, "Cape Henry Light abeam, sir."

Worden stared fixedly ahead.

Stodder dropped his glass and turned in surprise to the captain. There was not enough wind to have blown his words away, and the *Seth Low* was too far ahead for the sound of her paddles to have drowned them. He said again, almost reproachfully, "Cape Henry Light abeam, sir."

Worden made a small gesture of impatience. When he spoke at last he asked a question. "Mr. Stodder," he demanded softly. "Do you see smoke on the horizon?"

"Smoke, sir?" Stodder's voice had an almost humorous note of inquiry. They were in from the deep sea, they had reached shelter, they were absolved from the terrors of the night, and Worden was interested in smoke—smoke on the horizon. He searched the long mother-of-pearl levels of the bay obediently. After a moment he found it—a white haze of smoke to the westward, and under it a stretch of brown, and under the brown one small, insignificant stem of black. It was very far away: fifteen miles—perhaps twenty. Stodder said cheerfully: "I see it, sir. There's a considerable fire—"

"Listen!" Worden held up a warning hand.

Stephen, watching the two men, cupped his hand to his ear. He had heard the sound before, a moment earlier, an instant before Worden spoke. Something on the *Seth Low*. Something thudding in her engine room perhaps. Sounds came inexplicably over still water.

They heard it again: a single far-away thud with an inescapable impression of weight behind it; then a series of thuds that merged in a shapeless weight of sound.

"Thunder, sir? It could be thunder . . ." Stodder made the offering uncertainly.

"Thunder on the Chesapeake"—Worden was grimly scornful—"in March? And a clear sky?"

Again the thin reverberation reached them across the water. It had two weights, a lesser sound and a greater.

Stodder said: "Shore batteries, sir. The smoke bears over Norfolk—"

"The smoke bears over Hampton Roads, Mr. Stodder. Ship's gunfire. We are a day too late. The *Merrimac* is out. Mr. Greene!" His voice rose to the hard, authoritative level of command. "Mr. Greene, clear the ship for action!"

Chapter seven

PARRISH, the chief pilot, worked his hands together nervously. "Couldn't bring you closer'n a mile o' the *Minnesota*, Mr. Jones. It ain't possible. Tide's fallin' fast." He elongated the word, as if he felt it would carry conviction that way.

Catesby Jones rounded on him. "A mile is no good to me!"

"The tide—" began Parrish.

"Damn the tide! Get me in to her!"

Below, on the gun deck, the men could hear the argument.

Cahill, the captain of the pivot gun, said lazily: "Ain't half the man his uncle was. He'd a shot Parrish b'now and taken her in hisself."

"Who was his uncle?"

"Thomas ap Catesby Jones, the one as took Monterey."

There was a ripple of laughter among the older men.

They heard Parrish's thin voice again. "Touched bottom six times comin' down, Capt'n. You could see the mud."

"Get me in to the *Minnesota!*" said Catesby Jones with the stubbornness of a man unsure of himself.

"He won't," muttered Cahill. "He won't."

Lieutenant Wood came forward to the bow gun. "We'll be opening fire in five-six minutes: long-range, best part of a mile. See that you hit!"

"What's the matter with the pilots?" asked Cahill good-humoredly. "We can git closer'n a mile."

"Northerly winds the last three days," Wood answered shortly. "They've blown the water out of the Chesapeake."

"Blown the nerve out a the pilots more like," said a voice.

"That's enough!" snapped Wood. "The *Minnesota*'s hard aground. So's the *St. Lawrence,* far as they can make out on deck—'bout a mile down the Roads from her."

"*Their* pilots too!" commented the unrepentant voice.

A gunner in the starboard port said, "Hell, yes, she's aground a'right."

Two or three men climbed to their feet and crowded the deck.

Wood called: "All right, all right! Stand to! We'll be in range. . . ."

The men moved slowly, the verve and enthusiasm gone from them. Wood harried them.

The *Merrimac* seemed to hang in the shoal water. The engine note was uncertain, irregular.

At the gun the men waited. After an inordinate time a voice shouted through the speaking trumpet, "Open fire!"

Wood took it up. "Open fire! Open fire!"

He stood immediately to one side as Cahill, the gunner, made last-minute adjustments, and he stepped back as Cahill stepped back with the lanyard. The gunner fired. They waited while the smoke drove chokingly back through the port. When it cleared, they could see the ball skipping lazily between the ships.

Cahill said, "They'll have to take her a lot closer in, pilots or no pilots."

Through the gratings the voice through the speaking trumpet came down again: "Starboard guns open fire on the *St. Lawrence!*"

Wood bustled off, shouting. For a short time there was a wild confusion on the gun deck. The pivot gun was reloaded and fired again: the range was still too great. The starboard guns fired independently, raggedly, but after three minutes a voice shouted, "Hit on the *St. Lawrence,* sir!"

There was a lull. The bosun came up through the gundeck hatch. Wood intercepted him.

The bosun called: "Lot o' water in the forepeak, sir. Reckon the ram's busted clean away." They heard him go up the ladder, and he said, in answer to a quick question, "It's gainin', sir."

Parrish broke into the interchange. "Every ton o' water puts her head down. Best get back, Capt'n, while there's depth enough in the channels to float us."

One of the other pilots, speaking for the first time, said: "We done enough fer one day. Won't get her off this side o' mornin'."

The starboard guns fired again and drowned the argument.

In the next lull a voice called: "*St. Lawrence*'s off the mud! She's pullin' back."

"Hold your fire!" ordered Wood.

Above them in the hatchway and the gratings they heard the voice of Catesby Jones. "We'll finish her off in the morning. Take her in to Seawell's Point! We'll anchor off the batteries." He seemed utterly weary, utterly confused.

*   *   *

The smoke from the burning *Congress* rose like the trunk of a great tree. Then, as if the tree had been broken in a monstrous wind, it lay along the evening sky, drifting across the last pulsing of the sunset, staining it. The *Patrick Henry* moved across the brilliance, her wheels threshing the water. She came to her anchor two hundred yards above the *Merrimac,* close in to the beach of Seawell's Point, and lay there ridiculously self-conscious, steam coming from her stack in short, grumbling bursts like an old man clearing his throat.

Linden laughed at it, for the first time breaking the silence that she had kept since the *Merrimac* turned away from the *Minnesota.* She was suddenly lighthearted, suffused with content. She could not keep her hands still, taking them off the tiller at times and gripping them together in a small ecstasy.

Jeriel watched her, faintly scandalized. Finally he asked, "You want fer me to steer?"

She reached forward and put her hand round his wrist: the gesture was a rare one. "I'll steer. It doesn't matter. Nothing can happen to us tonight. We've won!"

"The *Minnesota*—"

"The *Minnesota* can wait till morning." Linden began to laugh again. "She'll still be there." She headed for a point upstream of the *Merrimac,* making allowance for the ebb tide.

The beach was encrusted with people. The colored dresses of the women made it brilliant in the very last light of the sun. The presence of the crowd altered the familiar outline of the batteries and filled in the open spaces. There were flags, and in the evening stillness she thought she could hear bands and cheering. Where the tracks came down to the water there were wagons and rigs, even oxcarts, men on horseback. The place had a festive and enchanted air. Excitement sparked in it— and glory.

The *Merrimac* lay across the lightheartedness of the pattern, swinging to the tide, her side dark, streaked with the grease that the men had spread upon it before the battle, scarred with the balls that had hit and glanced off her armor. Smoke poured out of the holes in her stack, and steam plumed silently through it, white where it began in the shadow, luminous and red where it caught the red of the sunset. Men were working at the fore end of the armor. One of them hung at the end of a rope with his feet against the greased slope, examining a point of damage. A group of officers stood on the deck gratings above him. But it was the ship that mattered, not the men: her huge, angular solidity, her dark, rigid stillness.

Slowly the skiff crept in to her, drifting half with the evening air, half with the tide. They began to see in sharp contrast to the grim solidity of her exterior the swirl of life within. Through the gun ports they could see men, naked to the waist, working about the gun carriages, cleaning, washing down. There were laughter and shouting. The whole interior of the ship pulsated with life.

They were very close when Revell hailed her. His voice was so near, so intimate, so known, that she heard it with a sense of shock.

He shouted: "Lindy, Lindy! We beat the hell out o' them!"

The nearest gun port suddenly framed heads and half-naked bodies.

Other voices called and whistled. Somebody shouted: "Come aboard
lady!" Another voice called: "Ain't seen a girl since we left port."
There was a confused chorus of mocking, inoffensive obscenities. Linden laughed and flushed and was aware of the exciting maleness, aware
too, of the female reaction in herself—half afraid of it, wholly bound
in it. Jeriel was chattering rapidly, chattering without ceasing, but she
ignored his soft, eager voice. She was savoring her body's responses.

Across her excitement came the remembrance of something old Sam
had once said: "War trips up more girls than love." And she remembered that when she had asked with an innocent idiocy: "What
do you mean: trips them up?" he had answered fiercely, "Lays 'em flat
on their backs."

The skiff drifted on. Linden drifted with it.

*   *   *

The keel of the *Merrimac*'s boat grated heavily on the sand, and the
noise was audible above the splashing of the men who hauled it ashore.

Revell's voice was full of importance. "Easy now, easy, goddamit!
We got wounded men here." The hauling men had reached the end of
their run. They stopped, holding the boat upright. People surged
forward as they do when a fishing boat comes in to land. They had the
same hard, eager curiosity. Revell bellowed: "Keep away, dammit!
These men are hurt bad."

Two doctors, one military, the other civilian, came forward with
the party that carried the litters. They made a way through the
crowd unceremoniously, borrowing something of Revell's importance,
adding something of their own. One of the wounded men groaned, and
women's voices made cooing noises.

Linden said sardonically, "Pigeons." They sounded like pigeons.

The crowd was cleared away from one side of the boat, and the
doctors and their men and Revell and his men began the process of
moving the wounded onto the litters. One of the gunners complained
in a harsh monotone. The complaint began before they tried to lift him,
continued onto the litter; it was still sounding, querulous, bitter, filled
with a deep injustice, when they slid the litter into the ambulance.
All the while the women and the girls murmured pigeonwise through it.

The two ambulances took all the wounded. Soldiers led the horses
across the sand toward the track. The women and the girls followed,
trudging through the sand in a fluttering wake of sympathy. Linden
watched them with scorn.

Suddenly she was aware of Revell standing beside her. He was very big, very conscious of strength and a new authority. He said loudly, "We'll have us a drink now."

One of the four men who had rowed the boat in, exclaimed, "That's talkin'!"

An artilleryman close by interjected: "Ain't no liquor at the battery. Colonel, he won't allow it. Not nohow he won't."

"Ain't no liquor store," grumbled one of the men from the boat doubtfully.

"What's that place there?" Revell jerked his chin at a house that stood in a narrow sheltering of pine, a tall house, gray-painted and weathered, having a remote and secret air.

"Th' Enwright place," the artilleryman said. "Ain't allowed in it. Colonel, he don't allow nobody."

"Why?"

"Mist' Enwright, he's gone north."

"There's someone living there?"

"Tu-three house slaves."

"Be liquor in th' cellar," said Revell with finality. "Come on!"

"Th' colonel . . ."

"Hell, he ain't *my* colonel!" Revell spoke with a deliberate roughness. "You kin come or not, as you like. We won a battle. We goin' to celebrate." He put his arm through Linden's, and she did not draw away.

There was a road on the near side of the pines and a rail fence; two gaunt pillars stood to the left of it, and a short avenue through the pines led to the house. The gate was shut and wired, but with a quick jerk Revell broke the wire. They went into the avenue: Revell and Linden, the four men of the boat's crew, and two girls they had collected from the group of women who stood staring down the road after the departing ambulances. The artilleryman walked a little behind, as if disassociating himself from the rest.

Revell looked up and saw a curtain move at an upper window above the pediment of the shallow portico. He said, "Someone's home."

The artilleryman, far to the rear, murmured again, "Tu-three house slaves."

*   *   *

The Negro woman said angrily, "They's comin' up th' drive." She was very dark. The bones of her face were strongly modeled and she had an arrogant beauty. Her eyes smoldered.

The man was undersized, as if he had shrunk in the process of aging, but he was not old—only a few years older than the woman, at most.

"You go tell them, th' cun'el says for them not to come."

"They's six o' them—seven."

"You go tell them! After, you kin run. You'll run anyways, but you go tell 'em firs'." There was a patient disillusion in her voice. She peered down through the window, pulling sharply at the curtain again. "Six. One of them's a girl in trousis!" The note leaped to an indignant scorn.

"What I do with six?"

"Aaron . . ." she began indignantly, then her voice trailed away in fresh disillusion. "Nuthin'," she said.

She continued to watch as the group came up the last of the sweep of the drive. It was noisy, shouting and singing.

She said again with a deep irony: "A girl in trousis. Aw right, I go down."

But she did not move; instead she lifted her eyes and stared out over the width of the Roads toward where the *Congress* was burning, its smoke darker now, its red angrier. "That ship's goin' to burn hisself right down to th' bottom," she declared somberly and, turning, walked with a magnificent, decisive grace out of the room.

The bell pealed harshly. She moved unhurried down the upper stairs until she reached the gallery. It shirred again, but she made no haste. Behind her the small man padded like an attendant animal.

As she unfastened the huge old-fashioned bolt, she heard Revell's voice outside, "We'll break down the goddam door then."

Instantly she opened it and made a quick, mocking curtsy that, meaningless in ordinary usage, held now a charged significance.

"Where've you been?" demanded Revell. "Didn't take you all that time to come down the stairs."

She looked at him with steady eyes, her face innocent of all expression. "Th' cun'el, he says for nobody to come."

Revell looked beyond her to the man. "We're usin' the house for a celebration," he snapped, crisply authoritative. "Get up some liquor from the cellar!"

Aaron hesitated in a paralysis of indecision.

The woman was watching Linden, studying her face, evaluating her body. She ordered quickly, her eyes still searching the girl: "Go get them liquor, Aaron. The gen'men is thirsty." She looked away from Linden

t last and, making again the mocking curtsy, said, "Th' ladies 'n'
en'men will sit down please in th' drawin' room." She shepherded
nem with the humility of a sheep dog and with the same underlying
xity of purpose. She had no definite scheme in mind yet, only an in-
ntion of revenge.

Revell said: "You talk too much. Go and help him with the liquor."

"Sho," she agreed, "sho," deliberately stressing the accent.

Linden watched her leave the room. She shivered a little. They
noved, a shade uncertainly, to the double doors of the drawing room,
nd Revell threw them open with a large gesture. The room was un-
xpectedly enormous, stretching the full depth of the house. The furni-
ure was elaborately solid. A piano stood athwart one corner, and the
valls were hung with tall, formidable pictures. One of the men walked
over to the piano and struck an uncertain chord.

Revell's eyes lit. "D'you play it?"

The man shied away. "Not me."

"If you could play it we could dance."

"Some darkies in th' quarters. They's always one's got a fiddle."

"When that dam' black monkey comes with th' liquor."

The excitement of the waterside seized them again. Linden felt her-
elf engulfed, her body freer, lighter than ordinary. She realized that
he had asked Revell nothing of the battle. All along she had been
onscious that he smelled of powder, powder and sweat, a dominant,
ll-pervading male odor.

She said, "Was it terrible, Revell?" not knowing why she framed
he question that way.

He looked at her swiftly before he answered: "We beat the hell out
of 'em. Would have finished off the lot if it hadn't bin fer the pilots."

She saw one of the other men look sharply at Revell.

He too might have seen the glance. When he spoke again it was
with a diminished arrogance. "Noise and smoke. You don't see nothin'
n a sea battle. Less you're in the pilothouse. It was noisier than hell
n there—noisier than hell. The crash when we hit the *Cumberland!*
Flat on my ass"—he eyed the other man hurriedly—"jest flat on my
ss."

One of the other girls asked, "Could you feel it when the shells hit
you?"

"Great, heavy slams," he answered, "heavy, like a tree fallin'. It
was our guns that made the most noise. Smoke! You couldn't see out
he ports. Couldn't hardly see the light, times." Suddenly he found one

word picture that had the conviction of absolute truth. "I saw th
Congress fire a whole broadside one time—ever' one of her guns. Je:
a sheet of flame. And the crash when they hit us!"

Linden had a sense of sharing, a knowledge of that awful momen
an exaltation.

The woman returned, carrying an immense tray with glasses. Sh
carried it ceremoniously, like a priestess serving a rite. The ma
shambled behind her with bottles and a jug of water.

"Is that good corn liquor?" Revell reverted to his ordinary crudenes:

"Th' bes'," replied the woman simply. She placed the tray on
mahogany table and began to pour.

Revell, watching her suspiciously, demanded, "You got a nigger i
th' quarters can play a fiddle?"

"We got," she answered mistrustfully.

"You got a nigger kin play piano?"

"No."

"Would of been better, but it don't matter." His voice had an in
creasing vulgarity. "Get him an' his fiddle! We goin' to have us
dance."

The woman's eyes flickered from the glasses to Linden. The girl fe:
them on her, was uncomfortably aware of the incongruity of he
trousers in this room, and flushed a little.

Revell chose the moment to put his arm around her. Immediatel
the male scent of him overwhelmed her again. She was conscious fo
the first time in her life of a desire for surrender. There was no particu
larity in her desire. It was not directed specifically toward Revell. I
was a desire in principle, a yielding up, an abstract celebration. Sh
had been allowed to take part in this triumph; she was a fragment of it
glory. She had so little to give in return—no more than her virginity
She could give this to the South. She made the decision without formu
lating it in words.

The woman watched her closely. There was a note of speculatio:
in her voice as she said: "Aaron, go fetch Estis and his fiddle. Go fetc!
One-Eye an' Murphy. They goin' to play for the gen'men"—she eye(
Linden again—" 'n' the ladies." She handed the bottle to Revell, an(
followed her husband out of the door.

In the passage outside, she whispered fiercely, "That girl—that gir
in trousis—she's virgin!"

"How do you know?"

"I know." A plan was shaping. It had no outlines yet, no structure
it was still only an inspiration of revenge.

They were drinking when she came back into the room. Her eyes immediately searched out Linden. She saw that the girl had a glass, but that she had hardly touched the liquor, conforming but not participating. Revell was offering toasts to the *Merrimac,* to Virginia, to the South, to Victory. Four of the bottles were already opened.

She went up to Linden. There were three more girls in the room now, and more men. Revell had sent out for reinforcements for the party; the thing was growing of its own volition. She said softly, "You cain't dance in trousis."

Linden looked at her, startled, feeling that the other woman had been reading her mind. "I have nothing else."

"There's a whole closet full o' Mis' Amelia's clothes. Reckon she's about your size."

Now that she was close to her she saw the faunlike beauty of the girl, the delicacy of the bone structure, the grace of the body under the heavy clothes. She was an artist in the care of women. She could make a butterfly out of this ungainly chrysalis—or not a butterfly but a dragonfly, something with a darting grace. "She got a frock would light up yo' eyes. She ain't never goin' to wear it again."

"Why?"

"Reckon the South's won." The Negro woman's voice was still soft, but it was toneless now. "Mebbe she never come south agin'."

Linden realized that she was being offered the spoils of victory, a tribute offering. The wine of it was heady.

Revell said: "You go 'n' dress, honey. It's goin' to be your ball." His voice had a caress in it, and a faint thickening.

The woman noted it but she kept her eyes on Linden's dancing eyes. "Yo' come with me. It's a blue dress; it'll light up yo' eyes. She had it made in N' York."

They went out together. More bottles were opened.

* * *

Her voice was soft, caressing. "Take off yo' things, honey. I got hot water."

Linden, without turning from the window, asked, "What's your name?"

"Agapemone," replied the woman gently. "Means the 'bode of love. They calls me Pemony. Take off yo' things, honey."

Linden made no move from the window. The flames were leaping on the *Congress* now. She could see the flick and return of them under the light of the sunset. The smoke was almost black. She began to un-

button the boy's shirt that she wore, peeling it away from her throat.
Finally she pulled it over her head, stood for a moment with her eyes
hidden and her arms above her head in a supple dancing posture, and
then dropped it.

"'N' yo' ves' too."

The girl put her arms across her breasts as if she were suddenly cold.
Then she pulled the vest up and stood naked from the waist. She said,
"I've got no stays."

The Negro woman looked at her appreciatively. "Yo' don' need no
stays. Yo' got firm breasts—breasts fer a man. . . ." She turned away
at once and began to pour water in a basin. "Yo' got salt on yo' face, 'n'
sweat. Come 'n' let me wash you, honey."

Linden flushed. There were more people coming up the drive, girls
and men. She came away from the window. Almost meekly she stood
over the basin, feeling like a child again, submitting herself to Pemony's
hands. The water was at precisely the right temperature, the face cloth
was soft and scented, the soap had a rich smell. She felt the woman's
hands moving over her shoulders, under her armpits, molding her
breasts. The sensation had the innocence of childhood, but coupled
with that innocence was something more, some expectation of sex. It
was as if she were preparing herself for love—or was being prepared
for love. She did not analyze the sensation.

"Take off yo' trousis. Yo' shouldn' wear trousis, honey." Pemony
fumbled at the buttons and released them suddenly so that the girl
stood in only her drawers, held round the waist by the tight drawstring.
Then she released that too.

Linden stood naked.

Her body had a docile line, a part surrender. The Negro woman's
hands, practiced and full of experience, both soothed and stimulated.
Linden felt the warm, moist cloth following the contours of her stomach
and her buttocks and her thighs.

She was washed. The woman powdered her. There was scent—a
delicate, subtle fragrance, like the wan, undeveloped magnolias outside the door. Pemony began to dress her: silk drawers and a silk
chemise, silk stockings, shoes. Her eye was exact; the clothes fitted,
the shoes fitted. She brought the dress. It was a mist of blue, a diapha-
nous thing of altering shades and values. A dress from a dream.

The woman slipped it over her head. She murmured: "It's a dress to
'maze a man," her words holding an infinity of insinuation. "He won
a fight today. It proper yo' dress yo'self fo' him." A strange little singing note came into her voice. "My people"—she hesitated for a

moment—"my people, when they in Africa, they dress themselves fo'
h' men when they come back from a fight. Th' girls, they lie down in
he path that lead to th' village."

"What were your people?"

"My people the Yoruba." The woman's voice was so proud that it
was almost strident. "Th' girls they lay down in the path, an' the men
loved them, honey. They loved them there, out in th' open." The black
hands moved caressingly around Linden's shoulders. "They loved them
there in the dus' in the long grass before they come to the village when
they won th' fight."

Linden could feel the shivering ecstasy of tribal remembrance in the
woman's fingers. It transmitted itself to her body in a hypnotic im-
pulsion. She shivered with an un-understood empathy.

The woman said abruptly, her eyes flashing: "Yo' man won th'
fight. Yo' go to him, honey."

*　　*　　*

Linden could hear the violin when the door opened—the violin, a
banjo, and drums—and there was somebody at the piano. The music
had a persuasive urgency, the beat of it was pulse stirring. There was
the murmur of a crowd over it and through it. Still more people had
come: soldiers from the battery, sailors from the other ships. The house
had an air of carnival. The candles in the great chandelier in the hall-
way had been lit now, and the candles in the wall brackets; the place
was a brilliance of light.

She walked out on to the landing above the big staircase, and behind
her she heard Pemony's voice, urgent and compelling. "Go to him,
honey—go to him!" and she walked to the head of the stairs.

She felt conscious—not self-conscious—conscious of destiny, as
if she were being moved by a power outside herself to play a role pre-
determined. She walked to the stairhead and began to step down it,
one hand on the balustrade. She was aware that the music had stopped,
that people were pouring out of the drawing room, that the hall was
full. She became aware that faces were turned to her, men were looking up at her, eyes concentrated on her.

She was conscious of pride.

She was a part of this, a part of an expression of loyalty, of an
emanation of spirit. She walked proudly, dropping down from step to
step, with her head high, her body lithe and supple and gracious.

She heard Revell's voice above an appreciative silence, "Linden

Cleave, you're beautiful." And there was an answering ripple of applause.

He came to the foot of the stairs and waited for her, his hand held out, and she went down the last treads, conscious now of power—the power of her womanhood.

The violin came alive in a sweeping, lovely arpeggio, and steadied itself into a minuet.

Revell led her forward, his voice saying thickly, over and over again, "Lindy, you're beautiful, you're lovely, you're wonderful."

She knew what Pemony had done for her, knew the deep outrageous cut of the dress, knew the beauty of her naked shoulders and the whiteness of her throat. She knew that Pemony had done something to her hair, turning it from a boy's crop to a delicate, surprising halo. She knew that she was beautiful and that she was a woman.

The minuet ended. There were few who knew the dance; it was archaic but it was utterly appropriate. There were sufficient to make the figure, though, and it had had a fragile beauty.

After it she danced and danced, passing from man to man like a trophy, coming back to Revell again and being torn away from him. Always she could tell when she was dancing with a man from the ships—not by the uniform, but by the scent of him, the smell of powder and of sweat, the smell of maleness.

Once again she was taken from Revell, and he went to the door that led to the back part of the house and stood there, waiting.

Pemony came up to him. She was no longer carrying a tray—Aaron carried it—and she moved among them as if she were ordering the ceremonies. Now she came to him and said softly, with her voice low, deep, and full of suggestion: "I done put the silk sheets on the bed," and then, as if she felt that he had not understood the significance of the words, "Mis' Enwright's silk sheets." And after a pause, as if she were explaining something patiently to a child, "Mis' Enwright, she had them fo' her weddin' night."

He imagined the feel of silk against his naked body and the silk of Linden's naked body.

He had had a lot to drink: old bourbon, sour mash bourbon a long time in the cellar; it was insinuating and potent. He knew what he was going to do now. He knew that everything was working for him. He had felt the response of Linden's slender body to his own under the blue silk of the dress, and the firmness of her breasts against him, the swell above the line of the blue dress, and their warm young color. There was consent in her.

Linden saw Jeriel at the end of this dance, and she asked him to dance with her, but he stood shy and awkward and terribly defenseless. She put her arm round him instead and held him, and he said with a patient wonder, "Didn't know you could look like that, Lindy."

Then she came back to Revell, and he said without any preamble, without disguise, the hunger naked in his eyes, "Let's go upstairs, Lindy."

*　　*　　*

The ship was still burning. She glowed sullenly in the night, spreading the red light over the long cloud of her smoke and throwing it high into the night sky. The stars were brilliant.

Revell came up behind Linden. Her heart was beating with the insistence of a drum now. She knew that she was frightened. She stood quite still, not daring even to move her hands, looking out at the ship as if by concentrating on it she could postpone what she knew could not be postponed, what she did not in fact want to postpone.

She felt his hands on her shoulders, groping, seeking, expectant. She felt them slide over her nakedness, and her nostrils caught again at the powder smell, and flared, startled. She felt his hands move under her arms and cup her breasts. And still she stood motionless, watching the ship with her lips parted.

She asked, though she knew the answer, "Which ship is it that's burning?"

"Aah, it don't matter, honey. It's the *Congress,* but it don't matter. Isn't nothing that matters excep' you." He was breathing roughly, unrhythmically. His hands became more urgent. There had been a gentleness at first but it was lost. He was groping harshly now. He withdrew his right hand from under her arm and thrust it down almost savagely inside the low neckline of the blue silk dress. He felt his hand alive in the double ecstasy of the silk and the fluttering silken warmth of the young breast. She quivered at the feel of it, the roughness of his fingers, the almost angry pressure on her nipples. She wanted to cry out to him to stop, to be gentle, to be kind. But she stood motionless, not knowing what she should do, not wanting to acknowledge her body's responses.

Out of her memory came the vision of the doe beside the swamp. She remembered her docile expectancy, her patient acceptance, the endurance with which she sustained the first crashing impact of the buck.

Revell pulled her away from the window and the burning ship. He was burning himself. He said thickly, "Come to bed, honey," and when she moved slowly, he thrust her forward with his own body.

*   *   *

Pemony, with her ear close against the sounding board of the door, heard Linden cry, "Oh, God, Revell!" She straightened herself and laughed with atavistic malice. Finally she moved away, satisfied, her fine-modeled mouth set in an unconscious smile. Her eyes glistened in the soft candlelight that came up from the hall below.

At the head of the stairs she paused for a moment and moistened her lips. "I evil-wished her," she said exultantly, "I evil-wished her!" She moistened her lips again, and then, with a sudden humorous acknowl-edgment of herself, she added: "I could have been evil-wished to bed wit' him myself, I could. Yes, sir. Ye-es, sir." She laughed, and began to go down the stairs.

The hall was almost empty now. One couple was linked in a corner; one man lay sprawled on the floor, asleep. The music had died a long while ago. The lights in the drawing room were out. She strode past the couple and walked with the assurance of use into the drawing room. There were other couples in the darkness of the drawing room.

She opened the door that led through to the kitchen, and as it shut after her, she said: "Ain't no punishment fo' a South'n girl. No, sir. That ain't no punishment!"

Aaron was in the kitchen, collapsed in a chair. He was drunk; she had known he would be drunk. She looked down at him contemptu-ously. "Ain't never been no good," she said with a weary malevolence.

She stood remembering casual infidelities. Four white men had used her, one of them when she was a child. She did not resent them; indeed, she valued her memories. It was not white men that she hated, but white women.

She watched Aaron's chest moving slowly up and down. At length she looked down at her foot. It was well shod, a fashionable well-designed shoe. It was her mistress' shoe; she always wore them when Mrs. Enwright was away, wearily indifferent to the possibility of detection. Finally she kicked at Aaron's leg. "Git up," she said as if she were speaking to a recumbent mule, "git up! Git to bed." She did not want to go to bed with him, and it was doubtful if in his liquored-up condition he would be of any use, but there was nobody else. "Git up," she said again, and added dispassionately, "Hawg."

*   *   *

The weight of his body was enormous, suffocating; she could scarcely breathe. Linden wondered suddenly if he were as ignorant as she. He seemed to have no restraints, no delicacies. She was being raped—she was conscious at least of that. She had wanted to give herself to him, but he had taken her, forcing, clawing, biting, lost in a red anger of passion. The worst of the pain was gone now. There was left in its place a lost feeling that was even more difficult to bear, a feeling of horror where there should have been peace, a feeling of humiliation where there should have been pride and fulfillment. She had stopped fighting him now; it hurt less that way, less physically, at least. Her shoulders were scratched, her breasts bruised, her lips sore and bleeding. She could not even speak to him now. A perverseness of pride suffused her. She would endure.

He reached a climax, but she had no answering response. She was indifferent now to everything.

He said obscurely, his voice spent and indistinct, "Oh, God, oh, Christ!" and fell away from her, one of his legs still pinning her leg to the soft sensual mockery of the silken sheets.

She lay absolutely still. Her father had once said to her: "It's wonderful, it's glorious, if you love the man. Remember that: you've got to love him."

She knew now, with certitude, that she did not love Revell. But she would not cry about it. She had suffered pain before—but not this sort of pain. And she had suffered humiliation—but not this sort of humiliation. She knew that she could endure, however, and the knowledge gave her strength. She pushed his leg away roughly and pulled herself upright in the bed, her arms hugged round her knees. After a little she allowed her head to droop, resting her chin on the little V between them.

She sat like that for a long time. Revell was asleep beside her. He began to snore, and she reached out and hit him deliberately. She was thinking over the day, remembering the battle. She used it half-consciously as an anesthetic, employing it to dull her consciousness of humiliation. The battle had been glorious, the victory absolute; it was at once her salve and her justification. Once she looked down at Revell in the faint light from the high moon. In her eyes was a measure of the same contempt that Pemony's had held looking down at Aaron, the same disgust with men. She had become a woman.

She wondered what her father would say. He would understand, she thought. If she could tell him her feelings and her motives, she was certain that he would understand. Aunt Deborah would be another matter.

She sat for a while without thinking, her eyes watching the faint flicker of red light on the window frame. It was not possible to see the *Congress* from where she sat, but the light was so brilliant now that the reflection was clear even under the light of the half-moon. The flicker of the flames was the last acknowledgment of victory. Her crew had failed to quench them, and the *Congress* was lost.

She wondered, abruptly switching from the burning ship to herself, if she would have Revell's child. Without any sense of shame or guilt, she pondered the curious, impenetrable mysteries of creation, and for no reason at all she said aloud, softly, "It's a fool way to make a baby."

Much later there was a brilliant red flash, so bright that it lit the whole window-frame and flooded the room. It happened in absolute silence, and the silence held as she leaped from the bed and ran naked to the window.

The *Congress* had blown up. The sky across the Roads was still red with brilliance, great parabolas of sparks descending through the purple darkness, spreading far out from where the ship had burned. A second flash, less brilliant, followed. Then there was only a small, uncertain line of flame upon the sea.

Long after she had reached the window the noise of the first explosion came. It smashed against the open space like a shock. Almost she could feel it on her bruised and naked body. It made her aware of the remembrance of pain.

It woke Revell, and she heard him turn on the bed and then sit up. As he swung sideways from the bed he said, "What in th' name of hell's that?" His voice was quite clear and ordinary.

"The *Congress* blowing up."

He came to the window. She was quite conscious of her nakedness and quite indifferent to it. There was no longer any room for shame, and she was certain that she had regained control. It was not so much that she felt she had control of Revell as that she was again in control of herself. He stood for a moment watching, then he said, "Maybe you're right."

"I am right," she answered calmly.

"Come back to bed." He reached out his arms.

"Damn you, Revell!" she said without heat or anger.

He stopped instantly, shocked into immobility. It was too dark to see her face or the expression in her eyes, but he put his head on one side, peering. "Come on, Lindy," he whispered. "Ah, c'mon, love."

He didn't even have the words, she thought contemptuously, to plead or persuade. "I'll never come to you again, Revell, long as you live."

"You can't say that, honey! We goin' to get married." He reached forward hastily and snatched at her.

She eluded him with ease. Her voice was acrid as she said, "Only a coward would do that."

He stopped at once, as if he had been clubbed.

She heard feet pounding on the stairs. It was unimportant; it was not dangerous, it was only sordid, and she had borne so much that she could bear that too.

A fist began hammering on the door. One of the men shouted: "Th' *Congress,* she's blowed up. We got to get back to the ship. Th' lootenant'll eat us out."

Revell shouted back, "Wait!"

"We ain't goin' to wait. You come back after—won't be no boat. We' goin'.'

Linden said, "You're going too."

"I don't care for no lootenant."

"You're going."

*   *   *

She went back to the bed and sat as she had sat before, her knees drawn up, her arms clasped round them, her chin resting on the notch between them. She was aware of little localized spurts of pain as she moved her legs, aware of the dull general ache of her whole body.

She sat there, thinking. Would it be very terrible to have a baby? She knew astonishingly little about it, except that she was familiar with the sight of women big and uncomfortable with child. Particularly she remembered them sweating in the hot weather—they had made her uneasy, afraid. There was very little else that she knew. None of her friends had had children, none of her aunts. Negro women did not count.

She heard the men clumping down the path. Revell said something which she could not distinguish, and the man who had called them barked, "Shet yo' big mouth!" The sound of their boots diminished, and there was silence.

Later she heard the pad of naked feet and a hesitant knock on the door. Jeriel's voice asked doubtfully, "You a'right, Lindy?"

"I'm all right."

He was silent, not knowing what to ask next. Through the silence she realized suddenly the depth of his faithfulness, the quality of his devotion. For an odd, tender moment she wondered what it would be like to have him here in bed with her. Would it soothe her, ease her disappointments, her frustrations? Would it reward his loyalties?

Jeriel asked at last: "Are we goin' out again, Lindy? Are we goin' to th' boat?"

She knew that they were going to the boat. There was nothing else to do. She knew that she could not ask him into this bed. She knew that her way was clear in front of her as it always had been. She called out, "I'm coming, Jeri, bless you!"

*   *   *

From the darkness Pemony watched them pass down the stairs. The explosion had awakened her too. She watched them go with a smoldering hatred in her eyes, hatred and envy. When they were gone out of the great front door, she padded up the stairs to the bedroom and took up her old place by the window. Linden and the boy were still visible in the faint light of the false dawn. Savagely she said, "She ain't goin' to wear them trousis long."

There were sounds coming up from the water: voices, and the clatter of an anchor cable, and steam blowing off. The night with its silences was in retreat. A bird sang distantly in the trees.

The girl and the boy disappeared at last, and the woman sighed. "Hit wa'nt no punishment," she said. "Would ha' done me good."

*   *   *

Along the beach men sat or stood in small groups. Here and there fires burned. The scent of wood smoke was pungent and exciting in the cold dawn air.

The *Merrimac* had sailed. She was already at the end of the spit, black smoke clouding her, trailing along the top of the armored structure from the holes in her smokestack, lying down on the still water in her wake. The *Jamestown* and the *Patrick Henry* were close astern of her; the *Raleigh* was getting in her anchor; the *Beaufort* was far down the channel toward Craney Island, coming along as fast as her engines would let her.

There was no cheering, no noise at all. An exhaustion of spirit was apparent; as if all celebration and thanksgiving were already expended. There were no flags, for the sun was not yet up.

Linden walked stiffly down to the skiff. For the first time, with the eyes of men upon her, she felt self-conscious. Once, stumbling slightly, she said, angrily and half aloud, "You fool, nothing shows."

Jeriel, close beside, glanced at her interrogatively, but she made no attempt to explain.

They reached the boat. Last night it had been dragged well above the high-water mark. The tide was low again now, the stretch of sand formidable. Wordlessly, each knowing what to do from old experience, she and Jeriel lifted the stern and began to drag.

Two men from a nearby fire got up to help them. A third man joined them. He said, "Hell, it's a girl!"

Linden waited for facetious remarks, for ribaldry, but nothing came. The solemnity of the morning seemed to hold the men in check. With three helping, the boat was run rapidly into the water. In a minute she floated. Linden climbed in and took her place at the stern and shipped the rudder. The men held the skiff straight. Jeriel gave a last push and jumped from the shallows with one knee on the gunwale. She floated out slowly.

The *Beaufort* was coming past now. Linden waited till the gunboat was clear, steaming down the deep channel, before she made sail. This time there was no shouting between them, and she did not follow the *Beaufort*. She stood over instead toward the shoals of the Craney Flats —she could not tell why. The morning was full of forebodings; there was a steely purpose in it. Slowly, the wind dropped.

The *Merrimac* had altered course and was standing over toward the *Minnesota*.

Jeriel muttered, more to himself than Linden, "She didn't get off with the night tide."

There was no need to answer him. The *Minnesota* was clear in the growing light, her spars sharply etched against the land darkness to the north, her mastheads inclined very slightly to port, her battle flag already brilliant against the morning sky. The tugs and small craft were steaming away from her toward the bight of Hampton Flats. The skiff waited in absolute silence except for the lap, lap of the quiet water under her bows.

The sound, when it came, was in the sky—a thin, ghostly noise like a pack of hounds.

Jeriel squinted up, searching until he saw the formation moving irregularly, lifting and falling, bright with the sun that had not yet risen for the boats. "Canada geese headin' north."

Linden did not even look up.

Chapter eight

THE messenger pulled at his shoulder as if trying to jerk him upright. Stephen woke hurriedly. He was lying on the top of the bunk, fully dressed. The night with its work and its alarms was over, but here in the depths of "Ericsson's Patent Coffin" it was impossible to tell that day had come. He came to his feet in one quick movement. "Has the *Minnesota* come afloat this time?" It seemed to him only minutes since the first alarm of the night.

The messenger answered: "Not the *Minnesota,* sir. It's the *Merrimac.* Coming down the river!"

Stephen buttoned his jacket. The moment had come, then. He made his movements deliberately slow: he put a comb through his hair; he put his uniform cap on and adjusted it; he found time even to grin at his reflection in the mirror. Then he went aft to the ladder that led through the bottom of the turret. Now he would be afraid or he would not be afraid; this was the test.

The air on the turret top was contrastingly cold. The ship was alive. She seemed to make more noise than a normal ship, to hold more echoes: the rattle and clank of the machinery, the thud of feet on iron plates, the groan and clatter of Ericsson's patent cable arrangement, the whirr and groan and slap of the blowers.

One of the tugs was already half a mile clear of the ship. The *Dragon* was getting under way; Stephen heard her engine-room bell and the splash of her side wheels.

In the same moment he heard a voice come sharp and clean-cut above the other noises: "One broadside from the *Merrimac*'ll sink her."

On board the *Minnesota* men at the battered rails were staring down at the *Monitor.* They talked among themselves, their speech less clear, less audible than the voice from the *Dragon.* Only occasionally was it possible to isolate a word from its context of tangled voices. Twice he heard the word "contemptible."

The engine-room bells below in the ship sounded with a hard, surprising clarity. The *Monitor* was moving with the tide. He could see the sheer of the *Minnesota* apparently sliding past them. Then he felt the iron of the turret top tremble below him and knew that the engines had started. They swung away from the *Minnesota* in an easy curve, and instantly, as if a curtain had been pulled aside, he saw the open water across the seaward end of the shoal. In the middle of it, harsh, brutally silhouetted against the sunrise, was the *Merrimac* with her trailing cloud of smoke, and beyond the *Merrimac* the hulls and the masts of the swarm of gunboats. He knew that it was time to go below into the turret.

*   *   *

Catesby Jones waited with a group of his officers on the grating of the *Merrimac*. He would go down to the pilothouse before the action began; that much the Minié ball that had struck down Old Frank had taught him. For the time being the view was better from the grating.

The *Minnesota* was like the center of a target, a dark center surrounded by emptiness. Neither the *Roanoke* nor the *St. Lawrence* nor the gunboats had come to her aid during the night. They had not clawed her off on the early tide. Nothing had happened to her. She lay where she had lain. She was utterly alone. Except for her and the one tug, Hampton Roads was swept clear of the Union flag.

Catesby Jones' task was made easy thereby. Long since he had decided to leave the Newport batteries alone. Magruder's force would never make use of the opportunities the Navy had created. Jones had made that clear to Buchanan before he put the wounded flag officer on a tug for the Naval Hospital in the darkness before the dawn. He had one task only: to destroy the *Minnesota*. After that he would think afresh.

To Wood, standing a little behind him, he said: "We will use hot shot on her the instant we make the range. See that the gun is ready!"

He was silent again. Half-consciously he knew that he was putting off the hour of decision, putting off the moment when he would have to brace his mind to order the ship through the narrows between the Rip Raps and Fortress Monroe. He would have to do that, he knew now, if he were ever to come to grips with the *Roanoke*.

He turned to sweep the narrows with his glasses, to assure himself that there would be no attempt at rescue for the *Minnesota,* and in that moment he heard Davidson say, "Sir, the *Minnesota*'s crew are leaving her on a raft." He swung his glass round anxiously, almost angrily. For an instant he had trouble with the focus. Then he saw the raft—a long construction, low in the water, with a large metal cylinder in the middle of it. He allowed himself a single swift examination. Then he closed his glass with a staccato finality. "Gentlemen, the *Monitor* has arrived."

* * *

Jeriel saw the *Monitor* first; this morning he saw everything first. Linden's eyes were focused inward; the past, the immediate past, was more important to her than this present.

Jeriel shouted, "B'God, what's that?"

Even then she looked incuriously, as if she had no wish to be brought back to a present consciousness.

"Chri' sake, Lindy, if you ain't goin' to use the glass, give it to me!" Scrabbling aft, Jeriel took it. After a minute he said wonderingly: "It's a tank on a flatboat. What in hell would they be wantin' a tank for? Mebbe"—he was searching in his mind for possibilities—"mebbe they're takin' her ammunition off to lighten her." He lowered the telescope. "Lindy, it's comin' this way; it's headin' straight fer th' *Merrimac*."

Linden said coldly, all enthusiasm drained from her voice, "It'll be the *Monitor*."

Only now she focused on the astonishing, improbable vessel. She could just see the line of its deck, as much as showed above the sea curve. There was an excrescence at the bows—what it was she could not tell at this distance. The round cylinder was amidships; it would be the turret that the *Scientific American* had described. Aft of the turret, smoke came up through two holes in the deck. There was nothing else. This was the *Monitor*.

Jeriel gasped: "Jesus, she's small! Ain't got more'n two guns."

"Two," she confirmed remotely, "eleven-inch." Yesterday she would have been in a fever of excitement. Today she was cold and indifferent; not even Jeriel's excitement could light in her an answering fire.

"She's little." Jeriel's voice held for the first time a shade of doubt. "*Merrimac*'ll wipe her out, first broadside! Reckon the Yanks is crazy."

Linden sensed his inarticulated fear. It lit a more tangible response than his enthusiasm. She was herself afraid, and she shivered.

Jeriel, his voice low and the hoarse croak for the moment gone out of it, said, "Did he hurt you, Lindy?"

They were both staring at the ships. There was no need to look at each other, no need for embarrassment.

"Yes," she answered.

He muttered malignantly, "Th' bastard!"

The ships were moving closer and closer together. The sunrise was making patterns of light on the rolling smoke cloud that trailed astern of the *Merrimac*. The far shore across the Hampton Flats was achieving color and solidity. The water was beginning to change, chameleonlike, to blue.

Jeriel spoke again. "You should've waited for th' real fight, Lindy."

"What do you mean?"

"You remember—the two deer in the swamp. That day . . ." The dying fall in his voice measured aeons of lost time.

"I remember." Of course she remembered. She had remembered last night; she had made the comparison then, but it was necessary to defend herself. "How was I to know which fight?" And then, when he did not answer, she asked impatiently, "*Which* fight?"

"This one."

Wildly she cried: "But Stephen's not here! How could he be here? He wouldn't be in the *Monitor*."

Jeriel's voice was harsh. "He could be."

She had a sudden awareness, an access of belief that was almost telepathic; Stephen was near, somewhere near. She said, whispering, troubled: "It's too late. It's too late."

Jeriel made no sign that he had heard.

The tension was growing with every moment now. The two ships were almost within range. The whole world, even the blue sky over them, seemed to be waiting for this climax. The gulls themselves were still. The smoke swirling across the line of sight hid for an instant both the *Merrimac* and the *Monitor*.

Jeriel shifted his position, easing his ribs. He said casually: "Mebbe Revell'll get killed. This ain't the *Congress* or the *Cumberland*. Thing is"—he explored the matter with the cruel, cold logic of the very young—"he's got t' get killed 'thout the *Merrimac* is sunk. It ain't so easy. Mebbe she'll get another shell in a gun port." He considered the matter again, and added, "Mebbe."

She faced his ruthlessness, and knew suddenly, because of it, that she hated Revell for all time. She felt a hot surge of anger against him, not because he had taken her virginity, which was unimportant, but because he had taken her sense of self-ownership, because he had taken her pride.

She sat watching the ships, her forehead creased with wrinkles, and a long time after—an infinity of time, it seemed—the bow gun of the *Merrimac* fired.

Chapter nine

THE look of strain, the hard gray-lined look on the faces of the men, was more apparent on the berth deck of the *Monitor* than it had been in the turret. Perhaps, Stephen thought, it was because the men in the turret were waiting to act, waiting for the physical activity of battle, while on the berth deck the ammunition parties were just waiting.

No man, he thought, knew what would happen. There were no precedents. No one knew if the engines, after the disasters of the passage, would function through a hard battle. No one knew if the ship, after the failure of her steering, would answer her helm properly in emergency. No one knew if the turret would train properly on the ring. No one knew if the guns would work. No one knew if the armor would stand its test. Everything was in doubt; there was no precedent at all.

The crew was untested. It had not worked together except for the brief trials in New York Harbor and the chaos of the passage over the shoals. It had not fought together—few of the men had fought at all. And this was no simple baptism of fire.

Slowly, as he made his way forward to the pilothouse, examining, checking, instructing, the idea formed in Stephen's mind that this was the first battle of a new age of the sea. In the explosions of the magazines of the *Congress* an age had vanished—the age of the wooden ship. All naval history had come in that moment to a climactic point. The tradition of a thousand years had blown up in a single thunderous coruscation of sparks and burning timber and flaming canvas.

An era was ended. Now, a bare six hours later, a new age had begun. For the first time armor would meet armor, and no man could do more than guess at the outcome.

He reached the foot of the ladder that led to the pilothouse. No water came down it now, no water and little light. The narrow box was dark with the shadows of three men: Williams, the quartermaster at the wheel; Howard, the master's mate of the *Roanoke* who had volunteered when the regular pilots refused the duty; Worden, his eyes close to the narrow slit between the armored billets of the housing. Stephen stood silent at the foot of the short ladder, waiting—he was not sure what he was waiting for.

Why had the pilots failed? He pondered the question. Yesterday the *Minnesota* had run on the Middle Ground under a pilot. The *Roanoke* had scraped and dragged under a pilot until she had lost her nerve and withdrawn behind the guns of the narrows. The *St. Lawrence* had gone aground under a pilot. It was easy enough to think in terms of treachery —too easy, perhaps. Perhaps it all came down to simple fear. These pilots were not Navy men; they were essentially civilians, most of them no longer even seamen; they had retired from the open sea; they were not conditioned to battle. Perhaps that was why they would not come to the *Monitor*. Or perhaps it was just simple communicable cowardice. He could understand that.

Worden's voice shouted, "She's opened fire!"

Stephen heard the crack of a gun, muffled and distorted through the slits of the pilothouse.

A long moment after, Howard's voice: "Missed us—over to the right."

"Keep her steady as she goes!" Worden ordered, and after a brief pause he added, "She's turning, opening up her starboard broadside." Into the speaking tube he called, "Mr. Greene, commence firing!" Stephen felt the grind and clatter of the turret machinery. In the same instant Worden called, "Broadside!"

More rapidly than the sound had come before, Stephen heard the crash of a salvo from the *Merrimac,* and with the sound, or a fraction of a second after it, he felt the ship shudder and give to a heavy impact. The grinding noise of the turret went on unchecked; there was no change in the beat of the engines or the purr of the blowers. The ship's motion was unaltered.

He heard Worden shout again, "Turret, have you damage?" The reply that came back was too faint for Stephen to make it out, but he heard Worden's satisfied, "Good!"

On the word the *Monitor* fired her first gun. He felt the blast of the discharge come through the slits of the pilothouse like a hot wind. This, he thought soberly, was the time when he should have been afraid, or was it the end of the time? An immense, uninhibited elation took him. If he were going to be afraid, he would have been afraid between the moment in which he dropped down from the grating to the turret and the moment that the first shells hit.

He had not been afraid.

*   *   *

Simms said exultantly: "We hit her! We hit her! We hit her twice!"

A sour voice growled beside him, "But we ain't hurt her."

The crash and shudder of a heavy shot against the armored shield of the *Merrimac* punctuated the words. At once everything was lost in the fury of the reloading.

Above them in the pilothouse they heard a voice shout, "She's comin' in to starboard!"

Revell stood rigid for a moment with a shell in his arms, staring out at the ellipse of the port, his eye held by the strange, flat almond-point of the forward deck of the *Monitor,* the featureless area of flat plates, the square hutch of the armored pilothouse. It seemed to be feeling toward them blindly, like the flat head of a water snake. The turret came into view, surging ponderously into the field of vision of the open port. It was as featureless as the iron deck. Only a ladder bolted to the side broke the smooth curve of plating and rivet heads.

Quite suddenly as he watched, it began to move, revolving slowly, silently, with an absolute inhumanity. Even as he saw the muzzle of the gun his gun captain bellowed at him, cursing, and automatically, more afraid for the moment of the gun captain than of the enemy gun, he shoved the shell into place for the rammer. Then, with a quick reflex of fear, he jumped back from the open port to the shelter of the armor.

Again there was a thunderous crash on the side of the ship. His teeth jarred in his head, his bones seemed to give and jar together again. Buckets on the deck lifted and fell, angrily metallic. His nose began to bleed.

The reloading was completed. The guns reported ready. A fresh broadside was fired. The range now was absurdly close: only a narrow lane of water separated the two ships. Down it the mud-yellow ripples of the surface appeared to race at an inordinate and incredible speed. Everything was magnified. Everything had lost proportion. The tiny world inside the armor had gone mad.

Three shells of the second broadside hit, but even at point-blank range there was no more damage than a scar on the curving armor of the Yankee turret.

Somewhere a voice said, disillusioned, "One hell of a cheesebox."

Stubbornly, doggedly, the ritual of reloading was begun afresh.

Catesby Jones came down from the pilothouse. He hurried through the gun deck like a small ship plowing through a tumbled and angry sea. Revell heard him say, "Can't see a damned thing." And Cahill, beyond him, said sardonically, "Now *he'll* get hisself shot." And in the darkness and the smoke and the smother another voice said, "Won't make no never-min'."

On the gun deck they began to lose sense of time and direction. The battle was fought in a series of intricate, inexplicable curves. All the while Catesby Jones carried out a private, personal battle with his pilots. The ship was continuously under helm, heeling one way, heeling another, dragging in the shallows, as heavy in her motions as a water-logged wreck, as hard in the mouth as a foundering mare.

To the gun crews it was early evident that their shot could not harm this terrible Yankee mechanism, this thing that ground slowly round and glared at them with one eye open and a muzzle poked through it, that lazily made flame and thunder and answering shock against the *Merrimac's* sides. Their own shells burst impotently against the curve of it. The few solid shot that they possessed made indentations, but nothing changed the remorseless swing and halt, nothing altered the black circle of the gun mouth. The thing was inexorable and inexpugnable. Slowly, frighteningly, a conviction of hopelessness took hold on the gun deck.

The nearer gun crews, in the brief, tense seconds before the order to fire, heard Catesby Jones' voice high above them, "We'll have to ram!" Immediately afterward they heard Simms' voice, "Fire!" Again there were hits reported, again there was no damage. Across the noise of the fresh reloading they heard wheel orders shouted and the clang of the engine-room bells, and below them the pulse of the engines died down unsteadily, and ceased.

Steam blew off through a damaged valve. Then an uncanny, terrible moment of silence seized the ship. Out of the gun ports they could see the *Monitor* swing away in a circle—a movement that by comparison with their own, seemed absurdly gay.

The battle developed into a macabre dance, a dance of death; the *Merrimac* swinging behemoth-like, ponderous; the *Monitor* making small circles, sudden, violent alterations of course that kept her always outside the desperate lunges of her enemy. It was like a game of chess on a board that had no squares, a conjuring up of move and counter-move, a pitting of brain against brain. For an hour it went on, a full hour before the *Monitor* made her first mistake.

Worden finished a curve and found himself suddenly in shoal water —shallow even for his eleven-foot draught. He made a full helm turn to swing out of it, and Catesby Jones, sensing rather than seeing what had happened, rang for full ahead on the *Merrimac's* ancient, hirpling engines, and steadied to a collision course.

*   *   *

Jeriel had undisputed possession of the glass now. He crouched in the bows with the end of it steadied on the gunwale, his face absorbed.

"Lindy"—it was only the third time he had ever called her "Lindy"—
"she's goin' to ram!"

Linden was trying to concentrate on what was happening, trying to
lose herself in the immensity of the event, in its significance and its
implications. She was trying to escape into it from herself—and from
last night. The only response she could make was to say, "You can't
tell from here."

It was, in fact, impossible to tell what was happening—impossible
to decipher the scrolls and arabesques of this most complex maneuvering. There seemed, from where they drifted over the Craney shallows,
to be no reason in the move and countermove. The two ships came
together and the guns fired, and the ships swung apart and fired again.
The *Minnesota* had joined in now, firing irregular salvos that sometimes
overpitched and sometimes fell short, and if they hit had no effect on the
slanted iron of the *Merrimac*. No more effect than the *Merrimac*'s salvos
had on the curved iron of the *Monitor*.

The South's wooden ships were lying well back now, under the cover
of the batteries on Seawell's Point. Their part was done, their age over.
Dimly, Linden recognized this.

Yesterday's battle had been simple; it had followed certain hard
rules of logic: iron against wood, fire against combustibles, steam
against sail. But this had no logic. Catesby Jones would try to ram because his shells had no effect, because Buchanan had rammed yesterday in triumph, because he had no alternative. But this time it would be
iron against iron.

Jeriel was right—the two ships were coming closer and closer together, drawing to a point of impact, as if they moved on invisible
tracks.

She said, "Give me the glass!"

Jeriel turned and handed it over with a wide smile. Linden had come
back to life, come back to the present. He could forego his share even
of this climax without complaint.

*   *   *

The manhole in the revolving floor of the turret slid across the manhole in the ship's deck and overran it. Through the gap came a confusion of voices. Stephen heard Greene shout, "Stop the god-blasted
thing!" and then the voices were cut off again.

Slowly the turret crept back again. Once more the manholes coin-
cided and, as motion ceased, they began to lower Stodder's body. The
navigator's face had a gray surface. His body was limp. Men took his

feet, Stephen grasped his middle, and they eased him down to the deck below. There was no observable injury, no sign of blood. The surgeon was there.

Stephen left him and shot up the ladder before the turret began to move again. "What happened?" he demanded.

"He was working the turning engine, leaning against the armor," Greene replied. "I told him not to—I told him . . ."

"And?"

"The *Merrimac* hit us. He must'a' got the shock of it through the iron. He fell on the deck—out—like a light."

"Anybody else hurt?"

"Not yet."

Stimers, with his hand on the lever of the turning engine, asked, "What does Worden say about the powder charges?"

"He says no."

"Damn it to hell!" exclaimed Greene. "We can't do any good with these. Give us a thirty-pound charge and we'll cut right through her armor. Fifteen pound's no good—not a damn' bit!"

"The Bureau's orders are definite."

"Damn the Bureau! We need thirty pounds." Greene turned away to the guns.

It was intolerably hot in the turret. It stank with sweat and the heavy, musty odors of unwashed bodies, powder smoke, hot grease, scorched wood, and the forward whipping of engine fumes. It was dark in spite of the grating and the manhole. It was full of noise and swearing and, Stephen realized with surprise, of laughter. The guns' crews were sure of themselves now; more than that, they were sure of their ship: the turret had justified its theory.

Greene shouted at him across the gun, "Can't your damned tinkers get the voice pipe working?"

He shouted back, "No," because there was no other way of making himself heard. The voice pipe had broken down completely; the whole system seemed to have collapsed in vibration and shock. He came close to Greene, and bellowed: "Keeler and Toffey are passing the orders. Can you hear them up here?"

Cochrane, one of the gun captains, shouted cheerfully: "Don't matter if we can't. Don't matter what them bastards in the pilothouse do."

The men laughed with him. They went in ordered disorder to the tackles and triced up the starboard pendulum, the cover over the gun port. They were a crew, they worked together, striving hugely, ribald, undisciplined, effective.

The shutter came up and Stephen saw the *Merrimac* very close, bows on, a black truncated triangle—the triangle of death that the men of the *Cumberland* must have seen—in the moment before the death blow.

Greene shouted like a maniac, grabbed for the lock string, and jerked. The gun leaped back on its recoil mechanism, grinding. The whole turret shook in conjoined identity of purpose. The ship shook. The men shouted and laughed, the pendulum fell, cutting off the light, cutting off the apparition of the *Merrimac,* cutting off the moment of doom.

*   *   *

The shot hit forward on the *Merrimac,* slithered up and to the left with the curve of the forward armor, and lifted, singing. The ship shrugged herself and went on. She was moving fast now, faster than she had moved all morning. The men at the guns could feel the pulse of the engines under their feet—irregular, uneven, but full of power. They knew now that the *Monitor* fired only at long intervals. They knew that in the minutes after a shot her turret was silent, the two eyes in it turned away, blind.

Revell crouched by the gun port, held there against his will. The ships were desperately close now, hurtling together. The alignment of the *Monitor* altered as he watched; she was trying to turn clear, but it was already obvious that her turn was too late, too slow—the ships were bound to collide. He was frozen in excitement, for the instant absolved of fear. A sense of the *Merrimac*'s size grew on him; he remembered her weight, and his mind went back to the first moment of the ramming of the *Cumberland.*

The *Monitor* was small; she would be overwhelmed; the iron of her sides would crumble under the smashing weight of the *Merrimac.*

He shouted: "We're going to run the bastard under. Drown the buggers—drown the buggers! Run her under!"

Cahill bellowed: "Shut up! Get ready to load!"

Revell stooped and hefted the shell, still watching.

The ships came closer and closer. Everyone was shouting now. There was pandemonium along the gun deck. They were very close—almost touching. They hit!

This time there was no splintering of shattered wood. This time there was only a dull grating of metal on metal, a ponderous thud—a check in the *Merrimac*'s movement.

The *Monitor* had achieved the beginnings of her turn. She accepted a glancing blow, already moving away from its direction. The timber and the armor of her sides stood up to it. For a moment she hung, held against the *Merrimac*'s bow by the movement behind the blow. Her deck heeled a little, water surged up it, almost to the turret ring; then she fell away, moving sidewise and diagonally at the same time. The moment passed; she slipped away from the *Merrimac*'s bow.

There was no ram. The *Merrimac* had left that yesterday in the side of the *Cumberland*.

The *Monitor* came to an even keel, swinging back on to a course parallel with that of the *Merrimac,* and, as she steadied, Revell saw her turret swing, saw the open eye of the gun port aiming directly at him. He flung himself, panicked, into the angle between the armor and the deck. The shell that he had dropped rolled away.

Somebody kicked him. Cahill rasped: "Get up, you gutless so'jer! Get that shell, one o' you. For Chris' sake, load! Godamighty, it's too late!"

The shot hit exactly level with them, fired at a distance of less than thirty feet. The man who had stooped for the shell was flung violently away by the concussion. The wooden backing behind the armor was forced in with an immense shriek of splitting wood. Revell was conscious long enough to be aware of the shriek, of the pain, of his paralysis, of the last limits of terror.

Cahill, in the smoke and the smother, shouted: "Put your boot in his ass. Get up, so'jer, goddammit!" The man nearest to Revell climbed up from his knees and kicked blindly. Cahill shouted again, "You bigmouthed son of a bitch!"

The man said: "Didn't shift him none. Reckon he's dead."

"He was a useless bastard when he was alive. Pull him back an' yell for the surgeon."

The man answered: "Cain't shift him; the timber's bruk. Guess he's pinned."

The surgeon came up from the berth-deck hatch. He dropped on his knees beside Revell and the broken timbers. After a quick look, he said: "Get an ax, someone. Cut away the timber—here!" He indicated the point with his finger. "There's a chance he's not dead."

"No call for you to sweat yo'self, Doc," said Cahill witheringly.

*　　*　　*

"What's she done?" demanded Jeriel urgently. "What's happened? She's still firin'."

Linden lowered the telescope. "The *Merrimac* hit her"—her voice was puzzled—"she hit her, but it didn't do any good. She didn't hurt the *Monitor*." She held out the glass blindly to Jeriel. "I don't think she can hurt the *Monitor*." Sitting bolt upright, she began to cry.

Jeriel, his eye fixed to the telescope, did not see her tears.

The two ships moved slowly apart, both circling. The *Merrimac* fired another broadside—and nothing happened. The *Monitor* fired —and nothing happened. They were like two tired fighting men, drunk with punishment, swinging great empty, air-cleaving, futile blows at each other.

Jeriel said, "Her smokestack's most gone now."

Linden remembered the broken metal as she had last seen it lying across the gratings of the spar deck. The black smoke trailed lower still. It lay along the water in dark coils. It was growing difficult to follow the ships in the smother. The gun smoke was collecting on the water in irregular, gray-brown patches. The *Minnesota* had ceased fire.

Linden asked through her tears, "Do you think he could be on her?"

"Stephen?" Jeriel nodded. "Could be." It pleased his sense of the appropriate. "Ain't no reason 'gainst it. He's a Navy officer. Good one, too, 'cept he went North." He paused for a moment, revolving the matter in his mind. "All th' same, he could be other places—the Gulf, Roanoke, anywheres. Hell, he could'a' been in th' *Cumberland* yesterday. Or the *Congress*."

She made no answer to that.

Jeriel said disgustedly, "Goddam Yank's fired again!" He offered the glass to Linden. "Look!"

"I don't want to see!" Her voice was dull, lifeless. "I don't want to see!"

Chapter ten

STODDARD, the old clerk in charge of the secretaries' office, listened to the voices in the White House Cabinet room with a strained attention. He made no attempt to disguise his purpose. He and Hay had an established understanding.

Now, as the younger of the President's secretaries came quietly through the door of the Cabinet room, the noise that had been no more than a blur of voices before was suddenly clear, Stanton's voice overtopping the rest.

Stoddard heard the words, high-pitched, emphatic, frightened. "Mr. President, she may be steaming up the Potomac at this moment. The shells of the *Merrimac,* sir, may disperse Congress before the morning is out."

Another voice—Stoddard thought it was that of Senator Browning —said: "Surely, sir, the . . ."

Hay closed the door. The voices became a blur again. His face was set and hard. Even the cynical understanding that existed between himself and Stoddard with regard to the Cabinet room had disappeared.

Stoddard fumbled for it. "The Secretary of War's riding the meeting?" His voice had a tentative appeal for a return to normality.

Hay answered grimly: "By God, he has reason! The *Merrimac's* out. She's sunk the *Cumberland* and burned the *Congress.* The *Minnesota's* aground, waiting for destruction. It's total defeat—a hellish defeat." He shook his head with an air of confusion. "I cannot understand it."

Stoddard sat bolt upright at his desk. "What does Mr. Welles—"

With a swift return to cynicism Hay said: "Mr. Welles is calm. He has nothing to propose—but he is calm."

Stoddard reached for and suddenly found comfort. "But the *Monitor?*"

"Nobody knows anything of the *Monitor,*" replied Hay savagely. "Welles does not know if she has reached the Chesapeake. There has been no report." He remembered the papers in his hands. "Mr. Stanton insists that the Governors of New York, of Massachusetts and Maine be warned immediately and instructed to put the defenses of their harbors in order. The President assents. This is a draft of the telegram which is to be dispatched. Have it copied immediately and taken to the telegraph office of the War Department." He stood for a moment trying to evaluate the news for himself.

Stoddard looked through the draft. "*Could* she go to New York?"

"I don't know," answered Hay somberly. "Nobody knows. We know only that she is impervious to shot. There is nothing she cannot do." For a moment he stood silent. "We must have information. We must have news. Mr. Stoddard, take the message to the War Department yourself! Find Lieutenant Eckert. Tell him the President must know at once the exact state of the telegraph between Cape Charles and Fortress Monroe."

Stoddard said, "The loss of the *Hoboken* on the twenty-fifth——"

"I know, I know!" interrupted Hay impatiently. "But they were to lay the cable again at the end of this week. Tell Lieutenant Eckert we must have news! He must speak with the engineers over the wire himself."

He went back to the Cabinet room and, as he opened the door, Stanton's voice, high, shrill, dominating, came clear again, "I shall recall Burnside." The voice altered in power as the Secretary of State for War turned abruptly away and scurried to the window again to look down the Potomac for signs of the *Merrimac*.

Stoddard bent over his desk and began to make a fair copy of the message to the Governors.

The buzz of voices increased and diminished in the Cabinet room but never ceased.

He finished the last sheet, got to his feet, walked to the stand and took his hat. Then he went to the stairs. His knees felt curiously loose, a faint, almost imperceptible trembling in them. He said to himself at the head of the stairs: "This is shockingly like Bull Run—the Navy's Bull Run."

The clerk's room stood empty for a little. Hay came out again. This time when the door opened Stanton's voice was silent; Seward was talking, his voice low and even. Hay shut the door, and waited. He tried to strike a balance. Since Stanton had rushed in to break the Sabbath quiet with the telegram from General Wool, it had been impossible to think. Stanton's voice was like a high-pitched saw. His ordinary control was gone; he had reached heights of incoherence at times. All his spleen, all his enmity for Welles had been allowed to come to the surface. How much of his panic was real? Welles showed no sign of panic. How much of Welles' imperturbability was real? How much was each man trying to score off the other in the eyes of the President?

The President himself?

The President was disturbed, profoundly disturbed—of that Hay was certain. There were a score of minute signs, signs that would be meaningless to an outsider; but Hay loved the man and, because he loved him, knew. The President had allowed himself to be taken to the window on one of Stanton's fantastic sorties. Sister Anne, Sister Anne . . .

He cocked his head. Stanton was talking again, a stream of words, a spouting.

The President—the knowledge settled itself in Hay at last—was steering a middle course; he was the proponent of the middle course.

He was working now halfway between the panic of Stanton and the calm of Welles. Presently he would find a course of action.

Someone knocked on the door of the room. Hay opened it abruptly. Mrs. Lincoln's maid stood there, half defiant, half obsequious.

"Go away!" said Hay with a quick, artificial fury.

The woman stood her ground. "Mrs. Lincoln says"—the formula was an ancient cause of hostility—"will the President be gettin' dressed for church?"

"God," exclaimed Hay profanely, "it only wanted that!" He shook his head wildly. "No. No. No. Tell Mrs. Lincoln that the President is occupied with urgent business. The Cabinet has been called to meet within the hour. There is a crisis, woman!" He shut the door, almost slamming it.

Had Stoddard got the messages to the Governors away yet? He tried to follow the messages through their course, to translate them from simple informative words to action. What would New York do? What would Boston do? He saw a swiftly increasing apprehension along the seaboard, perhaps panic in New York. Stanton was demanding the blocking of the Potomac. Would they block New York Harbor? What was the state of the forts at Baltimore and Philadelphia and Rhode Island? Was Stanton right?

Nicolay came through the door of the Cabinet room.

Hay almost ran to him. "What now?" he demanded.

"The President believes neither of them; he is going to take professional advice. He will see Dahlgren at the Navy Yard. The light carriage must be ordered at once. The full Cabinet will meet at his return at eleven o'clock, together with General McClellan. It would be best if you called upon them yourselves. Somebody must inform Commodore Smith—"

"Smith? As Chairman of the Ironclad Board?"

"Smith's son," answered Nicolay grimly, "commanded the *Congress*."

In a quick, perceptive flash of imagination Hay said: "If he had made up his mind to sign the contract earlier—if he had helped Ericsson at the beginning . . . He will not sleep o' nights."

There was another knock at the door, at once hesitant and peremptory—the woman again? "The Hellcat sent a message to tell him"—he jerked his head toward the Cabinet room—"that she wished him to dress for church."

"Nonsense!" said Nicolay brusquely.

"I told her that there was a crisis, that the Cabinet was meeting."

"Good!" Nicolay himself went to the door.

It was not Mrs. Lincoln's maid; it was a young messenger from the Navy Department, breathless, disheveled. "A message for Mr. Welles" —he waved the envelope dramatically—"from the *Monitor*."

Nicolay took it hurriedly and ran with it to the Cabinet room. He opened the door. "Mr. Welles, a message—from the *Monitor!*"

Gideon Welles was standing close to the door. He turned and, with a speed that belied his calm, snatched the envelope from Nicolay's hand.

There was an absolute silence in the room. Hay, listening with a quietly desperate eagerness, knew that no one was moving, that even breathing had almost stopped.

Gideon Welles said, with an immense expulsion of relief, "The *Monitor* is in Hampton Roads, Mr. President."

Before the President could answer, Stanton had crossed to Welles as if to take the telegram from him. He stood framed in the doorway with the light behind him, shining through the elaborate side curls on either side of the bald domed head. "How many guns has your *Monitor*?" He almost screamed the demand.

"Two," replied Welles slowly.

"The *Merrimac*, sir, has ten!" Hay saw the eyes behind the steel-rimmed spectacles screw up into a frenzy of anger and contempt.

Chapter eleven

CATESBY JONES watched the *Monitor* as she began another turn. She would come in again, he knew—come straight in, contemptuous of the *Merrimac*'s broadside, choosing her line of approach, warily keeping the shoal water under her lee, the shoal water where the *Merrimac* could not follow. He took out a heavy gold watch. "Eleven o'clock. Three hours and we are no nearer a decision. Mr. Davidson, you will order the Marines to fire on her gun ports as the turret swings toward us. We will try what bullets will do among her gun crews."

The pilot, Parrish, standing close to him, said, "Sir, we must swing her. We're getting into the shoal water again."

"Swing her!" ordered Jones reluctantly. He watched the bearing of the *Monitor* change. "We cannot penetrate her armor," he murmured, almost to himself. "We have no ram. Our bow by itself can have no effect on her." He had an orderly mind. There was one possibility left to him. Over his shoulder he said, "Call Mr. Davidson back!"

The *Minnesota* opened fire on the Southern ship again. One shot hit on the *Merrimac*'s armor, one splashed in the racing water that covered the foredeck. No one even took note of them. The *Minnesota* was unconsidered in this battle.

The *Merrimac* passed into the reeking bank of her own funnel smoke and came through to the sun glitter of the far side. Jones had a momentary vision of the ramparts of Fortress Monroe lying like a red headland at the mouth of the Roads, of the stranded, seal-like shape of the Rip Raps battery, of the forest of masts that stretched into the Chesapeake beyond the forts. Then the flat, raftlike hull of the *Monitor* came darkling across the sun glitter, with the black cylinder of her turret making a simple, somber shape in the center of it. His eyes were drawn to it as iron to a magnet.

Davidson came up behind him. "Captain, sir?"

"Mr. Davidson, We will make ready to board her." Hurriedly, as if to interpose his command between his words and any possible protest, he added: "I am aware of the difficulties, Mr. Davidson. The slope of our sides gives the men no proper footing for a leap across, nor does the grease and the tallow aid. It would be best to examine the possibility of getting the men through the forward gun ports onto the deck." He looked down at the bows. "There is very little water coming over the deck now, Mr. Davidson. We have used a great deal of coal, a deal of ammunition. The bows are rising all the time. It should be possible to maintain a foothold there at slow speed. The *Monitor*'s sides are not above two feet from the water surface. Ten men would be enough. There must be some opening in the roof of the turret, something through which they could fire." He paused. The Yankee ship was coming slowly up to them on a converging course, the turret still blind as she reloaded. He watched her for a moment. "I will endeavor to bring her alongside and to hold her there. Do you get your boarding party assembled and examine your plan!"

*   *   *

Captain Van Brunt walked to the taffrail at the starboard quarter of the *Minnesota* and measured the distance with his eye. "You may cease fire until she comes round again, Mr. Bryan." He spoke evenly, apparently calm. With continuing calm he said: "The *Monitor* is going into the attack again. She will accomplish nothing. For three hours she has accomplished nothing—more than three hours." He watched the movement of the two ships. After a pause he went on: "Mr. Purkis, you will instruct the master carpenter and the bosun to pile combustibles in the storerooms abaft the foremast. I will not permit this ship to fall into the hands of the enemy." He placed both hands, the fingers in line with the woodwork, upon the rail and leaned there, watching silently.

The distance between the *Monitor* and the *Merrimac* diminished. The *Monitor* fired her starboard gun. The *Merrimac* waited a long thirty seconds and fired a broadside. There was no visible result. The two ships continued their wide, sweeping curves. The whole area of the Roads was silent once more, and the last echoes of the gunshots rolled away. On the *Minnesota,* where men worked at the big hole above the water line made by one of the *Merrimac*'s earlier shots, there came the sound of hammering. Then that too ceased. Even the wind flutter in the halyards stopped. Smoke hid the *Monitor.* When it cleared, the ironclad was pulling in over the shallow water.

Van Brunt watched her morosely. "What in God's name has she got to do that for?" He had a curious feeling of developing hatred against this small ship that did what she pleased—and yet did nothing.

A voice behind him said, "The *Merrimac*'s altered course toward us, sir."

Heavily he answered: "That at least was inevitable. Mr. Bryan, you will wait till she is well within the range before you fire your next broadside. She will disregard it otherwise." He waited stoically.

Heavily the *Merrimac* crept up toward the stranded ship.

Van Brunt watched her, his face set. After a little he ordered, "Clear the tug away!" The *Dragon* was lying alongside the starboard quarter. "There is no need to take her with us." He did not turn his head to watch the movement of the tug. His eyes remained fixed on the Confederate ship.

The *Merrimac* fired first, a little early. One ball hit, a slanting blow; one passed overhead; one hit the *Dragon,* scarcely clear of the *Minnesota*'s side. The shell penetrated to the tug's boiler and she blew up in a ragged belch of steam. The *Merrimac* fired her bow gun, and a shell ripped through the *Minnesota,* wrecking the engineer's cabin and the mess room, bursting in the bosun's room, tearing a great hole and setting powder charges on fire in a single moment of intense, atrocious destructiveness.

At once, in the opposite reaction, men came rushing with buckets of water, with hoses, with wet coal sacks to put the fire out.

The *Merrimac* ran on, completing her awkward curve, and stood away again.

Van Brunt followed her movements narrowly. One more attack and that would be the end of the *Minnesota*. He had no faith left in the *Monitor;* he had had little to begin with.

One of the lookouts said, "The *Monitor* is turning now, sir, to come out again."

He made no answer.

A messenger came breathless to the poop and shouted, "Fire's under control, sir!" in a great outpouring of enthusiasm.

Van Brunt answered him grimly, remembering how close he had been to putting a match to another fire, "Good!" and let him go.

The *Merrimac* continued her curve, almost insolent in her deliberation. Van Brunt and his officers waited on the poop, the tensions building again.

A signalman called, "Cap'n, sir, the *Merrimac*'s aground!"

*   *   *

Linden's tears had passed. She sat silent. Everything was changed. This was a different picture; only the frame was the same: the frame of the low hills behind Hampton, the curve of the shore at Newport News, the shape of the forts, the flat gray levels of the Norfolk shore with its marching pines. Inside the limits of the frame the picture was altered; even the colors were changed. The smoke lay low today, graying the water, taking the blue out of the nearer sky. There was no longer beauty and brilliance in the picture, only dark grays and somber blacks. There were no high lights of victory, no dark shadows of disaster. There was nowhere, except in the momentary flashes of the guns, the heat of flame.

Slowly, intolerably, the knowledge pressed in on her that yesterday was a day, with its shouts and its triumph, its glory and its tragedy; and today was another day, without glory and without triumph—with only the hard, slow slash of the impotent guns.

Linden said to herself, "Three hours ago she went in to finish the *Minnesota*." Her eyes sought and found the high masts of the stranded ship, the spars that still crossed them, the black shape of her hull. The Yankee ship was still safe, still unbroken. The *Merrimac* was still held back from her by a tin can on a shingle.

Jeriel turned to her, puzzled. "He's takin' his time," he said skeptically. "Ain't nothin' goin' to happen for a bit, I reckon. Let's eat."

"You eat," she said with an effort. "I'm not hungry."

"The nigra woman give me a heap o' stuff. Lindy, you ain't ate nuthin' since befo' yesterday mornin'. You didn' eat midday yesterday, you didn' eat last night. You ain't had no breakfus'. You jest nach'relly goin' to faint or somethin'."

"I won't faint." She felt a sudden warmth toward him. "I'm sorry about you—and last night," she added reluctantly.

"You should ha' called for me."

"I couldn't," she answered painfully, her mind bruised by memory. "I don't think I can explain why."

"Don' need to." Jeriel shook his head. "Reckon you' sick 'bout today, ain't you?"

She realized that his mind was delicately perceptive—almost tenderly so. She knew that she could talk, now.

"I don't think the *Merrimac*'s what I—what everybody—thought she was." The words came out in a tumbled rush.

"Mebbe you 'spected too much out o' her," he suggested wisely. "Mebbe you thought she was better'n she could be, th'n anything could be."

The girl answered sadly: "I thought she could change the war for us. Now I don't think she can go out past the forts."

"She's as good as anythin' the Yankees got!" Jeriel was defiant. "They been talkin' about the *Monitor* fer a helluva time. She's been firin' three hours now. Looks like level peggin' t'me."

"Level peggin's not enough. We've got to have more."

"Pity Ol' Frank got hisself shot," said Jeriel obliquely.

"You mean . . ."

"Lootenant Jones, he's scairt o' his pilots, fer one thing. Ol' Man Parrish, he's never no good lest he's got a skinful o' liquor inside him. Rest of 'em's a poor lot. You know that, you know 'em. I heerd a bit las' night."

She began to feel more alive, more in touch with reality. The boy's rough, unsteady voice had a healing quality. It came from a fount of old, hard common sense. It was difficult for her to separate in her mind the reaction of the night from the disillusion of the day, to discover how much one was caused by and sprang out of the other.

The boy rummaged in the basket and produced an enormous slice of pie. "Eat," he urged. "Ain't no sense lettin' yo' belly knock against yo' backbone." He handed her the pie abstractedly, staring at the *Merrimac*. After a long minute, while his empty hand still maintained its position,

he said, without emphasis, "Looks to me like Jones has sat hisself up
on a mudbank—'spite o' Will Parrish."

She put the slice of pie down and reached for the telescope. "Why do
you think so?" Her voice was anxious.

"We ain't movin' hardly at all," replied the boy with caution. "You
take the li'l white house in line with the *Merrimac*'s fore end. We ain't
moved."

She felt a cold fear seize her.

*   *   *

Stephen called down to Greene in the turret. He waited while the
exec came up the ladder to the manhole. When he was clear of it he
pointed down toward the *Merrimac*. "Look!" Yellow water showed
in front of her bows, a long elliptical patch of it bright with the harbor
mud. "It's coming away from her with the tide. She's aground."

Greene, momentarily confused with the noise and the different eye
focus of the interior of the turret, said, "She could be going astern."

"But she isn't!" snapped Stephen. "She's aground. Worden ought to
know instantly."

Greene stared fixedly at the Confederate ironclad. Under his breath
he said: "By God, this is the best view I've had of her yet! She's a
damned ugly thing. You're right—she's aground. I'll pass the message."
He went down the manhole into the heat of the turret like a withdrawing jack-in-the-box.

Stephen stood where he was, watching. Presently he saw a boil of
white oddly divorced from the visible ship at the far end of the *Merrimac*'s submerged aftersection. The white became instantly yellow.
He said to himself, "She's reversing her screw," and added thoughtfully, "Take more than that to shift her."

Below deck Keeler shouted the message to the pilothouse: "The
Merrimac's aground!"

The news spread instantly through the Northern ship. It revived
excitement in her, heightened tension. Even before Worden answered
his paymaster, the ship knew that something would happen now, that
a climax was approaching.

Worden, from his position at the eye slit, said to Howard, the pilot,
"How much water is there this side of her?"

"Enough," answered Howard with decision. "More than enough
for us."

"Good," murmured Worden, almost lazily. "We will swing round and come in on her port quarter. I shall endeavor to wreck her rudder and propeller."

"Ah!" Howard gave a long sigh of satisfaction.

*   *   *

Catesby Jones watched the Northern ship make a wide half-circle. It was apparent that she was coming in astern. He had tried gunfire against that squat, round turret, and it had failed. He had tried ramming, and that had failed. He had tried rifle fire on her gun ports, and that had failed. He had tried boarding, but for that it was necessary to lay his ship alongside the enemy, and that had proved impossible.

There was still one thing left to try. Every ship had its Achilles' heel. If the *Monitor* had one, there was only one place left for it.

Davidson had returned after calling back his useless boarding party. Jones said: "Mr. Davidson, order all guns to concentrate on the pilot-house of the *Monitor*. Disregard the turret. Aim at the pilothouse."

Davidson dropped below to the gun deck.

Catesby Jones remained to watch the *Monitor*. He could see in the distance a man standing alone on the roof of her turret. It was the first time he had seen life upon her, the first time that he had had visible proof of her humanity.

Down in the smoke-filled gun deck Davidson pushed his way aft. He found Wood at the after pivot gun. "She's coming in on the port quarter. All guns to concentrate on the pilothouse."

"It's not as big as a good-sized coffin," protested Wood. "How does he expect us to hit it?"

Davidson replied bluntly, "Hit it!"

He waited while Wood raged along the line of the guns, shouting at the gun captains, cursing the men of the crews. He was loud-voiced, belligerent, full of energy. He seemed to fire the crews simply with the excess of his own noise. The place became a bedlam of hauling and levering.

The guns were trained round so that they were at the extreme end of their arc of fire.

"No allowance for wind," Wood was shouting. "Wait till just before your sights come on, and fire! We won't be movin'. We're on the god-dam mud. Hit that pilothouse and she's finished. Make sure you hit it!"

Davidson waited until he got back to the pivot gun. Then he said, his voice low and troubled, "My guess is she'll try to ram our propeller."

Wood laughed his enormous belly laugh. It roared above even the noise of the tackles, the crowbars, and the gun carriages, above even the shouts of the men. An excitement swept the gun deck again, building on apprehension.

Through the afterports now they could see the *Monitor*. She was coming up at her maximum speed. Water rose on either side of the broad, flat bow. The bow wave curled back now and again over the flat plating of her deck. Her turret was trained away. She was being aimed, coldly, deliberately, at the point where Worden knew the propeller and the rudder must be.

Wood exclaimed: "Old John Porter thought about that one! There's enough timber on the overhang to stop three ships like the *Monitor*." He bellowed at his gun crew and, stooping, grabbed the wheel of the elevating screw in his enormous hands.

The *Monitor* came closer and closer. The first of the Dahlgren guns fired.

Davidson, making his way back to Jones, heard Wood yell, "Missed, you miserable bastards!"

A second gun fired, a third, a fourth—all the guns that would bear except Wood's pivot gun.

Over the reverberation of the last shot he heard a voice scream, "Her turret's training!"

The *Monitor* fired her gun at the moment of impact. Davidson staggered slightly at the shock. He could not tell whether the *Merrimac* had given to the blow of the *Monitor's* bows or to the violence of the shell. An instant later Wood fired the pivot gun.

*   *   *

The shell hit level with the eye slit on the port side of the pilothouse. The sound of it had an unspeakable quality of shock. The force of its impact transmitted itself through the heavy iron so that each of the three men close-packed in the wheelhouse was stunned by it. But Worden, leaning against the afterface of the iron billets which made its structure, took the heaviest part of the blow. With the blow—in point of time indistinguishable from it—the blast of the shell drove a rain of tiny fragments of iron and cement and paint through the slit into his face. He was flung back from the slit and crumpled, his body wedged against that of the quartermaster.

The quartermaster, half conscious, put out a hand to steady him.

Howard, the pilot, fell forward against the iron and recovered himself, dazed.

From below Keeler shouted up, "Are you hurt?"

The quartermaster, least affected of the three, called back: "The cap'n's killed. Get the doctor! Somebody help us here! Somebody help!"

The quartermaster felt Worden stir, incredulously heard his voice: "Sheer off! Sheer off!" He put the wheel hard down, supporting Worden's limp body with his hip, pressing him against the side of the wheelhouse.

The place was full of light. The roof of solid two-inch metal had been shifted back by the blow.

Howard said thickly, "The pilothouse is wrecked."

Hands came up through the opening at the head of the ladder and eased him through.

Logue, the surgeon, shouted urgently, "Get him down to us!"

The *Monitor* surged away from the *Merrimac*.

The quartermaster, looking at Worden, said in a voice desperately shocked, "My God, he's blinded!"

The captain's blindness seemed to transfer itself to the ship.

*   *   *

A drift of cheering came with the south wind, from somewhere near Craney Island. It was like a rustle.

Linden asked, "What are they cheering for?" She was conscious for the first time of the immense ring of people that lined the batteries and the beach at Craney Island, that stretched out along the mainland past Hoffler Creek and Streeters to Pig Point and its batteries, that crowded the beaches from Tanner's Point to Seawell's, and the other, the enemy people who lined the great half-circle from Fortress Monroe to Newport News. Never in history had so many people watched a sea battle. She was not educated enough to think of Salamis.

She had a slight, momentary feeling of nakedness, as if her own griefs, her personal humiliations were exposed to that enormous circle of eyes.

Jeriel said, "*Monitor*'s pullin' out."

"She's pulled out before."

"Could be she has bum engines too."

Neither of them accepted as a possibility that the *Monitor* might have been damaged in her last attack. They sat watching quietly. Even Jeriel was drained of excitement now.

The *Merrimac* still lay aground. The *Monitor* moved steadily away, trailing a wake of smoke behind her.

After a long while Jeriel said, "She ain't turnin' none."

"No, she's not turning."

Linden sat stiffly silent, excitement beginning to build in her again. When she spoke she repeated earlier words, "She's pulled out before." And after a brief hesitation she allowed herself to add one word, "But . . ."

Jeriel's voice had passed out of control when he answered her. "She ain't never gone so far before!"

Cheering drifted down to them over the wind again like the sound now of surf on a sandy shore. They disregarded it, their eyes intent on the Northern ironclad.

It was Jeriel who broke the suspense. "Look at the *Merrimac!*"

Linden's stiffness collapsed. She turned rapidly, steadying herself against the thwart. A boat was rowing away from the *Merrimac*. Men crowded to their knees in water on her submerged foredeck, working. Men were on her armored top.

"Layin' out a kedge," said Jeriel. "Tide's still risin'. They'll get her off before that thing can come back."

The girl swept round, eager. Something of the old intensity of concentration, of identity with the protagonists had come back to her. "The *Patrick Henry* and the *Beaufort* are going out to her!"

"*Merrimac*'s signaling. They're goin' to tow."

Instinctively they abandoned both the *Merrimac* and the wooden steamers, and concentrated again on the *Monitor*. The Yankee ship was moving steadily, undeviatingly, across the shallows toward Fortress Monroe.

Jeriel exclaimed, "By damn, she's *runnin'!*"

Linden said, almost reluctantly, as if she could not bear to admit hope and to be proved wrong: "She could have been damaged that last attack. The *Merrimac* fired when she was right on top of her."

Jeriel insisted: "She must'a' been! She must'a' been! Else why should she run? Before, mebbe, it was her engines or somethin'. But she ain't never run so far."

Again the cheering drifted out to them. It seemed louder, more triumphant, this time like heavy breakers.

Linden said aloud, with only a faint shadow of doubt, "If the *Merrimac* pulls herself off, there'll be nothing between her and the *Minnesota*."

"Nothin'!" echoed Jeriel, triumph in his voice. "Nothin'—at—all!"

*   *   *

The boat had been damaged earlier by a shell; part of the gunwale was splintered, and she was leaking swiftly. Two boys knelt in water, bailing with a harsh, mechanical desperation. The men rowed raggedly. Davidson, in the stern sheets, was chanting the stroke and cursing in between. The heavy kedge anchor in the stern weighed her down so that water slopped in again and again over the stern sheets.

From the *Merrimac* they could hear Catesby Jones shouting through his speaking trumpet: "Keep her up, Mr. Davidson! Keep her up!"

Davidson, wrestling with the sweep at the stern, the stock of the anchor hampering every movement, fought to bring her head up to the tide. No one in the boat had any attention for the *Monitor;* they might have forgotten her very existence. They had no regard for anything except the fundamental necessity to get the kedge anchor laid, to keep the crazy boat from sinking, to fight the weight of the tide. They seemed to pull, sweating, for uncounted time. In the momentary pause at the end of each stroke they quivered with the violence of effort.

Jones' voice barked through the trumpet again: "Stand by to let go!" and then, after three more furious strokes: "Let go!"

Davidson slashed at the lashings with his knife; the anchor dropped. There was no noise; there was only a trick, instantaneous disappearance and a tongue of green water that splashed up and drenched him. The boat became immeasurably lighter, manageable.

Far back on the *Merrimac* Catesby Jones bellowed: "Heave in on that! Go full astern on the engines. Tell Ramsey he must lash his safety valves down. Give her every ounce of steam he can find. Where is the *Monitor* now?"

"Still running," answered Simms.

"Mebbe," said Catesby Jones shortly.

"The *Harmony*'s coming across the flat, sir. The *Teaser*'s under way. *Patrick Henry*'s about a mile and a half off, and coming fast. *Beaufort*'s just astern of her."

Jones grunted. "Watch the *Monitor!*" He pointed his speaking trumpet downward to the grating at his feet. "Come on!" he roared. "You can do better than that. Stamp and go! Put your guts into it! Heave! Heave!"

*   *   *

Greene crouched on the floor beside his captain. Logue bent over Worden, working at the captain's eyes with a pair of small forceps. Worden's face above the beard was a pulp of scarlet flesh.

After a moment Logue said: "That is all I can do here. Help me get him to his cabin!" Together they lifted the captain.

Through the blood that drained into his beard and mouth, Worden muttered thickly, "I can walk." Half lifting him they let him justify his pride. At the door of the cabin he halted. "Mr. Greene, I am blind. You are now in command."

Greene answered, "Sir, let us first get you on your bed."

Stimers came hurrying into the cabin. Keeler was already there.

Worden, sensing the presence of others, said very quietly: "Gentlemen, I leave it with you. Do what you think best. Save the *Minnesota* if you can."

Logue stooped over his eyes again. "He's hardly conscious but he will live, I think. Mr. Keeler, more clean water, please."

In the alleyway outside the cabin Howard, leaning against the bulkhead, rumbled: "We are going too far toward the Fortress. They will say we have left the battlefield. They will claim a victory."

Greene said: "There is time for that. We must make up our minds what we intend to do. Our orders are to save the *Minnesota*. Another hit on the pilothouse and the steering will fail. . . ."

Stimers growled angrily: "Our duty is to destroy the *Merrimac*. She is aground now. We will never have a better chance."

The captain's clerk came running forward to the cabin. He gasped breathlessly: "Mr. Knott says the *Merrimac*'s hoisting her boat. She's off the mud. She's under way."

"Mr. Stimers!" Suddenly Greene accepted the reality of command. "Get back to the turret, please. We will reverse course at once! Use the interval before we join action again to get as much ammunition into the turret as you may."

He allowed himself one more small hesitation. He bent over Worden's bed, his too young face staring down into the bloody ruin of the captain's eyes. He asked, half timidly, "You are sure he will live?"

"He will live," said Logue.

*   *   *

The furnace doors were red hot. The boiler room was thick with fumes and steam, harsh with intolerable heat.

Ramsey said: "We've used everythin' we have. We can get no more out of these engines—not ever. The smokestack must be clean shot away by now. If we cannot keep a draft going we cannot get steam. Someone must tell Jones. Tynan, take charge!" He stumped wearily up the ladder, his vitality, his mind, sapped by the heat.

Parrish met him at the foot of the ladder to the spar deck. He was wringing his hands. He moaned: "We're making water fast; she must have strained the bow when we went on the ground. If we take the bottom on a falling tide . . ."

"For Christ's sake!" exclaimed Ramsey dourly. "We're off the mud, Will Parrish. Ain't you never satisfied?" His temper broke abruptly and with finality. "You pilots," he snarled, "shit yourselves!" He stumped up the ladder through the reverberating noises of the gun deck. He had to carry the same warnings to Catesby Jones, to bear the same tidings of dole. He was utterly exhausted in soul and body. He had the bottomless weariness of stalemate.

At the head of the ladder a group was waiting. Ramsey asked, "Where is the *Monitor?*" His eyes were too tired to search, his brain was almost too tired to care.

Somebody answered, "She's still running—over by Fortress Monroe."

The engineer nodded heavily. "We'd best be gettin' home then," he said more to himself than the other, and plodded forward to tell Catesby Jones.

The new captain stood with one foot braced against the slope of the roof of the pilothouse. His face was gray. He growled at Ramsey, his voice ragged with the anger of a man unable to make up his mind, "You too?"

Ramsey answered: "We can't get steam. There's no draft through that ruin." He jerked his thumb back toward the battered smokestack.

Jones said: "They've been at me, all of them. The pilots, the bosun . . . Davidson says the gunners have lost heart. Might as well snap their fingers against her. We can't penetrate her armor. We can't ram . . ."

A voice said loudly, "The *Monitor's* still running, sir."

Parrish, who had followed him up the ladder, mumbled: "There'd be no disgrace leaving the field now, sir. She's gone a'ready."

Jones spoke, without certainty, without conviction. "Very well. Let's see what we can do with the *Minnesota.*"

Parrish almost sobbed: "If we touch again, we'll never get up the Elizabeth this tide. Take her in, sir, and patch the leak!"

Davidson said, "We can't leave the *Minnesota* . . ."

Jones made up his mind, abruptly, without balancing thought, without consideration. He croaked in his rough exhausted voice: "Bring her round, Mr. Parrish! Take her in to the Elizabeth. Mr. Davidson, fire the bow gun at the *Minnesota* as we come round. Give her the starboard broadside when the guns bear. At least we've driven the *Monitor* away!"

*   *   *

The heat of the turret was diminished; the long withdrawing had allowed the *Monitor*'s guns to cool, and the air had come back to some semblance of ordinary air. Men sat with their backs against the turret armor or crouched against the gun carriages or lay against each other. Their bodies were almost naked; they glistened with hot sweat. They were like bodies in a vision of Inferno—Doré-esque, damned bodies, waiting for some new aspect of Hell.

Stimers came up through the lower manhole. He grunted, "We're goin' in again."

In the same moment they felt rather than heard a shot fired, felt it as a transmitted shock through the armor, a sensation rather than a perception. Men who sat against the armor drew away wearily, angrily, remembering Stodder's injury. They waited in an uneasy silence.

Stimers, trying to interpret the silence, said: "He's not dead; he's not going to die."

There was a little murmur of satisfaction, but the tautness of the atmosphere in no way abated. Across it there was the roll of a distant broadside—not aimed at them.

The voice of the captain's clerk came up from below: "Stand by to open fire!"

Stimers bellowed back, "How does she bear?"

"On the starboard bow."

Stephen glanced automatically at the controls of the turret engine. The gun, he knew, was already loaded.

The men waited in silence, too tired to talk, too tired even to complain.

After what seemed an inordinate time, the clerk shouted up again, "Stand by!"

Again Stimers bellowed, "How does she bear?"

And the clerk answered, "To port."

"This goddam steel drum! What the hell's happenin'? You can't tell which way you're goin'! You can't see nothin'."

One of the men went to the hole in the shield, the hole through which the shaft of the rammer passed. He put his eye to it. "Seawell's Point's abeam, just abeam."

Stimers exclaimed, "And she's to port of us!"

A man suggested, "She must be goin' back to anchor."

Another said, "Headin' up the Elizabeth, more likely."

Somebody asked: "What's she want to do that for? She's clear o' the mud; she ain't busted."

Stephen went up the ladder to the manhole in the roof. Another man came up to help him work the heavy lever. He thrust his head and shoulders through into the cold, fresh air. For a moment he could not formulate words. There was a sense of shock in the scene, a sense of unreality. After the hours of fighting it seemed impossible. The *Merrimac* was heading up the Elizabeth at her full speed, the *Beaufort* in front, the *Patrick Henry* far ahead of the *Beaufort*. The position of the three ships, the aspect of them, the very way they moved in the water meant, could mean, only one thing: the Confederates were heading for home. The battle was over.

He shouted down through the grating: "They're going in. They've had enough. It's over!"

And to himself he said, "I will never again be afraid of being afraid."

*   *   *

Linden watched the three ships with wide eyes. There was no fire left in her, no eagerness of spirit. She could no longer be bewildered or angry or even sad. The ships were heading in, the battle was done.

After a little, gently, so as not to hurt Jeriel, she said: "It's finished, Jeri. Get the mains'l up. We'll be going home."

He said stubbornly, with an anger that was still alive, "The *Monitor's* comin' out again."

She nodded. "I know."

He persisted, raspingly, "They ain't finished the *Minnesota!*"

Once more she nodded. "I know."

He began to work on the mainsail rebelliously, clumsily, looking over his shoulder. "It don' make sense. She ain't hurt. She got off the ground a'right. It was the *Monitor* that bolted. . . ."

He began to haul on the main halyard, and the sail rose, creaking and protesting. A puff of wind from the north filled it and the skiff slowly began to gather way. The wind brought with it a sound like the first rustle of the cheering that they had heard from the southern shore, a sound like dry leaves in a light wind. "Yankees," he said acidly. "They reckon they druv us off."

Linden brought the boat's head round until she pointed at the gap between the guard ship and Craney Point. The Yankees would claim a victory. The *Minnesota* lay there black, whole, apparently unharmed; there was not even smoke.

A gun shot crashed across the water, and she jerked her head round. Above the *Monitor* a white banner of smoke above her showed that a gun had fired.

"They'll say they chased us back, God damn them!"

The shot splashed short of the *Merrimac* and set up a brilliant fountain plume in the afternoon sun.

She looked away again. It didn't matter. Nothing mattered now. The bright adventure had failed. So much effort, so much work, so much money, so much hope, and it had come to nothing. The *Merrimac* was outfaced. Yesterday had been triumph. Today was nothingness. She began to cry softly and secretly again, and even as she felt the tears cold in the light wind, she wondered if she were crying for the *Merrimac* or for her lost virginity.

The fitful wind died, and a puff came from the Seawell's shore. Southern cheering came with it, a wide, spreading contagion of cheering. Out of it two swans took off in fright. She heard the urgent splashing of their feet; then the water noises ceased, and she heard only the plangent, melancholy harp song of their wings, like a threnody for a lost cause.

Chapter twelve

THERE were boats moving everywhere along the shallows, sails going up everywhere. The coast line was abruptly, gaily alive. At Craney Island the garrison was firing rockets; back at Seawell's, answering rockets curled up and exploded in the blue afternoon. The shores were full of noise. From Seawell's up to the mouth of the Elizabeth, from Craney along to Pig Point the sound came out over the water and swelled and deepened. Heading across the flats for Craney Point, they seemed to be driving into a funnel of acclamation. The sound magnified itself with every hundred yards that they moved forward into it. Whistles bellowed their way across it. They heard the bells again: it was as if the ringers had never ceased, as if the ropes had surged down and up and the clappers had struck unceasingly ever since they left the Southern Branch yesterday—or an age of yesterdays ago.

The wind was settling in the north. The sun glitter on the water was almost unbearable. The glitter of flags along the beaches matched it in movement, in evanescence, in gaiety—in everything except brilliance. They were driving now into the apex of the great triangle of water between the Seawell's shore and the Craney shore. The figures along the beaches grew with every yard they sailed; the flags became larger, more triumphant; the roar of the voices stronger.

Linden looked back over the port quarter. The *Patrick Henry* was almost level with them, coming past them fast, steering to pass the *Germantown* by a bare fifty feet. The guns' crews of the *Germantown* had left their posts. They were standing on the broad rampart of the sand-filled bulkheads, waving their caps, brandishing sponges and rammers, shouting and whistling and cheering. The gap between the bow of the *Germantown* and the Craney beach was still wide enough for the skiff to slip past without interference. There was plenty of water at this state of the tide.

Linden handled the boat mechanically. Half of her watched the marks and the swirl of tide and the remnants of the old obstructions. The other half examined over and over again the fundamental reality of the day—the single fact that the *Merrimac* had gone out in the cold-ness of the dawn to destroy the *Minnesota,* and the *Minnesota* still lay there, black, resolute, unbroken.

The *Patrick Henry* passed the *Germantown,* and the *Beaufort* came threshing up, and the cheering began again—from the guard ship, from the small boats that crowded on either side of the entrance, from the shore at Craney and the shore at Tanner's Point. Behind the *Beaufort,* she knew, was the *Merrimac:* she would not turn to look at her—she was afraid.

They were almost up to the *Germantown* now. She allowed herself one look astern. Far across the empty water two tugs were closing the *Minnesota,* and a small steamship was heading toward her. The *Monitor* lay perhaps half a mile from her, between her and the Norfolk shore. At this distance she was no more than a round cylinder, the height of it diminished by the sea curve, its purpose dark, mysterious, obscure. To Linden it was the symbol of a broken hope.

They passed through the shallows. A handful of men on the bat-teries shouted at them jubilantly, with laughter, but beyond this they were not noticed. The whole of the attention of the multitude on Craney and on the boats and on the small ships that lay in the bight behind the island, and on the Norfolk shore and Lambert's Point was fixed, rooted, bound to the *Merrimac.* Even Jeriel was infected now. He stood in the triangle of the bows balancing himself with one hand on the forestay, watching eagerly as the armored shield of the *Merrimac* came through the narrows, caught up and drew level with the skiff. He could see the scars on the armor. At one point three or four strips of metal were broken. There were indentations at other points, long shining grooves and pockmarks and bruisings. Her smokestack was shot to a ruin of twisted metal, but on it her men had lashed a boarding pike, and from the pike, above the smoke that coiled black and greasy aft along the gratings of the shield, floated the Confederate flag over the flag of the Union: the claim of victory.

Catesby Jones stood by himself beside the peaked roof of the pilot-house. Behind him in a little knot stood his officers. Behind them the men had crowded onto the spar-deck gratings. They stood there naked to the waist, their bodies shining in the brilliance of the sun, black-streaked, powder-grimed, filthy, and triumphant. Other men crowded at the gun ports, leaning out precariously, sitting astride the muzzles of the cooling guns. They waved, they screamed, they cheered back as the cheering rolled toward them from the shore. High on the spar deck Catesby Jones lifted his cap and made the acknowledgments of a conqueror returned in splendor.

For a little the skiff, running before the wind, kept pace with the *Merrimac.* Then the wind diminished and she drifted. Slowly she crept up in the wake of the ironclad, rolling violently, dipping her boom end under, as the waves of the wake hit her.

Everywhere the boats that had lain on either side of the channel turned in after the *Merrimac,* making sail like the white wings of sea birds frightened from the surface, forming up in an enormous, joyous procession that stretched from Craney up past Lambert's Point to Pinner's, and on to the bend and the batteries at Hospital Point. Long before the skiff reached the hospital the *Merrimac* had swung round the bend. Now she slowed for the entrance to the Southern Branch, and boats began to catch up with her so that she moved with an escort of white triangles and squares and curves like the petals of enormous flowers.

She entered the Elizabeth. The noise had closed in on them now: bells and whistles, foghorns and saluting guns, rockets and firecrackers, and wild, irresponsible musket and pistol shots. And these things were only the accents, the overscorings, the emphases of the unending bourdon of men's voices.

Jeriel watched the afterend of the *Merrimac*'s shield disappear past the warehouses, and sat down again, with his knees trembling. He said, with a sudden savage irony that was frightening in a boy, "I suppose he's a hero now."

"I suppose so," agreed Linden wearily.

The wind came again and they covered the distance to the mouth of the Branch quietly and fast.

The Branch itself was a tumult of small craft. The *Beaufort* and the *Patrick Henry* and the *Jamestown* were milling round in a whirlpool of cheering boats. The *Teaser* and the *Harmony* were easing the *Merrimac* in toward the wharf.

Linden jibed the mainsail and headed the skiff in to the wood yard. Jeriel said nothing, but he turned and looked at her imploringly. The wind was light enough for them to come alongside the jetty with everything up. He turned again, missing the accustomed orders.

This time she said: "You take her, Jeri. Go on up to the Navy Yard. You've earned it." Slowly, stiffly, she began to climb up the vertical ladder at the end of the jetty, pushing the skiff off with one foot.

"Ah, jeez, Lindy!" Jeriel looked up at her with his eyes shining as he scrambled aft to take the tiller.

She walked slowly in to the shore. She had not known how tired she was, how close to exhaustion. She could feel the pain of her bruises, and the other pains with their more painful memories. Her face was white and distressed.

Cleave and old Sam, leaning over the wood stack, watched her come, Cleave with a cold foreboding.

She reached the path between the stacks, and for the first time the old man saw her face. He muttered, "God help her," and, turning, clumped heavily away up the sawdust-soft path.

Cleave called softly, "Lin! Lin!"

She came toward him, stumbling, and flung herself against him. He folded her in his arms. She said nothing; she was not even crying. She just leaned against him, waiting.

He did not know what to say. Essentially he was desperately shy. He worked his hand on one shoulder in a little squeezing, soothing motion. At last, deeply aware of the inadequacy of words, he said, "Everything passes."

She seemed to draw comfort from them—or perhaps only from the bond between them.

When something of the agony was drained out of her, he said, "Let's go home, Lin."

She hesitated, and he murmured carefully, without significance, "Your Aunt Deborah will want to know where you were last night."

"The Enwright house," she answered dully.

"And she'll want to know what you were doing."

"Dancing." Linden pushed herself away from him a little so that she could look into his eyes. Holding herself straight, not touching him, she added: "Dancing . . . and things."

He felt a stab of pain, but he put his arms out and pulled her to him again.

4

The
Clearing
Showers

THE lumber piles were mostly gone now except for the one on which Cleave and old Sam liked to lean. That still remained solid, foursquare, comfortably at its elbow-level height. It was a fixed point in a diminishing world.

Linden came to it tentatively, as if she were afraid and ashamed of being afraid. Her face was drawn and tired, and the skin under her eyes had a purple darkness.

Cleave turned toward her. He wanted to hold out his arms to her, but habit held him back. He waited, his heart beating unsteadily in his compassion.

She murmured, "What am I to do?"

For a painful moment he was silent, not sure what words to use. At last, while her eyes searched him, he said quietly: "Wait. It's all you can do. Wait. God's been unfair to women."

She looked at him, puzzled, her head a little to one side as if his answer had no meaning for her. "To women?" Then with a devastating candor she said, "You mean till I know if I'm going to have a baby?" Her forehead wrinkled in an almost mischievous incomprehension. "I wasn't worrying about *that*. If it happens, it happens."

For the first time in years Cleave lost his temper with her. "In God's name, what *do* you mean, then? I should have thought that was enough!"

She smiled a bleak smile, but it was enough to light her tired eyes. "That isn't anything. I'm only one person; I don't matter. Please"—her eyes pleaded for understanding—"the *Merrimac*'s failed." And when Cleave made no immediate reply, she said, "I believed in her."

He reached across the gulf between them. "I know."

They were silent. A drift of gulls went by, lazy-winged, lovely. A tug hooted twice on the Elizabeth, and boys shouted across the water.

She asked: "Are you angry with me?"

"No," he said, exasperated not with her but with himself. "No."

"Perhaps you ought to be."

"Perhaps." He let the word linger for a moment, then he went on: "No, I'm not angry. I'm trying to understand how you feel. It isn't easy." Then, as if to make clear to her that the misunderstanding was dissolved now, he added: "Are you sure that she's failed? Everybody I've talked to thinks that she won." He was genuinely puzzled. He too thought that the *Merrimac* had won.

Linden's eyes were somber again. "She went out to finish off the *Minnesota*."

"Does one frigate more or less matter after what happened Saturday?"

"She went out to finish off the *Minnesota*," repeated Linden patiently, "and she couldn't. I believed she could take on the whole Yankee navy. I was sure of it Saturday night."

Behind her, old Sam said: "You always want what you want, Lindy Cleave. No halfways."

She jerked round with a quick, frightened movement that showed more than any other thing the depth of her hurt. "I didn't hear you come."

"Don't signify. You want too much out of one ship. She's done pretty good."

For a moment Linden allowed a fleeting hope to come into her eyes, then the light faded again. "She couldn't do anything yesterday."

"You want too much. She come up against somethin' level with herself."

"I didn't think anything could be level."

"You and John Porter!" exclaimed the old man. "She did pretty well Sat'day. They tell me this mornin' there isn't a one Northern ship in the whole of the Roads. That's somethin'."

With the same patience in her voice she persisted: "It's not enough! She was going to clear them out of the Chesapeake."

"It's plenty," said the old man. "They been sittin' on the doorstep o' this town best part of a year." He shook his head with a quick exasperation. "Dammit, Lindy, it ain't for me to be speaking up for the *Merrimac* to you!"

Desolately she said, "You weren't there yesterday."

"All I heard, she done pretty good yesterday too. The *Monitor,* she's about the best the North's thought up so far this war. She didn't hurt the *Merrimac* none."

"The *Merrimac* didn't hurt her either, and she didn't hurt the *Minnesota.*" Linden came back again to the essential point like a hound dog returning to a mountain lion, worrying it, wounded by it.

"Ah, you want it all ways!" The old man allowed his voice to take on an edge.

"I was there," she said quietly. "She won't do more than she did yesterday—not ever."

Cleave shook his head impatiently. "Nobody can say that. Sam's right—she's cleared the Roads and the mouth of the James River. That isn't going to make things easy if McClellan's really heading up the Peninsula."

"She's done more'n that," said the old compositor. "When your pa's done bein' sorry for you, Lindy, he'll see that. Goin' to cost him a lot of money one way 'n' another."

"How?"

"Ain't nobody goin' to build wooden ships that can build iron after Sat'day," replied the old man succinctly. "Trade in grown timber looks like it's goin' to fall off."

Linden looked at him with a quick gratitude, grasping at anything that would ease her unbelief.

Sam chose the moment to head off the conversation. "Town was a mite crazy last night," he observed indulgently. "I don't know where the liquor come from—what with the bars all closed by Huger." He sighed reminiscently and added: "Mornin', Jeriel. You got a headache too? I seen you hellin' around."

Jeriel came through the alleyway between the diminished piles. "Mornin', Mist' Cleave. Mornin', Lindy."

Sam's quick eyes flickered at him and back to the girl.

She said quietly, "Jeri."

He settled himself in the place that he liked best, his back against the warm timber. There was a moment of quiet—except for the high-wheeling gulls.

It was Jeriel who broke the silence in the end. "You heard Rev Jordan's wounded?" he asked, his voice carefully devoid of expression.

Linden turned and looked at him doubtfully. Her hesitation gave him time to speak again.

"Bad," he said laconically. He did not look at her; his eyes were hooded.

"How bad?"

"Bad enough." A faint triumphant malice crept into the boy's voice. "He'll die mebbe." This time he looked directly at Linden.

"Wounded?" Her voice was puzzled, as if she could not understand.

"Yeah." The boy spat with care and precision at the end of a timber opposite him. Then he added carelessly, "But he ain't no hero."

Sam asked roughly, "What d'you mean?"

"You ask Cahill—he was the gun capt'n." Suddenly Jeriel's voice was all venom. "He was lyin' down when he was hit, trying to hide. Standin' up he wouldn't've been hit. You talk to them—you talk to his gun crew! He was a goddam coward." His voice rose on a high, scornful note. "Yaller," he said, and subsided, his back against the timber, his face set and still.

Linden forestalled Cleave, who was trying to find words. "It doesn't matter."

"If he's badly wounded . . ." Cleave began.

"I don't care, I don't care!" she cried wildly, and turned away down the path between the lumber.

Cleave looked after her helplessly. He made no move to follow: this was something that she had to handle for herself.

Sam was staring at the boy. Harshly he demanded, "What's wrong with Revell Jordan?"

"He's a goddam sonavabitch," began the boy evenly. He went on swearing quietly, calling up words from an adhesive memory. He ended, thumping the heel of his hand against the timber:

"Bastid—bastid—bastid!"

Neither of the men checked him.

Visibly the boy fought for control. When he had gained it, he said, almost conversationally: "If he hadn't bin wounded they would ha' rid him outa town on a rail. He's no good."

* * *

The long ward was full. There were no empty beds. For the most part they were occupied by men with fever and dysentery. There was only a handful of wounded from the action at Elizabeth City. There were the men who had been scalded on the *Patrick Henry*. There were the wounded from the *Merrimac*.

Revell lay with the wounded—with them but not of them. Even in the crowded ward there was a space on either side of his bed. He lay alone, separated from the others, a boundary about him as unmistakable as if it had been a high timber fence.

Linden walked down between the line of the beds. She moved with a deliberate, almost ostentatious dignity. Conversations stopped as she passed and picked up again in whispers. Girls at the bedsides turned to stare.

There were no flowers at Revell's bed.

This was the fourth day. He was conscious now; the doctors said that he would live. He lay silent and negative under the coverlet, not moving his heavily bandaged head. He did not greet Linden when she moved into the open space beside him.

She said without preamble: "I've brought more eggs. They say you can eat eggs tomorrow, perhaps."

He murmured: "You were here yesterday. I can remember now. I talked to you yesterday."

"A little; you weren't very clear." She sat down on the chair at the head of the bed and folded her hands in her lap. She looked straight ahead, not at Revell. She had sat like that through the four days when he had been first silent, and then rambling and full of words. She had not doubted ever that he was a coward, not since Jeriel had told her, but in his delirium he had condemned himself. She sat and thought about things: a little about herself, a little about Revell, mostly about the war.

The *Merrimac* was back in dry dock, where she was likely to stay for a time. Jeriel was busy ferreting out the details. There was little damage: a few of the vertical strips of the armor were broken and pushed inward, a few of the horizontal strips were curved and bent. There was nothing else, except that the ram was gone. They were to replace the ram, but it would be smaller this time, and they would add more armor—a new belt of it four feet wide around the water line. Catesby Jones had said that the knuckle was her weak point; that if the *Monitor* had only concentrated her fire there the *Merrimac* must have sunk. Porter said that this was a lie; that the armor went two feet below the surface of the water; that even when the *Merrimac* had burned most of her coal and spent most of her ammunition, there had never been a gap between wind and water, and that there had been no weak point.

Linden's world was crumbling in talk, in vituperation and argument. Catesby Jones was a man who made excuses: the pilots had deceived him; the armor had offered the enemy a gap; the engines were paralytic; the propeller and rudder were unprotected; the ship would not steer. One after the other she turned these over stonily in her mind. Before she had believed; now she questioned. How much of anything was true? How much of it was an excuse? How much of it was fear?

She sat considering the question of fear. The aura of coldness that made Revell's bed an island in the warmth of the ward was a by-product of fear. Yesterday she had heard that Revell would live. She had heard it when a man two beds away from Revell's said: "He ain't gonna die. I heard the doctors 's mornin'. He's goin' to live—scairt." And somebody beyond, whom she could not identify, had said, "Been better if he'd died, at that."

None of the other girls spoke to her in the hospital. Only the older nurses shared out their professional humanity with her. One or two of the girls she had known, friends, had tried to speak to her on the way home, but she had felt a hypocrisy about their sympathy; they all knew something and they all concealed their knowledge. After the second day they let her walk home from the hospital alone.

She could think, walking alone—think of the ring closing in on Norfolk and Portsmouth—think of the slow, long-drawn, festering end of the Confederacy. Nobody else thought in terms of defeat, but she was sure that death had touched the Confederacy when the *Merrimac* failed—the slow death of blockade.

* * *

As she started down the stairs, her father came out of his room. He stood for a moment on the second-floor landing, his hand resting on the slender, delicate balustrade. He said, "Good morning, Linden."

She answered him, her voice clear and completely divested of emotion: "Good morning. I'm not going to have a baby."

He looked at her awkwardly, a little shocked. His voice, in absolute contrast to hers, had a rich relief in it as he said, "Thank God!"

She nodded serenely. "Yes, I suppose so."

With a tinge of anxiety he asked, "Are you sure?"

"I'm sure. All I've got is a headache," she answered. "I always do." Then, without change of emphasis: "You were at the Atlantic last night. Did you hear anything about French Forrest?"

"No," he almost snapped at her, bewildered.

"They're going to throw him out." Her voice was skeptical. "I think they're getting ready to let the Yard go, and he won't do what they want."

"Who?"

"Mr. Mallory and the others at Richmond—I thought you knew. They're talking of shifting the machinery."

Cleave went slowly down the stairs. "I didn't know—but I think it's bound to happen. If they get past Yorktown . . ." He left the sentence unfinished. How was it that to her Forrest was more important than a child? What had happened to her sense of values? What were values?

Aunt Deborah had one hand on the coffeepot.

"You heard?" he asked.

"Thank God!"

Both of them listened with a conspiratorial self-consciousness.

Linden went past the door toward the kitchen.

Aunt Deborah said, "It isn't that she has no feelings . . ."

Cleave shook his head. "She has feelings, but none for herself. She put everything that she had into her faith in Virginia, and now she's lost faith."

"It's not natural."

"What is?" asked Cleave. "I don't know. I never had any faith in Virginia; I never had any belief that the South could win; I never counted on the *Merrimac*. I ought to be glad she's failed. The North will take Portsmouth back before long. I ought to be glad of that." His head made a little gesture toward the back of the house, toward where Linden had gone. "But I'm not. And I can't do anything for her."

Aunt Deborah said: "She sits at his bed day after day. She doesn't talk. I think she hates him. I think she sits there hating—but she won't stop going." She took her hand off the coffeepot with a gesture of absolute helplessness. "Perhaps it will be better now. I don't know. If I could only do something!"

Linden came into the room and kissed her aunt calmly. When she sat down her face was expressionless. The tiredness and the strain had gone out of it. It might have seemed to an outsider in its ordinary state of repose, but Cleave could see the inanimation of her eyes.

*   *   *

Revell said, "You're late this mornin'." He was full of self-pity.

"I'm late," she answered flatly. She put the basket on the locker that stood at the head of the bed and took out a packet of cookies and a small jar of honey. "These are from Aunt Deborah." She put the two small parcels away and sat down.

"I had a bad night." He said it as if it were important.

In the same flat tone she said: "You'll have more before you've finished. It stands to reason."

He moved uneasily in the bed. "You ain't got any sympathy, have you, Lindy?"

"No."

Defensively he said: "You ain't never been in a battle. You don't know what it's like. You don't know what happens to a man."

"I can guess," she answered laconically. "I know you, Rev Jordan."

With a sick cunning he demanded hastily, "Why do you come here then?"

"I don't know," she replied, thinking it over. "I suppose I'm sorry for you. There isn't anybody else but me to be sorry." And, as he started to mumble something, she slashed across his words: "Even if you'd come out of the fight a hero"—she gave the word a jarring, ugly sound—"I still wouldn't have spoken to you again after what happened at the Enwright house."

"Then why do you come now?"

"I've told you. Because there's nobody else."

He moved in the bed as if he were trying to avoid a physical blow. "Christ, you're hard, Lindy!"

A voice from the bed beyond him urged, "Aw, stop griping!"

Softly, afraid, he whispered, "I love you so, Lindy."

She said coldly: "You never loved anybody except yourself. In a little you'll begin to hate yourself. Maybe you do already—I don't know. But if you talk to me about love again, I'll stop coming."

He turned on his side with an immense and real effort. "You won't stop coming, Lindy," he begged. "Say you won't stop coming! I'd go crazy if you stopped coming. Promise me you'll come!"

Drearily she said, "I'll come."

*　　*　　*

Ulysses Hogan flicked over the pages of the notebook. "Joseph Tatnall," he repeated. "Don't know as I've ever seen him. Don't know nothing about him except he didn't do a lot o' good at Port Royal— but he takes over the *Merrimac* tomorrow."

Linden made no comment.

Old Sam, working at a form on the stone against the far wall, demanded without turning, "What they got against Catesby Jones?"

Ulysses consulted his notebook again. "He's inexperienced—too young—not enough time in command. . . ."

"Or didn't they like the way he handled her against the *Monitor?*"

"I asked that. Cap'n Lee said No, wasn't that at all."

Old Sam cleared his throat, and spat. "What d'you say, Lindy?"

Linden was sitting on a chair with her hands folded over her lap, as if the position that she had adopted at Revell's bedside had become habitual in her personal life. "The *Merrimac* won't fight. Doesn't matter who captains her."

Old Sam looked at her over his shoulder. "What about French Forrest?"

"Cap'n Lee said"—again Ulysses consulted his notes—" 'it was considered desirable in Richmond to have a change in the naval command at this juncture. This is not in any way a reflection on Commodore French Forrest, who has performed a Herculean task in circumstances of the greatest difficulty with extraordinary judgment and acumen.' "

"Make 'em say 'an Herculean task,' " said old Sam absently. "Don't matter about the truth so long as we get the grammar right."

He waited for Linden to make her comment. Ordinarily she would have been full of opinion, but she sat quietly, her hands quiescent in her lap. Again he turned and looked at her. Her hair was a little longer than was customary. She had not worn trousers since the battle. She had on a brown dress and an olive-green coat over it. Her spirit was quenched in the subfusc monotony of the clothes.

"He told me a lot more. The big steamer off Old Point belongs to Commodore Vanderbilt. They're gettin' ready to ram the *Merrimac* when she goes out again. 'Bout five other ships as well." Ulysses flicked another page. "Congress's voted two million dollars fer buying iron-clads in England." He looked up from the notes. "That'll show 'em!" His voice was suddenly full of buck and bounce. He in turn looked over to Linden. "What d'you think 'bout that, Lindy?"

"I think," she answered quietly, "that it will take a long time. Did you ask him about the Yankee transports coming back into the Roads again? They're back there *now*."

He shrugged. "You're that sour these days, Lindy Cleave. Just because Rev Jordan—"

Old Sam broke in: "That ain't nothin' to do with you, Hogan. You keep your big mouth shet!"

Linden said: "It doesn't matter, Sam. Revell's no good—everybody knows that now." Casually she added, "He's coming out of the hospital end of next week."

Ulysses said, as if he had been keeping the best for the last: "The *Merrimac* she'll be out in twelve days' time—out an' fightin'."

Linden muttered, "She'll go out and she'll come back again, but she won't fight."

Chapter two

JERIEL glowered up the Southern Branch to where the boats still clustered round the captured schooners. His face was set and sullen. "*Monitor* wouldn't come out," he said. "Wasn't nothin' they could do would make her come out. Not even when th' *Jamestown* went in an' grabbed th' schooners."

Linden made no answer. She did not appear to have heard.

"Two French ships an' a British Navy ship watchin'." The fact seemed to rankle in Jeriel's mind.

Sam, leaning against the bollard at the corner of the jetty, said: "Why should she come out? Long as she lies under the guns o' the fort, the *Monitor*'s doin' all the Yankees need."

Linden stared broodingly down at the water. Jeriel looked at the old man questioningly.

"Stoppin' the *Merrimac* from goin' round into Yorktown an' bustin' up their transports," Sam offered in full explanation.

"I thought she'd come when we grabbed th' schooners," the boy persisted.

"Look!" said the old man. "Sittin' there, she's like a cork in a bottle. Tatnall, he might try to get out between Monroe an' the Rip Raps, but he knows he can't get out between Monroe an' the Rip Raps *an'* the *Monitor*. Why would they take the cork out'n the bottle for the sake o' two-three schooners?"

Linden said drearily, "I told you she wouldn't fight."

"A whole month they bin workin' on th' *Merrimac* in th' dry dock, an' she goes out 'n' nothin' happens!"

"Who fired?" asked Sam.

The boy apparently ignored the question. "We went out 'bout half a mile astern o' th' *Merrimac*. Th' transports was on th' run a'ready. Ever' damn' thin' in th' Roads was runnin' 'cep' th' schooners in by Hampton. Reckon they thought they was safe." He recollected the question. "It was the Rip Raps firin'. Two guns, a long ways short. There wasn't anythin' else." He looked up at the old compositor. "Ain't th' *Merrimac* goin' t'do anythin' ever?"

"Depends what you mean. She's doin' a lot right now. She's stoppin' McClellan usin' the James River. If it wasn't for her, the *Monitor*'d be halfway to Richmond b'now and so'd McClellan. Yorktown wouldn't count. He'd be way past it."

* * *

Nicolay, the senior of Lincoln's secretaries, leaned one elbow on the mantelpiece and draped himself with what he considered to be a fashionable elegance. His thin beard made him look alarmingly young.

"The Tycoon's getting Napoleonic."

"We've got a Napoleon already," Hay said flippantly. "McClellan's enough for any one country at one time. What's he done now?"

"It's what he hasn't done," replied Nicolay slowly. "Yorktown. The President thinks he should have carried it days ago. But it's General Wool he's after, I think. He says Wool's done nothing since he was appointed to the command at Fortress Monroe."

"What does he expect Wool to do? He's the best part of a hundred years old."

"Seventy-eight," corrected Nicolay mildly. "He was one of old Fuss and Feathers' boys."

"In time we'll weed 'em out," said Hay, scanning the ceiling of the secretaries' room. "Trouble is, we'll both of us be so old by then they'll weed us too. What hasn't *he* done this time?"

"The President reckons he can take Norfolk." He looked challengingly at Hay as the younger man sat leaning back with his chair tipped and his head against the wall. "I think he's right, too, but he talks of going down to Fortress Monroe to see if he can find out 'by personal observation if some more vigilance and vigor might not be infused. . . .' "

Hay whistled shrilly. "When he talks like that he's mad as all get out."

"He's mad, all right, and I think he's got reasons."

"Goin to be uncomfortable for somebody," said Hay, unfeeling, "but who am I to defend generals? I'm only an undersecretary."

"He'll probably take you with him." Nicolay's tone was dry. He picked up some papers from the desk and turned to leave.

Hay said: "Don't go yet! There was a long coded message came into the telegraph room ten minutes ago. They should have it ready about now." He got up negligently and idled down to the door of the telegraph room. He opened it, leaning against the lintel, and asked, "What's the good news?"

The coding clerk looked up and said, his voice surprisingly loud in the night silence, "Confederate Army's abandoned Yorktown."

Nicolay dropped the papers on the desk. "Is that certain?" He hurrried over to the door in turn.

"That's what it says," replied the coding clerk. " 'Patrols report penetrated outer earthworks Yorktown. Enemy evacuation appears complete. Inner defenses abandoned.' "

"Who signed it?"

"McClellan hisself," said the coding clerk.

"I don't think he's gone to bed yet." Nicolay ran the short distance to the President's door.

The duty telegraphist said, "By golly, they're on the run, Mr. Hay!"

"By golly, they may be," said Hay skeptically.

*   *   *

Hay toasted the end of his cigar in the flame of the cabin lamp for an instant before he drew on it. When it was alight he said: "A bourbon then—a small one, and considered strictly as medicine." He grinned at the young lieutenant, and the lieutenant—he was Commodore Goldsborough's aide—grinned back and lifted the bottle from the little rack in the corner of the cabin.

The third man in the cabin was General Wool's aide. His mind moved more heavily than those of the other two. "The general does not approve of drinking on duty."

"I suspect," said Hay, "that a secretary is very like an aide. He has the same opportunities and the same problems. If he don't drink on duty"—he drew long and lovingly on his cigar—"he don't drink."

Wool's aide allowed himself a bleak smile.

Birkett, the lieutenant, laughed. He poured the drinks and said perfunctorily, "You won't change your mind?" and put the bottle down. He lifted his glass. "Here's to it, whatever it is! What's it all about?"

Hay put his glass down. "I'd say it was the capture of Norfolk."

Wool's aide snapped defensively: "We haven't at any time had the troops. The Confederates have eighteen thousand men in the defenses of Norfolk and the coast."

"Have they still got them?" Hay's tone was light but he was completely serious. "Johnston's withdrawing up the Peninsula fast. McClellan will be in a position any day now to put a force across the James River and cut the railroads into Norfolk. If I was Robert E. Lee, I'd be thinking of pulling out eighteen thousand good troops from a port that ain't going to be any use to me again—ever."

"There's still the *Merrimac*," Birkett reminded him.

Hay considered his glass with great concentration. "The Navy doesn't seem to be able to do much about the *Merrimac*," he said slowly.

"Under orders from the Navy Department!" Birkett challenged him.

"Navy Department . . . The *Merrimac*'s still afloat. Just being afloat she's stopped you doing anything about the batteries at Yorktown that might have helped McClellan. Just being afloat she's stopping anything being done about helping McClellan along the James River. Could be the only thing to do is to smoke her out of her hole."

Eldon, the general's aide, asked, "Is that the President's view?"

"The President doesn't confide his views to me," replied Hay dryly, "but at a guess I'd say that's the way he's thinking."

"What'll he do?" Birkett frowned heavily over his cigar.

"I don't know," said Hay. "I'd think he'd take twenty-four hours to look things over."

"And then?"

"Then," said Hay reflectively, "he'll do what he has to do." After a little pause he added with a seeming irrelevance, "When he lowers his horns and stomps with his right forefoot, I do what I have to do or I get out of the way."

The other two nodded.

They drank in silence.

"God knows what's being said in there"—Hay jerked his head toward the door that led into the Captain's cabin—"but we had a bad run down from Washington. The President was seasick this morning and he doesn't like being seasick, but he called the general for a conference on the *Miami* as soon as the anchor was down, and when he'd finished that he came across in that damned wet tug to this ship for a three-cornered conference with your master." He looked over at Goldsborough's aide. "I reckon I'd call that stomping with his right forefoot."

* * *

The room was an absolute contrast to the small cabin on the *Minnesota* that the three men had occupied the previous night. It was tall, well proportioned; the faded wallpaper was old and gracious. The fireplace was delicately molded.

Under Hay's prodding, Eldon had reluctantly produced whisky. Hay himself sat much in the position that he had adopted the previous night—one leg over the arm of his chair. He watched Eldon lazily as the aide fussed about.

Eldon turned at last and said irritably: "I still think it looked like sightseeing. We're used to visitors from Washington."

"All right," said Hay, "add it up." He ran over the events on his fingers. "Before breakfast the President looked at the *Vanderbilt.* He breakfasted here. After breakfast he went out to the *Monitor* and the *Naugatuck.* Then he went over to the Rip Raps and looked at the Sawyer gun, and then he came back and had a talk with the commodore"—he nodded at Birkett—"then the *Merrimac* showed herself off Seawell's Point." He looked quizzically at each of the men in turn. "You both know what happened then."

Eldon said morosely: "The general was right. It was necessary to cancel the review until we knew what she was going to do."

"Maybe." Hay's tone was noncommittal. "About the only thing I'd call sightseeing was looking at the ruins in Hampton. All the rest was seeing for himself. Whoever comes out of there"—this time he pointed directly at the door of the big drawing room where the conference was in progress—"will come out with orders. He went into that room with his horns down."

Eldon's voice was horrified. "That would be tantamount to the President's taking direct control of *military* operations!"

"Yes," said Hay succinctly.

Neither of the men seemed prepared to challenge him. They sat in the waiting silence of secretaries and aides.

When they talked again it was of Washington gossip and women and fishing.

An hour later Colonel Greer came out with three slips of paper. He handed the first to Birkett. "Read that! And if there is any action you can take on your way back to Commodore Goldsborough to expedite the matter, you are authorized to take it."

Standing, Birkett read the paper. It was in the President's hand: "If you have tolerable confidence you can successfully contend with the *Merrimac* without the help of the *Galena* and two accompanying gunboats, send the *Galena* and two gunboats up the James River at once. Please report your action on this to me at once. I shall be found at General Wool's headquarters." It was signed "A. Lincoln."

Birkett said: "If I may use a harbor tug, I will send a warning to the *Galena* and the gunboats, sir. They will require to get steam."

"Do that," agreed the colonel. He turned to Eldon, holding out a second slip. "You will inform the officers listed here, in the order of their listing, that they will hold their regiments in readiness from eight o'clock tomorrow morning in all respects prepared for a landing against Norfolk. This"—he held out the third slip—"will be duplicated and sent to General McClellan by telegraph and by hand to inform him of the President's intentions. You will use every expedition." He turned smartly on his heel and went back into the conference room.

Hay glanced from Birkett to Eldon. Then he grinned faintly. He did not bother to say, "I told you so!"

*   *   *

"Best open your mouth and put your fingers in your ears." The man had an almost patronizing manner. "They're 'bout ready to fire."

Hay opened his mouth, aware that he must look idiotic. As he put his fingers to his ears he heard the shouted command, "Fire!" He saw flame leap from the muzzle of the gun and a wide, brown flare of smoke follow the flame and envelop it and spread beyond the flame and change to white. The noise went shuddering through him. He saw the President clutch his tall black hat and then turn a little until his eyes were aligned to the line of fire. The shell fell to the left of the seaward battery on Seawell's Point, and a great cloud of sand and small bush and dirt was flung up into the sky and fell back again. Hay turned from it and looked over the upriver wall of the battery to the ships of the fleet.

The *Monitor* was leading now, the *Naugatuck* a little astern of her, and then irregularly the *Seminole,* the *San Jacinto,* the *Dacotah,* the *Susquehanna.* They looked extraordinarily dashing, full of color from their huge battle flags and the whipping signal hoists—a magnificent perspective of power, glorious and irresistible.

Another gun went off. He was not prepared for it. The shock of the concussion seemed to drive in his eardrums. He rocked on his feet. Again the President, in the center of a knot of Navy and Army officers, clutched at his hat. He saw Stanton crouch as if in actual physical pain. Once more he waited for the fall of the shot. This time it seemed to hit plumb on the battery. He saw the President brandish a hand triumphantly, and he thought: He's enjoying this. By God, it's like wine to him! This is what war ought to be.

The first gun fired again—the great Sawyer gun. Almost simultaneously the *Monitor* fired. Enormous clouds of white smoke rolled across the sea from the ships. There were answering smoke from the batteries and high splashes in the water. Two smaller guns on the eastern end of the Rip Raps wall were joining in now. The noise was continuous.

Perhaps because of that it was easier to bear. The concussion no longer hurt. He let his eyes travel from the Northern ships to the Southern batteries, from the batteries to the President, and back again to the ships. It was like being in the inside of a vast globe of blue crystal with all the hammers of hell beating on the surface of it—an inferno of noise, a glory of color and excitement.

Afterward he could never say how long it had lasted. He remembered the cheers when it was clear that the seaward battery was destroyed. He remembered the orders given to shift fire to the first of the batteries beyond the point. He remembered the *Monitor* steaming up into the deep-water channel almost under the muzzles of the enemy's guns. And then he remembered a black cloud of smoke in the far distance over the low ridge of the land, a black cloud of smoke far up over the Elizabeth

River, and a Navy lieutenant shouting at him: "The *Merrimac*'s coming! The *Merrimac*'s coming!"

He could remember Colonel Greer striding toward him saying: "We must get the President off—get him back to Monroe. The *Merrimac*'s coming down the river."

He could remember that the transports of the invasion fleet were already streaming back through the narrows to the open waters of the Chesapeake and that he could see the troops standing silent and motionless on their decks.

He could not forget the face of the President—grim and withdrawn and brooding.

* * *

Colonel Greer came stiffly into the improvised office. He returned Hay's greeting coldly. After an uneasy pause he said, "I find it difficult to understand the President."

"If I can help," offered Hay formally.

"I have heard of his custom of telling anecdotes upon serious occasions. I had not before believed it."

"What was it this time?"

"As far as I can remember it he said: 'General Wool, when I was a boy I used to steal apples. There was a farmer called Eickenberg. He knew that we crossed a field to get to the apple trees, and he put a bull in that field. I remember that it was a very angry bull.' And then"—Greer's face creased in distaste—"he bent down and took off his slipper and he said, 'General Wool, what do you think we did?'"

Hay kept the glint in his eyes from showing. "What did the general say?"

"He said, 'I am at a loss, Mr. President.' And the President said, 'We went round behind the house and slipped in through the yard.'"

Hay jerked his head upright. "By God, of course, that's it!"

Greer looked at him incredulously. "He's sent General Wool to examine the possibilities of executing a landing on the Chesapeake beaches—not, sir, on the Elizabeth at all!"

"Damned sound sense," said Hay.

Greer looked at him scandalized and, turning, walked out of the room.

Hay went back to his papers.

Eldon came in hurriedly. "The President wants to discuss the possibilities of a landing with the pilots. I've sent messengers for them." He

put down a slip. "These are the names. I've got to go with the general."
He hurried out again.

Commodore Goldsborough came in and was taken to the President.
Hay, sitting outside, could hear the voices rising and falling, Goldsborough protesting, Goldsborough arguing, Goldsborough acquiescing.

At noon General Wool came back with Chase and Colonel Cram.
Cram stayed behind with Hay when the others went in. "They
could land at Ocean View. We've examined the beach. There should
be no difficulty getting the men ashore unless the wind blows up from
the northeast." He looked a little anxiously at Hay. "It's none the less
unorthodox. They risk having to fight a battle of encounter without
artillery, without cavalry. It will take time to put guns ashore."

Hay said, "The President is convinced that General Huger and the
Southern Army are about to abandon the Norfolk shore."

"I hope the President is right," returned Cram heavily.

All through the afternoon the procession of people went on: pilots
coming to talk to the President, naval officers, soldiers. Stanton and
Chase were like permanent stars in a shifting firmament. At five o'clock
the President sent Stanton out. The Secretary of War said: "Mr. Hay,
the President proposes to examine the landing place for himself. I will
go with General Wool in the *Miami*. You will accompany the President
in the tug. You will inform the captain of the tug that he is to pick up a
boat with sailors from the Rip Raps. The President believes that he
has learned of a more suitable beach."

An hour later they were on the other side of the channel. The long,
low tongue of Willoughby Spit curved awkwardly up toward the Hampton Roads. Mile after mile of empty beach slanted down toward Cape
Henry and the sea. The low sun blazed with an unremitting brilliance.

Hay, on the foredeck of the tug, could hear the President's voice
above him talking lightly, enthusiastically, with the tug captain. He
thought: He's ten years younger. He feels he's doing something, something positive, something besides talk.

The boat was manned and the men from the Rip Raps began to row
in toward the shore. At once he heard a voice shout: "Beyond the trees
—cavalry! Look!"

The men in the boat stopped rowing, hanging on their oars ir-
resolutely.

From the *Miami* a voice shouted through a speaking trumpet to ask
if they should open fire.

For a time the President, in the cramped wheelhouse above him, was silent. Then Hay heard his voice. "No." It seemed reluctant. "No, reckon I've seen enough."

There was another brief pause. Hay watched the horsemen wheel and canter along the white wet sand. Then he heard the President's voice again. "Colonel Cram, will it be possible to embark the first of your troops by dusk?" And Cram's startled reply: "By dusk, sir?" Then, when the President made no answer: "Yes, sir; it will be possible."

"Let it be so," said Lincoln.

Chapter three

LINDEN was standing at the window. She did not move as he entered the room but she said, "Yes, Jeri?"

"They're pullin' out." His voice was unnaturally loud, full of grief and indignation. "Capt'n Emerson's come in from Seawell's Point. He brought back the last o' yesterday's wounded. He says they started pullin' out at sunup. They're leavin' the guns. *Leavin'* the guns!" He waited for Linden to speak, but she remained quite still, staring out the window at nothing at all. "They's on'y th' Jackson Grays left at Seawell's, and they was gettin' ready to move. They're the rearguard."

Again he waited for Linden to speak and again she said nothing.

He muttered pleadingly, "Lindy, they're pullin' *out!*" He could not believe it himself. He did not want to believe it. "Do you think they'll stand an' fight them outside Norfolk?"

She turned away from the window at last. Her voice was curiously gentle as she answered him. "No, they won't stand. It's over, Jeri."

He stared at her, open-mouthed.

She pressed her fingers to her eyes. "I'm tired; I'm going up to my room to rest." Like someone walking away from an accident she went slowly out of the door and began to climb the stairs.

He had always seen her take the stairs two at a time.

He waited, sitting in the corner of the parlor, on a low bead-covered stool that Aunt Deborah had worked half a year on. He thought, confusedly, that he would wait till Aunt Deborah came back. Linden, he felt, was ill. He tried to think while he waited, to think of what it all meant—what it meant to Virginia, to Portsmouth, to himself. It was immensely difficult. He could only think in terms of the batteries: at Seawell's, at Pinner's Point, at Craney Island, at the Hospital—the batteries that he had sat in and talked in, and dreamed victories in. Now they were empty. That was the one salient fact that repeated itself over again. No more shouting, no laughter in them; they were dead.

What would the Yankees do to him?

He was fourteen. They used boys of fourteen in the Yankee armies, he had been told. Could they conscript him? Could they make him fight for them? He wanted to go and ask Linden, to get assurance from her, to be told it was impossible. But he could not go to her—not now.

He was still mulling over his thoughts when he heard a thunderous knocking on the door. He did not go to it. Jacinta was about somewhere; it was Jacinta's duty. He would not admit to himself that he was afraid of the unknown.

He heard Jacinta pad down the passage, and he heard Revell's voice. It was almost hysterical. "I got to see Miss Lindy! I got to see Miss Lindy!"

Jacinta said, her voice shrill with dislike, "Miss' Lindy, she's took sick."

He heard what sounded like a scuffle, and Jacinta's voice indignant: "Mist' Revell, you shouldn't a' done that! You shouldn't a' done it." Then he heard feet pounding up the stairs.

He got up stiffly—he had sat in one position for too long. This time he was not going to wait for Linden to cry out. He looked doubtfully at the fireplace with its stand of heavy brass fire irons. The poker would do. He stood, waiting.

Revell was hammering on Linden's door, more gently this time but no less urgently. He called, "Lindy, Lindy, I got to see you!" The door gave. It had not been locked.

His voice changed in tone and in power as he went into the bedroom. "They're goin', Lindy. They're pullin' out."

He used the same phrase that Jeriel had used. "What am I to do? What must I do?" When she did not answer, he said irrelevantly: "The Rangers're gone already. They'll make me a prisoner." His voice rose in an immense surge of self-pity. "I'm too sick to be a prisoner. . . ."

The boy heard Linden's voice at last. It was completely without emotion. "Get your rifle and join your company."

"I can't! I'm too sick."

"You've not been too sick this last ten days to loaf round with

Wooleren and Purney and the other skulkers, drinking and doing what you liked. Join your company!"

Hurriedly, the words tumbling over themselves, Revell cried: "I haven't got a company. The Rifle Patriots are over the other side of the water. They won't have me anyways."

"Then go back to the Old Dominion Guard."

He was shameless, his voice had a whipped-dog cadence. "They'd shoot me if'n I went back to them. Lindy, I got to hide up somewhere, I got to get away. Till I'm well again, that's all—till I'm well. You got to help me!"

"You're well now—well as you'll ever be. If you want to hide, hide. But I won't help you."

"You must, Lindy, you must! Isn't anybody else can help me. I got to see you sometimes. I can't be made a prisoner, because I wouldn't see you again, ever. If I don't see you I'll go crazy. It's on'y because of you I ain't gone crazy. You don't need to do nothing for me, but I've got to see you, Lindy—I got to!"

Jeriel could sense, rather than hear, the alteration in his voice, the gradual thickening of it, the change in timbre. Now he could hardly distinguish the words, but he did not need to distinguish them.

"Lindy, if you won't help me, if I'm not going to see you again, if this is the last time, will you let me—will you . . ."

The boy waited in an unbearable tension, his eyes fixed on the poker. His hands clenched and unclenched. He waited for Linden's answer.

It was like the whistle of a whip when it came. "How rotten are you, Rev Jordan? I'd go to bed with a"—she paused, searching for an adequate pejorative—"with a water snake rather than you. You've always cheated, you've always lied, you've always let other men do the work, and hung around for the credit. You're a bully and a thief, but most of all you're a coward. You've got slime where other men have got guts. There's nothing where your heart ought to be, not even slime. . . ."

There was a breathless silence, and then came the sound of a blow, and Linden's voice saying: "Get out! Don't come near me again, ever. Don't speak to me. Don't look at me. Get out! Get out!"

The boy walked over to the fireplace and stood, half stooped, ready. Then, very slowly, he relaxed. He could hear footsteps on the stairs, slow, dragging.

Over them he heard Linden's voice again: "God, if I were a man I'd take my gun and go out and fight, even if I had to fight by myself—alone!"

Chapter four

JACINTA said: "She bin sittin' in her room since you all lef' this mo'nin'. She ain't et. Mebbe you c'n he'p."

The boy was white-faced, cold, frightened. "I got to see her," he said, and went stumbling up the stairs. In all his prolonged lieutenancy he had never been in Linden's room. His knock was an odd mixture of hesitancy and urgency.

Linden was a long time answering. All day she had sat alone, trying to think. Her world was shattered. For weeks now she had been cognizant of an increasing disillusion, of a growing lack of faith in the men who controlled the South. More and more she had grown aware of weakness and quarreling, of rivalries and instabilities, of folly and evasion and stupidity. But nothing had prepared her for the shock of surrender. She could not bring herself to believe in this final disaster.

Jeriel knocked again.

She said at last, dully, "Come in."

He saw her sitting drooped on the edge of the bed, and he said, without preamble, "They's shot Revell."

She straightened up with a jerk. "Who shot him?"

"Th' Yankees."

"Where?" She was standing up now.

"Him an' Elia Wooleren an' another man—they called him Nick—they took a boat an' they went on up the crik an' they lay out on a ridge over against th' town, an' a Yankee company come an'—an' they fit it."

"Revell?" she asked incredulously.

"An' Wooleren an' this man Nick."

"They fought? Just the three of them?" Her eyes were alight now.

The boy said with a cold, blunt harshness: "They warn't no heroes. They was all three o' them drunker'n a fiddler's bitch." He saw the light fade in her eyes.

"Drunk," she echoed bleakly. "Tell me!"

He took a moment to consider. The cold seemed to bite into him again, and he shivered. "They'd bin drinkin' an' they had a jug with 'em. I saw 'em go down to the shed by Cuffee's place. I got close to 'em."

"Why?"

"They was drinkin' an' they had their guns." Jeriel seemed to think it was explanation enough. "They was talkin' 'bout you."

"About me?"

" 'Bout you'd said if you was a man you'd go out an' fight even if you had t' fight by yourself. He kep' on tellin' 'em five-six times more. Then Cuffee come, but Elia Wooleren, he stuck a gun in his belly an' they took his boat."

"Did they shoot him?"

"No," the boy replied. "They reckoned it'd bring in half th' town. They took his boat an' they shoved off, an' I went back to th' yard an' I took th' skiff." He looked at her apprehensively, but she made no comment. "I follered 'em down the river an' they turned up Tanner's Crik. I was a long ways behind. Th' bridge was burnin' but they went up through it. They was shoutin' and singin'. Nobody took no notice." He stood silent again, marshaling his memories. "They went up far as the point t'other side o' th' Skinner place an' they ran the boat ashore there. They took their guns an' they went into th' woods." He thought for a minute. "They took the jug too."

"And you followed them?"

"I follered 'em but I was a long ways after. When I come out o' th' wood there was a Yankee company comin' down th' road." He paused, remembering the solid, close formation, the blue of the uniforms, the beat of the single drum, and the thin, almost inaudible sound of the fifes. The picture was burned on his memory. "They was singin'."

"And Revell?"

"Him an' the other two, they was lyin' on their bellies in th' bushes on th' ridge. You know, where th' swamp runs along th' road. Wooleren, he fired firs' an' then the other two. He was a deserter," Jeriel offered, as if it were an explanation.

Again he paused to collect his thoughts. The sound of the guns, the ragged answering fire from the company, the shouting, the screams were inextricably mingled—a huge, jumbled confusion of incident.

He went on: "Four men dropped that I saw. The res', they went fer th' ditch, most of 'em. Two-three here an' there, they stood shootin'. They hit Elia Wooleren right away. I saw him"—he hesitated for a second—"I saw him roll over. The one they called Nick, he got up after a coupla minutes, I dunno why, an' they shot him."

"And Revell?" she asked again.

"He run," the boy said contemptuously. "Run like a snipe, dodgin'.

They hit him before he got to th' edge o' th' wood, but he got up again."

Linden looked at him with horror in her eyes. "Are you sure he was hit?"

"He was hit," answered Jeriel bluntly. "They sent men, a sergeant. I went back through th' woods. When I come out, there was a pool o' blood on the far side where he must'a' waited fer a minute. He was hit bad."

"Did you look for him?"

"Why?" asked the boy simply. "He warn't no hero." He used the words again with an added scorn. "It was murder, that's all it was."

"Did he get away?" she demanded, not of the boy but of herself, of her own imagining.

None the less, the boy answered, "He couldn't git far." A deep, horrified respect for the Yankees had been driven into him.

"But he was still alive?"

He flared up at her, suddenly angry. "How in Chris' name kin I know? He was runnin' fast when I las' saw him, but he must'a' bin bleedin' like a stuck pig."

She considered this against the faint background of noise in the town, of shouting and crying and an occasional far-away explosion. She said at last, "We've got to find him."

The boy looked at her with an angry stubbornness. "Not me."

"I need you." Calmly she overrode his rebellion. "Get out now; I've got to change my clothes."

He answered automatically, "Yeh, Mis' Linden."

As he went out of the room she called: "Ask Aunt Deborah for bandages, lint, and salves—anything she thinks will help. Get some food from Jacinta!"

He went first to Jacinta, food being more important to him than Revell's wounds; also, he was afraid of what Aunt Deborah would say. He was only beginning a stumbling explanation to her when Linden came down. She was dressed as she had always dressed for their escapades. The old trousers, the shirt, the heavy jersey, the jacket were so like the old days that he forgot in an instant the months between.

He listened with an unholy joy to Aunt Deborah's greeting. "I thought you'd outgrown those things."

Linden—she was a new, a fresh Linden—outfaced her aunt. "I'm going out in the skiff."

"Tonight? It will be dark in an hour. . . ."

"Revell's been wounded. I've got to find him and bring him back."

"The ambulance men—"

"There wouldn't be an ambulance where he was wounded," said Linden grimly.

"Where is it?"

"Up Tanner's Creek, somewhere on the eastern side."

"You can't go there!" Aunt Deborah's voice had a sudden real horror. "The woods will be full of Yankee soldiers."

Linden turned to her and laughed—unbelievably, the laugh had no bitterness. "Too late. I've already been raped by the Confederate Army —remember? Are you going to give me the bandages?"

Aunt Deborah, stunned, handed over the small basket she held in her hands. "Lindy Cleave—" she began, but there was no rebuke in her voice.

"Hurry with the food, Jeriel!"

"I got it."

"Ask Father to wait for me at the yard." Linden spoke with a sudden humility. "If we're lucky we'll be back somewhere around midnight. We'll need help."

* * *

"Gordalmighty!" the boy exclaimed, his face awed and his voice husky with excitement. "It's the *Harmony;* she's burnin' like a tar bar'l on the fourth a July."

The tug swung slowly with the wind, turning on her heel in a fury of flame and smoke. Upstream beyond her was another tug, and beyond her again the salvaged hulk of the *Plymouth.* Coruscations of sparks leaped up from them; great banners and plumes of flame danced and sank and came alive again. Beyond the ships the Yard was burning. What had been spared by the North when they abandoned it was blazing now. What had been rebuilt since the South seized it was a blazing fury. All along the shore below the Navy Yard cotton was burning. Bales of it floated on the water, scarlet rafts flaring and hissing. Smoke from the great stack of tobacco hung across the Southern Branch, rolled and bellied across the harbor, hid Norfolk and its spires and the dome of the City Hall with the new-hoisted Stars and Stripes.

Along the wharves and the rickety jetties men moved with torches of pitch pine, burning, burning, burning.

Linden held a handkerchief soaked in water to her face. Jeriel coughed and buried his nose in his shirt. Their eyes smarted, their throats were sore and sour with the smoke, but the boat, clear of the bend now, moved fast, close-hauled for Hospital Point.

Gradually the smoke diminished. They ran into open patches, butted again through trails from new and separate fires and finally, abreast of the deserted batteries beyond the Hospital, found clear, clean air and the last brilliance of the evening light.

The *Merrimac* still lay at her moorings inside Craney Island.

Linden said, "We'll go to her first."

"Goin' to get dark soon," protested Jeriel uncertainly. He had no longer any ascendancy over this revived Linden.

"He can wait," she said brusquely. "Don't you go thinking I'm doing this out of softness for him, Jeri!"

"Then why're—"

"Because I made him go." Her voice was rough with guilt.

"He was drunk."

"Makes no difference. It was my fault."

They went on, the skiff moving, it seemed to Jeriel, more lightly, more eagerly than it had ever sailed for him.

There were two tugs and half a dozen small boats lying off the *Merrimac*. The tugs moved slowly, wheeling round to maintain their positions against the tide. The *Merrimac* herself lay utterly silent. A knot of men stood on the gratings above the armored casemate, looking up toward the smoke and flames of Portsmouth. Others stood at the gun ports, watching. No one moved.

Linden called to the first of the small craft—it was a Norfolk boat, but she recognized the man in the stern sheets—"When is she going to sail?"

"Reckon she ain't," replied the man in a deep, irascible voice. "She still cain't get up the James."

"Who says?" demanded Linden hotly.

"Pilots." And then, as if he felt that his hostility needed some explanation, he added, "My son's aboard of her."

She turned from him and looked long and silently at the *Merrimac*. The bow and most of the stern section were completely clear of the water. The great ironclad loomed enormous, three times the ship that had fought outside on the still waters of the Roads. With the western light behind her she was fantastic, forbidding, epochal, something more than a ship—a portent.

Linden let the mainsheet run creaking through the blocks, the skiff's head fell away, and she set course for Tanner's Creek. Neither she nor Jeriel spoke. Slowly the light in the west died. Across the Norfolk peninsula the afterglow hung in a great rose arc, clear in its northern half, stained, streaked, and at the last lost to the south in smoke.

The afterglow faded and the darkness came, and they had still not made the burned bridge. They saw it first as a faint flickering of fire: small, friendly flames like the night fires of a bivouac. They went through with Jeriel lying over the bow, an oar in his hand to fend off from the uprights. There was no challenge. They went on in silence.

A long while after, Jeriel, still crouching in the bows, said, "Take her in to the bank now, Mis' Linden."

She turned the boat's head instantly and, going forward, let down the mainsail with a run. They ran the boat ashore and made her fast. Kneeling, she lit the lantern and together they went up into the scrub pine.

In the darkness the landmarks were changed. There was nothing that Jeriel could recognize. The scrub where he had hidden from the sergeant could not to be distinguished in the dark from any other patch of scrub along the shore.

They walked between pine boles and through bushes, the lantern giving them little more than an illusion of vision. They were blind in the bottom darkness of a pool of pine branches.

Far away—Jeriel guessed that it was in the marsh between the last ridge and the road—there was a chorus of frogs. Intermittently owls hooted, and there were insect noises. Twice they heard human voices in the distance.

Linden said at last, "We'll do no good in the trees," and they headed back toward the creek bank.

The search became futile. They plodded on, Jeriel swinging the lantern to left and to right. There was nothing to see except scrub and scattered pine boles and tufts of grass. The boy began to be intolerably tired, and anger rose in him at this absurdity. He wanted to say what he thought of it, say what he thought of Revell—but he could not defy Linden in her present mood.

She heard the sound first. It was low, muted. It could have been a frog or a night bird or the experimental cry of some small animal. But she knew at once that it was not. She felt cold and her skin roughened. She knew it was Revell and that now she would have to do what she had set out to do.

He groaned three more times before they found him, holed up under a low tunnel of bush. He was unconscious, and from his right shoulder a great pool of blood seeped out across the sand.

She stood looking down at him as Jeriel flashed the lantern on his face, on his shoulder, on the blood. She said: "He's unconscious—that's something, anyways. How far are we from the shore?"

The boy answered dully, "I dunno."

"Find out, then! Leave the lantern with me. It won't do you any good. Find out and bring the boat up as close as you can."

She watched him as he looked up into the night sky to recover his sense of direction. Then she squatted down and held the lantern close to Revell's shoulder. The coat was soaked in blood, but it did not seem to be fresh. She thought that the wound must have clotted up. There was no point in doing anything for it now. She waited, squatting there beside him, trying to divine the impulses that had moved him, the forces that had driven him.

*   *   *

There was light enough in the night sky, red light enough, for the little group of men to see what they were doing in the lumber yard. The Negroes carried Revell without difficulty on a mattress that Eben had brought down to the jetty, but Cleave, watching them, asked, "How in God's name did you get him to the boat?"

"I don't know—I don't know!" answered Linden hysterically. She wanted to forget the brutality, the night-terror quality of that obscene hour. Her mind retained nothing now but a memory of the slipperiness of blood, and Revell's abject wailing, and Jeriel cursing and dragging and dropping to his knees and being sick, and cursing and dragging again. She wanted to shut her mind to it, wanted it expunged.

Cleave said: "I've sent Mullin for Doc White. I told him I thought we'd be needing him. There's a curfew, but he'll come. How bad is he?" He jerked his head toward Revell.

"I don't know," she said again. "Bad, I think." She was conscious of her exhaustion and, as if consciousness had relaxed the control of her muscles, she stumbled.

He put his arm around her and pulled her right arm over his shoulder. "Take it easy! There's nothing hurry will do."

Behind them the boy plodded, moving his feet as if he were walking through heavy clay.

They put Revell on the table in Isaiah's cabin.

Old Sam woke at the noise. He looked blearily at Linden. "Found him? I reckoned you would."

Cleave said sharply to Isaiah, as the Negro began to unbutton Revell's coat: "Leave it till Doc White comes! We don't want to start it bleeding again."

Sam stared at Linden for a moment or two. Then he walked over to Jeriel, picking up a bottle on the way. "Take a slug of this! You look like you need it." He watched the boy's face as he drank.

Cleave led Linden over to the old man's still-warm chair. "There's nothing you can do. Rest!"

She lay back for a moment, flaccid. Then in one movement she shifted onto her side and was asleep, as swiftly as if she had fainted.

Cleave stood looking helplessly down at her.

Doc White came in. His greeting was hard. "They found him? Pity they did. General Viele's looking for blood over this. He's a dangerous-tempered man. All right, let's look at him!"

He unbuttoned the front of the coat, found it caked to the body with dried blood, searched in his bag for heavy scissors, and began to cut at the material with quick, incisive movements. After a few minutes they lifted Revell and the doctor pulled the remains of the uniform jacket away. Then he cut through the shirt. Soon he had freed enough of it to see the livid bruising under the collarbone. There was a high lump projecting above the bone.

White felt at it exploratively. "Humph! Shot in the back. He would be. The bullet's come clean through. It's in the muscle here. God knows what it's done on the way. Sam, give me that bottle of whiskey you're sozzling!" He swabbed away blood that had welled out over the front of the shoulder. Then he said to Cleave, "Give me the scalpel there!" Holding it in his hand he bent down, put his ear to Revell's chest, and listened perfunctorily. "We'll get it out before we look at his back." Neatly, quickly, the scalpel cutting crisp through the bruised flesh, he cut the bullet out and tossed it behind him on the floor.

The eyes of the two Negroes followed it with horror.

He swabbed the wound with whisky, stitched it rapidly, and ordered, "Turn him over!"

It took long minutes to clean enough of the caked blood away to see the damage. Obviously Revell had been hit while crouching—crouching as he ran. The bullet had gone in through the ribs. Splintered bone stuck out through the first shallow groove of it, then it dug into the body.

"There's not a lot I can do for this. It's missed his lung, far as I can judge. Come up inside the cage of the ribs. I can clean it a bit." White's voice was doubtful. "Have to open up the whole of his back to be certain about it. Probably kill him anyway." He put cotton on the end of the probe, soaked it in the whiskey, and began to swab out the entry wound.

Patiently, meticulously, he worked for a long time. Then he said abruptly: "Nothing more I can do. I won't sew it up—it'll have to drain. What are you going to do with him now?"

Cleave replied, "It wouldn't do any good getting him to a hospital."

"They'll go through the hospitals first thing in the morning. In Viele's mood they'd string him up in the hospital grounds." White stared down again at the bandaged wound. "I wouldn't lift a finger to stop them."

"Last half-hour you bin tryin' to save his life," old Sam said sardonically.

"My job," snapped the doctor.

Cleave harked back to the original question. "We'll have to send him up the Shingle Run." He looked over at Isaiah.

"That was how you brought them down?" White asked. "I wondered sometimes. In a load of shingles. Yes, I see."

"You've known all along that we ran the route through here."

"Been called in to 'tend enough of them! You don't think I believed your stories about accidents, did you? If you're going to move him, move him now while he's unconscious."

White wheeled suddenly and looked down at Linden, his harsh face softening to tenderness. "And while she's still asleep, or she'll go up into the swamp with him." He studied her face, smoothed by the lamplight and by exhaustion to a child's innocence. "She's been runnin' herself ragged these last weeks. You'll have her breakin' down on you."

"Isaiah," Cleave ordered, "you and Eben get the flatboat ready. You'll put him in the side space. Ballast the boat with bricks on the other side. The Yankees won't be on the Branch yet. You'll have to get help to get him round the lock. Best wait below against the bank and send Eben up to Andy's cabin on foot. You'll be doing things the wrong way round all the way back to the island. You'll have to work it out for yourself."

The Negro looked speculatively at Revell. After a perceptible hesitation he said softly, "Yes, suh, Mister Cleave."

"And what about the people in the refuge?" asked White dryly.

"Meanin'?" Sam cocked a doubtful eye at him.

"Meaning that the Yankees are here and they may be thinking in terms of the Jubilee."

Tersely the old compositor answered him: "They're a mite cautious in the swamp. Reckon they'll wait a while to find out if the Jubilee's come—long enough to last him out, anyways."

The doctor looked down at the unconscious man. "You could be right," he said.

Even as he spoke the cabin shook in the blast of a heavy explosion.

Old Sam waited for an instant before he said: "The dry dock. I bin waitin' fer them to blow it. Reckon that's the end."

Linden sat bolt upright without speaking. The doctor turned and fumbled in his bag.

The old man went on: "The Yankees left it and look what it cost 'em. If it hadn't been for the dry dock, there wouldn't have been no *Merrimac*."

White handed Linden a pill. "Swallow that! Give her a cup of water, Isaiah."

"What is it?" she asked.

"Never mind," he answered brusquely. "Swallow it!"

Childlike, she took the pill and then frowned at him with the resentment of childhood. "What are we going to do with him?"

Cleave said, "That's all taken care of, Linden."

Unemotionally she asked, "Is he dead?"

White answered, "He's being taken up into the swamp to one of the slaves' refuges."

She heaved herself wearily out of the chair. "All right, let's go."

White said, "You're not going anywhere!"

"I've got to."

"Linden Cleave, you're about as full of opium as a Chinese. In three minutes' time you'll be dead to the world, and you'll stay that way for a bit. If you won't use the sense God gave you, other people have got to use it for you."

Slowly, very slowly, she sank back into the chair. A combination of exhaustion and the assurance in his voice made her feel as if the opium were acting already. Her stomach had an odd internal warmth, a faint happy tingling of the nerves. She lay back and looked at her father.

Cleave asked, "Are you going to give him one?"

The doctor shook his head. "Opium's damned scarce, Ash Cleave— and damned expensive! This lot came through the blockade. I've none to waste on men like him."

Cleave said reasonably: "If he wakes going up past the lock gates and makes a noise, there'll be trouble. I'm thinking of Isaiah."

White considered. At length he took out a pill and wrapped it angrily in a screw of paper. "He couldn't swallow it now anyway. Give him this if he wakes. Bring it back to me if he doesn't!" He handed the screw across to Isaiah. "I'm going," he said with finality.

*   *   *

The second explosion came just before dawn. This time it was from the northwest. Distance gave it a drum-roll quality, a deep, rolling reverberation of sound.

The cabin shook hardly at all, but Linden half woke through a complex dream of swamp stillness and weathered tree stumps, singing frogs and snakes, and the harsh croaking of night birds.

Through the dream she heard her father's voice say: "It'll be the *Merrimac,* Jeriel. She's been blazing like a hayrick for the last hour."

She heard Jeriel's voice say, "Yes, Mist' Cleave."

And her father's voice again, deeply comforting, deeply generous: "You don't need to grieve for her, Jeriel. She's done her work—she's saved Richmond."

Chapter five

LINDEN stretched experimentally, ran her tongue round the inside of her mouth, and said, her voice still heavy with sleep, "I feel like hell."

Jeriel looked her over with a friendly malice. "You look like hell. Doc White filled you up to th' gills with opium. You ain't moved none since they blowed up the *Merrimac.*"

She sat upright in one awkward movement. "The *Merrimac?*" Then her voice went dull. "Yes, I remember. My father said something about—"

"About she saved Richmond," the boy interjected. "I don' know what he meant, but if he says so . . ."

Her mind moved forward. "Have the Yankees come yet?"

"Not to the yard, they haven't. There's plenty o' them gone past along Crawford Street, to the Navy Yard an' such. Jacinta says they been movin' up the High Street, outa town."

"Jacinta?"

"She's waitin' in the office for you to wake. She's got your clothes."

Linden disregarded the information. "Have they been searching?"

"Dunno." The boy shook his head. "Ain't seen nothin'. Reckon they'd search the Norfolk side firs'. Yankees—they wouldn't guess we'd used a boat to bring him here."

She climbed up from the low bunk. "We've got to go over to Norfolk and find out. We'll take the skiff"—her face went white for a moment —"there'll be blood all over the skiff!"

"Washed it out," said Jeriel laconically. "Pulled the plug and let the water in—whole bottom of her colored up red. I didn't know blood spread so. Then I bailed her out. They won't find nothin'."

Reluctantly she came at last to the crucial question. In a small voice she asked, "Was he still alive?"

"When they started for the swamp, you mean? Yeh, he was alive. Doc White fixed him up. He cut him open and took out the bullet." Jeriel pulled his hand from his pocket, tossed a misshapen lump of lead into the air, and caught it expertly. "That's it."

She went white again. "Where is everybody?"

"Ain't back yet."

"What time is it?"

"Dunno, one o'clock maybe."

"It can't be! I ought . . ." She shook her head as if the lost hours were of immense importance. "Get the skiff ready while I wash."

"Nope." The boy shook his head in turn. "Ain't nothin' movin' in the harbor e'cept Yankee tugs an' the ferries. They stopped traffic, I guess."

"Old Sam will know."

"Nope." The boy dropped the bullet and bent down to retrieve it. "He ain't back neither. He went up to the swamp with them."

"Old Sam? He hates the swamp."

"The nigras don't like Rev Jordan special," said the boy dourly. "Nobody does."

"What are we to do?" With a sudden warmth she appealed directly to the boy.

He hesitated uneasily. "You could dress like your aunt says, an' we could go down to the ferry an' see kin we get across." He turned and opened the door of the cabin as if his suggestion were an order which he knew would be obeyed. As he went out he said over his shoulder: "Don't look purtier'n you kin help. There's a lot o' Yank soldiers about."

Crawford Street was coldly empty. Single men walked along it separated by wide distances. They moved apprehensively. There were no soldiers. All the while Linden was conscious of eyes. She saw curtains move at windows and shadows in the darkness of rooms. All Portsmouth was waiting and watching.

There was a thin crowd at the ferry dock. Jeriel saw a small boy whom he knew leaning half-hidden in a doorway. He left Linden and went to him. After a brief interchange he rejoined her. "Ferry's for Yankees only. They movin' troops. They's a tug runnin' folks. Comin' across now."

They waited, backed into the inset angle of a shuttered store, trying to look inconspicuous.

A company of infantry came ashore from the ferry and formed up almost opposite them. There were whistles and occasional calls as the men saw the girl. A sergeant shouted them down. They fell in smartly, moving with ease, handling their weapons well. The dark-blue uniforms, the touches of gold were smarter than the worn Southern gray that Linden had grown used to. They were young men, well fed. After a moment or two they were marched off.

The tug berthed. A trickle of civilians, four women among them, came off and hurried up High Street.

Jeriel said, "Now!"

One of the tug hands was a friend—an old man, dark and gnarled. He moved jerkily and unnaturally and, as they passed him, he said: "Keep outa th' way! There's a Yankee guard."

Halfway across he came sidling past them. "You seen th' *Monitor*? She's lyin' in th' *Merrimac*'s ol' berth. Th' *Naugatuck*'s 'longside too. *Susquehanna*'s anchored off." He fiddled with a coil of rope. "Watch your step!" he warned them. "You kin get took up easy as spittin'. There's somethin' happenin'. Th' *Baltimore* come up the river an hour ago. They're all fussin' an' fumin' t' get aboard her, generals an' sich."

They landed without hindrance. Water Street was thick with troops. Jeriel knew an alleyway—he always knew alleyways—and they worked up almost to Town Point, found an open space and crossed, again unhindered. Perhaps there had been no need for furtiveness.

They headed for the office of the *Day Book*. Linden knew two of the reporters. At Granby Street near the Atlantic Hotel they heard horses, the clatter of innumerable hoofs, a clashing of accouterments.

They were stopped by a little tide of people running across the intersection. The horses went by: cavalry, ill-mounted but still cavalry, men sitting high with drawn sabers, stiff with pride.

There was a carriage behind them, an officer riding close beside it. They jingled past; there was a long-drawn word of command, and the cavalcade came raggedly to a halt. The carriage stopped almost level with Linden. The officer's horse moved backward and then forward uneasily and stopped half a length clear.

There were two men in the carriage, a general on the far side, a tall man in black on this—a tall man in a tall black top hat. He was looking at something on the far side of the street. Slowly he turned until he faced them. It was not necessary for her to see all his face, to see the short chin whiskers, the high, exaggerated cheekbones, the heavy brows. The eyes were enough—the deepset eyes, dark, filled with an illimitable sadness. They seemed to rest on hers for a moment. Then suddenly the carriage jerked forward.

She heard Jeriel's voice behind her. It was awed, unbelieving. "Ole Abe Lincoln hisself," he whispered.

Chapter six

AS she picked her way between the type cases, old Sam held up the proof, wet from the press. She could read it almost the whole length of the long composing room:

MURDER!!

$1000 REWARD

to ANY PERSONS supplying information that will lead to the apprehension of REVELL SEBASTIAN JORDAN, private of the Norfolk County Patriots DEAD or ALIVE

Brig Gen E. Viele
Military Governor

"Murder!" she said desperately. "Why must they call it murder?"

Old Sam considered the matter. "Popes an' archbishops an' such the last thousand years bin tryin' to draw a line between war an' murder. Result's th' same."

Her hands were clasped in front of her, the fingers working. "Why did *you* have to print it?"

The old man looked at her sourly. "I'm a workin' compositor. I set up what I'm told to set up." He had turned the proof now, and as he spoke his eye ran down it. "This could do with a comma after 'private.'" He looked up at her ironically. "Reckon I'm the only comp that's set up th' bill, kin claim th' reward, and is li'ble to swing if he does."

She said: "Thank you for going up with him. I would have gone myself." Her voice had an unaccustomed humility. "What are we going to do? A thousand dollars . . ." Her voice trailed away.

"Nothin'," he said shortly. "Ain't nothin' we can do."

"But a *thousand* dollars!"

"All right—who knows about it? Ain't nobody saw you up Tanner's Creek. It was dark. Anybody see you on the water comin' home?"

The girl shook her head.

"Nobody saw us on the way up to the swamp 'cept Andy and his boy." The old man began to count on his fingers. "Your pa, Jeriel, Doc White, Isaiah, Eben, Andy and his boy—ain't nobody else that I know of. Oh, yes, old Mullin. Any of them 'cept Jeriel could ha' got more'n a thousand bucks for your pa's head any time the last five years. It wasn't never offered official but they know'd they could ha' got it. They all bin workin' fer th' underground railroad since I kin remember. Doc White's the only one who wasn't in. D'you think he'd claim?"

She shook her head again, her face white.

"All right, then. Ain't nothin' we can do 'cept wait. Thing that's puzzlin' me is how they knew his name so quick."

She thought for a moment. "Maybe one of the other two men was still alive when they found them."

"Ah!" The old man slapped his knee. "Must'a' bin that. Why didn't I think of it? The boy said they was shot, an' I reckoned that meant dead. That's all right then!" He seemed enormously relieved. "Sooner or later they're goin' to get round to askin' you questions, Lindy. Somebody'll tell them you was his friend—on'y friend he had, barrin' those other two. They're boun' to question you."

Cleave came into the composing room through the outside door. "Jeriel told me you'd be here. Sam, what's this about a bill?"

Sam held up the proof. "I wanted to put the runaway nigger cut on the top but editor said he'd fire me."

Cleave grunted. "A thousand dollars—that's a lot of money."

"I bin goin' over it with her." The old compositor jerked his head toward Linden. "Ain't nobody knows 'bout it that isn't workin' with us 'cept Doc White. And he ain't goin' to talk."

Linden said abruptly, "I'm going to General Viele."

Old Sam looked at her scornfully. "You ain't goin' nowhere. You heard Doc White Sat'day night. No, maybe you didn't—maybe you was asleep. He said Viele's that mad if he found Rev Jordan in a hospital he'd swing him from the firs' tree outside the windows."

"It's not murder. He's got to see that. It's *not* murder!"

"Depends which side you're on. Viele lost five men. He'll take a lot o' convincin'."

She turned in appeal to her father.

Cleave said: "He's right, Linden. Viele is the military governor. This is the most important city the North's taken yet. He's got to hold it down and he's got to do it with the smallest possible number of men. They can't waste troops. One man's life counts very little against considerations like that."

Stubbornly she persisted, "Who's above General Viele?"

"General Wool. You won't get anywheres with him. He's got to back Viele. Ain't done so well himself, an' he's a dry old bastard anyways."

Cleave said: "It's no good, Lin. They're soldiers. There's only one way they can look at it. They can't afford to consider an appeal."

"Who's above Wool?"

"I don't know," said Cleave. "McClellan perhaps, or maybe the Secretary of War."

"I'm going to appeal to the President."

"You can't, Linden!"

Old Sam snorted. "Abe Lincoln? They say he was the general behind this. Ol' Wool, he wouldn't ever ha' done anythin'. Ulysses says they told him Lincoln come down an' made him. Anyways, he's gone now. The *Baltimore,* she sailed five o'clock yestiday. He's back in Washin'ton by now."

"Then I must go to Washington," she said evenly.

Old Sam was looking at her curiously, his head on one side.

Cleave said gently: "There's no way to get to Washington, Linden. They'll not open up transport. This is a conquered city."

"Leave her be, Ash! What's on your mind, Linden?"

She answered slowly, in the same cool tone: "I saw him yesterday. I saw his eyes. They were—" She hesitated, searching for a word, and then said simply, "They were kind."

Both men were silent, watching her.

After a moment, her voice humble again, she went on: "I don't know about the underground. I don't know what you've been doing. I never saw anything. At least, I never knew that I saw anything. There were strange niggers about the yard, times. I know there were places back in the swamp—refuges. Will you tell me?" She looked at her father pleadingly.

Old Sam said: "She knows about the Shingle Run. Tell her the whole of it. It's all over now, anyways."

Cleave nodded slowly. "Sam wanted me to tell you long ago. I couldn't. You had your own loyalties toward the South. It wouldn't have been fair to burden you with it." He paused, looking to her for a sign of comprehension. She stood quiet, waiting, and he went on: "There's nothing heroic in it—no romance. It was Sam's fault." He looked over at the old man with such a warmth of understanding that the girl was aware of a deep envy. "There was a boy over at a truck farm in Suffolk. He was the son of a slave woman who'd been in Sam's family—"

"I owed her a debt," said the old man in a deep, unfamiliar voice.

"He was sold down into Carolina." Cleave picked up the story. "Virginia's been a slave-breeding state too long, Lindy. He'd been happy enough in Suffolk—there was a girl, I think. He ran for it. . . ."

"Dogs got him on the edge of the swamp, but he got away again." The old man turned to the type case and began to search for a comma.

"He got to one of the refuge islands—I don't know how. He was badly hurt. Sam asked me to help get him out. It was just after I'd freed Mullin and Isaiah and Eben. I think he felt he could trust me. We got him out. It wasn't difficult." He made the statement in a flat voice. "There were others afterward. It grew of itself; these things do."

"Are you an Abolitionist?"

Sam whipped round. The word was the nadir of Southern abuse, the word from which there was no turning back.

But Cleave, watching the girl's eyes, saw that she needed, for some purpose of her own, to know. He answered softly, "I hate slavery, Linden."

"I've never thought enough about it to know what I feel. I've just— just . . ."

"Accepted it," suggested Cleave.

"Yes," she agreed candidly. "Even with Jacinta and Mullin, I think . . ." she stumbled over words. "They were black. . . . I knew that they were free, of course, but I didn't—it didn't mean anything to me. They were black."

He nodded heavily. "That's my fault, perhaps."

She came across to him and put her arms round his neck and kissed him. "Thank you."

Old Sam said caustically: "You finished now? I got to run off a couple'a hundred o' these bills."

She kissed him in turn. "Bless you!" She stood beside him as he locked the form. "I know about the Shingle Run but"—her attitude was one of pure curiosity—"what did you do with them after that?"

The old man looked up at her with a dancing light in his eyes.

Cleave said, "We put the boy on an English ship that was just pulling out."

"And after that?"

"We had hides in the yard. We could hold them for a day or two if we had to. Revell found one of them that time, but he was so mad to get at Stephen that he didn't think it out."

"It was near enough," growled Sam.

"Mostly we brought them down from the swamp just before we had a cargo ready to go up the bay. That's why I bought the *Chula*."

"That's why you'd never let me use her?"

"That's why." He grinned at her.

"Where did she take them?"

"Mostly to ships off Cape Henry, ships going up to Canada or to New England—anywhere north. Sometimes when there wasn't a ship they went up the bay. There was a land route up through Maryland—I never liked it, but it mostly worked."

"Where did it begin?"

"Galesville," replied Cleave.

"Did you have a—an agent there?"

"Methodist parson."

Old Sam glanced up at Linden's face, the dancing light still in his eyes.

"Have you used it since the war?" she asked.

"Twice, I think, or three times perhaps."

"How did you get the *Chula* out?"

"Fog was best—evening mist sometimes."

"But the Harbor Guard?"

"Captain Elleck helped us."

"That was why he took his tug over to Monroe on Saturday?"

"He reckoned he'd lasted out his luck," said Sam reasonably. "Wasn't worth risking anything for another two-three days."

She nodded, and again there was a little silence. Then she turned back to her father. In a voice drained of every vestige of her ordinary impulsiveness, she asked, "Could the *Chula* take me to Galesville?"

Cleave frowned. "Galesville?" he repeated incredulously.

"It can't be more than twenty-five miles from there to Washington."

"It's not possible, Linden. The bay will be full of patrols. They won't lift the blockade just because they've taken Norfolk."

She looked directly at him, something of the old determination already back in her voice. "I've got to go to Washington. It's the only way I can see"—she hesitated for a long moment, as if she were trying to decide among the innumerable names, and then said—"President Lincoln."

"It just isn't—" began Cleave.

Old Sam broke in: "Lindy—Lindy Cleave, you go an' find Jeriel! If you goin' up the bay you'll have to take him. Ain't fair to talk it over without him."

She turned to him gratefully.

He said, "Git!"

She glanced at her father and, when he made no move, she accepted his silence for assent.

When the door closed behind her, Cleave said: "We can't let her go up the bay, Sam. It's madness!"

"You'd let Isaiah take somebody on the run?"

"That's different."

The old man lifted the brass lead that he was working with and pointed it at him. "She's on the run, Ash. She's on the run from herself, and it ain't so crazy at that. For one thing, it gets her an' the boy an' Isaiah an' Eben—Mullin too, if you send him—out o' the way when the Yankees come questionin'. That's five out o' the bunch that knows. Looks a lot safer to me that way."

Chapter seven

THERE were lights along the Roads from Newport News past Hampton entrance to Fortress Monroe. With the blowing up of the *Merrimac* the shipping had come crowding back. There were lights off the Craney narrows. There were scattered lights along the invisible shore of Seawell's Point.

Twice before they picked up the dark loom of the land they saw small craft. Eben spotted them each time, and they altered course to pass well clear. Seawell's Point itself was utterly dark as they ran by. The *Chula* was moving very fast now; the sea was making. The land went by darkly, ghostlike, and fell away again, and out of the darkness to starboard Willoughby Spit came up.

Jeriel, crouched close beside Linden in the stern, said, "Ain't been close as this to the Rip Raps since befo' the war."

She looked out to port and saw the lights over the Rip Raps, flaring and insolent and bright with victory.

Two miles beyond the Spit Isaiah called the other two men aft. "Git your mainsheet in! I wan' her to sit nice and close. We got to run up over th' Horseshoe. They got their patrols there fo' sho.'" He waited while the main sheet blocks creaked, and put the helm down slowly.

The *Chula* heeled and the noises altered: there was a harsh pounding of spray under the bow, a wind song in the shrouds. She seemed to acquire new life, new vigor.

Isaiah said, "Wind's freshened a mite."

Jeriel snorted. "Win's freshened a whole damn' lot."

A long time later, a long way farther up the bay, they saw one small boat moving in toward the land across their course. Eben was steering then. He said: "Looks like he's goin' in under the land fo' shelter. Hit's goin' to blow."

Isaiah came back to the tiller when they were clear of Buckroe Beach. He sat for a while without taking over, watching the sail against the intermittent stars, feeling the movement of the boat. Finally he said: "Right thing to do, Mis' Lindy, would be t' go in an' anchor off the sho'. Wind's goin' t' blow his belly out over the York River. You want fo' us to go in, ma'm?"

She laughed in the darkness. "The patrols will be in for shelter."

She heard Isaiah's answering laugh, high and with a new excitement added to it. "Sho, ma'm, sho, Mis' Lindy—the patrols'll be in. Reckon we reef down an' keep on."

They reefed in darkness, spray whipping aboard, the boat spinning wildly out of control, sails thundering, the spars lunatic and unamenable. They were wet and chilled. They fought wet canvas with stiff fingers. They were bruised and hurt and in a sense shocked before they got the reef points tied and the storm jib set. When they backed the jib and swung her head round on course again and the *Chula* answered her helm, the wind had risen so that even with the reef she was still overpressed, still slammed into the rising sea, still heeled furiously without rhythm, without sense.

Sometime after midnight they came in under the lee of New Point Comfort. The short, vicious sea subsided. The boat lay down less. Linden felt that the wind was less violent, less angry.

She heard Isaiah shouting in the darkness: "Keep yo' eye on th' Wolf Trap, some o' you!" And she knew that he had seen the light before them.

Four minutes later, with the wind definitely lighter and the sea easy under them, the mainsail split across in one great shriek of torn canvas. She knew she was frightened then.

*   *   *

Before dawn it was calm again with the full unpredictability of the Chesapeake. Through a long, exquisite day they moved up the bay. Tangier came up, lay abeam of them for a little, diminished and faded astern. Out in the deep water they could see steamers moving, a Navy frigate under sail, and small craft farther over. Nothing came near them. The hot sun baked into them, the ship dried, and when the mainsail was whole again they hoisted it.

The *Chula* picked up speed and hurried, graceful and agile, to the north. They lay on the deck and talked. The Negroes sang, making close harmony. Isaiah sang by himself from time to time in a smooth, high tenor. There was little sense to their talking; yet through it and through the songs she knew that she was getting to know Isaiah as through the past years she had never known him—beginning to know his wisdom, his courage, his faith, and his wry, impersonal humor.

Late in the evening they found the lights of Galesville, and as they nosed slowly in a dying wind into an ancient wharf, Isaiah said, "Go straight up th' street till yo' git to th' church an' go on one block to a white house on th' corner an' ask for the Reveren' Clayton."

She walked up the road slowly, Jeriel with her till she should find the house.

*   *   *

She asked for Isherwood at the gate of the Navy Yard, as Clayton had told her to do. She was sure that he would be there or at least that they would know of him. She knew no one else in Washington, and Stephen had said of Isherwood, "He's tough but he's fair." She was surprised when she was taken to him without delay.

The engineer was standing at a desk of drawings. Over his shoulder he demanded, "Who the hell is it?"

"Linden Cleave," she answered.

He whipped round then, the astonishment palpable. He said accusingly: "You're from Portsmouth. You're the girl . . ." He prowled up to her—there was no better word for it—whistling tonelessly "The Girl I Left Behind Me." "On the scrawny side," he said, "but you'll fill out. Good bones. Good eyes. Good teeth." He was like a horse trader. Abruptly he lifted his head and barked, "What d'you want of me?"

In spite of his manner she was not afraid of him. "I have to see the President. Will you help me?"

"The President?" he snapped. "Anybody can see the President. Washington's full o' people seein' the President. God knows what they want! What do you want?"

She hesitated.

"Well," he snapped again, "what *do* you want?"

For no obvious reason, she knew that she could tell him. The words came in a flood.

He moved restlessly while she talked. When she came to the handbill and the reward, he stood still. "Revell Jordan . . . That was the man who hunted Stephen through the wood yard."

"I was with him," she admitted with a tinge of despair.

The engineer began to laugh. "And you come to me!"

"I had to." Her voice was humble. "I know no one else. If I knew where Stephen was—"

"You'd ask him." Isherwood laughed outright.

"I have to ask," she said, still humble. "It was my fault. He went because of me."

"He went," retorted Isherwood brutally, "because he was drunk. What d'you want? The President to pardon him so you can marry him when you get him out o' the swamp?"

"I never want to see him again!" she answered desperately.

He stopped in front of her, crouched slightly, staring at her. Speculatively he said, "You know, I think you're telling the truth." He asked no further questions. When he spoke again it was in a conversational tone. "He won't help you, you know. He's the President. He's got to follow the law. On the story you've told, *any* court'd hang Jordan." Again he thought for a moment or two. Then he continued: "Don't listen to me. Go and see him! I'll give you a note to McManus; he's the doorkeeper at the White House. Times he thinks *he's* the President. A little man, Irish; jigs around like an organ-grinder's monkey."

She was aware that he was trying to comfort her with nonsense.

*   *   *

The horsecar rattled wildly down the slope from Capitol Hill. Pennsylvania Avenue was a seething confusion of carriages and hacks, of buggies and horsemen, of ambulances and small groups of cavalrymen. The pavements were full of soldiers, women with parasols, men in top hats, bootblacks, candy hawkers, and newsboys. Officials and citizens. Righteous and unrighteous. Active and idle. It was so full that separate identities had ceased. The street itself had an identity, however: it was the aorta of the heart of a nation, the main artery—the vital, indispensable vessel.

It terrified her. There was an acceleration of mood, a velocity of spirit here that was outside her experience. It was not possible to compare Portsmouth with this. It was not possible to scale herself into it. She was too tired. She could only think, with her eyes half closed to occlude the kaleidoscopic movement of it all, that it was not possible to win against anything so beating, so palpitant, so vigorous.

A voice said, "Get off here fer th' White House, lady."

Chapter eight

THE little Irishman was as Isherwood had described him: small, full of an odd, undirected vitality, a village cunning that seemed incongruous in this place. He nodded. "I'm Mister McManus."

"I have a note for you," said Linden warily. She was afraid.

McManus read the note, his manner dispassionate and professional. "You will be wantin' to see the Presidint." He spoke as if he had divined her intentions by some special act of cerebration. "I am glad to do an assistance for Mr. Isherwood." He called to a Negro messenger. "Take Miss"—he consulted the note again—"Mistress Cleave up to the waitin' room. See that she has a good place. Then take her card to Mr."—he paused, giving his gravest attention to the matter—"to Mr. Hay."

She was led through the main vestibule, with its towering portraits of past Presidents, and up the side stairs to the clerk's room and thence to the waiting room. There were perhaps a score of people there already. For a while she could not bring herself to look at them. She stared over their heads at the heavy, embossed paper on the wall, at the elaborations of the fireplace, at the pictures, at the moldings of the cornice.

After a delay the messenger came out of the secretaries' room with a young man. Linden examined him anxiously. He carried himself stiffly upright, as if trying to add years by dignity. His hair was parted a little to the left of the middle and hung lank and slightly untidy. He had an indeterminate mustache that drooped. Clean-shaven and left to itself it would have been a kindly, humorous face. Hay—she was sure it must be Hay from what Isherwood had said—evidently felt the need of a reinforcement of hauteur against uncertainties. The Negro messenger pointed her out and he stared at her distantly. Then he went back into the secretaries' room again.

After that she began to look at the people who had arrived before her. These were Yankees. They were like the people who waited in the vestibule of the Court House at Portsmouth. There was no difference.

One by one she studied the faces. One old couple sat close together, almost ostentatiously not holding hands. She knew with an instinctive sympathy that they were frightened. The man next to them was not frightened—he was impatient. He twitched with an air of offended importance: obviously he was not, in his opinion, being accorded his due. Next to him was an Army lieutenant in uniform. He looked uneasy, as if he were not sure of his right to be there. There was a woman beyond him, in black like so many women in Washington, remote-looking, withdrawn. Linden could not make up her mind whether she was sad or angry. One by one she studied them all, noting mannerisms, trying to decipher expressions.

And all the while she knew that she was only trying to postpone the moment when she would have to decide what was truth. For she knew instinctively that she would have to tell the truth when she faced Lincoln.

The room receded, and she remembered for an instant only the agony and anger of finding Revell's blood-covered body.

The room came back and was suddenly commonplace, like the descriptions she had read of a dentist's waiting room, or a lawyer's office at the reading of a will.

What was reality?

How real was the President? Lanky Linkum came to Town in night and wind and rain, sir. Lincoln the Baboon. Mass' Linkum. Mass' Linkum give us our lives to live. Was Mrs. Lincoln as dreadful as they said she was? Caricatures: an immense and elongated body; a hat as tall as the unfinished Washington monument; long, disproportionate hands and feet; enormous boots resting on a White House windowsill. A President measuring himself against all comers with pencil marks on the wall. A President telling barroom stories. A President singing in an ambulance on a field of the dead. *"There has never been any reasonable cause for such apprehension. There has never been any reasonable cause for such apprehension. There has never been any . . ."*

An old Negro, immensely full of importance, opened the door that led to the President's room. He announced, "Th' Pres'dint will receive yo' now."

There was an instant, nervous rush to the door.

She went through it with the crowd—the businessman and the soldier, the widow and the old country couple.

She saw him uncertainly at first, her eyes blinded by the light of the great windows that looked out over the Potomac. She could see that he was tall, even though he was sprawled in his chair; that his face was hacked out of a harsh bronze, deep-furrowed, with high, exaggerated contours. She saw all this, but she saw nothing in detail. But as the crowd divided, as a little opening appeared between the desk and herself, she saw his eyes again—the deepset, deeply sad, profoundly human eyes.

He took the soldier first. She could not hear what he said but she could hear Lincoln's voice. "I have every confidence in the courts-martial." He paused. Evidently the young man protested. She saw the great rough-boned hand make a sweeping movement. "I am of the opinion, Lieutenant, that you were more fortunate than you deserve. I have read the papers. I can do nothing for you. Good day, sir."

The businessman thrust himself forward. She thought she saw a look of wary blankness on the President's face; her eyes were used to the light now. The President let the man talk. A rumbling, monotonous, faintly hectoring tone reverberated in the room. She saw Hay at his desk holding himself even more upright.

The rumbling went on, and then she saw the hand rise again, heard the President's voice, sharper this time: "Sir, you are aware that matters such as this are in the purview of Mr. Chase. Mr. Chase is master in his own Department. You have no business coming to me."

The rumbling resumed, more loudly. The hand rose again; she watched it, fascinated. "No, sir!" The monosyllables had suddenly an absolute authority.

The man turned away, his face gray and strained.

The President watched him. When he turned back to the waiting people, his face was clear once more, curiously gentle. He held out both hands to the elderly couple in a little welcoming gesture. When they reached his desk he rose again and bowed. She heard him say, "I think you must have come a long way." And then when they had answered slowly and with difficulty, he said: "I used to ride circuit through there. What can I do for my country-folk?"

Again there was an indeterminate exchange of voices. She could hear only the words, "My last son."

Afterward she heard the President's voice clear again. "Yes, I can do that for you—even if Mr. Stanton *is* mad at me. I've done it before —I'll risk it again." His voice was almost gay, young again. He pulled a card from a pile on the desk and began to write. "Give that to the doctors. They'll honor it." And then, cutting short their thanks, "Tell me, how much land did you plow this year?" Through the simple, conventional words Linden sensed a longing for country things, a gentle, deep nostalgia.

The three talked together, their heads close together, for four long minutes. Then the old couple withdrew, walking pridefully.

He called the woman in black next. Again his voice changed and his manner with it. Before she reached the desk he asked, "Have you brought the papers with you?" Then, when she hesitated, he said: "I see that you haven't. I did not think that you would. Madam, I believe your claim to be false. You waste your own time and mine. Good morning."

He watched her back as she walked resentfully away; then he turned and scanned face after face in the line that waited against the dividing rail. Linden had lost her place at the rail, edged out of it as much by her own uncertainty as by the urban thrustfulness of Washington. Yet the sweep of his glance stopped between the heads of the man and the short square woman in front of her and his eyes searched her for a moment, faintly puzzled. He indicated her with a gesture. The man made a move forward and Lincoln's voice said, "No, the young lady!"

She went through the little gate that Hay, on his feet now, indicated. She walked with difficulty. She could feel her nervousness coursing under her skin, washing over her nerve ends in hot waves. But she kept her eyes all the while on Lincoln's.

He rose and sketched again the brief momentary indication of a bow. Before he sat down again he said: "You are afraid of me. Why?"

She answered the assertion, not the question. It was possible to speak without difficulty, she found. "I am afraid, yes."

He sat back in his chair, the great loose-modeled head slightly to one side. "Why?" he asked again.

"I'm from the South," she answered simply.

"There are many in Washington from the South." His voice was ruminative, as if exploring other considerations. "They aren't afraid of me."

"I am not from Washington. I came here last night, from Norfolk."

"From Norfolk?" His voice rose. "I did not know that communications . . ." He let his voice trail away as though the matter were of no importance.

She said quickly, knowing that she had to tell him the truth, "I came in a small boat."

"Through the patrols?" He was sitting upright now. "I know of the patrols. I was in Norfolk on Sunday."

"I saw you," she said quietly. "That is why I came."

He was silent for a moment. "There was a storm on Monday night, a strong gale."

Linden nodded. "It was very bad for a while. The mains'l ripped."

He smiled at her for the first time, a rueful, humorous smile. "I would have been sick—and scared, I think. I'm not a sailor." He went to the point suddenly. "You must want something very badly. What is it?"

She abandoned her prepared speech, her demands, her appeal to chivalry, all the elaborate methods of reaching him that she had thought out on the deck of the *Chula*. She knew now that they would be of no use. She knew also that they would not be necessary. This was a man who would not be moved by rhetoric or by emotion, a man who could be reached only by direct and simple truth. She held out the bill that had been ready in her hand since, some intolerable time ago, she had entered the White House. "This," she said.

He took the paper and opened it. The light from the window was strong enough to shine through the rough paper, silhouetting the coarse black lettering. She could read the words in reverse: "$1000 REWARD TO ANY PERSONS . . ."

His eyes were held by it for a moment, then he looked back at her. "I know of this. I was told of it, in Norfolk." He looked searchingly at her. "Do you think that this is unjust?"

"Yes," she answered passionately.

"They murdered."

"It was not murder, Mr. Lincoln! They were soldiers. They had a right to defend their cities, their homes."

"Norfolk had surrendered."

"No," she said urgently. "No! It happened before Norfolk surrendered. An hour at least—more. They did not know of the surrender. A soldier's duty is to fight."

"A soldier's duty is to obey his orders." The President's forehead creased. "You see, I *know* about this. One of the men killed was a deserter. The other was a—a throw out. This man"—he lifted the bill with its glaring death-black lettering—"was sick, wounded."

"They went by themselves to fight—"

He looked at her sharply. "What do you know of them?"

"I made them go," she replied starkly, her face drained of blood, her lips so dry that she could hardly utter the words.

"You made . . ." The President leaned forward in his seat, his elbows among the untidy papers. "You knew them?"

"I knew Revell Jordan." Her fists were so tightly clenched now that the nails were cutting into the skin. "He was afraid. I taunted him, I told him that he was a coward. I told him that if I had been a man I would have taken my gun and fought."

"In front of the others?"

"I never saw the others."

"Then why did *they* go? A deserter, a useless man—why should they go because a coward was taunted?"

She was silent.

"I think you know." He was not the President now; he was Abe Lincoln, the small-town lawyer, the circuit rider—Abe Lincoln with his teeth in a witness.

She could not evade his eyes, the deepset dark eyes that seemed to pierce hers. She said in a small, desolate voice, "They were drunk."

"Aa-ah!" He slumped back in his chair. "That might be the truth of this. There was a madness in it that escaped me. There was nothing heroic. It might have been, but it was not. This man"—again he lifted the paper—"is still alive? You had better tell me everything that you know." He raised his hands in a light, compelling gesture.

"I found him. I went to find him." Somehow it was easier to talk again. "He was shot through the left side, above the heart. I took him— a young boy helped me—to a boat, and we crossed in the darkness to Portsmouth. The Navy Yard was burning—the warehouses. . . ." She gave a little shudder. "We got a doctor for him, and when the doctor had done what he could he was taken away."

"Where?"

Piteously she asked, "Do I have to tell you?"

He smiled at her, his face creased and gentle. "To the Great Dismal —it would be there."

"Yes." She nodded.

"And then you came to me. Why?"

"You are the President," she said simply. "I thought you could pardon him."

"No"—he shook his head slowly—"I cannot pardon him *because*

I am the President. The President is the guardian of the law, and the servant of it. This man must stand his trial."

She stood looking at him, trembling very faintly.

"I want to know more. He was taken to the Great Dismal—it must have been dangerous—and then you came here to Washington in a small boat, through the patrols and the storm. Do you love him very much?"

"I hate him," she declared, passionately grateful that she had been given the chance to say so, "I hate him!"

Again Lincoln leaned forward and studied her face. His own eyes expressed bewilderment: it was clear that an elaborate theory had been demolished. "I do not understand." He enunciated each of the words slowly and distinctly, emphasizing the negative.

She accepted the words as a request for information. With a simple candor she said: "I loved him once—or I thought I did. He was a soldier. He was for the South. He talked about what he would do, how he would fight."

He interrupted her. "And you—you were strong for the South?"

"I loved Virginia," she answered quietly.

If he noticed the past tense he made no sign. "And then . . ."

"He volunteered for the *Merrimac*—because of me. I went out to watch the battle in a boat. Afterward, on the first night, he came ashore. Must I tell you—everything?"

"No." He was strangely like her father. "These things happen in war."

She nodded gravely. Then she said: "He was a coward. I didn't know it, but there was trouble the first day. Then on the second day, when the *Merrimac* rammed the *Monitor,* they had a chance. The turret was turned toward them thirty feet away. If they could have fired, they would have hit one of her guns." She paused for a moment, trying to visualize the scene. "He broke down," she went on. "He hid and he was wounded. The gun never fired. Afterward nobody would help him."

"You did?"

"There was nobody else," she repeated drearily.

"Hating him"—Lincoln pondered the question for a moment—"because he was a coward?"

"No, because of that night."

"Aa-ah!" He understood now. "And after?"

"Everything has gone wrong! The *Merrimac* failed—not because of anything that was wrong with her but because—because of what people did and thought. They quarreled, they let things slide. They cheated and lied and argued. Hatteras, Roanoke, the work on the *Merrimac,* the pilots, the officers—everything!" She could not frame her case properly; she could only offer him these confused, unrelated phrases. "I think"—her voice was very small again—"I think I lost faith."

"In Virginia?"

"No!" She lifted her head. "Never in Virginia—but in the men who are fighting this war."

"Aa-ah!" He was still, watching her.

In Norfolk she had seen his eyes and thought that they were sad and kind. When he talked to the young soldier they were sad and angry. When he talked to the businessman they were just angry. When he talked to the old people they were just kind. But now she saw them as deep wells of compassion, as if upon his shoulders rested all the responsibilities of war and all the understanding of it, and of what it meant to each person who was caught in it, and shaped by it, and hurt by it.

His voice was gentle as he murmured, "You are so young." Then, as if switching the direction of his thought, he said: "There is one more thing. Tell me"—it was as if he were filled with curiosity on a lower plane—"he was taken into the Great Dismal—you found a boat to bring you here. How?"

"They were my father's boats. He was the link at Norfolk of the underground railroad. He helped Negroes to escape."

"Why didn't you tell me of this earlier?" He put his head a little on one side. "Didn't you think it would help? Didn't you think it would influence me?"

She shook her head. "Revell had nothing to do with it. I had nothing to do with it. It was all my father's . . . I had no right. I did not even know about it until I had to get Revell away."

Again there was a long silence. The murmur of the crowd outside the railing was growing louder. There was a hint of impatience. He murmured at last: "I said in a speech once 'a house divided against itself . . .'" Then, suddenly businesslike, he continued, "I won't bargain with you." He pulled another card from the pile, took a pen, and wrote slowly and deliberately. When he was done, he handed the card to Linden.

The sloped, spidery writing read: *To General Viele. Miss Linden Cleave will deliver to you the Confederate soldier Revell Jordan. He will be tried in due form. The papers in the case will be sent to me for confirmation.*

It was signed *A. Lincoln.*

He watched her read it. When she looked at him again he said: "I can do no more for you, but"—he fumbled for the right words—"there is much that you can do for me. When I spoke of a house divided I meant the States, the Nation as a whole. But a nation is made up of its houses, of its homes. Your own home was divided." He paused and looked at her searchingly.

"Yes," she whispered.

"Your father with his work for the slaves, you with your fervor for the South."

"Yes," she whispered again.

"Your house has come together again?"

For the third time she whispered, "Yes."

"It is my task to make the Nation come together again." His voice was so low, so deep that she could scarcely hear him. "I believe that we will secure the victory"—he looked up at her—"but I do not know that victory will bring peace. For that I must have help, I must have understanding. Will you go back to Norfolk and help spread that understanding? The Nation is greater than the States—greater even than Virginia. I was born in Kentucky—it is greater than Kentucky. But it is not greater than the homes which added together, make the Nation. You can go into some of those homes. You have seen us here in Washington in a moment of victory. We are not savages. You have talked to me. I"—a wide, utterly human, utterly charming smile suddenly spread over the deep furrowed face—"I am not a baboon, despite my appearance. Will you go back and do what you can to bring the Nation together again?"

"Yes," she said for the fourth time, but this time it was not a whisper.

"Even if I cannot save Revell Jordan?"

"Even then."

Chapter nine

THE light made patterns of brilliance and counterbalancing patterns of shadow. It was a design complicated by the difference between the values of the lights on the ship and the lights on the wharf. Sometimes they overlaid each other. The boilers were blowing off steam in short, shuddering bursts. Men were shouting. Somewhere beyond the wharf Negroes were singing.

Linden leaned on the rail, watching the scene with an eagerness that shook her. It was for her the beginning of another cycle in life— that much she could recognize—but she had still to clarify for herself the significance, the precise meaning of Lincoln's words. She tried to recall them, but only the memory of a deep compassion remained unclouded.

She was still remembering it when she heard Stephen's voice—and her heart leaped. There was no exceptional quality in his voice, no unique distinction; it was only that the timbre of it had its place in her heart; and in the moment that she heard it she knew for the first time that she loved him, that there was no one else, that there never had been anyone else.

She waited against the rail, quite still. She heard the words: "A young lady, Miss Linden Cleave . . ." A roar of steam blurred them. Then: ". . . special order of the President."

She continued to wait. It was not necessary for her to do anything; she had the feeling that this was all foreordained. She heard one of the officers say, "Upper deck."

She made no move.

Stephen came to her in the darkness. He said only, "Linden."

She put out her hands and seized his wrists and held him as if she were afraid that he would vanish in the cubes and triangles and broken, irregular patterns of the lights.

After a long while he said, "Isherwood sent me. I was at Alexandria. I got back an hour ago. He had my orders ready. I have to inspect ships and engines at Portsmouth and Norfolk."

With his wrists still imprisoned in her hands, she said, "I had no right to expect you to come."

"Because we took different sides?" His voice was incredulous.

"No." She shook her head.

"Why, then?" His voice was suddenly apprehensive.

The whistle blew above them, raucous and stunning, and he accepted the interruption with an inexplicable relief. He was afraid of what Linden might tell him. The moment was lost in shouting as the gangplank was hauled away. An officer's whistle blew from up near the bows, shrill, mocking the deep-toned steam whistle. A voice called, "Let go aft!" The boat came alive, moving slowly against the light patterns, so that they changed and altered in a kaleidoscope of two simple, essential colors. Under their feet the engines began to throb. A peace came to the ship, and the night wind grew cool and lovely.

He said at last, breaking the spell, "Come inside, Lin, and let me see you."

"No." He felt her hands tighten on his wrists. "No. I've got to tell you something. In the dark it'll be easier." There was a childlike honesty in her voice.

"You don't need to tell me anything, Linden." With a quick movement he freed his wrists and put his arms round her, and bending, kissed her. "I love you. You don't need to tell me anything."

"I've got to tell you!" Courage and terror were inextricably mixed in her voice.

"No," he said in his turn, something of her terror infecting him.

She lifted her face again, groping for his lips in the darkness, and when she had found them she kissed him hurriedly, humbly, and drew away. "Listen, Stephen! I'm not—oh, Stephen . . . oh, please don't look at me! Hold me while I tell you. After, you can let me go." She did not wait for his answer but went on hurriedly, breathlessly: "The night when the *Merrimac* came back, the first night, I had to do something, Stephen—I had to give something. There wasn't anything I could do while they fought. There wasn't anything I could give—except myself. I let Revell take me to the bedroom—to the bed. I let him . . . I let him . . ."

He had not loosed his arms. She felt them stiffen slightly and she heard him say, "Do you love him?"

She heard and despised the wail in her own voice as she answered: "I hate him! I hate him!"

"Why?"

"It was horrible," she said with such a childlike directness that he almost laughed, his spirit inexplicably lightened.

"He's a coward, Stephen."

"We're all of us cowards at some time." It was as if her honesty forced a corresponding honesty from him. "Why did you go to the President for him?"

"Because I made him do what he did. Because I shouted at him— and jeered at him till he went out . . . and the others were killed and he was wounded, and it was my fault. I'd have hated myself always if I hadn't tried to do something."

"Where is he now?"

"In the Swamp. He's wounded, badly wounded. I had to come, Stephen." With her instant devastating candor she added, "I had to come for myself."

Through the disjointed sentences, perhaps because of their disjointedness, he saw clearly into her heart and mind. Her romanticism, her self-deceit, her young, fragile integrity were plain for him. He was lost in a flood of compassion. He said only, "I love you, Linden."

She clung to him, not crying, but trembling faintly. After a long silence she said in an almost ordinary tone, "There's one thing I can do."

"What?"

"I can lie with you."

The archaic biblical phrase shocked him almost more than the offer. "No," he said.

"You don't understand. I must! It wouldn't ever be the same between us after if I didn't. We'd always remember it."

"There's no need, Lin. I love you."

"I love you too; that's why I've got to. I'm going to my room now. It's the first one inside the door. Come to me!" It was a cry for help.

"Lin, listen . . ."

She broke away from him, almost running.

He thought: She's only got herself to give this time too.

For a time he watched the dark waters of the Potomac, then he turned slowly on his heel and walked forward to the door that led to the passengers' cabins.

*   *   *

The thin dawn light came in through the louvers of the shutter. It was enough to see him by. She sat as she had sat in that other bed, her chin in the notch between her clasped knees, her eyes studying his face. He was not so handsome as Revell. His face was rugged and the planes of it were broad, but it had strength, even in the surrender of sleep. It was a good face, and she knew that when the eyes were open they would be kind eyes.

There was no sound except for the thresh of the side wheels and the water noises; not even the gulls were awake yet on the Chesapeake. She sat and thought, tracing patterns on the blank pages of her ignorance. She wondered what Abraham Lincoln knew of love. Somebody had talked of Lincoln and a girl called Ann. She wondered if the young Abe, the tall, shambling, sinewy boy Abe, had loved Ann—as she had been loved this night. She hoped that he had. For the girl's sake she hoped he had. And there had been a girl called Mary Owens. She remembered about Mary Owens. One of the innumerable waspish clippings in Ulysses' files had said that he had jilted Mary Owens, but she remembered also that old Sam, snarling, had said, "She throwed him over," and quoted from inexhaustible memory a passage of an article on Lincoln. There was Mary Todd. He must have lain with Mary Todd—there were the sons to prove it. He must have loved her. Was it possible that he still loved her?

She recalled the planes of the gaunt, gentle face. He'd grown the whiskers because a little girl had written to him suggesting it. They were grotesque but they fitted into the composition of those deep-seamed sculptured contours. The voice he had always had—low, roughly gentle, assured. And the eyes, always it was the eyes that she came back to: the eyes that she had seen first in that brief moment on Granby Street: the eyes that had stripped her of all pretense and fantasy. Those eyes would penetrate her mind now, would know the simple honesty of her intention, and the innocent gurgling wickedness of her joy that her honesty had not led her again into horror but instead into —she paused, searching in her mind for a word, and knew that the only word was fun. Nobody had told her that to love with a man was fun, not even her father. Perhaps it was difficult for a man to formulate the words. Perhaps there weren't any words.

She let her mind go back to Lincoln, to the tall, stooped frame that had uncoiled itself from his chair to say goodbye to her. What was it that he wanted her to do? She had not shaped it in her mind yet. She was allowing her joy and her gaiety and her silent laughter to postpone decision.

Outside on the deck there were voices and the heavy sound of feet. Stephen stirred, half turned toward her, and shook himself free from the blanket as far as his thighs. She gazed at him absorbed, studying the power of his chest and the great muscles, still flaccid in sleep, of his arms, and the square strength of his shoulders. She studied his maleness—in a sense it was hers too now—wondering at its capable power for joy. He was defenseless here in sleep, and she had a quick access of maternalism, so that for a moment she felt as if he were not her lover but her child.

Her train of thought changed at once, by a quick, inevitable association of ideas. She wondered if she would have his child. It would be a glory to have his child. She could not even remember that she had once thought: It's a silly way to make a baby.

He moved again and his eyes opened. The seagulls were raucous outside now. He put out a hand and touched her back and for a moment, still not wholly awake, he looked puzzled, then his hand flattened and ran up the silk of it, joyously exciting.

At once, as if she were prompted by something outside herself, she knew that there was still a sacrifice that she had to offer—that even now she was not altogether absolved. As if someone else were speaking through her voice, flatly and without expression she said, "You don't need to marry me, Stephen."

His hand fell away from her back; he raised himself on his elbow and looked at her. She dared not meet his eyes, though she was sure that they would be kind. "You don't *need* to," she said again, and this time there was a little note of despair.

Then she heard his answer: "I need." And that was all. And she knew that she was safe.

* * *

They were dressed and on the deck when the steamer went in past the Rip Raps. Fortress Monroe was behind them, red and still menacing in the sunrise. The wall of the Rip Raps was low and angry-looking. The Roads were very blue.

The steamer turned at Seawell's Point and headed in for the Elizabeth River, with the houses of Norfolk growing and the spires and the dome and the masts of ships. Linden had an impulse as they passed the abandoned batteries at Seawell's to point to the square, gray bulk of the Enwright place and say, "That was the house." But she knew there was no need.

They came, slowing down, to Craney Island.

The wreck of the *Merrimac* was lying in the shoal water. Her bows were toward the shore; the great casemate was open to the sky; the steel bars that had cost the work and the thought and the emotions of a town were twisted and riven and worthless.

She stood looking at it, desolate, the joy and the hopefulness fading out of her. Stephen saw that she was crying silently, that she was alone again, and he put his arm round her and drew her against him. "She was a great ship," he said gently. "She nearly did it—God knows it was near."

Through her tears she asked, "Did you hate her?"

"No"—he shook his head positively—"No, we were afraid of her; but we respected her. You did a wonderful thing in Portsmouth when you built her, but the luck wasn't with you, we knew that. It was with us—another hour of the wind on the shoals and we'd have drowned." He felt her arm tighten convulsively. "Sometime I'll tell you, but not now. It was a near thing."

"You won," she said, but he saw that the tears had stopped.

"No," he said, almost sharply, "nobody won. It was the fighting on the Albemarle that defeated her, and the loss of Yorktown. She held McClellan up for three months. That's more than any single ship has done in history. She was a great ship."

She said nothing; there was no longer any need of words between them.

They swept in across the wide bight inside the island and headed for Hospital Point. The guns had been dismounted from the seaward batteries. The place had an empty and a desolate air, but at the tall flagstaff, the flagstaff that dominated the Point, that seemed to dominate by its straight delicacy the whole entrance to the Elizabeth, the Union flag flew out steady and brilliant in the morning wind.

He felt her hand contract and he looked down, searching her clouded face. He said, "Lin, you've got to accept it now."

Desolately, so that his heart almost failed him, she answered, "Yes, I know."

He put his arm around her shoulders. "You've got to do more than accept it; you've got to work for it. We've all got to work for it."

"I know, I know"—she had a break in her voice—"only, I've seen the other one there for so long, Stephen. I'd gotten used to it." She gave a quick, half-acknowledged little sob. "I loved it so!"

After a moment she added, "He said . . ." and paused—Stephen knew that she meant Lincoln—"He said a house divided against itself . . ." And Stephen wondered if Lincoln had remembered the phrase and used it perhaps as a talisman, perhaps as a catalyst, to release the girl's inhibitions.

"He said that, and he was right. This is going to be the greatest country that the world has ever known—if it holds together. If it doesn't, it will break into"—Stephen hesitated, searching for a simile, and came back to Lincoln's own, original, intensely personal illustration—"into the pieces of a house divided, a wall standing up, a beam, a chimney piece . . . a house that was a home."

"I never thought of it," she said simply, "as a home."

With anxiety he said, "It won't be easy, Lin."

"They always hate people who've changed sides." She turned and looked up at him. "It won't be easy for you either." Then, with a swift insight, "It hasn't been, has it, Steve?"

"No"—he shook his head—"but I had plenty to do." Carefully he framed the question: "What are we going to do about Revell, Linden?"

She put her hands on the rail, turning away from him. She flushed with gratitude at the pronoun. But when she spoke her voice was reckless, almost hard. "You can't do anything, I'm going to do it. I'm going to fetch him out of the Dismal. My father ran a depot for the underground railway, did you know that? They brought the Negroes down to the town in the loads of shingle. They had a hide in the lumber there, and he shipped them out in the *Chula*. One way was out through the Capes to a boat from Massachusetts. The other was up to the Maryland shore."

"I knew."

"Seems as if everybody knew except me," she said humbly. "I didn't know. I didn't know, Steve, until they helped me take Revell away—until they took me up to Galesville."

"I knew," he said again. "I went out that way, the time—the time you helped me in the lumber yard."

"I might have helped them to hunt you, Steve." There was a terror in her eyes as she turned and looked at him—terror and an absolute honesty.

"You didn't," he said gently.

"I couldn't." She sighed, and was unaccountably happy again. "Perhaps I knew even then."

"I think you always knew"—he nodded reflectively—"but you were afraid."

"Yes, I was afraid."

There was a brief, considering silence.

"And after you've got him to the wood yard?" Stephen went back remorselessly to the problem of Revell. It was necessary that it be settled now, that a decision be reached before the boat docked, before the contacts were reestablished and the old influences began to work again.

Almost lightly she said, "We'll get him up to the house, and Aunt Deborah will nurse him."

"You can't do that!" He was inexplicably shocked. "They're likely to search your house any minute."

She shrugged. "They've searched it already by now. They won't search it again. It'll do Aunt Deborah a heap of good to have a man to look after." She smiled again the wicked, infinitely youthful smile that had always wrenched at his heart.

"You can't! They'd jail you if they found out."

"I've got the President's letter."

"That letter was meant to be taken to General Viele right away."

"That letter"—she almost mocked him—"was given me to do what I liked with."

"And then?"

"When he's well enough he'll give himself up."

"Revell?"

"I'll make him." She spoke with an absolute confidence. "And Abraham Lincoln will stand by me."

The world had come clear now, the way was open.

Stephen, looking at her, shook his head in wonder.

She made a tiny answering gesture with her hands. "He's not guilty, you see," she said reasonably. "He didn't know that there was a flag of truce."

"He was drunk."

"He was drunk," Linden agreed without question. "So he thought he was a hero. Sober he'd have known what he was."

Stephen, remembering that first moment on the deck of the *Star of the West,* threw up his hands in surrender.

She turned and kissed him lightly, disregarding the deck hands who were making ready the landing plank. "You see, if there's trouble, I won't be Linden Cleave—I'll be the wife of an officer of the Navy of the United States."

"Linden Cleave," he almost shouted with the sudden release of tension, "I ought to beat you!"

The ship was swinging in to the wharf now. She moved very slowly through water brown with mud and juniper stain and fouled with oil and little islets of debris. The wharf was crowded with men in blue uniforms. Beyond them was a rank of sullen townspeople. Groups of Negroes stood watching with an odd self-consciousness.

As they began to close the gap to the black and battered piles of the wharf, Stephen had one last moment of doubt. "What will your father say, Lin—about us?"

The glint in her eyes was ribald. "He'll say"—she mimicked her father's long-jowled look—" 'You'd have saved a sight of trouble if you'd done it a year ago, boy!' "

*   *   *

The men nearest to the ship were soldiers. There were other men in civilian clothes, their Northern voices hectoring. The man who appeared to control them leaned against the door of the warehouse. He was tall, lean, and the long cigar that he smoked hung a little from the horizontal as if he were too indolent to support it. He had a vulturine, predatory air.

Jeriel was sitting on the top of one of the piles of the wharf, far up near the bows of the ship. His feet dangled under him. He looked uninterested and he looked wary. He saw Linden first and raised one hand, but his face showed little sign of welcome. When he saw Stephen he dropped the hand and sat lax. One of the Yankee roustabouts came up and harried him away from the pile. He slipped down with the slightest shrug, walked over to the warehouse, and stood slouched against it.

It was ten minutes before they were allowed ashore—time enough to see that the Yankees were riding the town hard, that the townspeople were cowed and spiritless, that the Negroes were wholly uncertain, moving like dark gazelles in a forest of carnivores.

Behind them on the water the gulls cried, and the morning wind died and was silent.

When they reached the worn, rough planking of the wharf they saw Jeriel still leaning against the wall, and they walked over to him. He watched them, his face wiped of expression.

Linden cried: "Jeri! You got back safe. I'm so happy!"

He gave the ghost of a nod.

Linden did not appear to notice anything odd in his manner. She asked, "How did you know we were coming?"

"Didn'," said the boy carelessly. "I bin meetin' th' boats from Washington. This is the third."

"It was good of you, Jeri."

The boy looked at Stephen in his uniform with a smoldering hate. "Where'd you find him?"

"He found me." Linden spoke with such an overflooding of happiness that in three words she betrayed everything.

"Yankee," said Jeriel softly, so softly that she did not seem to hear. But Stephen heard, and tensed.

"Have you seen Revell?" Linden ignored the whisper.

"He's daid," replied Jeriel indifferently.

Chapter ten

SHE felt numb, but there was no surprise in her. In a sense she had known all along that he would die. Her journey had perhaps had little to do with him, as she had told Stephen. It had been necessary for her to go to Washington, out of the orbit of Gosport and Portsmouth and

Norfolk, to go to Lincoln. The war was an entity, a whole. For its wounds, salves were conceived. She was absorbed now in a healing process. War tore down, but even in war, or perhaps especially in war, some equal and opposite reaction built up.

She did not formulate these ideas to herself; she could not have expressed them aloud; she felt them, vaguely and movingly.

Stephen held her arm in a grip that was almost painful. He whispered, "I'm sorry, Lin."

She shook her head. "I think he would have died anyway. There wasn't anything left for him to live for. I thought I hated him, but perhaps I never did, perhaps I never had any real feelings for him." She accented the word "real" with the unconscious cruelty of a fulfilled woman. Finally she asked Jeriel, "When did he die?"

"Two days ago."

"Was anybody there?"

"The nigras."

"He must have hated that." She made the comment dispassionately, as if she had had no actual connection with or personal knowledge of the man who had died—as if he were a name only.

They came to the ferry landing. The boat was ready to leave, and they climbed on board.

Stephen made an effort to turn the conversation away from Revell. "Where's Seth Pritchard?" he asked.

"He's daid too," replied Jeriel with a macabre relish. "That's a Yankee bastid in th' wheelhouse." He looked sidewise at Stephen to see how he would take it.

Stephen heard but ignored the calculated insult.

Linden said, "Jeri!" and waited till the boy turned to her. When he looked at her she went on with a bubbling happiness, "Stephen and I are going to be married."

"I know." His voice was flat.

"How did you know?"

"It shows," he growled brutally.

The ferry started in an unaccustomed flurry of steam whistle and cursing. It backed out of the shaped dock and scurried with a great protest of engines into the river.

Linden said: "I'm glad it shows. I want everybody to know. Jeri— I saw the President."

"Him!"

Stephen made a small involuntary movement and restrained himself.

Linden looked steadily at the boy. "I know him now. He isn't what

I thought he was. Jeri, he made me understand that whatever happens we've got to come together again after the war. North and South."

"And for that he give you a free pardon for Revell?" The boy's voice was bitter with disillusion. "He's a goddam fool."

"No," she said evenly, "he didn't give me a pardon. He said that Revell would have to stand his trial. He isn't a fool."

"Would've been if he had. Revell was a no-account sonavabitch."

"He's dead." Stephen felt that he had to try somehow to get through to the boy. He could sense the desperate pain, the hurt, the impulse to lash out at anything and anybody.

"He was a coward all th' time, on'y he was so big-mouthed nobody saw it."

The Yankee skipper came aft and saluted Stephen with an exaggerated formality. "Mornin', Lieutenant. Got to keep these mushmouths in their place." He was referring evidently to the fuss at the moment of departure.

Stephen looked at him distastefully. "You'll do what you have to do, but I wouldn't make more trouble for myself than I had to."

"They'll dance," said the skipper darkly, and went on.

Stephen watched Jeriel's eyes, cold with hate, as they followed the skipper down the deck. "Jeriel," he said, "the war's over for Portsmouth and Norfolk. There won't be any more fighting. We won't let go again. Portsmouth did well with the *Merrimac,* but now that's over too. Now we've got to live together. The President's right."

Jeriel said painfully, his voice so low that it was scarcely audible above the thresh of the paddles and the river noises: "It's easy fer you. You're *goin'* to live together."

Stephen realized with a shock that for years the boy had been Linden's shadow. What happened to a shadow when the sun went in?

The skipper passed them again, looking sidewise at Stephen. At once an uproar of bells and curses began as the ferry headed into the narrow V of the Portsmouth dock.

Before she was made fast, Jeriel said acridly: "You don't need me no more. I'll be goin'," and was gone.

Linden turned to Stephen when they were on the wharf. "We could have stopped him."

"No"—he shook his head—"I don't think we could. He's growing up, Linden."

Because of Stephen they passed the Yankee pickets without question. Oddly, there had been no one they knew on the ferry coming across. Now, though there were not many in the streets, everybody knew them. People waved to Linden, smiled at her, called to her. Then they saw Stephen, and some of them recognized him at once, and some remembered him only when they had passed and turned and looked again. Only one man greeted him. He shouted across the street: "Hi, Knott! What you doin' here . . ." And suddenly realized why Stephen was there, and turned his head away and almost ran.

Stephen had expected things like this; Linden did not notice them. She was absorbed in an interior happiness that was proof against anything. Stephen looked down at her sadly once and knew that she had forgotten even Jeriel—at least for the time being.

They came to the lumber yard. Linden had wanted to go there first. Her father, she knew, would be there, leaning over the timber stack at this hour.

Cleave heard them coming. He turned swiftly and cried, "Lin—Lin!"

Her memory went back instantly to the day of the *Merrimac*'s return, and, as she had done on that afternoon, she ran to his arms. It was a parallel but it was also an opposite. Then she had had desperate need of him because of her hurt and despair; now she had intense need of him because of her happiness.

She said against his cheek: "Everything's going to be all right. We're going to be married. Mr. Lincoln . . ."

He pushed her away from him, infected by her laughter, laughing himself. "One thing at a time! Where did you find Stephen? And who are you going to marry?"

She took Stephen's hand. "We're practically married already." She had the shamelessness of absolute innocence. "I didn't find him, he found me."

Cleave smiled wryly. "Should have happened a year ago. Would have saved a lot of trouble." He held out a hand past Linden to Stephen. "I tried to tell you once."

Sam came down the path. He walked more slowly, with less spring in his step than Stephen had remembered, but his eyes were still alight and sardonic. He called from a long distance: "Mornin', Lindy! You caught you a Yankee officer?"

Stephen said, "I captured her."

Sam belly-laughed: "That's what you b'lieve. You go on b'lievin' it, it's easier that way." He stared at him for a long moment. "I'm glad you're back, Steve. Ain't goin' to be easy here, not anyways." Over his shoulder he asked casually, "You know Revell's dead?"

"I know," Linden replied patiently.

"Best way out," said Sam, dismissing the whole affair. "Doc White told me he wouldn't live anyways."

"And you let me go to Washington?" The girl looked at him, puzzled.

"You was set to go," the old man answered simply.

Cleave smiled.

With a momentary flash of her old fury the girl cried, "I went to the President when——"

"I reckoned Abe Lincoln'd do you more good than a strap to your bottom. Didn't he?"

She opened both hands in a charming gesture of surrender. "Bless you, Sam," she said humbly. "I love you."

"Pity you didn't say that a month or two back," growled Sam. "I'd ha' took action. You seen your Aunt Deborah yet?"

"We came straight from the ferry," Stephen said.

"You'd better git, then. Your aunt'll forgive you anythin', Lindy, even that you ain't waited for the preacher, so long as Mrs. Shermadine don't tell her news of you first."

"How did you know——" she began indignantly, and stopped.

"Lindy Cleave . . ." He drawled her name in gentle derision.

Stephen thought how easy her task might be if all Portsmouth were peopled with men like these two with their quiet understanding.

Cleave nodded. "We'll go to the house now. Your aunt's been worried sick."

"I wish Jeriel was here now," said Linden inconsequently.

"He's growin' up." Old Sam's voice was cryptic.

They went through the gate of the wood yard out into the road. Stephen glanced once or twice at the old man's face—he was trying to warn them of something, trying to bring Linden down to earth. He turned away and smiled at her and she smiled back with such joy in her eyes that his heart missed a beat.

They had turned up South Street before they saw anyone they knew—anyone who mattered. Then it began: whispering voices, a window shut with an indignant slam, a door banged. Stephen was acutely conscious of it all, sensitive to every overt expression of hostility. But Linden moved through it with an absolute serenity.

Stephen remembered his last journey down South Street, stifling in the narrow box under the seat of Aunt Deborah's brougham—the box that was never seen because it was so perfectly in view.

Aunt Deborah was in the parlor. She called out, "Is that you, Ash?"

When he answered, "And Linden," she came swiftly to the door. She said, "I was afraid for you, Linden," and took her into her arms.

Only when she had kissed her did she see her face, and only then did she look beyond her and see Stephen. She held out one arm to him and, as he came forward, she kissed him, still holding Linden. "I've waited a long time for this!"

Nobody cried. It was not the fashion with the Cleave women to make a fuss about their private lives.

Chapter eleven

THE boy was sitting between two trees that grew a little away from the main body of the scrub pines. The last light of the sunset was still enough to color the spread of dogwood above his head. He sat quite still, watching them.

Linden called to him when they were still forty yards away. He lifted one hand in greeting but made no answer.

Stephen saw that he had a rolled blanket over his shoulder and that there was a knapsack on the ground beside him and what looked, even at that distance, like a rifle.

Linden said uncertainly, when they reached him, "You wanted us, Jeri?"

"Wanted t' say goodbye." He put it bluntly, almost harshly.

Automatically she asked, "Where are you going?" though even before she spoke she knew the answer.

"Through the lines." There was no boasting, no vainglory; it was a simple statement of fact.

"Why, Jeri—why?"

"Ain't nothin' else I can do," he answered her simply. "I'm a Southerner."

For a moment she allowed herself to be betrayed into a sentimentality. "You're so young!"

"Reckon I'm old enough. War goes on another two-three years I'm li'ble to be drafted into th' Union Army. I'd ruther fight the way I choose."

Stephen looked carefully at him. "Jeriel, the South isn't going to win, you know."

"I know," he said calmly.

Deflated, Stephen tried again. "England isn't going to come in on her side, now. The South may go on winning battles but she'll lose the war. You saw it with the *Merrimac*. She was good—she won the first day—but she wasn't good enough. She wasn't good enough because the South has no foundries, no factories, no machinery. The blockade'll be worse as it goes on. It'll strangle the South in the end."

And again Jeriel said calmly, "I know."

Stephen made a gesture of despair. "You'll always be falling back; there'll be no ammunition, no food, no doctors. It's hell on the losing side, Jeriel."

"It's my side," said Jeriel, still without a vestige of heroics. "I been thinkin' about it. Reckon I'd as lief be shot as live under some o' th' Yankee bastids I seen the last few days."

Linden groped for some way in which she could reach his mind. "They're not all like that. The President's not."

"He made the war," said Jeriel flatly.

"Nobody could have prevented the war."

"You're the one told me he made it." Jeriel's voice was carefully void of expression.

"I didn't know him then!" Suddenly she became passionate. "He's a good man, Jeriel—he's a great man. He's like one of the old saints in a way. He wants us to be one Nation again, when it's over."

"Mebbe," said Jeriel noncommitally.

"He does." She made the words urgent. "I was wrong, Jeri—I didn't understand. My father knew . . ."

"Your pa, he's a nigger lover." Jeriel spoke without rancor. "He run th' underground—him an' old Sam, and I reckon your Aunt Deborah. He wasn't never South." Like a judge delivering a carefully considered judgment, he added: "He never claimed otherwise. You did!"

"I know," she admitted humbly.

He shrugged. "I ain't talked to the Pres'dent. All I know is I was born in the South, and I was raised in it. An' I got to fight for it even if it *is* beat." He considered his words and amended them. "Because it's beat," he substituted with the wisdom of the very young.

With an overwhelming sadness she realized that there was nothing more that she could do. In a sense the boy was the incarnation of the South, with its stubbornness, its pride, its gallantry, its hope, and its despair.

He had grown up.

Stephen put his arm round her. He made one last effort: "Jeriel, I think I could fix it so that you wouldn't have to fight. . . ." Even as he said it he knew that it was useless, unworthy. The boy had an active identity; he would never settle in a conquered town.

It was implicit in his answer: " 'N live with bastids like the skipper o' th' ferry?"

"Conquering armies throw up men like that," Stephen conceded. "They won't all be like him."

"I'd ruther fight," said Jeriel.

Stephen admitted defeat. "Where did you get that rifle?"

"Offn' a dead Yankee." The boy's voice was suddenly hard and wary. "One o' the ones Rev killed."

"Throw it into the swamp!"

"A good rifle?" He gave a little harsh laugh.

"Throw it in," said Stephen peremptorily. "You've still got to get through the lines. If they take you with the rifle, they'll hang you. They can't hang Revell now."

The boy looked at him uncertainly, disconcerted for the first time. Stephen took three ten-dollar bills from his wallet. "Throw it in the swamp and take this. You can buy a Yankee rifle with it when you get across the lines. God knows they've got plenty!" His voice grew a little bitter.

The boy's face crumpled. Stephen was painfully anxious that he should not cry.

When Jeriel spoke, his voice had lost definition; he almost mumbled the words: "Thank you." Then he climbed to his feet and, picking up the gun, swung it once and let it fly toward the nearby water. It made a brown, stained splash and sank instantly, and the water ruffled a little and was quiet. He took the money, stuffed it into his pocket, and swung his knapsack onto his shoulder. "Reckon I'll be goin'," he said.

Linden went to him, put her arm around him, and kissed him—an adult, generous kiss.

When she released him he stepped back, confused. "Thank you, Mis' Linden."

"Lindy," she corrected.

"Lindy." He grinned, suddenly boyish again. Then he nodded to Stephen, and, turning, began to walk away, not hurrying, moving with a complete and positive confidence.

Linden whispered, watching him, "I've failed already."

Stephen tightened his hold of her. "We've got to reckon on a deal of failure."

Jeriel reached an open stretch where the afterlight of the sunset was brilliant between the trees and the water. He looked ten feet tall. His voice came back to them:

> *"I got a gal*
> *In Cumberland Gap.*
> *She's got a . . ."*

This is a full-length portrayal of one of the most crucial battles of the Civil War. For the background of his novel, David Divine has chosen the dramatic events leading to the duel between the great iron warships, the *Monitor* and the *Merrimac;* for his characters, he has created men and women whose divided loyalties alter the course of their own destinies.

The story begins shortly before the firing on Fort Sumter, when the action that Virginia would take in the event of war was still unknown. In the Cleave household in Portsmouth, opinion and allegiance are at variance. Ash Cleave, grimly aware of the tragedy inherent in the threat of a war between the states, works secretly for the Underground while professing a guarded neutrality. His proud and defiant daughter, Linden, is vehemently pro-South. When war does break out, Linden's two suitors, Stephen and Revell, follow separate paths: Stephen retains his U.S. Navy commission and Revell enlists in the Confederate army. It is then that the fate of these two young men—and that of the vulnerable and passionate Linden—become intimately involved in the starkly opposed, bitterly contested struggle between the two ironclads.

From their conception on the drawing board through their construction, launching, and fateful meeting, the history of these two ships is painted with an exciting immediacy of the first order. Here are scenes of violence and mounting tension—the firing of Portsmouth by retreat-